KT-226-731

SARA SHERIDAN

The Secret Mandarin

AVON

This novel is entirely a work of fiction.
The names, characters and incidents portrayed in it are
the work of the author's imagination. Any resemblance to
actual persons, living or dead, events or localities is
entirely coincidental.

AVON

A division of HarperCollins*Publishers*
77–85 Fulham Palace Road,
London W6 8JB

www.harpercollins.co.uk

A Paperback Original 2009

Copyright © Sara Sheridan 2009

Sara Sheridan asserts the moral right to
be identified as the author of this work

A catalogue record for this book is
available from the British Library

ISBN-13: 978-1-84756-189-3

Set in Minion by Palimpsest Book Production Limited,
Grangemouth, Stirlingshire

Printed and bound in Great Britain by
Clays Ltd, St Ives plc

All rights reserved. No part of this publication may be
reproduced, stored in a retrieval system, or transmitted,
in any form or by any means, electronic, mechanical,
photocopying, recording or otherwise, without the prior
permission of the publishers.

Mixed Sources
Product group from well-managed
forests and other controlled sources
www.fsc.org Cert no. SW-COC-1806
© 1996 Forest Stewardship Council

FSC is a non-profit international organisation established
to promote the responsible management of the world's forests.
Products carrying the FSC label are independently certified
to assure consumers that they come from forests that are managed
to meet the social, economic and ecological needs
of present and future generations.

Find out more about HarperCollins and the environment at
www.harpercollins.co.uk/green

Thanks are due to many, for it takes a village to raise a book.

To Syd House, who mentioned in passing that I might find the Victorian Plant Hunters interesting, especially some guy called Robert Fortune (thank you, Syd!). To Mrs Campbell – a wonderful history teacher. To the staff at the Botanical Gardens in Edinburgh who generously gave up their time and helped me in the library and the herbarium. To the staff at The Scottish Plant Hunters Garden at Pitlochry who answered questions ad nauseam. To the brilliant archivists at the National Library of Scotland who were enormously supportive and continue to be so – much appreciated – David McClay and Nat Edwards in particular. To those who read the book in its early draft and gave detailed criticism – the fabulously enthusiastic Jenny Brown, Maxine Hitchcock and her wonderful eyes, the exuberant Val Hoskins and the ever-inspiring Elinor Baginel. To the Kay Blundell Trust for generously giving money when I needed it most – the faith you put in me means a great deal.

Lastly, but in no way least, to my friends and family for putting up with me going on about tea plants for a bloody long time – so many of you lovely people have been kind and patient all through the writing process and then genuinely happy for me when I finally sold the manuscript – I am entirely blessed to have so many wonderful friends. Thanks are due in particular to Lorne Blyth, Monica Higgins and Lucy Gordon for the top party, the gorgeous and supportive Gemma Tipton for knowing me so well, the generous and ever-upbeat Jan Ambrose (head of list-making), the Goodwins and the Faulkeners who bore the brunt along with my lovely daughter Molly and my very own rock, the stupendous Alan Ferrier.

The Secret Mandarin is dedicated to
the memory of Daniel Lindley.
I do wish you were still around.

Prologue

Indian Ocean, 1842

When the ship went down the other women were praying. The captain had ordered us stowed below decks, out of the way, while the crew battled the storm. I sat silently in the candlelit gloom, keeping my balance as best I could while the boat pitched violently. As the others mumbled on their knees, my heart was dancing along with my stomach in a strange, whirling tremor that brought me out in a sweat. We did not know what would happen and there was nothing any of us could do. It had been hours.

In the end it was sudden. The ship was noisy, the timbers creaking before they finally broke, the wind screaming. Outside, the scale of the weather was titanic and I remember thinking that we were so tiny, so vulnerable. The whole ship split open like the cracking of an egg – just one almighty crash and then the shrieks of terror, my own among them, quickly silenced by the rush of water.

There was no point fighting the storm. Besides, it happened so fast there was little opportunity but to move where the water threw us. Another world, it was completely silent under there – a relief after the long, noisy hours of terrifying anticipation. I became an observer, my panic quelled, as if this was only a strange dream that I was swimming through. The currents rushed, all bubbles and smashed pieces of the ship, as the faces of the others loomed in and out of my line of vision, never close enough to reach out, to cling together. I surfaced once into a blinding torrent of tropical wind and rain and grabbed three long, desperate breaths before the waves crashed over me once more. The towering currents were impossible to scale. It seemed safer, somehow, under the surface.

'Just swim upwards,' I told myself. 'Watch for the bubbles and swim upwards as much as you can.'

Swimming was familiar and the action itself rid me of any anxiety. The water had always been my friend. I was put in mind of my sister, Jane, and our childhood outings to the pond at the bottom of the big hill about half a mile from the house where we were raised. We used to discuss our plans endlessly at that pond. In the summer we splashed about in the sunshine, squealing as we jumped off the rocks. Now in the middle of this wild monsoon, my mind transported itself to happier times. I comforted myself that I was safe and at home again. Truly, I must have been hysterical, half out of my mind. But I did not struggle. The storm was nothing. The storm was gone and in its place my childhood swirled around me.

'I want to be married,' Jane said down by the water, 'to a gentleman. A gentleman is always kind and looks after his wife.'

I spat at her as I surfaced – a long jet of ice-cold water. Jane was barefoot in her pinafore and blouse, sitting at the edge while I dived in and out like a baby seal that sunny summer day.

'A gentleman,' I scoffed.

Such people were above our station. Jane, however, had decided. She was in possession of a novel, which she read in secret. She hid it under the washstand. In my opinion, it had given her airs.

'Yes,' she said, attacking my dreams because I had laughed at hers. 'Better than wanting to be Fanny Kemble.'

'When Fanny Kemble played Juliet grown men cried. Gentlemen,' I told her. 'Anyone with the talent for it can be a great actress, Jane. But gentlemen marry ladies.'

'Then I shall be a lady,' she said simply.

I moved off without a splash.

Now Jane was Mrs Fortune and I, well, I had failed.

I cannot remember any more of the storm, only swimming and swimming. The water felt like a living thing as it moved around me. I truly believed my dear Jane was waiting on the side, dangling her feet as she read passages aloud from her foolish love story. And then, warm and very drowsy, my vision narrowed to a tiny beam of light, the arms of the ocean entombed my body and I was gone.

When I opened my eyes again the storm had faded and I could see a beach. I had come up on a rocky outcrop. My clothes were torn and my arms purple and yellow with bruises that ached as I moved. Confused, shaking and dry-mouthed, I crawled over the rocks, pushing aside the splintered flotsam and jetsam that had ridden the current with me. The shattered dreams of the others. Wedding trousseaux. Photographs torn at the edges, still trapped beneath the glass – families far away. They would never see Calcutta now.

The sand was bleached a dazzling white. It stretched a long way in both directions. The sea, now completely calm, was the colour of bluebells. A strange, spicy fragrance hung, intoxicating in the hot air. I had hardly an ounce of strength and lay dreamless for a long time. Then I heard voices.

'*Une femme. C'est une femme!*'

I opened my eyes and blurred, through the haze, I saw two, half-naked, black children running towards me, and a white man, leading a horse. His tunic was dark with sweat and his grey hair had come loose and shielded his eyes. He was old – fifty at least.

'*Mon Dieu!*' he said.

I was safe, thank God. The man gave the reins to one of the children. He leant over and gently poured warm water from his flask into my mouth. It tasted heavenly.

'The others?' I said, still woozy. '*Les autres, monsieur?*'

My French did not extend very far. The man shrugged his shoulders and shook his head sadly.

'*Personne.*'

Even in a daze, half battered to death, I could hardly believe that I was the lone survivor. Were they all gone? The stinking deckhands, seadogs every one, the gruff captain with his two surly officers, the elderly, unsmiling chaperones who had attended our cabin and, of course, those like me, the companions of my shameful voyage – Miss Cameron, Miss Hughes, Miss Lucas, Miss Thornton and more. Punished by our families – sent away forever. Each on the run into the arms of the first Company man who would have her. And now, every soul aboard swallowed up by the wild and tropical sea. Every soul that is, except me.

'*Où est ici?*' I hazarded as the man lifted me up and placed me, floppy as a rag doll, on his horse.

I could not sit upright and lay flat instead with my head on the animal's long mane and my fingers curled loosely around the reins.

'*Ici c'est* Réunion,' the man smiled.

'I want to go home,' I said.

My heart was in London. I had never wanted to leave. The whole journey had been forced upon me, after all.

A banishment. A casting out. I had hated every minute even before the sea reared up. Now it occurred to me, perhaps the storm was a sign.

The old man clicked his reins and the horse began to walk up the beach. The movement below me felt awkward on the uneven sand and even my bones ached, but I smiled through my exhaustion. I had survived.

'*Allons nous à St Denis*,' the old man said. '*Il y a un docteur.*'

Chapter One

I think my family were glad that I had died. It must have been a relief. Crystal clear, I can see Jane now, wringing her tiny hands while she reads out the news from the evening edition – the first they know of the storm. As her lips form the words she is all too aware that her tidy navy dress with the red buttons is inappropriate attire in the circumstances, and that she will have to unpack the mourning clothes she used when our mother died. She wonders if she will be expected to organise a memorial service or a monumental stone.

'What is it one does,' she thinks, 'when there is no body to bury?'

Robert, her husband, in his dark jacket and carefully chosen cravat, is pacing the thin carpet of their Wedgwood-green drawing room, circling around her like a wiry, wily woodland predator as he listens to the article read out from the paper. It is five weeks after the ship went down and all they have are the scantiest of details – a dry little column about the ferocity of the storm and the notorious waters of the Indian Ocean – fifty souls on board, no survivors and no mention of me.

Even if you are at sea, the weather in England is unlikely to kill you. Drama on the high waters off the Cornish coast or in the North Sea is not unheard of, but fatalities are very rare. Of course, there is plenty that will carry you off. The pox, the cutthroats fired up on gin who will burst your skin for a shilling, or the sheer poverty, the circular fortunes of the slums. If you have no money you can't eat so the poor are thin, the unlucky starve and, for the most part, the likes of Jane, Robert and I don't notice. But whatever filthy, threadbare, rat-infested, desperate horrors you might encounter in London, the weather all on its own is unlikely to take you, whatever Miss Austen might have her readers believe about the frailty of English women subjected to a summer rainstorm.

In the Indian Ocean it's quite different. I can't imagine Jane cried at the news of my demise. Her soft voice doesn't waver as she reads the report aloud. My sister does not find it strange or tragic that I have been borne away by the sea. I imagine she thinks of it as the 'sort of thing Mary *would* do.' Always stoic, her dark eyes dart emotionless, like a tame bird. She copes uncomplainingly with everything and causes no fuss. I am the wild one.

She did cry, however, three weeks later, when I came back. I paused at the front door, wondering if I should have sent word from Portsmouth rather than simply a note from St Denis. The doctor had had good English. He made idle chatter as he inspected my bruises and cuts, pressing gently where the skin had swollen.

'You will be marked for life,' he pronounced, 'but you will recover.'

Then he had them feed me bone marrow and a little brandy. Now, weeks later, the bruises were gone but there were scars that still ached. I was back in London after an uncomfortable voyage home on a trading ship. The city was my lifeblood and I was glad to be there, but my heart was pounding too, for I did not know what my family would make of my return. It had been five months since

I was here last and I had disgraced them. I reached out and let the knocker strike and then waited.

The maid opened up and revealed my nephew behind her in the hallway. He froze as soon as he saw me and I thought he looked rather like a photograph, a perfect picture of England. His little body was already taut and strong in the image of his father and his skin was so pale in his charcoal grey shorts that his knees seemed somehow luminous against the shiny, dark, wooden floorboards.

'Aunt Mary!' he shouted when he found he could once more speak. There was panic rising in his voice and his eyes were wide.

'Now, now, Thomas,' I said to comfort him, as I advanced into the house past the plump, open-mouthed serving girl and laid my hat on the satinwood table. The poor child backed away as if I was a spectre and I realised straight away that my note had not yet arrived. They had evidently been mourning me.

'A good thing that I can swim, don't you think?' I said gently, smiling to make light of it.

Thomas was taking lessons at the new pool in Kensington. We had discussed the subject on many occasions and he had vouched that it was his ambition to dive into the deep end from the balcony. Now, far braver than taking a fifteen-foot drop, he put out his hand and touched my cheek.

'There now,' I said. 'Don't ever believe a bad review, Thomas. Let that be a lesson to you.'

By this time we had been too long without being announced and Jane appeared from the morning room to investigate. She was holding the baby. My baby. I think it was only there in the hallway that I realised how much I had missed him. He had grown in my absence and there was a rash on his cheek. I found I was smiling quite involuntarily as I stared at it. It was a relief to see that he looked chubby and healthy, dressed in a little smock. They had kept their word. Jane hesitated at the sight of me and seemed to deflate – the black skirt of her mourning dress was huge and she too small within it.

'He must be almost six months old now. He looks well,' I smiled.

'Mary,' she mouthed.

I reached out to hold her in greeting and as I pulled back I saw there were tears in her eyes.

'I was washed ashore,' I whispered. 'I wrote to you but I must have overtaken the letter . . .' My voice trailed.

I put out my arms and she gave me the baby. I hugged him close. I never will understand how it is possible to so love a child – a child you cannot possibly know. A new baby. Heavens, a new baby can turn into anyone – a family disgrace or lord of the manor. How ever do you know if you will like him or not? Clutching onto my son, though, after all those months, finally I felt whole again. I felt like myself.

'What have you called him?' I asked, giving him my finger to grasp as I stared into his handsome blue eyes.

But the shock of seeing me again had been terrible and instead of replying, my sister folded over and landed on the carpet.

I loosened the stays of her bodice with my free hand. I swear she was as small as a child. My niece, Helen, came out of the morning room in a jumble of mahogany ringlets and black, lace-edged ribbons. I sent her to fetch water and told Thomas to bring a pillow for Jane's head while the maid fanned my sister's prostrate form with a copy of the morning paper.

'I told Mother you couldn't die,' Helen said defiantly.

Carefully, I sprinkled water on my sister's ashen cheeks. As she opened her eyes I couldn't decide whether she was simply shocked that I was alive or dreading that I was home again. When she sat up the pins in her hair had loosened and a strand fell down like a blackbird's broken wing. It trembled in the wake of the maid's vigorous attempts at fanning with the *London Times*. Jane waved her off to one side.

'Stop that at once, Harriet,' she directed. 'And bring us some tea.'

Harriet had taken the children to the park. The day was bright if a little cold. My sister said nothing as she poured. After the initial exchange of information, there was, I suppose, little to say until the details had been digested. Jane bit her lip. She was thinking. I examined myself in the mirror over the fireplace. I looked respectable enough – my chestnut hair was piled into a bun and my hazel eyes shone bright and healthy. I had healed well. In fact I looked better nourished than my pale sister. I always thought Jane worked too hard and was thin as a waif, albeit a ladylike one.

After a few minutes the front door opened and crashed closed and I heard Robert storming across the hallway – a familiar pause as he removed his hat, coat and gloves. I caught Jane's eye and a flicker of a smile crossed both our lips. As children and, truth to tell, sometimes even as adults, we used to play hide and seek. Until Jane was ten we could both fit in the cupboard in my mother's kitchen – behind the loose piles of crockery. Now we said nothing and didn't move an inch, only sat waiting on the plump pink sofas by the fire. There would be no games today.

'Jane,' he roared.

She did not call back to him, only raised an eyebrow and went to the door. I stared into the fire. There was anger in his voice already. It did not bode well. Right enough, Robert's eyes were alight as he pushed into the room past his wife and stood on the carpet in front of me, staring.

'After all your indiscretions! Mary, have you no shame?'

'I was washed ashore,' I started.

But he was not listening.

'We have tried everything for you.'

Jane slipped back into her seat. She must have sent a message to the Gardens while I was talking to the children and dandling baby Henry on my knee. Robert never came home in the afternoon except in the middle of winter when it was dark early and his beloved plants could not be tended. I had often remarked to Jane that her husband treated his orchids with more care than his three children.

She used to shake her head. 'Don't be silly, Mary.'

I realised that we should have discussed this between ourselves before Robert returned. I also realised that Jane had decided not to.

'You are reckless, Mary Penney,' Robert snapped, the fury dripping from his lips. He ran a hand over his dark hair, in desperation, I expect. 'The worst of it is that you are reckless not only for yourself but for all of us.'

He strode to the chair beside Jane's and sat down. He was wiry but strong and his body was tense with anxiety. When he was angry he did not blink. Jane tried to calm her husband. I knew that she wanted me to stay, however shocking my return.

'You do not feel it time enough then, Robert?' she asked. 'A few months?'

I hung my head. I could see the difficulty I brought them. They could have done far worse than send me away to start a new life. Many in their position would have.

'I will go back to the theatre,' I declared.

At that Robert jumped out of his chair with his cheap pocket watch bouncing against his peacock-green waistcoat.

'And forsake us all?' he raised his voice. 'You go back to the stage and you will be dead to the children. It is enough, Mary.'

He meant it. And in that moment I knew that I'd never act again. Having the baby had changed me. It had changed everything. The day had come and gone when I would risk anything for a chance to play Rosalind. I had been foolish but still my blood rose and I could feel the colour in my cheeks. If I did not leave and could not go back to the stage then I would be a spinster – the children's penniless, spinster aunt. I was unmarriageable to anyone in polite society for all my tiny waist, my smooth skin and indeed, my talent. Still, I did not want to leave. England was my home and I was sure all that awaited me abroad was a string of second-rate suitors. My choices were limited and I railed against all of them. As far as I was concerned, I had been happy before all of this in London. I wanted to be happy here again.

'They die in Calicut,' I said. 'There is dysentery and worse.'

Jane sipped her tea silently. Between us we had scarcely caught a chill all our lives. When little Helen was only two she had a fever. Both Jane and I had been shocked. We had so little experience of sickness that we had to nurse her from a household manual, learning page by page. Penney women were small but strong. Our mother had been a full sixty years of age when she died.

'You will not catch it,' Jane said.

'We will secure another passage,' Robert added. 'We will send you to India again.'

This, of course, would take some weeks and I resigned myself to the decision slowly. For a woman like me there are few options. I had, I realised, come back to London hoping for something that was no longer there – an insubstantial promise of love that I had trusted like a fool – a promise, that, despite everything, I could not believe was truly gone. I had hoped that a few months' absence, might, at the least, allow me some shadow of the life I had before. I missed my friends in Drury Lane – the bright-eyed actresses and their dowdy dressers, our plump and jolly regulars back-stage who accompanied us on afternoon trips to Regent Street and Piccadilly, shopping in Dickins, Smith & Stevens or setting out to James Smith's to buy umbrellas or fancy parasols. I missed the fun of sherry and shortcake in the early evening and the backstage parties later on, the lazy band tuning up in a side room and the whores plying their trade on our doorstep. If I had expected to return to any of that I was mistaken – in the event of wanting to keep my son respectable, that is. I was at my family's disposal once more. It hurt. Still there were many women in a far worse position than I.

It's so easy to fall. From my sister's house in leafy Kensington, on Gilston Road, it is but a small drop to some damp room down by the river where you grow very thin and are used very harshly. I wanted no son of mine to dwindle to a stick. Too many children, half abandoned, live their lives hungry. Open your eyes and you'll see them in the filthy, dark corners, angular and ravenous. Even their hair is thin. Their mothers, poor souls, have nothing to give as they disappear into the quicksand, penny whores if they're as much as passingly pretty and washerwomen if they're not. Most people of our acquaintance do not even notice the desperation of the thousands, but there are plenty who regularly pawn their clothes for a little bread and would sell their honour, their spirit and their children if they could, for a life less comfortable than a nobleman's dog.

We were doing our best to salvage my mistake and, with a little stake money, India at least offered a decent chance for Henry (who, raised respectably with his cousins, would be free of my disgrace) and for me (since abroad I might still marry tolerably well).

*   *   *

14

I moved into my old room at the back of the house. Like a beating heart, in the background the city pulsed with vitality, but I might as well have been in Calcutta for all I could partake of it. I had nothing to do apart from spend time with the children for a few hours in the morning but I accepted that, for Henry's sake.

'He has your smile, Aunt Mary,' Helen said.

'I am not sure I am pleased by that,' I told her. 'Henry has no teeth yet.'

And this set us giggling. We drew pictures with coloured pencils and I kept Helen and Thomas amused with stories. I liked to hold Henry. I allowed myself to dote on him for hours until Harriet came to take him out in the perambulator after lunch.

Then, most afternoons I read an old copy of *Moll Flanders* and pondered on a woman, fallen like me, and attempting to be practical while indulging a hopeless love. I ran over again and again what had happened and cursed the unfairness of it. Damn William and his upper-class sang-froid that had left me abandoned like this. And yet I did not believe I was capable of settling for what Jane had. My spirit is too unruly. I loathed Robert and his like – their grasping, scraping self-righteousness. The lack of passion. The awful fear of what Others May Think. It seemed to me preposterous that Jane should love him – a man who calculated every step from a very high horse. To Robert what I had done was incomprehensible. For myself, I regretted what had happened, but running over the events in my mind, I knew why I had made my choices. I had been unlucky.

The night Henry was conceived William had been courting me for a year with what gentlemen call 'no satisfaction'. He took me to his private rooms for dinner. The hangings

15

on the wall glowed sumptuous red in the candlelight. We ate roasted boar with pear relish and crisp parsnips studded with rock salt, all served on silver platters that seemed to dance as the light flickered down from the sconces on the wall. As he downed French burgundy, I sipped champagne and William wove a wonderful spell. He would keep a house for me, he said. Anything I desired. Anything. Of course, such promises of devotion fired a passion in me that was blinding. I lived to be adored and here was a Duke's son, on his knees.

When I surrendered he kissed me all over and I hardly blushed. In the end he was so gentle that it surprised me. William was a large man and so much of the world that I expected him to make a hearty lover. Instead, 'You beautiful woman,' he moaned, the sweat dripping off him as he fumbled like some schoolboy. I should have known then how weak he really was. Instead, his vulnerability touched me and excited by the jewels and promises I took pity on him and forgave his physical frailty. I trusted him completely.

Now, in the cold bedroom at the back of my sister's house, the pale walls blue in the fading light of the afternoon and my cheeks already wet with tears, I cried for myself and my poor baby boy – whatever might become of us. I was sequestered – all respectable doors bar these were closed to me, and though Drury Lane would have welcomed me back with open arms, I had Henry to consider. It was a sacrifice all right and a shock to find that in six months nothing had changed. Still, I comforted myself that there is always hope and I did not wish for one second that the storm had done its job.

One afternoon about a week after I returned to Gilston Road, Harriet knocked on my bedroom door. She curtseyed, unwillingly, I thought, and held out a tiny salver with a calling card. I expected no visitors and eagerly turned it over to see who might have arrived. My stomach lurched as I read the name – William. A warm surge of hope fired through me. Perhaps everything would be all right after all. I told Harriet that I would come down shortly.

'Where are the children?' I asked as she left.

My voice was casual – at least I hoped it sounded so. My hands shook.

'Upstairs, Miss Penney.'

'Thank you.'

In the mirror my colour was high, my heart racing. Of course, I had rehearsed this moment – meeting William by chance in public, perhaps in Hyde Park, or seeing him on the other side of the street. But since his absolute abandonment, my letters returned, the long hours of waiting, the humiliation of being shunned, well, I had never imagined that he would actually call. All my thoughts had been directed to being beautiful at a distance. Of taking him by surprise and prompting him to adore me once again. The father of my child was downstairs. And Jane – Jane was out.

I laid my palms on my cheeks and took as deep a breath as I could, confined by my corset. Usually when I acted I did not tie my stays so tightly. The night I met William I had not worn a corset at all. I was Titania, Queen of the Fairies, all flowing chiffon and trailing beads. He had kissed my hand and remarked that the part had become me – henceforth he would think of Titania no other way.

'Do you think of Titania often, your Lordship?' I drawled, all confidence.

'From now on I shall,' he bowed.

Now, blushing, I hurried downstairs to the drawing room, my confidence much dented since my fairy days. William was standing by the fireplace. He looked as handsome as ever. As I entered, Harriet brought in a tray of tea things and laid them on the table next to the sofa. She curtseyed and left. I kept a steady gaze on the tall figure by the mantle. William did not meet my eye. I would not, I swore inwardly, take him back unless he begged.

'You are well?' he enquired at length.

'Yes.'

'You look well.'

I waited and in agony indicated the teapot. 'Might I offer you . . .' My voice trailed off.

William nodded. My hands were shaking too violently – I did not want to attempt pouring the tea so I crossed the room and sat down instead. I couldn't bear it.

'Monsoon, eh?' he commented. 'I expected you to be battered and walking with a limp! Half drowned when the *Regatta* went down and look at you. You're some gal, Mary!'

I stared. What on earth was the fool trying to say?

'William, why are you here?' I asked.

His eyes fell to the carpet.

'It was a boy, I heard,' he said. 'We have only daughters. My wife has never borne a son.'

My heart sank and I felt a rush of anger. A female child would not have prompted the visit and, clearly, neither had I.

'The claim of a natural child in such circumstances is strong. I will recognise him, Mary. I have discussed him with Eleanor.'

I got up and poured the tea after all. It would occupy me at least.

'Eleanor is one of seven girls, you know,' William continued. 'It runs in the family.'

It seemed impossible I had ever kissed the mouth that

18

uttered these words. Of course, a wiser woman might have flattered him. A wiser woman might have tried to woo him back. A wiser woman might not have felt anger rising hot in her belly or at least might have ignored it. Not I.

'And so you plan Henry to be your heir?' I said, 'and I will be nothing to either of you. I will sail again for Calcutta. Henry will stay in this house.'

'Oh, of course,' William said. 'Certainly until he is old enough to go to school. I have no objection to it.'

'You have no objection! No objection! You have never *seen* the boy, William. In point of fact you have not seen me since last summer and by God, you were not a man of honour on that occasion!'

I was working up a fury. A vision of Henry at twenty-one visiting his half-sisters. Him being whispered of as the bastard child of his wealthy father. 'To some actress, I heard,' they would nudge and wink, my name unknown. I saw William an old man, paying the bills, passing on a lesser title. While in Calcutta or Bombay I would outlive a husband I was unlikely to love. I would not matter to anyone.

I thought I might pelt William with the shortbread that Harriet had placed on the tray. Perhaps pick up the poker by the fire and smash something, hit him, anything. Had I survived the shipwreck just for this? I was searching for the words to shame him, ready to launch an attack, when, like the angel she is, Jane swept into the room. She probably saved me from a charge of murder.

'Your Lordship,' she curtseyed to William.

'Mrs Fortune,' he smiled.

'I have asked Harriet to bring down the baby so you might see him,' she said. 'I hope I have done the right thing?'

It was so like my sister to easily fit in with whatever was going on and simply make the best of it. William looked relieved.

'Yes, yes. I have told Mary that I will own him. It is all decided.'

'I have not decided,' I said.

Jane sat down next to me.

'Shush, Mary,' she soothed, before turning her attention to business. She was right, of course. This was the best thing that could have happened for the baby even if William's offer was somewhat late. Scarce more than a year ago he had said he loved me. He had sworn on his life.

Jane picked up the plate of shortbread and began to serve, passing the biscuits smoothly as she spoke. She, at least, was thinking with logic.

'Now, your Lordship, might I ask how much you were thinking of annually?'

Money was always tight. When Robert had his first appointment at the Royal Horticultural Society he earned a hundred pounds a year. Before my disgrace I was paid three times as much at Covent Garden – and then there were the gifts. Trinkets, baubles and fancies. Frills and sparkles. A dressing room so full of flowers it made you sneeze. I was never a star but I had admirers, a retainer and a portion of the receipts.

After Mother died I began to give money to Robert and Jane. Five pounds a month sometimes. Robert kept an account so he could repay me. He had an eye to the business of plants. Once when I had scoffed at his obsession, his ridiculous interest in soil types and root systems, Robert pulled out the newspaper and read a report of an auction – prices paid for tropical flowers arrived the week before from the East Indies. It ran into thousands.

'Rubber, tea, sugar, timber,' he enumerated, leaning over the dining table counting on his fingers. 'They've all been brought back to London. Tobacco, potato, coffee, cocoa beans. I will find something,' he muttered, 'and it will pay.'

At the time Robert's ranting seemed like the crazy ramblings of a Lowland Scot. Not that Robert had kept his accent. It diminished daily.

'I will not end up like Douglas,' he swore, 'mad, penniless and alone.'

I nibbled the cheese on my plate. You could not argue with Robert about plants and my interest in any case was limited.

The thirty guineas a year most generously settled on Henry was the first money that had come from my side of things in eighteen months. It had been difficult for Robert and Jane, I knew. As in any household, extra money was a boon. So this windfall provided a nanny, covered all Henry's expenses and, with what William had referred to as his 'dues for the last several months', Jane paid for another ticket to send me back to India, for, unspoken as William rose to leave, was the understanding that I was troublesome and the money would only be forthcoming if I was removed. If I had daydreamed of dallying in London, I had been squarely woken from it.

The *Filigree* was due to sail at the end of the month.

I found myself restless and unable to sleep. Things weighed uncomfortably on my mind. One night, some days after William's visit, I was late and wakeful. I visited Henry in the nursery but at length I grew tired of watching him and had it in mind to cut a slice of bread and have it with some of Cook's excellent raspberry conserve. I sneaked down to the kitchen like a naughty child, barefoot in Jane's old lawn nightdress. I had not bought anything to wear after the wreck and had only the clothes kindly provided for me on the island – Parisian cast-offs, well worn – and some hand-me-downs from my sister.

The slate was cold on my feet. The air in the house heavy

and silent – not even the ticking of a clock. The bread was wrapped in cloth and, as I unwound it, I jumped, spotting Robert, red-eyed, crouching beside the stove. He looked worn out – far more than I. His skin was as white as the nightshirt he was wearing over his breeches and the curl of hair that protruded at the top of his chest, clearly visible above the linen collar, looked dark against it.

'Sorry, Mary,' he said. 'I could not sleep. I have not rested properly in days.'

The house, it struck me, was a shell and we were restless spirits within it, seeking respite. Though I could not see what reason Robert had to prowl about in the dark.

I had planned on opening the heavy back door and sitting on the step while I ate. Everyone in the family had done that from time to time. It was something of a tradition. That night it was too cloudy to see the stars but the moon was almost full. It cast an opaque light through the misty sky.

'Well,' Robert said, 'perhaps we should have some milk?'

He brought the jug from the pantry and poured. I cut two slices of bread and spread them thickly with butter and jam. We swapped, pushing our wares over the tabletop. I glanced at the door.

'Oh yes,' he said. 'We should sit down.'

There was a breeze in the garden. Very slight but delicious. The fresh air blew in as we sat companionably on the step listening to the church bell sounding three. As the night wears on, the chiming sound echoes so. It is different once it's dark and the streets are quiet. I thought this could not be anywhere but England. The touch of cool night air on my skin and the bells in the distance. There were those, I knew, who had been out half the night at cards or dancing or worse, who were only now in some dark carriage on their way home. Robert shifted uncomfortably. He had a fleck of jam on his forearm and when I pointed it out he brought his arm to his mouth and sucked the sweetness away. This left, I noticed, a pale pink mark on his skin.

'I am going, Mary,' he said. 'I am commissioned.'

Robert did not look at me though an eager, almost shy, smile played around his lips. He had been given his chance. I assumed that he meant that the Society was sending him abroad to collect botanical specimens. It had been his ambition for some time.

'Where will you go?' I asked.

'China. *Camellia sinensis*. Tea plants.'

'You would think they had tea plants aplenty at Kew.'

'Those are Indian tea plants, not Chinese ones. Besides, I am not going for the Society,' Robert whispered. 'They do not pay anything more for travelling and whatever I bring back is not mine. I will go for the Honourable East India Company, Mary. Whatever new plants I collect outside the terms of the commission will belong to me. I will sell them to a private nursery for profit.'

'How long will you be gone?'

Robert stared towards the garden wall. 'More than one year certainly. Perhaps two or three. If I can find something it will make us, Mary. And of all the specimens to come from the Orient I cannot believe I will not make a discovery there.'

He had not touched the food. It lay in his hand. When Robert had secured his position at the Society it seemed the pinnacle of his career. This was a leap beyond. For all his efforts to fit in, all his fears about my behaviour, Robert was audacious on his own part. He worked every daylight hour. I could not find it in my heart to begrudge him this success, however difficult a time I was having.

'Well done,' I said, holding up my milk in a toast. 'I hope you discover something England cannot live without!'

We tapped the cups together, though as he drank I could see a flash of uncertainty in his eyes. Robert had fought hard to scramble up the rough battlements of advancement. He had become everything his betters wanted – a hard worker, a respectable family man and a prudent and underpaid employee. Now he had thrown over the Royal Society and struck out for himself. A mission to a barbarian land would be both dangerous and difficult. It was daring. No wonder he couldn't sleep.

'If anything happens to me,' he said in a low voice, 'I worry that they will fall. They will go hungry. I could stay at the Society, of course, but then we will never have the money to move up. I want the children to marry well.'

A few months ago I would have considered these words only proof of Robert's desperate desire for his own advancement, but now, having Henry, I recognised the father in him. Besides, he showed more spirit that evening than I had seen in him in ten years.

'No one could know more than you do. You have an eye for it – a feel for the plants that has brought you this far and will take you further. Strike out for yourself, I say, Robert. Jane will not be for starving if I know my sister. You are doing the right thing,' I promised him.

He took a hearty bite of his bread and jam.

'They do have a fund at the East India Company,' he murmured. 'For widows.'

We said no more.

The following afternoon I took the atlas from the morning room and sat by the fire. The tea countries are hilly and lie away from the coast. Robert was set to travel far further than I. With my finger I traced the outline of Madagascar, the largest island in the Indian Ocean. Réunion lies to its

24

east. My fingers followed the fine line of the coast. The map seemed too small to contain the vast, empty sea, the expanse of beach, the two miles to St Denis that I had been led on horseback, half dead. What lay for me in the maze of streets behind the tiny black dot that marked Calcutta and where was my sense of adventure that I so strongly resisted its allure? Unlike Robert I would not travel in unwelcoming territory. Bohea and Hwuy-chow were closed to white men. In India I would be welcomed with open arms.

I stretched my hand across the open page, my thumb on London, my fingers lighting on Calcutta and Hong Kong, Robert's landing point in China. We would be very distant. Weeks of sea between us. William did not love me any longer. He had dispatched me as easily as a lame horse or a hunting dog. Bought and paid for.

That week, Jane ordered two trunks from Heal's. We packed them together.

'I did not expect to love Henry so much,' I admitted.

'You cannot have everything you want, Mary,' she chided me.

The truth was I had nothing I wanted. Neither William nor Henry nor my life on the stage – only a sense of doing what was expected. I had fought against that all my life.

'Mother should have come with you to London,' Jane said wistfully, as if that might have kept me in check.

I giggled. Our mother loved a rogue. She probably would have encouraged me with William, if I had the measure of her.

'It is not funny,' Jane retorted. 'You treat everything as if it doesn't matter. It matters when you hurt people, Mary.'

But as far as I could make out I had hurt no one but myself and I let the matter drop, instead lingering by the open window. I love the smell of the horses wafting up as they pass. You can only just catch it. The sound of hooves and the whiff of hide that reminds me always of the stables near our old house, where we grew up, Jane and I. She and the children were my only family now and there was a bond between us that I simply could not bear to break.

'Do you remember Townsend Farm?' I asked. 'Father took me there once. He let me ride a pony. A white one.'

Jane stiffened. She banged the lid of the trunk down. She thought we were better off without him. Mother had agreed. 'We might have no man about the house but we can do for ourselves,' she used to say. I missed my father though, for I had been his favourite. I was not quite eight and Jane perhaps only ten when he died. Why he had cared for me more, I have no idea. Nor why he had taken almost a dislike to my sister – for he had been fierce with her, though I could not remember much of it. The bonds between a family are strange indeed. Jane had sheltered me when many would have slammed the door in my face and yet she would not talk about him. If I mentioned our father she simply clammed up, drawing her protective armour around her. Saying nothing. Our children make us so vulnerable. Our parents too, I suppose.

'It's all right for you,' Jane snapped. 'I have to pack, Mary. I have to organise everything. There is no time for your dilly-dallying. Come along.'

I had lost everything aboard the *Regatta* – love tokens, letters, my books and clothes. With William's money in hand, such replacements as could be procured arrived daily now, packed with sachets of lavender and mothballs. A notebook wrapped in brown paper from Bond Street as a present from Jane. Ribbons, a shawl for the evening, a bible, two day dresses from King Street and an evening gown from Chandos Street – everything I would need. And in Jane and Robert's room the other trunk, identical to mine but packed with a few clothes, a box of Robert's favourite tobacco from

26

Christy's ('No one mixes the same,' he always blustered as he exhaled), some botanical books, a map, more books to read on the journey (all on the subject of the Chinese). And then items for sale – prints of London and of the Queen for the homesick abroad, copies of *Punch* and the *London Illustrated News*.

Robert continued to be tired. I saw him mostly at dinner if he came home in time. He was working out his notice at the greenhouses in Chiswick, determined to leave everything in his care in perfect condition. Our only family outing was to a photographic studio in Chelsea ten days before we left. We took two hansom cabs and as the horses picked their way along the colourful West London streets I sat straight and eager with Henry asleep on my lap. I was delighted to see the city at last after being confined for so long.

On the route there were market stalls and apothecary shops, rag-and-bone men and ladies out walking. Even the strong smell of hops from the brewery delighted me but the children scrunched up their noses and complained. Towards Chelsea my attention was drawn particularly by old posters for the plays at Drury Lane that had opened weeks before. The tall, dark lettering on thin paper captured me immediately – *Othello* and *The Dragon's Gift* at the Theatre Royal. I wondered who was on the bill and if the parties were as much fun backstage as they used to be. Did the ladies still drink laudanum for their nerves and the gentlemen arrive with garden roses and boughs of bay? Helen followed my line of sight, seeing my eyes light a little, I suppose, on the thin, posted papers, and being a girl who was naturally curious, she leaned forward to read more easily and Jane, sitting next to her, pulled her daughter firmly back against the cushion as if out of harm's way.

At the studio Jane held Henry in her arms with Robert

behind us, and the older children to one side. In the photograph none of us is smiling and Robert looks exhausted, the sepia only highlighting the bags beneath his eyes and the indents of his hollow cheeks. At least we would have a record of the last weeks we were together.

'You will carry it with you, Father?' Thomas asked.

'All the way to China,' Robert promised. 'And when I return you will have grown beyond all recognition. You will be tall and speak Latin perfectly.'

A mere five years before, we had had another photograph taken. John, their eldest boy, now away at school, was held by Jane while I had little Helen on my knee. All of us were in jovial spirits that day. I was playing Cleopatra at the Olympic and had not yet encountered William. The kohl around my eyes had been almost permanent that summer. The dark lines did not come off fully until weeks after. They lent me an air of mystery, a sense of the forbidden.

In India the women wear kohl. They paint their skin with henna and scent themselves with moonflowers. The Hindus will not eat animals. But there is gold cloth as fine as muslin and as many servants in each household as work a whole terrace in London. I studied Hindustani from a book. 'Fetch this. Bring that.' So I could give orders. But still I did not want to leave.

In my last week, Jane and I engaged the nanny together. Harriet whistled as she worked, very pleased at this development, for it would greatly ease her workload. Jane's too, I suppose, for though principally in the house for Henry, the girl would also undertake duties for Helen and Thomas. With William's money in hand, Jane had placed a newspaper advertisement. She offered ten pounds a year plus board and we had over twenty enquiries.

We interviewed the more eloquent applicants – a mixed

28

bag of ages and experience. Jane was drawn towards the older women, the more prim the better. They came with references, of course, each woman from one wealthy family or another fallen on hard times and making her way as she could. For my part, I wanted laughter in the nursery and I took to asking, 'What games do you play with your charges?' The women Jane favoured invariably faltered at this. I despaired that we would come to an agreement and I had to concede that it was my sister, after all, who had to live with the successful candidate.

Our second but last interview was with a younger girl, new to the city. Her name was Charlotte. As soon as she opened her mouth and we heard her accent, it was as if a spell was being cast. Charlotte came from a little town not ten miles from where Jane and I were raised. Scarce seventeen and plain, there was a familiarity about her that we liked immediately. As a nursemaid she had looked after a family of two children outside London as well as having experience of her own, large family. 'There are many at home. I am the eldest of eight,' she grinned. She was well versed in poetry, I was glad to hear, and her favourite game was hide and seek. On Jane's list of priorities, Charlotte's manner was businesslike and respectful and although she had only one reference, it was excellent and, in addition, she was acquainted with many of the farming families we remembered from our childhood. After a fifteen-minute interview, Jane and I knew we had found someone who fulfilled our requirements and we offered her the job.

Charlotte's trunk arrived later that very afternoon and the children took to her immediately. Jane was quietly delighted at having another servant in the house.

'You will call her Nanny Charlotte,' she told Helen and Thomas, proudly.

It seemed to me she might have added, 'In the hearing

of as many of the neighbours as possible', for to have a third domestic servant in the house was a leap up the social ladder indeed, whatever circumstances had brought about the engagement in the first place. We ordered a uniform of course, and Jane wrote to William to inform him of what she had done. I had no heart to add a post-script of my own.

'I will miss you horribly,' I declared as Jane and I mended the last of the packing together, darning stockings and sewing buttons. The five months of the shipwreck was the longest we had ever been apart. 'I know I will be lonely.'

'Don't be silly,' she chided me. 'We will write every week. India will be wonderful. It is the perfect place for you, Mary.'

My sister lifted the cotton shirt up to her nose as if it was a veil.

'You will write to me of dusky beauties,' she twitched the material. 'And I will write of the children.'

I noticed that she breathed in, smelling the shirt before she put it down. Perhaps the soap and starch reminded her of Robert. The way he smelt on Sundays, freshly pressed, freshly dressed. When she took his arm and they walked together along the crescent, to church. That was how my sister loved her husband – well turned out and in public.

'Well,' she said, 'he is getting on. Nurseries pay well for the exotic and this trip will bring in a good fee plus anything Robert can sell on top. God will bring him home again and keep him safe.'

I had no fear for Robert. Nor for myself. After all, I had survived a shipwreck a thousand miles from London and still come home. I am of the view, however, that it was less God's business and more blind luck. And no one could deny that we were of a lucky disposition, all of us.

'He will be fine,' I said. 'Of course he will.'

*　　*　　*

30

When the trunks were packed we had sherry in the drawing room. Robert was booked on the *Braganza*, due to set sail for China from Portsmouth on the same tide as I. Jane had arranged for us to travel to the port together. She was stoic, of course, but had placed vases of lilies in each room. The funereal scent pervaded the house and matched her hidden mood. Jane might be exasperated by me but we had been close all our lives. This time it was not only I who was leaving but her husband as well.

Robert was late home from work that night. We did not wait for him. Cook sent up sandwiches and we ate them by the fire, toasting the cheese until it bubbled and spat. It made us thirsty and Jane had more sherry than usual.

'He must have made you feel wonderful,' she mused, drawing her hand down to smooth her navy skirts. 'Did you like it? What William did to you?'

I sipped my sherry and let it evaporate a little inside my mouth before I swallowed. Jane and I had never discussed our carnal desires and the truth was, William was not my first, though neither of my other lovers had inspired me to the heights that the ladies talked of in the dressing rooms. For myself, if anything, I missed being held. I like the strength of a man's arms around me. I avoided my sister's question entirely.

'Do *you* like it, Jane?'

Her eyes moved up to the shadows dancing on the ceiling. 'I love my children,' she said, 'and it does not last long.'

It is true that I had never seen Jane flush for Robert. They never seemed like lovers – did not lie in bed all morning or dally on the stairs. But this was a step beyond what I had imagined. It seemed so cold.

'William,' I said, 'was a terrible lover. But I know it can be . . .' I paused, 'very satisfying.'

31

My sister sighed. 'Before I married Robert, Mother tried to warn me, but it is beyond imagination, is it not? She said that it was like rolling downhill. But that scarcely touches the truth and makes it sound pleasant. The whole business is just so animal. I think I will never get used to it. A gentleman becomes quite unlike himself. I am lucky I fall pregnant so quickly and can have done with it.'

I was not sure what to say to that. Robert and Jane had been married a long time and they had only three children. If she had fallen pregnant quickly each time, they had perhaps only rolled down the hill on a handful of occasions in all the years.

'He is doing so well,' I commented, and topped up our glasses from the decanter.

'Oh, yes,' she enthused. 'God willing.'

My poor darling.

The day we left London it was raining. It rained all day. Jane rose early and saw to it herself that the children were breakfasted and dressed. By eight they were waiting to say goodbye, assembled uncomfortably in the morning room. These are awkward moments, I think, the moments of waiting, the time in between. Robert gave a short speech, advising them to be good, saying he was going away for everyone's benefit and when he came back he would expect great things of them. Thomas' lip quivered. Helen stared ahead, emotionless. I said nothing, only climbed up to the nursery where Henry was asleep and silently kissed his little head goodbye.

'Look after him,' I said to Nanny Charlotte.

'He's a lovely baby, Miss. Don't you worry about him,' her syrupy vowels soothed me.

I gave her a shilling and stumbled back downstairs. I shouldn't be leaving. I shouldn't be leaving. But here I was, almost gone, my sister kissing my cheek, her hands shaking.

'You can trust me with Henry,' she whispered. 'Never fear,' and then she turned and kissed Robert smoothly – a mere peck to which he scarcely responded. It was difficult to go. I stood on the steps until Robert grasped my arm and guided me firmly to the kerb.

When we mounted the carriage I could see the shades of self-doubt in my brother-in-law had hardened into righteousness. At the Society he had always been treated shabbily – a garden boy made good. Brave men have been broken that way. Douglas risked his life to bring fir trees from Canada and the seeds were left to rot in the Society's offices. He died unrecognised for his achievements, an irascible old drunkard, half blind and mad. Robert was now privately commissioned.

'On our way! On our way!' he said gleefully as the carriage pulled off. It seemed he had no thought for those he left behind.

Jane remained dry eyed. The last time I saw her was through the coach's moving window. The children were bundled upstairs. She stood on the doorstep of her house alone. It felt to me as if too much was unsaid, that words would have helped her if only she had used them. Everyone dear to me was now in that white, stucco house on Gilston Road and all in Jane's care. For the second time that year I waved goodbye as I watched the house recede. When the carriage turned left I saw my sister spin round and walk through the doorway, the sweep of her skirt slowing her haste. She slammed the black door quickly, almost before she was fully through. And we were gone.

Chapter Two

The road was muddy and it slowed us down. The hired carriage, uncomfortable to drive in at the best of times, bumped along the uneven surface. If I lost hold of it, the rug simply jolted off my knees.

When I had first arrived in London I walked there. It was more than a hundred miles and took me a week. I left home with my mother's blessing. I was fifteen by then and fired with visions of myself on stage, my name on billboards, fêted. I arrived with a shilling in pennies, a change of clothing and a fanatical light burning in my eyes that made me shine in any part I was offered. I bribed the scene-changers, forced my way into auditions and, once I had hijacked the part, stole the attention of the audience by fair means or foul – anything to act, to lose myself for a few brief hours on stage and bask in the limelight and the applause. My tactics worked. In my ten years in London I had managed everything I had hoped for – even two love affairs that had not inspired a single sentence in the scandal sheets and which, for a long time, saw me better provided for than most young actresses. Then I had met William. I hated being swept under the carpet like this. It was simply not in my nature.

Robert, by contrast, was in good humour. He clutched his pencil eagerly and wrote notes in a moleskine – comments on the weather or trees he had spotted by the road or over the tops of the brick-walled gardens as we rode out of Fulham, past Wimbledon Common and Richmond Park.

As we left the reaches of the city we followed a route now familiar to me, scattered with villages along the way – Claygate, Chessington and Esher. The clean air cut unexpectedly through the dampness, my head cleared and I felt calmer. I realised that I had been closeted too long in my sister's blue back bedroom at Gilston Road.

'I will simply have to make the best of this,' I thought. 'Perhaps I am an exotic flower and Calcutta will have me blooming. Maybe my instincts are wrong.'

Outside the window the puddles splashed as we drove through.

Robert sat back smugly. 'Headed for warmer climes, eh, Mary? We English travel well,' he remarked.

'You are not English,' I laughed.

Robert pulled at his greatcoat. I had irked him. So far from home I could see he would enjoy not being placed. He could be born a gentleman, an Englishman, whatever he chose.

'I'm sorry. I did not intend to hurt you,' I apologised.

'It is the least of what you've done, Mary,' he retorted tartly.

I straightened the rug over my knees and lowered my eyes. I did not wish to quarrel. We had hours until we reached the port. He drew a small volume from his pocket and settled down to read. Glancing over, I could see maps of India, drawings of tea leaves and tables of humidity readings. I contented myself with the thought that Robert was insufferably dull.

The rain made the countryside doubly green and lush. The dripping sycamores were beautiful. I watched the passing of each field. The tropics would be very different and these, I realised, were my last glances of England. The last time I had passed in this direction, many months before, I had been so distressed after Henry's birth and William's abandonment that I did not look out of the window once. My recollection was that I had been distracted by my own body – it was so soon after the birth that I ached all over. Coming home again I had willed myself every mile to London and was so intent on reaching the city that I scarcely noticed the scenery on the way. Now, entirely recovered and not at all intent on my destination, my curiosity was piqued by the view from the carriage window.

'Robert,' I enquired, 'are there sycamore trees in India? Are there horse chestnuts?'

Robert looked up. His blue eyes were bright. 'No,' he said. 'Not in Calcutta,' he tapped his pencil against the cover of his notebook. 'The seed does not travel easily. I know of a nursery on this road. We could obtain cuttings. The Society would be fascinated, Mary, if you could make the trees take on Indian soil.'

'No, no,' I insisted. His eagerness was simply too bookish. What did I care for the Royal Society and their no doubt copious information about what trees will grow where? 'It was not for that. I only wondered,' I said, cursing inwardly that I had started him off.

He laid down his notebook and continued.

'They have been cultivating tea plants in India for sixty years, you know. The bushes have died even on the high ground. It is in the tending of them. That is the thing. If I can crack that conundrum I will be there.'

I could think of nothing more tiresome.

'Does nothing else in China interest you?' I asked in an attempt to stave off the information that was coming, no doubt, about soil alkalinity and water levels. 'Strange dress or customs? The food?'

Robert looked thoughtful. 'I heard they train cormorants to fish. The Chinese keep them on leashes. Perhaps I will collect bird skins. I can dry them with my herbarium specimens.'

A sigh escaped me.

'And what of you in India? What interests you?' he snapped.

It saddened me. 'It is not by choice I am sent away,' I said. 'I have no interest there. I am cast out, Robert. You know that.'

He simply ignored me. He picked up his book and continued to read.

In the middle of the day we stopped in the muddy court-yard of an inn. Robert and I sat silently over a side of ham. I had not thought that we would stop. It was only for the horses. The road was hard on them.

Robert said, 'We will go faster in the long run if we see to them now.'

I wished we had travelled by train or taken the public coach. When the innkeeper stared at me, half in recognition, Robert became flustered. Perhaps the man had seen me on stage. We were not so far from town that it was inconceivable. Robert hurried our host away from the small side room and closed the door.

''Twas not the end of the world if the man had been to Drury Lane,' I said.

Robert checked the tiny window to see if the carriage might be ready.

'You do not fully understand what you have done, Mary. You have some regret but you do not understand. It is as well you are away.'

My jaw tightened but I could not stop the tears.

'You have never been in love,' I spat. 'There is no love in you.'

Robert rounded on me. 'It is not love to beget a bastard out of wedlock, Mary. *That* is not love.'

It was a comment I could not allow to pass.

'Henry will be fine. As you are fine,' I said pointedly.

Robert's parents were not married when he was born. Only after. Jane had told me about it years before, when she had been considering Robert's proposal of marriage, in fact. It was a secret he had not known I possessed and it infuriated him now.

He pushed me against the mantle. His eyes were hard and I realised how strong he was. The material of his great-coat cut against my neck and his voice was so furious that the words felt like barb-tipped arrows.

'You will never say that again, Mary Penney.'

Robert was often short-tempered but I had never seen him violent. I thought to strike him but I believe in that state he would have struck back. His cheeks were burning. Jane's husband had not a Lord for a father. Not like Henry. Robert's father was a gardener, a hedger on an estate in Berwickshire, or had been until he died. The man's talent with plants was not a wonder. No, the wonder of Robert was how effectively he had expunged the two-room cottage where he was born and in its place put all the comforts of his house on Gilston Road. The carved wood of the mantle cut painfully into my skin.

'Let go, you brute,' I squirmed. 'Are you set to beat me because I defended myself? What would Jane say, Robert? Get off!'

Robert's hands fell to his side as he brought his temper under control.

'You try me, Mary,' he said.

I hated him horribly but I bit my lip and said nothing. It was clearly fine for Robert to insult Henry, but not accept-able for the same words to be used of him. I comforted myself that this journey would be over soon enough and then I would be free of the tiresome bully. I stalked back out to the carriage and, refusing help, I took my own seat. Robert said not one word the rest of the journey and that was fine by me.

On the coast it was not raining but it was cold. At Portsmouth we were to stay with Mrs Gordon. Jane had written and reserved the rooms. All being well with the weather, we had a night to wait. Jane had thought we would prefer to spend the time on land together rather than make our way to separate cabins. This was a treat that I had not been accorded before William's money came to bear. I regretted the arrangement, but now we had arrived there was nothing else for it.

Mrs Gordon's house was on a busy side street close to the docks. At the front door, I dismounted and was welcomed by our cheery landlady, a fat woman wearing a plum-coloured day dress that set off the copper hair beneath her starched white cap.

'Come in, ma'am, sir,' she smiled. 'I am Mrs Gordon and you will be Mr Fortune and Miss Penney, I'll be bound,' and she swept us inside on a tide of efficient courtesy.

The house was clean and comfortable and smelled pleasantly of sage and lavender. In the generous, wood-panelled hallway Mrs Gordon ushered our luggage into place and told us the arrangements for dinner.

'Your rooms are the two on the left at the top of the stairs. They overlook the street,' she informed us. We were set to ascend when a door opened and a cross-looking lady emerged from the drawing room with her husband. Mrs Gordon introduced them as the Hunters.

Mrs Hunter fiddled with a chain around her neck. She reminded me of a dog playing with its tail, the links twisting round her fingers never quite satisfying her, the amethyst and pearl locket constantly out of reach.

She inspected me plainly while Mrs Gordon introduced us. 'We are off to inspect the *Filigree* before it gets dark,' she said. 'We sail tomorrow.'

'You will be my shipmate, then, Mrs Hunter,' I smiled.

'How nice. What takes you to Calcutta?'

Behind me, Robert froze.

'I will visit relations,' I lied smoothly, aware of his eyes on me. 'And my brother here is to board the *Braganza*.'

Mr Hunter nodded towards Robert. 'Well now, you must envy your sister, Mr Fortune. Hong Kong is no match for the delights of India.'

This topic was no better for Robert than that of my reasons for going to Calcutta. The East India Company did not wish his mission to be common knowledge. I realised my mistake and tried to divert the conversation. This chance encounter was rapidly becoming unexpectedly difficult.

'So you have been to India already?' I attempted.

The Hunters giggled good naturedly as if I had said something particularly amusing.

'Half our lives,' Mr Hunter replied. 'Is it your first voyage to the East, ma'am?'

I shook my head. 'This time I hope to arrive, though.'

'It was you who survived the *Regatta*? Oh my,' Mrs Hunter's voice rose, 'how exciting! Freddy, Miss Penney shall be our lucky charm. No one has ever gone down twice! You must wish very much to visit your relations. What are their names? Perhaps we are acquainted.'

Myself, I would have concocted a name, but before I could answer, Robert cut in, unable to bear it any longer.

'Mary will marry in India,' he barked, staring pointedly at Mrs Hunter. 'There is no more to tell.'

My cheeks burned with discomfort and quickly the Hunters excused themselves and hurried out of the front door. Such rudeness was entirely unnecessary and I rounded on Robert as the door closed behind them.

'Did you think I would be able to embarrass you halfway across the world?' I snapped, though in truth I pitied him. The poor man would never be free of himself. He pushed me forward a little to escort me upstairs, past the trunks that were now piled on the landing – ours and the Hunters'. He could scarcely wait to stow me away.

'I have enough to think of, Mary. You and your bastard child are the least of my worries.'

That settled it – I had had enough. Incensed, I turned on him and as I did I saw a cricket bat piled up among Mr Hunter's things. I grabbed it.

'How dare you?' I raised the bat, furiously swiping as hard as I could. 'You pompous, self-important, short-sighted fool!' I lost my temper.

Robert backed downstairs, away from my blows and nonchalantly and with his hackles down, easily wrestled the bat from my hands, tripping me up so that I landed with a thump on the thin carpet. The man was all muscle. My blood boiled even further.

'You must rest, Mary. You leave tomorrow,' he said coolly to dismiss me.

I scrambled to my feet and, disarmed and furious, I ran to the first room, slamming the door behind me. There were tears in my eyes. I cursed Robert as I sank onto the bed. How dare he? After a minute there was a soft knock at the door. I threw a pillow at it.

'Go to hell, Robert,' I said.

I thought he surely must regret behaving so callously but when the door opened it was the ample figure of Mrs Gordon that entered.

'Now,' she said, her tone comforting and motherly, 'here is some arnica cream, Miss Penney. My guess is that fall will leave a fine bruise.'

'Thank you,' I sniffed.

Jane had picked our lodgings well. Mrs Gordon's kindness only provoked me to cry more. I was in a torment of anger and humiliation. I felt like hammering the mattress with my fists.

'Some polka you danced there with your brother,' Mrs Gordon remarked. 'I keep an orderly establishment as a rule. But,' she smirked, 'the look on his face when you took up that bat has me inclined to allow you to stay the night.'

I had no idea we had been seen.

'I am glad to be gone tomorrow,' I snivelled.

Mrs Gordon nodded. 'Perhaps I will see to it that you have dinner in your room. I shall send the girl with a tray at seven.'

'Thank you,' I sniffed as she helped me unhook myself and I smoothed on the cream.

That night I dreamt of my dressing room at the theatre. I was drawn back vividly to everything I was leaving behind. I could smell the jars of rouge. The broken handle on my dressing table had not been fixed. There was a door in the corner that led to dark rooms, new places beyond the scope of backstage. There were fur rugs and long benches padded with comfortable cushions, and the wax had burnt very low so the flames flickered, lending the dimmest glow to the endless labyrinth of windowless rooms. The place had the air of a funfair with a dark helter skelter in one corner and a Punch and Judy show too. And somewhere I knew there was a baby, but I could not find him. I dreamt of myself wandering, tormented, searching and moving on. Leaving Henry had disturbed me.

When I woke after this restless sleep it was already light. I shook off my misgivings and dressed for breakfast. Downstairs, Robert was just finishing. He drained his glass. I wished him a good morning and slipped uncomfortably into a seat. It transpired that the Hunters had gone to church early. St Peter's held special services for travellers about to embark and my shipmates were, it seemed, of a pious disposition. It would be awkward now but I would do my best to befriend them once we were underway. It was a long voyage, after all.

In silence, I sipped some cocoa and nibbled on a slice of bread. Outside the little window the weather was perfect for getting off. The dockside was bustling with activity, ships loading last-minute supplies and sailors turning out of the waterside inns, some drunker than others. Robert paid our bill.

'I will escort you to the *Filigree*,' he said. 'I promised Jane I would make sure you were safely aboard. I have sent the luggage.'

I felt like a schoolgirl, but there was no point in arguing.

'Lead on,' I replied, falling into step along the cobbles of the sea front. I told myself it would be fine. I was set to try. Perhaps India would be wonderful and I would lead a life of exotic adventure in the Raj. Shortly, we came to a halt at the ship, right under the name, emblazoned in white above our heads. Robert gave me my passage money. I squared up to him and held out my hand.

'I know you only want rid of me. You might not believe it but I wish you the best, Robert. Come home safe and wealthy from your adventures.'

Robert peered at my hand and then reached out to take it.

'Goodbye, Mary,' he said. 'It seems unlikely we will meet again.'

He did not stay to watch me up the gangplank. I held the railing studiously. William's money had secured a more expensive passage for me this time. The ship was bigger than the *Regatta* and well finished. Mostly she was laid out to cabins. Up the other gangplank they were loading boxes and casks – the final supplies for the voyage. I stood at the top of the plank and with some satisfaction, my gaze followed the figure of Robert as he made his way towards the *Braganza* and disappeared into the throng of bobbing heads.

'Well,' I thought, 'at least I am on my own reconnaissance now. I shall find my cabin.'

I drew myself up and turned to face the deck, and my future.

This resolve, however, did not last me thirty seconds for I had no sooner moved than Mr Hunter appeared from a doorway near the poop deck.

'Miss Penney,' he greeted me curtly.

I nodded back, at a loss how to explain Robert's poor behaviour the day before. Mr Hunter, however, showed no sign of discomfort at all.

'I have come to check our cabin. Clara will follow me shortly. Perhaps I could help you to yours?' He took my arm.

For one moment I thought perhaps it would be fine, and then my blood ran cold as Mr Hunter placed his free hand on my waist, coming too near to whisper:

'I realised last night that your face was familiar. No one on this ship or indeed in Calcutta need know, Miss Penney, of your particular talents or your misfortune.'

I pulled back. Would I never be free of the reputation afforded me in those damn scandal sheets?

'We can come to some arrangement, my dear. I did not expect you to be childish.' The blaggard pushed up against me so that I could smell the tobacco on his skin and the claret on his breath. His contemptible intentions were all too clear.

'Would Mrs Hunter find it childish?' I challenged him.

'A man being married never troubled you before as I understand it.'

'I can find my own cabin, thank you,' I retorted and turned away, catching the sneer he gave me, the half-muttered threat under his breath.

'You don't have a choice, you harlot.'

Robert, it occurred to me, would probably agree with him. For that matter so would William. I was fair game.

But there on the deck, quite suddenly I found that I did have a choice. I did not have the choice I wanted, of course, but that was by the by. In a flash I realised that if I was to be labelled with my shame and preyed upon wherever I went, then why should I go anywhere? Especially not on William's say-so or indeed, Robert's. Damn them all, why should I do what they say? It was for Henry's welfare, certainly, but then who was to know if I didn't embark? Who was to berate me or penalise him? In fact, the only thing that mattered was that William wouldn't find out. Robert would be gone, I reasoned. Jane hardly left the house and certainly never went as far as Drury Lane. I had lost my family whether I went to Calcutta or not and I was never expected to return. I had tried to come back and it had not worked out as I had hoped. Now I might as well make myself happy, or as happy as I could be. I would not be subjected to Mr Hunter's odious desires. Why should I?

Once the idea presented itself I was taken. My heart fluttering with anticipation, I climbed the steps to the poop deck without a word, leaving Mr Hunter behind me. Above, the captain was not at his post but the first officer presented himself. I had made the decision.

'Take my trunk off,' I said. 'I will not be sailing today.'

'But Miss Penney, your passage is part-paid. We cannot wait for you.'

'I am not going,' I said very definitely. 'Keep the money.'

Mr Hunter had left the deck when we came back down. No doubt he thought he had the whole voyage to prowl me. I watched as my trunk was carried off and I paid tuppence to have it taken back to Mrs Gordon's. A plan was taking shape, even as I walked away from the *Filigree* and all my good intentions. I could pitch up in London and use a different name. I had always wanted to be named Georgiana. The more I thought of it, the better it seemed. Would William even recognise me, I wondered, if I changed my name and my appearance? Dyed my hair darker with the walnut, plucked my eyebrows thin and wore an old-fashioned mole? I would disappear into the world of London's theatres. Better for me to stay in England surely, than go to Calcutta. Why should I be banished when I was not the one who had broken my word? I had tried what they wanted, now I would make my own way and best of all they never need know.

Fired up, I cut along the dock, avoiding the *Braganza*, and walked uphill towards Mrs Gordon's. With luck I could take the public coach back to London the following morning and have, if not everything, at least some chance of happiness. I would be in Shaftesbury Avenue in time for the evening shows. I still had friends there, people I could call on easily and who would welcome me back with a role if I wanted it. They would keep my secret, I knew, for Drury Lane is full of confidences and cover-ups and its residents are adept at their workings. Quite suddenly I felt exhilarated. I had been so cooped up that even walking alone along the narrow streets was an adventure and now here I was unexpectedly at the start of a new career. Another twist in my life prompted by a damn blaggard, I reflected, but still this felt good.

'I shall call myself Georgiana Grace,' I decided. It had a ring to it. Oh, yes, I would dine well at Mrs Gordon's house and, better still, I'd play Rosalind yet.

I rapped on Mrs Gordon's door and the maid answered. The trunk had followed me up and was now deposited in the otherwise empty hallway. Mrs Gordon hurried down from her chamber and I made my requests, checked the Hunters were now gone and, paying one night's lodgings, I settled by the fire with a bottle of burgundy to myself, a plate of cheese and some bread.

'I do not wish to be disturbed,' I said and Mrs Gordon asked me no questions. It occurred to me in any case that she was the kind of person who knew the answer before the question was posed.

'The London coach leaves at nine tomorrow. I'll have the maid rouse you with time to spare,' she said.

I ate, read and daydreamed. I thought perhaps that after some months had passed I might manage to see Henry in the park. I could walk there when Nanny Charlotte was sure to be taking the children out and I could keep my distance, but watch him nonetheless – see him grow up a little. The loss of Henry was at the heart of me and while I knew I would never see my sister again – that simply was not possible – perhaps, I hoped, I might be able to keep an eye on my son. The more I thought of it the more I liked my plan. At length the *Filigree* sailed and when it was gone, and I could no longer change my mind, I felt freedom beyond measure and I decided to take an afternoon stroll. The weather was fine and I was eager. I pulled on my gloves, checked my hat in the glass and set out to work up an appetite for my evening meal.

I wonder often what might have happened had I not left Mrs Gordon's that afternoon. I wonder what might have happened had the *Braganza* set sail an hour or two before she did. For I had made my decision to disappear and it was not in my mind that Robert, of course, was still in Portsmouth. In fact, I was not thinking of Robert at all and, while I avoided the docks and set out in the opposite direction, I had no thought that he might see me. I expected him to be in his cabin or sitting on deck reading some dull and worthy textbook as he set out to sea.

Robert, however, believing I had gone, had repaired to a public house to celebrate before his ship set off. He was not a drinker as a rule but I expect I had tried him and he had hoped to blow off some steam. The place he had chosen was not a bawdy house. It lay away from the docks on the path I happened upon for my afternoon stroll. It was frequented mostly by naval officers, many of whom followed Robert into the street when he spotted me through one of the small windows and dashed outside in rage and disbelief. He bellowed my name so loudly it echoed.

I froze and so did he. Both of us stopped on opposite sides of the narrow street, staring in incredulity and horror at the sight of each other. We hesitated. Then I turned and ran, pelting up the cobblestones, cutting into a muddy alleyway with no thought but to flee, blood pumping through me so fast that my heart was hammering. Of course, a lady is at a great disadvantage when it comes to a chase and I did not get far.

He caught me roughly and bundled me back down the hill, dragging me most of the way. I could not imagine where he was going, could not make out the furious muttering under his breath. His fingers were gripping my arm so tightly that I thought he would draw blood. People avoided us, stepping out of the way and deliberately not meeting my eyes.

I was crying. As we came closer to the port such was Robert's fury that I feared he was going to throw me over the side and into the stinking, green sea. Instead he clutched me by the shoulders and pushed me aboard the *Braganza*.

I shouted, 'No, no, no,' over and over. I cursed him for his hateful snobbery. I shrieked every insult I had kept to myself all the weeks I had been home. 'You liar! You bastard, Robert Fortune! You are nothing but a Scottish pretender! Even your wife can't bear to touch you! I'll embarrass you now, by God! What would Jane say if she could see you like this? You're a beast and a bully! No gentleman at all!'

Robert did not reply. He bundled me across the deck and flung me through the door of his cabin, slamming it shut and turning the key before I could round on him. I sank to my knees, pulling the clothes off the bed, flinging papers, scattering his precious tobacco on the bare floor. I wanted to rip everything apart, to smash my way through the thick, wooden walls and destroy everything.

'Let me out,' I screamed, hammering so hard my palms hurt. 'Let me out! You have no right, Robert! No right!'

No one came. As my wrath wore down I lay on the floorboards and cried until at last my tears ran out. I waited a long time, the ship creaking, footsteps passing by the doorway, until at length the sounds of the ship changed, voices were raised and we cast off. Outside the tiny porthole the skyline seemed to move. We were in motion. Robert had clearly decided that if I could not be trusted to leave England alone then he would escort me himself. I could imagine nothing worse.

I sank down onto my knees and for once I prayed. 'Dear Lord, please,' I said, 'not to sea with Robert. Not with Robert. Anything, anything else.'

But as the ship rocked this way and that, setting out from Portsmouth on her long voyage, it seemed that that was exactly what God had in mind.

Chapter Three

Robert and I did not speak for a month. He waited until we were suitably far from shore before he let me out of his cabin. He had it in his consideration, I expect, that I might have jumped ship and swum back had he not left a few miles of open water between England and me.

'You swine,' I hissed at him, my voice acid and my heart black, as he led me to my own quarters that first afternoon.

I had never hated anyone as much as I hated Robert then – not even William. If I had had the opportunity I would have cheerfully pushed him overboard but our passage to the cabin newly assigned to me took us nowhere near the fringes of the ship. As it was, my trunk had been fetched from Mrs Gordon's, a small ship's cot had been made up for me and from there on, as Robert closed the door, not a word passed between us as we sailed south. My meals arrived from the galley on a wooden tray. Robert dined with the captain and the officers. Everyone avoided me. I had been hauled aboard red-faced and screaming, and I could only guess what Robert had told them.

My isolation made the days and nights both long and lonely. There is little enough to do on a voyage, no privacy outside the dark, wooden cabin and scarcely any space or, indeed, occupation outside your own mind – if no one will speak a civil word to you, that is. I passed Robert frostily on deck every day that first week or two and neither he, the officers or the main body of the crew acknowledged me once. I was a pariah.

At night I had a strange dream, that Henry, his body still that of a baby, but his face as old as his father's, screamed abuse at me for leaving him behind. As the ship sailed further I felt the lack of him like a hunger – a physical sensation – that woke me often in the night. I had not had this on my last voyage for I had not known the child at all and my mind had been focused on William's betrayal. Now, I tried not to dwell on these dreams and, during the long days and their endless line of blue outside my porthole, I continued with my Hindustani lessons out of sheer boredom, and read about India's history and the customs of the Bengali region around Calcutta. Of elephant-headed goddesses and golden temples. Day after day after day, my hours in the dark cabin were punctuated only by a short and uncomfortable stroll along the deck with all eyes upon me. With a sinking sadness I resigned myself to this punishment and to my banishment once more.

One such dreary afternoon, the line of blue at the porthole grew a streak of vibrant, tropical green and, unable to take my eyes from it, I flung open my cabin door to discover we were pulling into dock. I rushed across the deck, excited, halting in my tracks only when I saw Robert standing at the rail, his brown suit buttoned up and cravat in place. As if he sensed my movement he swung round, his blue eyes hard.

'Is this Tenerife?' I asked in a breathless rush, quite forgetting my hatred of him in the excitement.

We had stopped here on the *Regatta* and the ladies had bought trinkets. Robert strode across the deck towards me and almost swept me off my feet with the force of his anger as he pushed me to the side of the steps that led up to the poop deck. I still did not immediately understand what he was doing and I continued to babble.

'They have parrots here, as I recall,' I said, pushing back against him. 'Let me pass, Robert. It is quite a spectacle.'

The crew were all about their business on the deck, securing the sails and making ready. The captain was above us, instructing his officers. I heard a snippet of their orders – a list of provisions required and names of the men who were allowed ashore.

'Robert,' I started, distracted and enthusiastic still. 'What are you doing?'

He had taken a thin rope and expertly tied a knot, which he slipped quickly over my left hand and then the right, before I had time to set myself free. Then he tethered me to the post at the foot of the stairs.

'No. No. I promise,' I whispered, desperate with embarrassment. 'I will not jump ship here. Please, Robert, don't. Please.'

But it was no use. He grunted like an animal about to attack and then he moved off.

'How could you? How could you?' I shouted.

My cheeks were burning. My brother-in-law turned, his eyes as sharp as a hawk's trained on its kill. I knew he was thinking of hauling me back to my cabin if I made a fuss. Damn him. My stomach turned over in fear and a single tear slipped down my cheek as I bowed my head, trying to contain my fury. I did not want to be confined to my cabin for the rest of the trip. I could not have borne it.

'I will be quiet,' I said, tight-lipped and unwilling.

It was better at least to stand on deck and see the loading and unloading on the shore. I kept my head high. The whole crew were in good spirits as the stocks of fresh water, fruit, meat and vegetables were replenished.

'Excuse me, ma'am,' they said, tipping their caps as they passed me, acknowledging my existence for the first time since I came on board.

No one mentioned the rope that bound me or even looked at it and I tried not to dwell on what Robert had done though I was furious with him.

Robert had written to my sister and now at length I saw her name on a packet that was passed down to the dockside. As it passed me by, I felt sad that Jane would know I had been caught trying to get away. She always worried so, as if the spectre of our father might be waiting in the wings to punish any wrongdoing. I did not wish to add my own missive home. I could think of no words that would calm her. Robert, I surmised, would make a better job of that. My apology could wait. Had he told her, by postscript, I wondered, that he had tethered me to the ship? That he had confined me by force? That in a matter of weeks he had struck me, kidnapped me, bound me and bullied me? He had a fire in his belly that belied his bookish existence in London – how could my sister have married such a brute? But then I could not be sure whether Jane would be more horrified by my behaviour in sneaking off the *Filigree* or her husband's in press-ganging me to his own voyage.

All in all, I was left for four hours tied to the deck that day in Tenerife. My wrists were as painful as my furious heart as I tried and failed to loosen the bonds. When we sailed away from the port at last, heading back to sea, I watched the yellow houses on the dockside recede until they were only tiny pinpricks on the blue horizon – a final goodbye to all that was even vaguely familiar. The coast of Africa lay ahead.

When Robert came to cut me free my body tightened with fear and anger. God knows what he might do next.

I said nothing, only regarded him with clear disdain and held his gaze defiantly as he removed the ropes. Still he did not speak, only stood back to let me return to my cabin.

Over the following week Robert maintained his silence. Whenever I saw him he was tending his plants. Glass cases like huge trunks had been bolted into the deck. He watched over them devotedly, like a child with a fallen fledgling. And they thrived. As the weather became warmer he appeared to relax. He worked without a jacket, or when he was not working he sometimes sat reading. The day he first said something to me it was a week since the ship had pulled out of the Canaries. I had taken to walking the deck for an hour each morning, as there were gulls and jumping fish to watch where we followed the coastline.

'These Ward's cases have done well,' he said as I passed him on my way down the deck.

There was no sign of viciousness in his voice. It was as if we were in the habit of passing our time chattering to each other and this casual comment was not a landmark – he sounded just as he used to in the drawing room at Gilston Road. For a moment I found it difficult to comprehend that Robert had spoken to me at all and I was not sure how best to reply.

'Ward's cases,' Robert repeated, tapping the top of the glass box.

I could see out of the corner of my eye the cabin boy stop coiling rope and silently watch us. The child was the only person on board who routinely acknowledged my presence. He never spoke but always nodded in recognition when I passed him and was often sent to deliver my tray. One time I had offered him a scrap of cloth to bind a cut on his arm, but he had fled from my cabin in terror. It made me wonder what reputation I had been afforded among the crew. Robert sat down on the deck and continued.

'At first I was troubled by weeds. But what I realised, Mary, is that if unwanted seed can germinate on board so can wanted ones. On the way home I shall try it. I shall embark with bags of seed and arrive with saleable seedlings worth a great deal more.'

He poked his trowel at a bougainvillea plant he had brought on board. The flowers were a beautiful, deep pink. They bloomed in abundance all over the wiry stems. Robert picked one and passed it to me.

'Robert, you know that you have bullied me half to death,' I accused him. I was not that easy. 'And you seem to expect simply to take up normal society. I am angry.'

I held the flower in my hand.

'Yes,' he said, a slight tremor in his voice. 'I am angry too, Mary. You lied. You did not keep our agreement. But we are beyond Europe and there is no point in argument now and every point in coming to terms.'

'No apology then,' I suggested.

Robert's body became tense at once and he leant forward, his voice too low for anyone else to hear. I think he wanted to strike me, but he was holding himself back.

'And did *you* apologise? You are headstrong, Mary Penney. You simply do whatever you please. I took in your son for Jane's sake but that lodging did not come free of charge. If you leave he will be recognised a Duke's grandson, one day a Duke's son, too, with a title of his own. Don't you want that for him? For us all? And I catch you in Portsmouth and your ship has sailed. Come now.'

I bit my tongue but I am sure my eyes flashed with fury.

'Think on it,' he said. 'I have done what's best for the boy.'

And he returned to his work as I stalked away. He had a point, of course, God damn him. I knew he did.

In my cabin, I placed Robert's flower in a tiny glass of water on my bedside table. It was the brightest thing I owned by far.

That night, after dinner, I took my life in my hands and crossed the deck to Robert's cabin. The weather had become hotter and I was uncomfortable despite the breeze. My only sleeveless gown was of a pale eau de nil tulle. I coiled my hair in the French style to keep it off my shoulders. I had come to try for a peace. Some kind of resolution. Robert was right – there was no point in quarrelling so far from home though it was difficult to quell the anger in me. I paused a moment, took a deep breath and then knocked.

'Come in.'

Inside, lit by two oil lamps, Robert was surrounded by his books. He stuck stringently to his suits the whole voyage and was still wearing evening dress, having dined earlier with the captain. His face was dark from the sun and lines of paler skin showed at his wrists. If he was surprised to see me he showed no sign of it.

'Mary,' he said. 'Can I offer you . . .' he gestured towards a decanter on the side table.

I shook my head.

'Robert,' I started with my heart pounding, 'I have come to ask you, where am I heading? You have kidnapped me and I don't have a clue of your plans.'

'I had no choice, Mary,' he started his defence.

My fingers quivered. I did not intend to fight with him – that would not get me what I wanted and I knew now that he would simply force me to do whatever he decided was best. Straining against my instincts, I stepped further into the room and shut the door behind me.

'You were probably right,' I conceded. 'I had promised

to leave. Only that fellow Hunter recognised me. He threatened me and I walked off the ship. He wanted . . . relations I was not prepared to accord. And now, Robert, I merely want to know where I am going and when I might get there.'

Robert shifted uncomfortably before he replied.

'Oh, Mary. I had no idea that man had . . .'

'It doesn't matter,' I said miserably. 'You are right in that I intended to stay in England and I should not have done so.'

I waited momentarily and Robert nodded, clearly deciding that I was at least rational.

'The captain's plan is to dock somewhere on the western side of the Indian continent but he told me he must consider weather conditions to the other side of Africa before he can be sure.' Robert jerked his head to the left indicating the general direction of the land mass. 'It is only then he will make his judgement where we will port.'

'Will you leave me there?' I asked plainly.

My hands were still quivering.

'We are bound for Hong Kong,' he said quietly. 'I have paid your passage.'

The truth was, of course, that Robert did not trust me to stay in India. I can hardly blame him. Shortly after we embarked he amended his original plan. He discarded Calcutta and chose to take me somewhere remote that had the advantage of a less regular passage, as well as being a hub for his own voyage. His plan was to use Hong Kong as a rallying point at the end of his trip. He would there-fore be able to check on me over time. It made sense now I thought of it.

'I see,' I said, hiding my surprise.

'We have another eleven weeks or so. The current to the other side will bear us more swiftly.'

I hung my head. I knew the currents around the African coastline only too well. I had to be practical and control myself. Robert took my silence for fear.

'There are no monsoons at this time of year, Mary. I trust Captain Barraclough. He is prudent.'

This half-hearted attempt at comfort annoyed me but I said nothing. I was further and further from London, that was all. At least now I knew.

'Did you tell Jane that I am here?'

Robert nodded. 'As briefly as I could,' he said.

I suppose that was fair of him.

That night I stayed up late. As the humidity increased I found myself keener on the clear, balmy, black skies than the midday swelter. I excused myself from Robert's cabin and took a turn around the deck. The wide sky was breathtaking, more pinprick stars coming into focus every minute. The only sound was the boat cutting through the water, slapping against the swell. I have always been a night owl rather than a lark. It felt like a very long voyage as we sailed into the inky blackness ahead. I was childish, I suppose, but with tears on my cheeks I surreptitiously snapped the stem of one of Robert's stupid plants in a silent rebellion. I ripped the bright flower to pieces and threw it over the side.

When we came to cross the equator, the traditional initiation to the Southern Hemisphere was due for anyone who had not passed that way before. The ship was all excitement and the cabin boy – the only person on board who had not been that way before – was nowhere to be found.

On my first voyage it was only the ladies who had not previously crossed the line. The crew showered us with buckets of seawater on deck and we toasted our luck with Madeira.

It had been a fête of good spirits. The *Braganza*'s cabin boy, however, was not treated so kindly – he was found hiding in an empty barrel. They bound his hands with rope and then hauled him over the side. He emerged minutes later, spluttering, bruises appearing on his childish skin and bad cuts where the rope had chafed him. The crew made him drink more than he was able, holding his nose and pouring rum down his throat.

'Enough of that!' I said, horrified. 'Enough. Stop it!' But no one listened and my voice was lost in the jeers of the horde, while Robert held my arm tightly in his grip as we watched from a distance. I expect he worried that I might fling myself among the sailors and attempt a rescue.

My eyes filled with tears though I knew it was foolish. It had not been so long since I spluttered seawater myself.

'It's cruel,' I said simply. 'That boy is so young.'

'Sometimes you are too soft, Mary,' Robert chided me. 'I hope you are not going to make a fuss. It will be worse for the lad if you do.'

I let it be though my blood boiled. The life at sea is hard and I did not at that time realise that being half drowned was the least of the child's worries. Drunk and exhausted they let him fall asleep.

Later that day, alone in my cabin, I put my mind to remembering everything I had heard about Hong Kong. It was an island; I had seen that on the map. And it had not long been British. *The London Times* had been sceptical when China had handed it over. They said the place was hardly worth taking. The truth was that it sounded even worse than Calcutta – some god-awful backwater full of second-rate pioneers. As I stacked the now useless Indian books in one corner of my trunk, I resolved to ask Robert to let me read some of his books about China because, apart from this scanty impression, a Chinese embroidered shawl the wardrobe mistress used at Drury Lane, and a beautiful lacquered cabinet William had in his London drawing room, I knew not one thing about where we were going.

My bougainvillea was already wilted and I slipped the faded bloom inside a flyleaf to press it as I packed my things away. 'The colour was bound to dampen down,' I thought sadly and wondered if Hong Kong might supply as steady a contingent of suitable husbands as had been expected from the Indian colony.

'Is this the best I can hope for?' I asked myself but, of course, there was no one to reply.

There was still a long way to travel. Even by the time we had reached the Cape of Africa we had not yet covered half the miles. It felt as if I had spent a whole year at sea. When we encountered the storm it scared me more than I expected. Thankfully, my voyage home through these waters had been uneventful, the variety of weather limited. This time the sea reared mountainously and we were closeted below decks. The petty officer escorted us to the hold. The ship was keeling so hard that it was difficult to remain on the wooden bench, though it was bolted to the floor.

'You will not lock us in,' I begged.

The officer did not answer me. He directed his comments to Robert.

'Stay below decks,' he said. 'It is safer. Some will be swept away in this.'

Then he fastened his greatcoat and left.

We were below for hours as the weather raged. The winds were high, the water towering exactly as it had the day the *Regatta* went down. Robert paced up and down, worried only about his Ward's cases, while every tiny creak had my heart pounding as I waited for the ship to split in two. This time would I be lucky enough to be driven towards the shore or would I be swept further south to the open ocean? Robert hardly noticed my anxiety, such was his concern for his plants. He muttered under his breath about the ropes holding the canvas covers he had fitted in place. He worried about how low the temperature might drop or if the cases would flood. He had no sense of our mortal danger at all. From time to time a sodden deckhand passed and sent up another man to relieve him.

At last, after several hours, Robert could not bear the uncertainty. Despite the petty officer's warning he pulled on his coat and went to check the damage. The ship pitched and rolled. The storm had not abated. I thought longingly of home. Not London, but my childhood home. I admit, it crossed my mind that should Robert be swept away I would return there. When he did come back I could see he had properly realised our peril. He was drenched to the skin, his pink flesh icy and a cut on his leg.

'One case has smashed,' he reported, indicating the bloody slit. He must have fallen against the broken glass. 'The one with the bougainvillea,' he said absentmindedly, for the plants were less important to him now he had seen the height of the storm.

At that moment there was a loud crash above us as some part of the rigging came free on deck. I screamed, my whole body taut, waiting for the force of the water to smash everything and toss us away. Robert placed a hand on each of my shoulders and shook me.

'Stay calm, Mary,' he directed sharply.

At first I could not speak for terror. Then I found my voice.

'This is how it happened before,' I said, trying to explain, 'the ship split. That noise . . .'

Robert cut me off. 'Your panic serves no one.'

'Those who have not been stung will not fear a bee the same as those who have,' I retorted.

He really was hardly human sometimes.

Robert took his handkerchief from his pocket and bound his wound. He took a draught from his hip flask and offered it to me. I shook my head.

'Go on, Mary. It will help,' he said.

I took it but did not thank him. The man was unbearable but his brandy warmed me. I could feel myself flush.

'I know you want sympathy. But my sympathy will do you no good, Mary. We have to do our best if Captain Barraclough does not succeed in riding the storm. If we will die, we will die.'

I snorted, handing back his flask. The brandy instantly made me drowsy. I have never been one for spirits on an empty stomach and now I sank down on my knees. Low to the boards I was rocked by the movement of the ship without fearing I might fall, and, despite all my apprehensions, the lateness of the hour prevailed, exhaustion overtook me and I drifted fretfully to sleep.

When I awoke the ship was steady and Robert was gone.

'We are safe,' I breathed and climbed the wooden ladder onto the deck.

The sky was clear as far as I could see. It was as if there had been no storm at all. As I emerged into the scorching heat Robert was salvaging battered plants from the end case. The bougainvillea petals were smeared over the shattered glass, the soil soupy with seawater.

'Help me, Mary,' he directed.

My fury stung me. It was clear these stupid plants meant more to Robert than I or anyone else. I could not forgive the fact that his first comments did not concern the welfare of the crew or our good fortune in surviving the storm. I surveyed the battered plants with no pity.

'If they will die, they will die,' I pointed out and swept past him back to my cabin.

I was not allowed ashore at the Cape although Robert must have trusted me more by then because I was at least allowed my freedom. I sat on deck under a makeshift parasol and watched the supplies being loaded. Bare-chested men with gleaming ebony skin carried boughs of fruit on board. They brought sacks of cornmeal and barrels of palm oil on their heads while I fanned myself regally with an ostrich feather, which I had bought leaning over the side and bartering in sign language with an old Indian man on the dock who seemed fascinated by the whiteness of my arms. While the loading of the ship diverted me, I admit that the views above the bay held my attention more. The flat mountain and the verdant countryside were entrancing. I found it difficult to harbour a grudge in such a setting.

Robert repaired his case and restocked it. He chose grape vines that were delivered in terracotta pots and slotted into the empty spaces under the newly puttied glass.

'Perhaps,' he hazarded, 'we shall start a vineyard or two in China. They make rice wine, you know. And five grain spirit. Now they can try a hand at a decent claret.'

This amused the captain, who had come to stand with us as Robert bedded down the vines and soaked them well.

'Are you recovered from the storm, madam? My petty officer tells me you were distressed,' he said.

Before I could answer this Robert stood upright.

'My sister is now quite recovered,' he said as if this should end the matter.

Captain Barraclough, however, persisted. 'I can imagine how frightening such an experience must be for a lady.'

'Tell me,' I asked, 'are the crew all right? Did anyone . . .'

The captain nodded. 'All present. One man hurt an arm

when the rigging snapped but everyone was held fast with rope. No one overboard.'

At this news my eyes filled with tears, a vision of those long past, another crew, another captain. Barraclough looked concerned.

'I was on the *Regatta*,' I said simply.

Robert looked furious at my admitting this but Barraclough's face softened into understanding. He evidently thought that here he had found the reason for my behaviour when I boarded ship.

'I knew James Norman,' he said, naming the captain.

There was a moment's silence. I could think of nothing more to say. Then Barraclough bowed, having evidently decided I was not mad after all.

'Will you do me the honour tonight of dining with myself and my officers?'

'Thank you,' I replied. 'I will.'

When the captain turned back towards the poop deck, I waited for Robert to reprove me. Instead he surveyed his planting.

'I will say nothing to cause you embarrassment,' I promised.

'I suppose 'tis well enough,' Robert nodded curtly.

That evening, like a debutante, I enjoyed dressing for dinner. I put on my finest dress and piled my hair into a bun with trailing wisps. For scent I chose lavender oil with a touch of violet. I pinched my cheeks ferociously to heighten my complexion and gazed at myself in the tiny glass with pride. To enter society again was exhilarating. I blew myself a kiss.

The tales I had heard of high jinx and drunkenness in the captain's cabin aboard British ships proved unfounded that night. Barraclough and his two officers, Matthews and Llewelyn, were easy company and civil. All had been to

China before and were patient as I quizzed them about our destination while the very cream of our replenished supplies were served – a side of boar and some exotic fruits I had never tasted before, which were as honey in their sweetness. As the salty night air seeped into the candlelit room I simply felt happy to have conversation and company. No one mentioned the storm or my time on the *Regatta* and I was grateful for that.

'The highlight of London on my last visit,' Llewelyn admitted, 'was *Hamlet* with Mr Charles Kean.'

Barraclough smiled indulgently. 'Llewelyn is one of our artistic officers,' he explained. 'He takes drama very seriously.'

'I know the production. So tell me, sir,' I ventured, 'how did you find the tights?'

Llewelyn shrugged his shoulders. 'Tights, madam?'

'Why yes. It was the chap playing Horatio. For you know, Hamlet – that is Mr Kean – is a most exacting gentleman and the young fellow, at the Royal for the first time as it would happen, lost the dark tights that were provided for his role. His "mourning garb". He scrabbled about everywhere but could find no replacement save a scarlet pair, that were rather patched. For Horatio? Can you imagine? Knowing that each of Horatio's scenes are played with Hamlet and that Mr Kean would not let such slovenliness pass, he visited the great man's dressing room to explain and receive permission to wear the scarlet hose until a replacement could be procured. "Ah," said Mr Kean when he heard the story, "I will forgive you, but" and here the great man pointed skywards, "will you be forgiven there?"'

'Actors!' I declared as the men laughed. 'They do take the whole business rather seriously, don't you think? Did you as much as notice the famous tights, Mr Llewelyn? That's what I want to know.'

Robert cut in, of course, as soon as the laughter subsided. 'I shall tell you the story of the cultivation of the potato now,' he announced and diverted the attention away from me just as the cheese came to the table.

Although I sighed inwardly, I do admit that the details of his tale did appear more interesting somehow at sea than they ever had in the drawing room at Gilston Road.

When the ship's bell struck ten Robert walked me to my cabin door and bid me goodnight.

'I enjoyed myself,' I said. 'Thank you for letting me attend.'

In my cabin, alone again as I pulled off my gloves and considered getting ready for bed, I heard a footstep on the corridor. I waited a moment or two as it receded and then checked the door. At the footplate Robert had left two books. One was on the subject of the Han Dynasty, the other an examination of Chinese porcelain production. I took them in greedily and flicked through the pages. It was difficult to sleep in the heat. Even in the dead of night it was humid and uncomfortable. I often read until my eyes were dry with tiredness. It was comforting that this gift meant Robert was set to forgive me a little and was entering into the spirit of the peace pact I had hoped for.

In the second tome a detail caught my eye – an unusual china plate with a star pattern. At dinner the captain had mentioned how different the stars were when he viewed them from the south and I thought to show him what I had found. Perhaps he might be able to identify the stars in the illustration. We had a long way to go together. I grabbed the book and left my cabin once more.

In the moonlight I crossed the deck and rapped on the captain's door, not waiting for an invitation to enter. I had left him so lately that I still expected there to be company in the room. As it turned out there was. The cabin boy. As the startled child ran past me, a flash of bare flesh and rags, it struck me that he could not be more than twelve years of age. His breeches were not fastened properly and I could smell a grown man's sweat – the smell of sex on his skin. My blood ran cold.

Barraclough squared up with his shirt tails trailing. He ignored the boy's flight entirely.

'Ah, Miss Penney,' he said. 'Can I help you in some way?'

I am no prude and no innocent either. I know of such things. Unlike Jane, I have moved in many circles and some are circles of the night, of gambling dens and seedy brothels, of smooth young boys and richer men. There were reasons Robert did not wish me to admit to my life in Shaftesbury Avenue, Drury Lane and Covent Garden. Talent might not be thoroughly unrespectable but some of the places it can take you are. This child had been tampered with. I thought of the bruises I had seen on his arms and legs over the weeks, his treatment at the equator, the way he had fled from me when I offered to bind his wound and now this. Barraclough was despicable. Had he done this every night of the voyage? Had he dismissed the company he entertained at dinner in order to terrorise this child? And if I accused him openly what might he do? Buggery is no mild offence. At home they hang you. For the captain, the stakes could rise no higher. I did not want to corner him and make him fight. I only wanted to save the boy if I could.

'It is nothing. It doesn't matter,' I said and left at once.

The child was nowhere to be seen. I ducked inside my cabin with my mind racing. My only point of appeal for injustice was to the captain. On the water they are as kings. I thought of telling Robert. I almost did but the captain was the captain and Robert cared for no one.

The next morning I approached the child on deck at his duties. He was afraid and lashed out at me.

'Go away!' he hissed.

'What is your name?' I tried.

He regarded me plainly.

'I am Mary,' I said.

He hunched his shoulders, clearly calculating whether talking to me could cause him any harm.

'Simon,' he said. 'I am Simon Rose. Please leave me alone, Miss. They will beat me.'

No child should have to endure such wickedness but on board there was little I could do. I resolved, however, to take whatever action I could think of. When the invitation came to join the captain's table that night I declined. I declined every night from then on.

Perhaps a week later, Barraclough passed me as I strolled on the deck. He tipped his hat. 'We miss your company, madam,' he said.

'Manners maketh not the man,' I replied, gliding on. 'I have seen what you have done.'

He did not answer and kept away from me then.

'Lord, Mary,' said Robert, some time later, when he realised finally that I was avoiding the captain. 'You are never at ease. What fuss is it you are making now?'

I almost rebutted him. I almost told him, but it would have done no good. He was not a person who cared for cabin boys and servants, actresses or illegitimate sons. I had no more power to help the child than my sister had had to help me. I offered what little I could but the child would not accept even a scrap of food from me (for I tried that) or the whispered offer that he might, if he wished, sleep outside my door for protection.

When Robert later wrote the memoir of his travels he

did not dwell on the voyage. He said, I think, that his passage of four months to Hong Kong was 'uneventful'. After all, of more interest to his readers were his wanderings in China, the allure of the East and the plants he found there, along with some account of the people. The book sold well. It secured his children's education and saw Gilston Road polished and repaired, hung with fine curtains hand-embroidered in Soo Chow and fitted out with intricate papers on the walls. I can see Jane pulling her cashmere stole around her, enjoying the spoils. Of course, I was not mentioned – his companion on the uneventful voyage. He did not tell of the storm at the Cape nor mention any of the crew. Those days are unrecorded. The late night games of rummy in my cabin. The night we ate spices off the coast of Alleppey. Or the day Simon Rose's body was committed to the Indian Ocean, covered in bruises and swaddled in sackcloth, for the child did not even have a hammock to be buried in and had slept on the bare floor.

After that I retired to my cabin for the rest of the voyage, tiresome though it was to be closeted and alone. I read and pondered, thinking often of my baby, wondering about his progress and hoping Nanny Charlotte was right and he was fine. The tiny porthole allowed me to daydream, my eyes on the cloudless sky and my heart in London still. It was a heavy burden. I decided to write to Jane when we got there.

By Hong Kong I was the only person on board who had not been off the ship in eighteen weeks. The air in the bay was dripping with humidity. I put on my most fitted corset for the disembarking, aware that I would be noticed and commented upon. I piled up my hair and wore a hat. The atmosphere was so full of water I noticed every hot, heavy movement, my legs damp with sweat. Still, as the lush, green bay grew closer my heart pounded. I looked up at the Peak, making out one or two houses being built.

'Bamboo scaffolds,' Robert said delightedly. He had brought up his binoculars. 'An excellent idea. Ingenious.'

My notice, however, had fallen to the dock, which was coming steadily closer. It teemed with tiny figures despite the fact there were only five other ships in the bay. I took a deep breath or two, as if I were waiting in the wings, and decided that I would try my best. The island looked lush and green and not at all the unpleasant, arid rock I had expected. Perhaps my time in Hong Kong would pass well if only I could make myself amenable. By now I could make out individual faces in the mass of people going about their business. Wide-faced women were selling noodles and hot tea. Coolies with wooden chests balanced on their backs were scurrying from the docked vessels towards the town. And rows of Englishmen in red uniforms wearing pith helmets to protect their flushed faces from the sun were overseeing the activity, checking papers and directing traffic. Back from the main bustle young Chinese girls in brightly-coloured satin dresses lazily eyed the soldiers.

I watched Barraclough disembark, the first to stride down the gangplank and towards the harbour master's office with his lading papers in hand. I was glad to come down after him and stared icily as Robert shook his hand and we said goodbye. Perhaps Robert did have some notion of what had gone on, for Barraclough was in Hong Kong a week or more and Robert did not invite him to dine.

As we watched our trunks unloaded and waited for the Ward's cases to be unbolted and brought down, Robert breathed deeply with satisfaction. I crept off to one side, finding my land legs hard to come by. The ground seemed to sway and I felt quite in a haze, as if I had taken a swig of laudanum in the backroom at the theatre as was pleasant from time to time. Along the dock there was a wooden shrine with a cloud of incense around it and I decided to try out the solid ground and make for that. There were two old women there on their knees before it, praying, one whirling a wooden clacker and the other beating on a brass gong. The latter approached me and offered a handful of incense sticks, gesturing for payment. I scrabbled inside my purse for a small coin, which she inspected, shrugged her shoulders and then carefully stowed away. I suppose it is normal to use English coins around the world. The island was ours, after all.

'Come, come,' she gestured me forward and then put her hands together to indicate that I should pray at the shrine.

As I came closer I saw there was a figure, roughly hewn from wood, and small pots with tropical flowers beneath gold and red Chinese script. There was so much incense already stuck into piles of sand, I was surprised that the whole thing had not ignited, but I decided that I would light my own anyway as a gesture, foolish perhaps, for my arrival. As the sticks started to smoke I made a wish, concentrating hard on it. Please let us be all right, I prayed, as the fragrant smoke wound like a spell around me. Henry and I. Jane and the children. Let us all do well. And it was only as I walked away from the little temple that I realised I had not included Robert in my thoughts. I had just spent months on end with him and now, two minutes apart, he was the last thing on my mind.

'A place of adventure, Mary,' Robert commented stiffly on my return, surveying the dock with obvious delight. 'And full of adventurous men.'

His plans for me had evidently not been changed in any respect other than location. However, I liked this little city. I bought a cup of green tea from a stall and sipped it. I had become accustomed to the island quickly, enjoying the feel of solid ground. And, as Barraclough strode back up the gangplank to give his directions, I was only vaguely uneasy that perhaps an adventurous man was not what I was truly looking for.

Chapter Four

Robert busied himself with his preparations. There were only three weeks before he was due to sail for the Chinese mainland and leave me behind. In that time he had to engage a guide, sell the plants he had brought with him and make plans for his journey. I was to settle. Given that I liked the island and was most diverted by its delights after the long confinement of the voyage, I found this surprisingly difficult. Banishment is an unpleasant sensation. I continued both angry and frustrated but hid my feelings from all around. The August weather was stifling and without the breeze of the moving ship the humidity sunk me. There had been a malaria outbreak at the barracks at Happy Valley and the town was greatly concerned – hundreds of soldiers had died and there seemed no containing the spread of the disease. Some of the ladies refused to go out at all.

Robert was pragmatic. He had no time for such fancies. Major Vernon, the head of the battalion, visited our lodgings shortly after our arrival. The marshy ground at Happy Valley was conducive to the epidemic and Robert recommended vegetation to counteract its effects. Vernon commenced planting straight away. Thus introduced to the British community as an expert and a welcome addition to their ranks, Robert's now-forsaken job at the Royal

Society made him friends easily and he visited someone new every day. He brought plant cuttings for the enthusiasts and snippets of news about London – changes to familiar streets, accounts of mutual acquaintances and detailed descriptions of new planting in Kew Gardens, Hyde Park and Chelsea. It seemed such was the excitement of receiving fresh news that most people were prepared to disregard the danger of us contaminating them. Nor did Robert consider that our new acquaintances might contaminate us. The contact was too valuable.

His new friends helped him plan his journey, poring over maps for hours, telling of the dangers in taking on the mandarins, who were the ruling class in the interior, and volunteering letters of recommendation to the few European missionaries living inside. China's borders were closed to white men. Only five of her ports had any kind of British community and those had only become official since we won the war the year before. The ports supported British trade in the region, but the Chinese were hostile and resentful of our victory and the enforced terms we had imposed. We made them buy our Indian opium but the Emperor had banned his people from taking the drug as he considered it dangerous. I had seen what opium could do – there were dens in the West End, I knew, where some chased the dragon to the detriment of everything else. But then there were those who could not rise without their shot of brandy either. Some people will fall victim to anything for it is in their nature, but that is no reason, to my mind, to ban a drug outright. Such extremes are a far cry from the laudanum that I and my friends sometimes relied on for a touch of comfort. Why, even Jane used the tincture from time to time, when she had the cramp and the apothecary recommended a grain or two. The Emperor's stance seemed some kind of hysterical reaction to me.

Of greater threat to his empire, as far as I could see, was Robert's mission. Tea was China's greatest export and the Emperor's men guarded the tea plants and the secrets of their production carefully. In this venture my brother-in-law was taking his life in his hands – the Chinese would kill him and his entourage if they knew what he was up to. In Hong Kong, however, everyone rallied to the pluck of Robert's expedition and in the fine mansions on the slopes of the Peak all appeared to have one or two scraps of information about the interior that were invaluable in planning the trip. It would have been difficult to continue without such help and people were extremely generous.

I was invited on all these visits. I expect Robert was keen to present me as much as he could to maximise my chances of finding employment and also to establish me so I was less likely to leave.

'My wife's sister has decided to settle here,' he would say. 'Might I ask you to keep an eye to her interests while I am gone? No, no she is *Miss* Penney. Quite unmarried. For the time being in any case.'

Had my skin not been swollen pink and puffy with the heat I am sure it would have crawled with discomfort, but his words washed over me as if the opium that had won us the island was embedded in the hot, heavy air. Distracted by the activity that Robert generated in making his plans, it was as if I had simply disappeared.

One afternoon Robert returned to the lodging house with a Chinaman he had engaged down at the bay. The man was underfed and fell upon the bread and tea sent up for him from the kitchen as Robert quizzed him in my presence. In a mixture of Cantonese, which Robert had studied for some months now, and the man's patchy English, it became clear he was from Hwuy-chow, one of the tea countries Robert had determined to visit. His name was Sing Hoo.

I admit I did not take to Sing Hoo. He had been poorly treated and unlucky in seeking his fortune, that much was clear. But he had a shifty look about him as if he was always sizing up the possibilities. When he finished his tea he tapped the side of the porcelain surreptitiously as if checking its quality. When he realised I had seen this he shifted uncomfortably.

'The Chinese will not meet a woman's eye,' Robert commented sagely for he had not noticed Sing Hoo's action – only seen my stare and the Chinaman turn his head away.

I said nothing.

Over the following day or two Robert listened to everything Sing Hoo had to say about tea. He had been brought up on a smallholding and had grown tea plants there since his childhood.

'Can you take me there? Can you show me this?' Robert asked each time a particular process was detailed.

Interspersed with more general questions of horticultural interest, Robert took copious notes of everything, any detail about the soil, the weather or the farming of the tea plant. When Sing Hoo explained the process of drying the picked leaves, heat levels used or aromas added, Robert drew what he understood – a drying rack or a mixing bowl, and Sing Hoo hooted with laughter, grabbed the drawing paper and amended the sketch.

After two or three days the man lost his hungry look, but my view was still that his eye was to the main chance. When Robert opened his maps and called Sing Hoo to help plan the expedition he became vague and uncooperative. Distrustful, I expect that if he told what he knew he might

76

no longer be needed. Robert's face showed his frustration as he tried to find details of jurisdictions and journey times, navigating the strange interior at a distance to foresee as much as he could. I knew he was finding ways to send home seeds and plants no matter what might happen to him once he crossed the forbidden boundary into China's interior.

I passed my time walking out. I felt an affinity with the island. The freedom to wander was most welcome after the confinement of the ship and Hong Kong felt like a vast and exciting half-discovered world – an alien dream that entranced me with its lush greenness. There was plenty to see. Splashes of vibrant colour burst from the foliage – an abundance of fascinating, angular pink, red and orange flowers I did not know the names for. I never asked. I did not want Robert to launch into an explanation that would diminish their exotic magic with details of pollination or water systems.

I liked the calm water of the bay in contrast with the bustling dock. I liked the stacked baskets of chickens and the sheen of the brightly coloured satin displayed in its bales. The toothless ancients outside the little temples fascinated me, their bodies like stick insects, angular and dry as they sat in the shade and begged alms. Dusty-skinned Chinese children hovered nearby their fathers who had fought in the war. There were many missing an arm or a leg and others with scars on their faces where hand-to-hand combat had torn their skin to pieces. Still-eyed, bony and eager they watched me as I passed. Their children, fingers twitching, all set to cut my purse should the chance arise, the bolder ones circling at a safe distance like birds round a fishing boat, ready to swoop. With my heart racing at the thrill of my proximity to something so foreign and dangerous, I hovered only on the fringes of their territory, never entering the fetid shanty town itself. I peered down the narrow, hot streets that ran with stinking, steaming excrement over the beaten earth and came as close as I could. It was like holding an entrancing but venomous snake that might strike at any moment. I was fascinated, but I kept it at arm's length.

It was on one of my expeditions I encountered Wang. Abandoning my attraction to the shanty for the day, I had decided to hike up the hill to take in the view of the bay. It was a difficult climb with only a muddy pebble track but I was sure it would be worth the effort. The top of the Peak was very high and the outlook undoubtedly spectacular. Robert had gone to the other side of the island to sell some of his plants and had no need for or interest in my company. After lunch I set off with only a flask of boiled water to sustain me.

I started fine. The road was not too steep but as I climbed higher the gradient increased dramatically. I was not a third of the way up when I decided that this was not an expedition for a solitary lady. My boots stung and I was perspiring furiously. I found a large rock to lean against and sipped the water.

'I had best go down,' I thought.

I did not want to be beaten by the hill, however, and I resolved to try again another day with more appropriate footwear and stays less closely bound. The view was already opening out. To the west I could see smoke rising from a thousand cooking fires down in the grubby settlement and ant-like figures moving along the makeshift alleyways. Every one of them appeared to carry a parcel of some kind either bound to their backs or carried in front. I would come back, I decided to enjoy this view again, and climb even higher.

The air had been thick all day. Close to the sea my guess

was that a refreshing breeze might come off the water, but the weather defied such expectations. We were not in Europe any more. Now, within seconds, a tropical rain shower broke. I pulled myself under a large, flat-leafed tree but it did not afford much protection. My skirt was soaked immediately and I watched horrified as the path I had followed up the hill flooded into a muddy morass and the pebbles that had helped me to keep my foothold became as slippery as polished glass. I had been gone from the lodgings less than an hour. Getting back was going to take far longer.

In the midst of this I saw large branches suddenly thrashing beside the path, as some creature made its way through. I glanced round frantically, calculating where I could run. My first emotion was a reserved relief when it was a man who emerged. His loose trousers and coolie shirt were thoroughly soaked and a brace of dead pigeons was slung over his shoulder. He was as startled to see me as I was to see him. It cannot have been common to come upon a muddy white woman underneath the dripping trees. I backed away, noticing a sheathed knife slung through a scarf of material binding his waist. There was no one around for at least a mile. My breathing became shallow as I contemplated bolting despite the treacherous path ahead.

Then Wang said something in Chinese. I did not understand so he pointed first at me and then down the hill, motioning me to follow. He smiled a brown-toothed grin and did not make for his knife. I weighed it up for a moment and, heart in my hands, I decided to go. Getting down by myself would be too difficult.

Far more slowly than he would have made the journey without me, I am sure, we picked our way through the trees. It was the natural way to descend the slope when it was so wet. Roots bound the earth together and there were branches to hold. But the jungle was very overgrown and if you did not have your bearings it was easy to get lost. Wang led me sure-footedly down. We emerged near the town.

'*Um goi*,' I said. Thank you.

He seemed so competent I doubted he was hungry but he had done me a good turn and I wanted to reward him. I motioned him to come with me this time. Back at the house I could give him a coin or two. Now we were in the city he walked behind, the sodden game still over his shoulder, splashing whenever it hit his body. The pigeons were as effective as sponges.

'This way,' I said.

By the time we entered the front door Robert had returned. He strode out of the drawing room in a bad temper.

'Where in the devil have you been?' he snapped. 'Look at you.'

'This man brought me home through the storm,' I explained.

Robert fumbled in his pocket, gave Wang a small coin and directed him to the kitchen for some food.

'I think I shall go up,' I said.

It was odd Robert had not pushed me for an explanation of where I had been or exacted any kind of punishment – it was not like him when his blood was up. But, as I alighted the first step, I could see the reason. There was a figure in the drawing room. An old man. He inclined his head and came to the door.

'This the girl?'

Robert nodded.

'Yes, my sister-in-law, Mary. Rather overtaken by the weather,' he said.

My stomach turned over so fast my kidneys felt as if they had been hit. Robert was plotting. The old man eyed me avariciously. Even in the heat my fingers drained ice cold.

'Well, my dear, you have settled upon Hong Kong, then?' he said. His teeth were yellowing and his thin lips seemed almost blue-grey. He was seventy, this fellow, if he was a day.

'I must get changed,' I replied coldly and walked up to my room.

I would rather be a spinster than be sold off, traded in, whatever they might call it. I had lost all my trust after William and the world of love and marriage was no longer somewhere I wished to travel. Marriage carried with it a long list of things I could not, should not do. Some say once you're married you can do as you please but that isn't true if you marry someone who wilfully restricts you. You have a great deal less control over a man's life than he has over yours. I began to look on Robert's plans for me as if they were some kind of unhealthy obsession on his part. I knew that he had good intentions. He wanted a rich husband to support me. In Hong Kong I must make my living and the pickings for a woman on her own were slim. Robert would leave me with a little money, of course, and I might find a job that would earn a meagre keep, but the drop here if I did not marry was no less than it would have been in London. I tried to ignore this.

Once I had dressed I sneaked down to the kitchen. Wang was still there, eating noodle soup from a bowl. Between ugly, gulped mouthfuls, he asked a question in Cantonese and the maid rebuked him.

'What did he say?' I asked.

The girl had good enough English.

'Stupid man. He ask if you have seen the ship that sails without wind. No such thing.'

81

'I have seen it. A steam ship. The *Sirius*.'

'He wants to work on this ship.'

'Tell him it is in London – a long way from here.'

Wang continued to eat and as my words were relayed he barely stopped long enough to laugh.

'He come from inland,' the girl motioned. 'No good sailor anyway. From Bohea.'

'Bohea?' I said gleefully. What a stroke of good luck – this was Robert's other tea country. The home of black tea.

'Fetch the master,' I directed. 'Bring him now.'

Much to the maid's displeasure I picked up a spoon and tasted the noodle soup from the pot that still lay hot beside the range. Unlike us, the servants ate exotic fare. There were noodles and dumplings, chickens' feet and rice. The cook made a plum sauce that was delicious. The plums were delivered fragrant, still ripening on the bough. They smelt enticing. Unlike the mangoes and bamboo shoots, the melons and fresh ginger, they reminded me of home.

'Fetch him,' I motioned to her, ignoring her look of disapproval as I took another mouthful.

Robert's acquaintance had evidently left and Robert had retired to his study. He arrived in the kitchen seconds after the maid had bid him and his eyes lit up when I explained where Wang came from. He was so excited that thankfully he did not mention his friend, rebuke my coldness or tell me, as he had become accustomed to, that I really must play the hostess more. Instead he asked Wang a series of questions that he fired like bullets. Wang answered slowly. He knew how to grow tea and how to dry it. He had made black tea but preferred to drink green. Bohea was hilly and the best way to travel in the province was by sedan chair. By the end of the conversation Robert had engaged Wang for his trip. Like Sing Hoo, despite the obvious dangers, Wang was tempted by the money, and, of course, at first he did not fully understand the import of what Robert was to do. While principally interested in tea, Robert asked general questions about geography and did not concentrate overly on the tea plantations that were his real prize. Neither Wang nor Sing Hoo were to know for some time that Robert had their country's main export in his sights. Meanwhile the man nodded furiously and beamed whenever Robert spoke, for he had been engaged at a monthly rate two times what he might expect in the normal run of things. His information about Bohea would prove invaluable.

'Well done, Mary,' Robert pronounced and disappeared upstairs once more.

Sing Hoo and Wang did not take to each other. From the beginning it was clear they were constitutionally opposed. At first I wondered if the natives of Bohea and Hwuy-chow were generally at odds, like supporters of opposing teams, but this was not the case. The men simply disliked each other on sight. I think their rivalry was not helped by the fact that Robert could not tell them apart. While their facial features and general size was similar, I have to say they were not indistinguishable by any means. Sing Hoo was a good ten years the senior for a start. Robert simply did not appear to see this or any other difference and clearly felt they were unimportant in any case as long as one or the other did his bidding.

The last few days in Hong Kong were punctuated by bickering between the men that degenerated rapidly into sly punches, nips and kicks whenever they could manage.

'I do not fancy a year's wanderings with those two,' I jested to Robert. 'They will kill each other in a month.'

Robert was unperturbed. 'Servants,' he said vaguely, as if the other staff could regularly be seen punching each other and the enmity between the men was perfectly normal.

Supplies for the trip were piled high in the hallway. Robert had procured a gun, a stove, a tent, a trunk of goods for barter as well as Chinese currency. This last was a strange-looking collection of coins that he secreted in the internal pockets of his coat, in the hollow heels of his shoes, in the false bottoms of his travelling trunks, and sewed into the hems of his trousers. The large coins were silver. The smaller, bronze coins were called *cash*. They had holes through the centre and came strung together.

During his time in Hong Kong Robert had bought goods to be sent home and sold. There were ten inlaid chests, several bales of embroidered fabric, sundry porcelain items and a selection of carved ivory and mother-of-pearl fan sticks. He split this consignment in two and organised transport back to London on separate ships to halve his risk. It would be sold for a profit at auction before he returned and provide Jane with a nest egg.

'It will be cheaper still in the interior,' he said gleefully. 'I shall send more from there. This is only the start.'

I admired Robert's tenacity and determination in Hong Kong. He had arrived with only an outline plan and had succeeded in filling it in great detail. He organised the trip in the three weeks allotted, set up a line of credit for his export plans and tried his best to see me settled. It was to his mind the honourable thing to do and I was glad that we were settled on friendlier terms than on the *Braganza*. Sometimes in the evenings we talked nostalgically of England as if we had been away for years rather than months. As if we were friends rather than enemies. I have to admit it was pleasant to have such society once more, albeit with a man I scarcely ever agreed with. We came to an uneasy truce, putting the journey to Hong Kong behind us and, in the face of his departure, I found some real forgiveness within me at last.

Still, it was not all easy. Twice more he brought elderly men to the house to peruse me despite my evident unwillingness to participate in this activity. He mentioned to everyone he met that I required some form of employment. One or two families offered positions teaching English to their young children. Among those brought up by Chinese nursemaids some had started speaking Cantonese more than English. The horrified parents sought to redress the balance. Robert accepted both positions on my behalf. Two visits a week would hardly keep me but it was, he pointed out, 'necessary to have *something*, Mary'. The money might, I thought, go at least halfway. The fact I had little interest in other people's children was neither here nor there. Robert also took lodgings on my behalf and paid six months in advance. The rooms were fine but I could not see how I was going to afford them beyond the allotted time. There was little to employ a lady on the island and if I was going to survive on the longer term I would have to capitulate a very great deal. I wondered how far my credit might extend, given that Robert was set to return and could be relied on to settle my debts. I had no idea how long as a white woman I might last in the shanty, if it came to that, and, if the worst came to the worst, how I was ever to afford my passage back to London if I did not even have enough money to pay rent.

'Perhaps,' I said to Robert one evening after dinner, 'I shall export. I could pick out things myself. I have a good eye. I could charter a ship and send goods to auction in London.'

Robert laughed.

'But *you* have done it . . .' I started.

Robert held up his hand to prevent any further discussion.

'You are a woman,' he said and downed his drink. 'It is not done.'

He was right. I had a notion that over the several thousand miles I could conceal my identity so the merchant in London would not know. That somehow I would manage it. They would know, of course, in Hong Kong.

'You may teach,' said Robert. 'You may keep books, perhaps. Something will turn up if you are willing.'

'I could perform,' I countered.

'For God's sake,' Robert exploded. 'Will you never stop?'

He had done everything he could. I realised I must have tried him horribly. Robert was fulfilling his lifelong desire to make his fortune. I was far from realising any of my dreams. I told myself that I must keep my eyes open. There had to be something – surely the choice was not between a decrepit husband of advancing years or a bookkeeper's role.

'Is this where I am meant to be?' I thought to myself. A drawing-room lady in a remote colony. A spinster. As good as invisible.

'What is the point of travelling so far in order to become so small? I am not a teacher, Robert. I am not a convenient wife for some old soul you might meet in planning your excursions. I want to be *myself*.'

Robert's face wore an expression as if he had tasted sour milk.

'Yourself,' he echoed. 'There is no place anywhere I know for yourself, Mary. It is pure indulgence.'

'I like Hong Kong,' I said.

'Good, good.' He was not listening.

'But I have nothing worthwhile to do here.'

I had written letters to Jane all the way from Cape Town though I had not included the truth about the cabin boy and Barraclough or, for that matter, her husband. Instead they were full of my observations from the deck of the ship, details of exotic and unusual foodstuffs and lively questions about Henry. I had not dispatched one of them. Robert had forwarded a single short missive telling his wife we were well and had arrived thus far. I found myself unable to communicate with my sister, probably for the first time in my life. The truth was that I was afraid, I missed my son and I felt truly lost to the world. I could not tell her any of that.

Robert was, as ever, unperturbed. While brief in his writings to the family, he had regularly furnished a gardening journal with his lengthy observations on the plant life wherever we had docked. These were set to appear monthly in the form of a regular column. It irked him that they would be published out of their proper season but there was nothing he could do. The passage west was as irregular as it had proved eastwards and his words would appear in print whenever they happened to arrive in England. Should my sister wish to see what her husband had been occupied with some five months out of time she need only subscribe to the periodical for his views on exotic blooms, ferns, palms and unusual fruits and vegetables.

It was this that held up Robert's departure by two days, for he was committed to sending copy and in his rush to prepare for the journey had not done so. Hong Kong had proved a font of horticultural excitement and Robert paced the drawing room as he attempted to edit the weeks' experiences down to a page or two. Plants were not a subject about which he was naturally abrupt, and he had some difficulty. In the end he settled upon providing material for two columns – one on the subject of Hong Kong's indigenous flora and fauna and another on the cultivation of imported species. Many of these had been brought recently to the island by our new friends and reared from seed.

I made myself scarce. The prospect of Robert's departure

unsettled me. He would sail to Amoy first, via Namoa. I had traced his route on the map. I knew the flat paper was deceptive. What was a finger or two's width could take weeks to traverse and once on the mainland the overland route would be arduous. Robert was not set to return to Hong Kong for at least a year and I would be alone. He was the only person in a thousand miles who knew me or had my interests (or so he thought) to heart. I felt hemmed in by my homesickness and fear – the trepidation of not knowing what was to become of me and the sinking feeling that I was between the devil and the deep blue sea. In all likelihood there was no way forward that was in the least appealing. Though Robert and I were settled on friendlier terms, it surprised me now to realise that I was going to miss him. The truth was that I would by far have preferred to stay with my brother-in-law for all his faults than take on any of the ancient worthies he had lined up as my suitors.

I decided to sit in the garden. A long pagoda had been erected on the lawn and it afforded a good deal of shade. I set aside my worries and instead decided to try once more to write to Jane. It was difficult to know what to say but before Robert left I was determined to send her something. There was no option but to square with her what had happened but whenever I sought to write it down I knew my sister's reaction would be so horror-stricken that I was inhibited. After an hour I had merely three lines.

Dearest Jane
I have arrived in Hong Kong. Here Robert can keep a close eye on me. I have taken a teaching position. The island is lovely although malaria is rife. I am trying hard. My dear, I am so sorry, to have let you down once more. Please forgive me.

I laid down my pen. On the *Regatta* I had written pages posted home from each port en route. Missives arrived from exotic locations at least twice after my family thought I was drowned. I had committed every thought to paper. Now I felt I had nothing to say. At least, nothing pleasing. I was being abandoned on this rock, left to fare for myself. There were no doubt far fewer single men here than in Calcutta and little employment to speak of. In two days Robert would be gone. I was acutely aware that there was no middle way that was acceptable both to my family and to me. Something would have to give.

That evening we ate at the Governor's mansion. The hallway was splendid with candles. I wore my shoulder-less evening gown and the sheen of the material came to life in the glow.

'My dear,' a lady resplendent in a carved jade necklace that matched her intricate bodice said to me, 'your brother is leaving. You must be very proud. But will you manage alone?'

I smiled. 'We each have our adventure,' I said. 'He has taken rooms for me but I must find something to do.'

It was not the answer she had expected and I think she did not know what to make of me. I had been supposed to simply say I would miss him but that I would be fine. I had never had an appetite for glossing over such things and I was unsure how to develop one.

We had ten courses for dinner, and afterwards withdrew to hear Miss Pottinger, the Governor's niece, play the piano. It was a lovely night. The mansion had been ransacked some months before but the insurgence was quelled and every piece of looted finery replaced. Our people in the colonies lived daily with such things. No one seemed to find it alarming.

As his niece stepped down from the piano, Sir Henry rose. 'Who shall be next?' he asked. 'Miss Penney?'

He said this teasingly, no doubt expecting me to blush and giggle – Fortune's quiet sister-in-law, all set to disappear. However, I rose to his challenge. I was in the humour for it.

'I cannot play the piano, sir. Certainly not. But I *can* recite,' I said.

The Governor's eyebrows rose. As I got up from my chair Robert blanched. He put out his hand ineffectually in a motion to stop me as I moved to the front of the room. It seemed no one else noticed him and I ignored it.

'Delightful,' said the Governor. 'A recitation. What will it be?'

It was Lady Macbeth. I chose the speech where she urges Macbeth on, calls him half a man. I always found it stirring. The company fell to absolute silence. The Governor sank into his chair. I had missed Shakespeare. All the passion I could not express personally flooded into his words. I recited for five minutes to the point where Macbeth leaves his wife to kill his king. It was wonderful to act again, even if only for a moment. When I had done there was a long silence. Then, to my relief, everyone clapped and there was uproar. Miss Pottinger rose to her feet in a standing ovation.

'My, my,' said Major Vernon as he escorted me back to my chair. 'We have a great talent among us.'

Robert eyed me with silent ferocity. No amount of praise would convince him that my performance was anything other than a betrayal.

'The Governor asked me,' I whispered in his direction, but it was no good.

'You shall come to dinner once your brother-in-law has sailed,' an older lady next to me declared. 'Do you know *The Tempest*?'

'I know the part of Ariel.'

'Excellent. Why, Miss Penney, we must sponsor you to recite some more. Capital entertainment. Capital.'

I sat back in the mahogany chair and I admit that I felt a good deal better.

We were scarcely out of earshot in the rickshaw on the way home when Robert turned to me, his blue eyes blazing.

'I wash my hands,' he said. 'You are incorrigible.'

I did not reply. Instead I looked upwards. The clear sky was studded with huge stars as if a whole constellation had come to rest on the Peak. After midnight, there was an unaccustomed stillness to the island. It was beautiful.

'The stars are lovely, Robert. Look,' I said.

'You are all pretence. All show, Mary.'

'I will not fight with you,' I said. 'You are gone the day after tomorrow. If I must make a life for myself here so be it.'

'You shame me.'

'By taking a round of applause? That is preposterous! I wager Sir Henry is not berating his niece for her skill with the piano.'

Robert was so agitated that he began to pick at the material of his trousers distractedly.

'They will uncover it all now,' he said. 'We should have altered your name. Someone will write of it to a relation in London. Someone will realise what you have done. There will be talk of it. You were in the scandal sheets, Mary. Your name is known.'

I began to fear he would make a hole in his trousers.

'Try to remain calm, for heaven's sake,' I said. 'You must let me be.'

'I shall have to remove you, Mary. Don't you understand? If I cannot trust you I must take the responsibility. But to

Amoy? Ning-po? The interior?' he said as if he was really considering it.

'Robert, please get hold of yourself,' I parried.

These ports were, by all accounts, rough places and tiny. If there was little occupation for me in Hong Kong there would be even less on the mainland where no white man could possibly expect his family to live.

'Bad terrain. Too harsh for a woman,' he went on.

'There is no need to overreact,' I said.

'Overreact?' Robert was now shouting. 'When you persist in publicly embarrassing me? You take enjoyment in the threat of humiliation. I will return some day to Hong Kong and must rely on the good will of its citizens, Mary. I cannot leave you here to shame me further.'

At this moment we arrived at our lodgings. Robert sprung from the chair and entered the house without helping me to descend. When I came into the hallway I could hear him barking orders I could not understand at the maid who had appeared sleepily to greet us. He pointed at my valise that lay packed for removal the following day.

'What are you doing?' I asked.

He was a man possessed.

'I cannot trust you, Mary. Your judgement is too poor. Within six months they will know it all, if not sooner.'

'Will you have me spend my whole life running?' I said. 'It is madness. Sleep on this, Robert, and you will see the foolishness of your concern. It was a recitation. Women everywhere amuse themselves so.'

Robert ordered the maid below stairs. He grasped the banister in fury. I feared he was about to strike me, but then he appeared to deflate, as if defeated. Things had shifted since he had hauled me aboard the *Braganza* by force.

'I do not know what to do,' he said wearily. 'You frustrate me at every turn. I only wish things to be right for us all.'

I scarcely slept though I could not imagine that Robert would carry through his threat. Everything I had read or heard about China proved that it was no place for a white woman to make her home. Still, the tales were intriguing. There were pleasure cities, masked dramas, snow-capped mountains, white tigers and mystic temples. There were legends of carved jade so exquisite it was priceless.

In the morning Robert finished his column and dispatched the text. He said he had particularly concentrated on azaleas and a lilac foxglove we had seen which was a member of the tea family. Dark eyed and heavy footed, it was clear he had not slept either and was under a considerable strain. In point of fact the whole household was ill at ease. The maid, our packing complete, had started to prepare the house for the next tenants with gusto. She spent the entire morning polishing. Wang had taken to checking the bags, counting them and ticking off a list he had made. He brandished the parchment proudly, perpetually rolling and unrolling it. Sing Hoo it transpired had never learned to read or write and jealously eyed his rival.

'I thought the Chinese always respected their elders,' I said in passing to Robert.

We were all of us waiting.

Clearly it was my duty to put Robert's mind at ease. I had no desire to make things more difficult for him. I wondered if perhaps I had been hasty in my recitation after all and I should have left it until after he had quit the island. I could have chosen another night. I never seemed to be able to get things right. To fit in. To behave as I ought. Now both Robert and I were miserable and with our minds buzzing we agreed to walk down to a bird market of which we had heard. It would at least distract us.

The market, it transpired, was a small collection of rickety bamboo cages that had been assembled off the main thoroughfare along a narrow, dingy, muddy track. We made our way in silence. I really could not see what I had done was so dreadful, but then given Robert's fears about me, it was perhaps understandable that he had reacted so strongly. I supposed Robert and I were never going to see eye to eye.

The first few stalls were set out with trinkets and incense but these soon gave way to the cages. Some were hung from bamboo poles. There were pretty little songbirds and white doves that fluttered from side to side. The larger creatures were stowed on the ground and they were more exotic. There was a blue bird the size of a dog, a retriever perhaps, but on long, spindly legs like a heron. It had a fascinating red plume. Robert had settled upon his idea of collecting bird skins that he could dry, ready to be stuffed on his return to England. He examined the creatures carefully and I was glad that this would take his mind away from the immediate dilemma that he faced and I hoped that perhaps if things could only feel more normal again, it might allow him to relinquish his control over me.

'It will make quite a show,' he said, bending down to look at the peacocks, 'although I would prefer to catch the birds myself in the wild, I think. I have heard there are white ones.'

'You will make a sport of it?'

'Indeed.'

He was clearly downhearted and I felt unaccountably sad. I wanted to make him understand that I knew what was really best for us all – those in London and the two of us abroad. I was coming to accept that I should submit and lead a quiet life. At least until Robert had made his trip and departed again for England. It was only a few months, after all. A year or two. Not so much to lay aside for my sister, her children and my only son. Perhaps I had been hasty. I had baited Robert and I regretted it. As we walked back from the market I found my courage and took my chance to apologise before he sailed.

'I will live small if I have to, Robert. I am sorry to have distressed you last night. I know what you want of me. I assure you I will do it.'

Robert nodded. He seemed taller at once as if the burden of my behaviour had weighed upon him. He had never wanted to bring me on his travels. I was a dreadful consideration for him. It was, I suppose, the promise he had been waiting for and now I had given it we both felt better.

We turned up to the house. A barrow had been brought from the dock and loaded. My bags were piled separately beside it, only waiting for the bearers to arrive. Wang still had his list to hand, the spidery Chinese writing running up and down the page in black ink. When he caught sight of us, he came over, reverently bowed and passed me a sealed note that had been delivered while I was out.

'What do you say, Robert?' I asked as I tore open the wax. 'Will you take my word? Will you see me settled in my new rooms?' The letter was from the older lady at dinner the night before. Robert did not answer my question. He was reading over my shoulder.

'So looking forward to your Ariel. Wherever did you learn to recite so beautifully? Please come on Thursday,' it said.

He glowered. That little piece of parchment changed everything. His hand was already tightly gripping my arm as he began to steer me towards the carriage.

'I am sorry, Mary. It is too late. I cannot let them find out. Sing Hoo,' he shouted at Wang, who still stood before us, 'come now! Take Miss's luggage to the ship.'

Chapter Five

On the dockside I hurriedly amended the letter I had written to Jane, scribbling that Robert was taking me with him further on his travels.

'This way we can look after each other,' I wrote at the end. I could scarcely tell my sister that I was once more furious with her husband. That I had tried everything but it had done no good. 'I will write again as soon as I can,' I promised.

I dated it August; and the last thing I did before walking aboard the ship for Amoy was to leave the envelope, carefully addressed for dispatch, in the harbour master's care.

As we came aboard the captain greeted us and a member of the crew made to lead me to my cabin. I scarcely noticed the man but I had no more than moved off when Robert pulled him up sharply, calling the captain over.

'This man looked at Miss Penney,' he said. 'I will not have it.'

My mind was in London and I did not understand at first, though the man flushed and lowered his eyes.

'Sir?' the captain asked.

Robert pulled him aside. 'He looked at her inappropriately,' he whispered, though not too low for me to hear it clearly.

'Seaman Lewis.' The captain turned immediately.

'Miss Penney is a lady. We will have none of that on my ship. Report to my cabin once we are underway and you best apologise. Now.'

The man stood to attention, his eyes straight ahead.

'Sorry, Miss Penney,' he barked in naval fashion.

'Let me take you to the cabin, myself, ma'am,' the captain offered. 'I will punish the man later.'

And Robert nodded, satisfied. He might feel he had the right to force me on board but Lord help a simple sailor who looked longingly at my bustle.

I must admit my immediate thoughts were that I had brought upon myself a terrible mistake. White tigers and priceless jade aside, on closer inspection the ship upon which Robert had taken passage was ramshackle and the weather as we moved northwards became increasingly stormy. As the Peak shrank from view, disappearing, it seemed, into the ocean, I was overwhelmed by a feeling of hopelessness. Had Robert disappeared I would have gone home immediately. In those circumstances I was sure that the Governor would have forwarded the funds for the ticket. Quite apart from Henry, I wanted to see my sister. Indeed, I think I missed her far more than Robert did.

As children it was Jane who was the natural carer. She was the one who had helped to rear Mother's animals. At lambing she always picked a favourite and took it on. One summer I recall her leading several piglets round the bottom field and teaching them to jump the stile. I was too selfish, my mother pointed out. Perfect for churning butter or bottling berries, where your thoughts are turned inwards. All my childhood I churned butter to John Donne's poetry or pickled vegetables to Marlowe, while Jane tended lambs and piglets at the back of the shed.

Having spent all summer rearing the litters Jane had no

difficulty in slaughtering them. In fact, by the time Jane was thirteen, she was a proficient butcher. She calmed the animals before she slit their throats and most died like loved ones, lulled in her arms. One autumn Mother had sold six pigs to the big house, to be delivered butchered. Jane slaughtered every one. When she emerged from the shed she was covered in their blood and not one squeal had come from the outhouse.

'They went happy,' she told me. 'They had no idea.'

There was a steely core to my sister, very brave and terrible. And yet, despite that, there was a softness that bound us together. Like all of us, Jane had myriad of facets, different sides to her nature, though these, it seemed to me, decreased the older she got. For years after Da died, Jane woke often in the night, vulnerable and terribly fretful of having hurt him somehow.

'I never told him,' she said as I hugged her in the darkness of our tiny, shared attic room.

'Told him what?'

'That I loved him,' she said.

Poor Jane. It was almost as if he was haunting her. Even then I knew it and cold fingered, though it was July, I stroked her hair and said, 'He knows that, Janey. 'Course he does.'

The small house in which we were brought up was still our own. The path that leads to the front door is the highway to too many memories for either of us to part with it. If Jane finds those memories haunting, I have often thought it is those same reminiscences that animate me. We talked, before I fell pregnant, of using the old place now and again as a country retreat – I think perhaps Jane thought if she took possession of the house it might exorcise her demons. It was not a grand building but very amenable, and we both had a fondness for its pretty pan-tiled roof and rough stone walls, half covered with ivy and wisteria. We thought to take the children, to teach them something of farming and the countryside that no town-reared child can possibly glean. John had shown his father's aptitude for horticulture and we considered it would be good for him to spend some time there during the holidays.

I think autumn is the prettiest time in the countryside. The hay is baled and stacked, the berries are out and the leaves are set to turn. There is blue-flowered scabious growing wild and the birds are finished nesting. 'I will never see it again,' I realised. The fields and woods with their hidden pools. The secret pathways and the muddy horse tracks.

'Are you never homesick?' I asked Robert now.

But it was no use. He did not even reply. The man had no feeling whatsoever.

We were to dock briefly at Namoa before continuing to Amoy and then we must change ships to go up the Formosa Channel to Chimoo Bay and the island of Chusan. Thus far the restrictions placed on white men were not as stringent as Robert had feared. In London some had said he would be entirely banned from Chinese soil, as was the agreement with the Chinese government. But, close to the five agreed British settlements, it seemed that as long as a man did not take a permanent residence he was allowed some freedom of movement. Trade was brisk and ships docked and sailed so quickly that it would be difficult to administer a ban on Europeans in any case.

I stayed mostly in my cabin, thinking of home. Apart from the few hours I spent walking on the deck and reading, I devoted most of my time to sitting on my bed, cursing William or crouching beside the small window daydreaming about how things might have been. Had I not fallen in love I would be still in my dressing room at Drury Lane, visiting my sister on a Sunday afternoon and playing hoops with my niece and nephews on the nursery floor. Or better still, had William kept his word, I would have a place in the theatre still, a house of my own and Henry too. I could not completely regret the affair now Henry was born, of course, but try as I might the truth came back again and again. I would far rather be in England.

To make things worse, the journey itself was in stark contrast to what had gone before. Until this part of our trip, we had docked only at large ports accustomed to accommodating travellers' needs. Hong Kong had been enough of China to be exotic and enough of England to be familiar. Now we were travelling northwards and close to the coast everywhere was truly alien and the settlements impoverished. We passed cottages open to the weather and Chinese nomads with scores of half-starved children camping in makeshift tents and fishing from the rocks. I saw one tiny boy eating his catch raw and still alive. There were rivulets of blood dribbling down his chin.

When we reached Amoy it was the filthiest place I have ever seen. From the opium warehouses with their sackcloth bales stacked behind slatted gates to the grubby shanty that stretched acres away from the port, the whole place stank so badly that my stomach turned. Robert showed no sign of notice and his attention was drawn instead to the strange rocks on an island in the bay called Koo Lung Soo. Misshapen trees hung like fronds from the angular rocks, their trunks growing straight out over the ocean. I spotted one entirely upside down. Amoy harbour was stowed out and there was hardly space to lay another anchor. Most of the ships were ferrying opium and, armed as usual with news of London, Robert found himself easily in demand with the merchants and captains alike.

There was nowhere suitable to stay on land so we arranged to keep our berths until we found our onward passage, for here we must change ships. While Robert called on the more promising-looking vessels I remained in my cabin. My soul was swamped with regret. I do not think of myself as unduly maternal – clearly I am not – but there was a bond between my baby and me that pulled him continually into my thoughts the further I travelled away.

In my cabin I went over and over the details of Henry's birth and then imagined his future marriage. William's money could procure my son a gentleman's match, but I wondered if he would want one. I willed with all my might that Henry should have spirit – the manly bravery that William so clearly lacked. I hoped that quality, more than anything, might come from my side of things. Strange, really, to long for someone you do not know – to plot and plan for them. I tried to comfort myself that at least Henry's fortunes were safe now. He was no doubt set to attend Eton and then Cambridge as his father had. William would provide. It was fine. Fine. And yet still I wondered if our features might be similar. If my son had inherited his father's sly smile and his aristocratic bearing. His taste for forest green, roast lamb and malt whisky? Or if perhaps there might be a trace in him, a whisper, of my love of cherries, steaming bowls of hot chocolate and the very English scent of lilac.

In Hong Kong I had bought a book on the subject of Chinese mythology and to distract myself I read my way through the tales of fabulous creatures – phoenixes, unicorns, dragons, fox spirits, earth gods, the Buddha and the Monkey King. I began to understand more of the elaborate shrines set up on the dock by resident merchants with their display of gold and red ribbons, figurines and incense holders. I picked out the amulets worn by the sailors, offerings to Tien Hou, goddess of navigators at sea.

After a few days we picked up a passage with a British ship journeying as far as Chusan. Though the vessel was smaller than those to which we had become accustomed, the berths were comfortable and half the crew European. The captain, Landers, was from Northumberland. A cheerful, red-faced giant of a man, he towered over Robert. He had been at sea for fifteen years and claimed he had never slept a night on shore since he was twelve.

'Unusual for a lady to travel here,' he commented. 'Amoy is no place to linger.'

Robert bristled, but Landers continued uninhibited.

'Are you missionaries?' he asked.

I adopted my most pious expression. 'No, Captain Landers,' I said. 'I am merely accompanying my brother-in-law in his research.'

Robert attempted to change the subject.

'The conditions these poor heathens live under!' he exclaimed. 'As bad as Scotch cottages!'

I restrained myself from pointing out that living in a Scottish cottage appeared to have done Robert little harm. Though I expect a wry expression played on my face.

'Yes,' I said. 'Poor things.'

Landers restored my faith in the honour of captaincy. He did not possess the polished manners of Barraclough and was not turned out at all well, but he proved a hearty and genuine soul and both Robert and I became fond of him. We moved our berths onto his ship, the *Dundas*, had the Ward's cases bolted into the deck, and little by little my spirits rose.

It was at Amoy that Robert collected his first plants. Thus far he had always bought his specimens but now he decided to travel away from the dock to the hills behind and see what he could find for himself. The *Dundas* would sail the following day so we were at our leisure. He took Sing Hoo and Wang and they set off just after dawn.

I admit I had little to occupy my time. Perhaps, I thought, the next occasion Robert hiked to the hills I would beg to come. Certainly, if Amoy was anything to judge by, it was so unpleasant to be at dock that it would be a relief to get away. I passed my time as usual, reading and taking a turn along the deck. Despite the rank air and the stench that rose from the waters, to watch the teeming crowds about their business was great diversion. It was easy to pick out the few Europeans from the throng even at a distance. The mass of Chinese somehow moved differently. I walked the boards, my handkerchief to my nose, trying to emulate the Cantonese women I could spot here and there, with their tiny steps and high shoulders, the beautiful stillness of their thin eyes and their wide, high-boned faces. I wondered what mistakes they might have made, as they moved smoothly through the crowd. Adultery. Dishonour. They could have done anything. Were any as wicked as I?

When Robert returned he was laden. The hillsides had been fruitful and the plants he brought aboard were fragrant in the thick, evening air. Wang stumbled under two small fig trees and there were vivid gold and bronze chrysanthemums in canvas bags strapped around his shoulders. Sing Hoo carried various Chinese roses of a delicate pink so pale it was almost white, while Robert was laden with jasmine. The metal vasculum boxes they had taken were brimming with cuttings and tightly strapped over Robert and Sing Hoo's shoulders.

I was delighted. Who would believe so close to the squalor of Amoy such beautiful flowers bloomed? I helped Robert bed down the plants in the cases. My hands were filthy with mud but the scent was heavenly redemption. We worked by lamplight while Robert explained where he had found his treasures, and complained of Wang and Sing Hoo's incompetence when extracting the plants from the soil.

'They pulled them,' he shuddered. 'I have shown them now but both are so lazy that I will not be able to trust them unsupervised.'

'I can help,' I offered.

'Wang pulled an olea. The only one I could find. He has quite ruined it though I have kept it to dry for the herbarium.'

'And in the herbarium,' I ventured, taking an interest, 'the plants are all dead?'

Robert looked as if I had slandered the memory of some dearly-loved relation.

'Dried,' he said acidly. 'We have herbarium specimens more than a hundred and fifty years old at Kew.'

That evening Robert set up his plant press and opened the drying racks. He carefully labelled each leafy specimen, laid it between thick papers and left the air to do its work. Then he turned his attention to the seeds. He cleaned them minutely with a small brush and put some into tagged canvas bags. The others he laid out to dry. From this I took it that some required airing while others did not. I watched this process carefully, holding open the cloth bags for him and tying the twine tightly. His concentration was intense though he looked very tired. It seemed he never stopped planning. His mission consumed him entirely. I tried to take in everything he was doing. After all, I might as well learn to help. As he piled the last of the bags into a wooden box he looked up, realising that I had watched all the while. A smile broke out on his face and he reached for the lamp to escort me back to my cabin by way of saying goodnight.

104

Really, I think Robert was stronger than the servants. He kept longer hours and often worked twice as hard. I could see the muscles in his arms as he reached for the lamplight.

'I can send these back from Chusan,' he said, indicating the drying racks of specimens. 'They will be ready then.'

The Formosa Channel was stormy. The boat rocked badly in the choppy swell and Sing Hoo became sick. Wang cooked food as close to him as possible and made it highly spiced. The poor man kept down scarcely anything and vomited over the side half a dozen times each day. The men were berthed with two other Chinese travelling, as I understood it, only to Chimoo Bay. Occasionally at night, above the breaking of the waves, I could hear Sing Hoo wailing in the distance. We were in no danger whatsoever, of course. The water was high and uneven but we could hardly have called it a storm. Sing Hoo, however, was inconsolable.

For several days Robert watched over his specimens as they aired. A knock or a bump could dent them easily so he held them in place with a crisscrossed twine secured to the drying frame with nails. He changed the pressing papers daily, kept his eye on the plants in glass cases and made meticulous notes in his journal. I was eager to help and here and there an extra pair of hands made a difference. Robert often explained the process as he went along. Mostly I simply enjoyed the flowers, but I noticed as my competence increased I could tie knots easily and prepare different seeds for storage without needing instruction. It was pleasant to have something to do.

One evening I was helping with the drying racks when Sing Hoo started to moan very loudly in a cabin along the passage.

'Do you think we ought to go to him?' I suggested.

Robert shook his head. 'No.'

The truth of it was, of course, that Robert would not leave his specimens.

'It might hearten him to see us,' I persisted.

Robert shot me an angry look. 'He has his own people,' he growled.

I was about to point out that it could not have escaped even Robert's notice that in no measure could Wang and Sing Hoo be said to be kinsmen, when the ship keeled very suddenly and I was thrown to the floor. Robert fell likewise on top of me and in his attempts to hold the rack upright he snapped off one of the legs. The whole thing tumbled. I was dazed and struggled to my feet. Robert was on his knees with the papers in his hands.

'We are lucky these are not fully dried and still have some pliancy,' he said. 'Only two are crushed.'

As if time had distorted, I got to my feet and helped him stack those we could salvage in a pile of papers. We bound it with twine. I was still reeling, realising slowly that he had less concern for me than for the specimens.

'Damn this weather,' Robert exclaimed. 'I suppose they are safer this way.' He patted the parcel. As the ship keeled again and we both almost tumbled once more we could hear Sing Hoo's voice raised in terror.

'He is not much of a sailor,' I said.

Robert laughed. Now the specimens were safe he relaxed and, I suppose, realised there would be no harm in indulging me. 'I expect he will be better when we are travelling overland. I suppose we can go to him now, if you still wish it.'

We made our way along the dark, wooden passage clinging to the rail and entered the Chinamen's cabin without knocking. Inside Sing Hoo was huddled in a corner. He was shaking and wild eyed, and sprung to his feet,

106

shouting in a babble that neither Robert nor I could understand. His cabin mates regarded him with plain disgust.

'Sit down,' Robert ordered and reached out to take Sing Hoo's arm. Like a cornered dog, Sing Hoo lashed out wildly, flaying with his arms and baring his teeth. Robert moved more swiftly than I would have expected. In a mere second Sing Hoo was floored and Robert held him there, his foot on the man's back, his arms held tightly behind. My brother-in-law was competent in hand-to-hand combat – I knew that for myself already, ever since our spats at Portsmouth.

'Are you all right?' I asked Wang, who looked delighted at Robert's assault on his rival and inclined his head eagerly.

Robert removed his foot and let Sing Hoo's arms go but the man did not rise. He remained silent on the bare boards.

'It must break soon,' Robert observed in the direction of the others who had stationed themselves edgily in the opposite corner to the fracas.

There was nothing more to be said so I bowed as I had seen the Chinese do, my hands clasped before me, my eyes lowered, and I wished them all a peaceful goodnight.

Robert was a brute but, I suppose, sometimes he needed to be. That night I dreamt myself as a warrior and I attacked him. I wrestled Robert to the floor. I bound his hands and made him watch as I shredded his stupid specimens right in his face. Then, scissors in hand, Jane materialised beside me.

'Shush, Mary,' she said.

And suddenly I wasn't a warrior any more. I was in a garden, on my knees. I still had the scissors but I used them to prune a rose bush. Coolies were watering the other plants around me. Everyone was Chinese. When I woke again I sighed deeply.

'That man is driving me crazy,' I whispered to myself.

What infuriated me was that, despite his hateful behaviour, so often he was right.

It was the habit of the smaller ships in these straits to feed the crew with fish foraged during the sailing but the sea was so unsettled that the nets could not be cast. After days of biscuits and grog the crew became surly. I saw Wang selling small portions of his cooked rice to some of the deckhands – rice that Robert had bought to supply him and Sing Hoo. Robert and I ate with Landers. The captain's table was stocked with preserved food and after a while even these supplies began to dwindle to a spare diet of salted beef and tasteless crackers over which we discussed the Chinese coastline and, upon occasion, the recent war. Landers had fought, of course.

'Sorted them out and no mistake,' he said cheerfully. 'Imagine refusing to trade! Cheeky beggars!'

As the days progressed I tried to encourage Sing Hoo to eat something to sustain himself, but it was hopeless.

'Many days more?' he kept asking earnestly.

All I could do was assure him that the weather would change.

To divert myself from these troubles, I took to visiting Landers on the poop deck. Like all the naval officers I have met, he was fascinated by the stars and he offered to guide me round the night sky once the sun had fallen below the horizon. I never knew that stars rose and set. Landers instructed me good naturedly. To be so competent in making your way in the world as to need only the sky for guidance was intriguing and the man's relaxed company was pleasant. With Robert I never knew what he might do next whereas Landers was easy – the kind of chap you could rely on.

'The stars here are amazing,' I said.

'Yes,' Landers replied enthusiastically, 'the sky is a huge map. You can tell the time by the orbits, you know – just like guessing the time of day when the sun is up.'

I enjoyed learning about Orion and Gemini, seeing the moon move across the sky and learning what time of year one might expect a meteor shower or catch sight of a particular planet.

One such evening I was on deck, staring at the sky with him when we hit a squall. These straits were infamous for poor weather but even counting that we had a bad run of it. We moved to the shelter of the poop where Landers gave orders to guide us through the swell and the men set to it. The waves were rising higher and higher. Then, all at once, there was a crash directly over our heads. I screamed as the timber roof shattered and the splintered wood rained down. Was it happening again? I crouched instinctively as a huge, grey mass quivered beside me out of nowhere. The fish was enormous and it seemed to have been stunned by its fall. The rest of the ship was clearly intact. We were not wrecked.

Landers leant over to examine the trawl. He was admirably unruffled.

'What have we here?' he said.

'Is it a shark?' I asked, rising slowly to my feet again.

'No,' Landers laughed. '"Is it a shark?" Don't know the name of it to tell the truth, Miss Penney. Look at the ugly thing. But she'll cook up delicious.'

He called the bosun who reckoned the catch at thirty pounds, netted it and had it dispatched to the galley immediately to feed all hands.

That evening the captain's table was fine – the fish was fried and the cook had found a lemon to juice on it. We were ravenous, our appetites piqued by monotony.

'This is why I love to journey,' Landers said. 'Delicious! A fish from the skies, who would have thought it?'

By the time we reached Chimoo Bay and the Chinese travellers had disembarked, the herbarium specimens had dried. Robert packed them in fresh papers, labelled each carefully, put the lot in a large tin and sealed the lid with wax. He pasted the instructions to the front along with the address of the Royal Society. On the dock he commissioned parcel passage back to Hong Kong on an opium vessel at anchor. The box's onward journey was to be made from there with the first Royal Navy ship returning to London. The seeds were given a similar treatment and dispatched to a nursery in Wiltshire with which Robert had an arrangement.

We were to be at port for two days. The next stage of our journey as far as Chusan Island would take over a week. In the meantime Robert declared his intention to collect more specimens. After some enquiries it became clear that there was no plant nursery nearby, which was most disappointing. It was far easier, Robert said, to talk to someone who knew the local planting.

'A good hour or two in a nursery can yield more than a week on the hillsides,' he swore.

'Robert,' I asked. 'Might I come with you?'

Robert regarded me plainly and I could not tell what he was thinking. Then it seemed as if he had made some kind of calculation and he nodded.

'You must do as I ask,' he said.

I was excited. This was to be my first expedition on the mainland. The next morning we caused quite a commotion at the dockside, the two of us side by side with Wang and Sing Hoo in our wake. Already we were in a place where Europeans were a rarity and European women practically unknown. For the first mile a curious crowd moved in the same general direction as Robert and I, observing us from a distance. Children gaped and pointed. I felt uncomfortable

110

in my skirt. Not that it was fancy, or indeed, particularly wide. However, it irked me to see one boy explaining to his younger sister that white women were all shaped like bells and that my legs fitted snugly under its frame. With elaborate hand gestures he made it clear the extent of my limbs and the apparently hilarious size of my feet. Robert gripped my arm tightly and guided me onwards. I was not in any position to remonstrate with the child and would not have lifted my skirts to prove myself, of course, but the turn of my ankle had been commented upon in more than one review and I felt outraged. Robert, sensing this, moved me on firmly.

'It is only natural for them to be curious,' he whispered. 'Pay it no heed.'

As we walked further from the settlement I noticed rats moving in the squalid shadows. There were dingy pawn shops and ships' chandlers and huge warehouses, their produce piled up on display, the eyes of the merchants expectantly upon us as they stood in the doorway.

'You want to buy, mister?' one man asked Robert. 'Come in and I will prepare some tea.'

'No, no.' Robert waved him off.

We walked on. Near the end of the town I spotted two corpses in the street, side by side, covered only with a thin, white cloth, the still outlines clear in the sunshine. They had not started to smell yet. I wondered how they had died. Was there malaria here, or typhoid? But we did not stop. As we reached the very fringes, the crowd dispersed saving one elderly man who continued to follow us most of the day, never coming close enough to hear our conversation but never far enough away to lose sight.

The hills rose steeply and it was not long before Robert spotted one or two interesting plants that had him climbing rocks and excavating root systems. When I suggested pressing onwards and leaving the men to dig, he insisted that all the work must be done in his sight. Sing Hoo, evidently feeling far better now he was on land, loitered behind Wang so all three men were stationed around the muddy excavation. It was very dull and I was keen to get on. I wondered if we might come across a cottage, or indeed, a family. I had yet to speak even indirectly to a native other than our own servants. The hills were charming and it was in my mind that we might find the elevation for some stunning views.

Robert would not budge, however. He worked carefully. Sing Hoo kept his eyes fixed on his master. Since Robert had toppled him during his screaming fit he had a new respect for my brother-in-law and watched reverently as Robert jotted down Latin names in his journal and made rough sketches of the terrain. Waved on by Robert, who seemed discomfited by my lingering, I decided to climb ahead alone and hiked a further four hundred yards. I rested on a flat rock looking down onto the valley though I stayed, of course, within sight.

Settling to wait I wondered if it was raining in London. At this time of the morning Jane or now, I supposed, Nanny Charlotte, would be supervising the nursery lunch. If I were at home I would only just be rising to a breakfast tray in the small brick house I used to rent in Soho. My maid had been called Mary – a fact that had always amused me. Jane became cross if I mentioned it in company, but I liked that we shared a name. Mary, as far as I know, had done well when I had dismissed her. Jane would not have my staff in the house and I had become too big with Henry to ignore my situation any longer. Without any money coming in and with respectable hopes for my unborn child in mind, I had had to comply. My dresser, who visited me in Gilston Road during my confinement, told me that Mary went to work for a courtesan in Chelsea when I had disappeared from society entirely. It struck me as a strange hand of cards. I wished I had not met William or better still that I had snubbed him. I wished I was sipping my chocolate and Mary was still in my employ.

Close to where I sat, the ground levelled out and there was a banyan tree. Robert was not interested in these, I knew, and already had cuttings and seeds from several. However, some unusual foliage by the trunk caught my eye. The smooth, long shape of the leaf and its pretty reddish colour drew my attention. There was an extended seed pod. I decided to investigate but as I came closer I was caught by a foul aroma. It was like a cesspool in the height of the summer. I drew my handkerchief to my nose and gagged, backing off.

'Robert,' I called from the flat rock. 'I am coming down.'

Robert looked up only momentarily from his diagram and was still working on it when I reached him.

'It smells dreadful up there,' I said. 'Worse than the port at Amoy. There must be a carcass or something of that nature.'

'Which way?' Robert questioned.

'Up there at the banyan tree. There is the strangest plant but the stench is dreadful.'

Robert sprang to his feet and scrambled up the hillside towards the horrible odour.

'Show me the plant,' he said.

I pointed laconically, unwilling to return to the vicinity of the smell.

'Come on,' he insisted and grabbed my arm, hauling me up in his wake.

'You do not attend me, Robert,' I protested.

But he merely continued to pull me up the hill.

* * *

113

Of course, there was no carcass. It was the plant that stank.

'*Poederia foetida*,' Robert said triumphantly, packing it into the vasculum eagerly.

Wang and Sing Hoo scrunched their noses and looked on disbelieving. I hung back. Though the vasculum was airtight the odour lingered all afternoon.

'Wonderful,' he said enthusiastically. 'Well done finding it, Mary. Well done.'

This was not my idea of entertainment. Things got worse and worse the longer I continued, the more I decided that I would try.

Robert said nothing, only passed me his hip flask. I think he had no idea.

Coming back to Chimoo we attracted once more a large entourage. Robert had decided to hike to the north and re-enter the settlement from that direction. He did not wish to re-cover old ground. Wang had taken charge of the vasculum with the *poederia* and tramped sullenly at a distance. Sing Hoo was laden with equipment and a few smaller flowering plants that Robert had identified. He had, it seemed to me, the far better deal.

'They think all white men carry firearms here,' Robert commented, nodding his head to indicate the first few of our followers. 'The war saw to that. We are devils to them. They will come no closer.'

Then, an hour or so from the harbour, one or two of this company began to remonstrate with Sing Hoo, gesticulating wildly and trying to turn us back. Within half a mile the company had swollen. They were all Chinese, a mixed bunch, though mostly men, hands outstretched, pointing us back in the direction we had come from, trying to make us stop. It made me uneasy and I tried to keep an eye on the figures milling around me. I did not know what they might do.

Robert was ever single of purpose. The East India Company had evidently chosen the right man for the job – nothing would sway him.

'We are not supposed to leave the port,' he said. 'The cheeky blackguards are telling us off for straying outside the allowed boundary. Come along. They dare not touch us. Ignore them.'

The crowd grew to a dozen. They were ragged people, thin and dishevelled.

'Perhaps we should go back,' I urged.

They were coming too close now. It was not normal.

'We are returning to the bay by the most direct route. Show no fear, Mary. It is fine.'

It did not feel fine and, besides, Wang and Sing Hoo were becoming anxious. The old man who had followed us all day was no longer anywhere in sight and I took this to be a bad sign along with the fact that now and again I felt a pull at my skirt as if someone was pawing the fabric.

'Robert knows what he is doing,' I told myself. 'Simply get through this and in an hour you will be in your cabin.'

The crowd, however, had other plans. All at once a young man suddenly pointed at us and shouted. I have no idea what he said but Wang and Sing Hoo took off, bolting at full pelt and leaving us behind. Two or three ran after them but the rest of our hangers on became still, as if hesitating, and then all at once fell upon Robert and me. I let out a whimper.

My scarf was pulled from my shoulders, the remainder of our provisions was seized and several hands ripped at my skirt, tearing it badly. Robert was flailing his arms, fighting his way out. The crowd had a natural wariness of him and in a temper he was especially strong. They stole his hat and a pocket watch he had been carrying, but when someone removed his journal Robert launched such a

115

furious defence that it was dropped. Three of Robert's assailants lost their footing and rolled down the slope. I did not like to hit out. I have never brawled in my life and worse, it was two old women who had fallen on me. But they were ripping my skirt to shreds. I plucked up my courage and punched hard, catching one squarely on the jaw. It felt surprisingly good to vent my anger. My blood was high. Then, kicking and flaying my arms I fought my way over to station myself behind Robert for protection. He was bleeding from the nose and still thrashing out at all comers, but as it stood so far, he had seen off over half the mob. His face was covered in sweat and he was breathing very deeply. The remainder of the crowd poked and picked for a minute, tearing the pocket of Robert's jacket so that a couple of coins sewn inside fell to the earth and were stolen away before he could catch the assailants. Some were not so lucky and felt the full force of his blows. I was glad to be able to shield myself with Robert's frame and my fighting became quite tactical as a result. One man tried to grab me and I kicked him hard in the shins for his trouble before he backed off. Robert had a good right hook, I have to say, and after a few more rounds the remainder of the crowd scattered.

We sat on the dry, yellow earth, our sweat turning to mud in the dust.

'Are you all right, Mary?' he asked.

'Yes,' I said. 'My skirt is ripped to a shred that is all.'

'I don't understand it. Do you think they would have attacked us if we had turned back?' he said.

'I don't know.'

I pulled a small piece of fabric loose and mopped Robert's nose where there was blood. My ankle was aching but the skin had not been broken. I thought I might be sick.

'Come on.' He pulled me up. 'They may return.'

We hurriedly made our way to the south, back towards the bay.

Wang and Sing Hoo were sitting on the ground five minutes on. The plants they had been carrying were ripped to pieces. Petals and leaves were strewn across the ground. Those fleeing Robert had mined through the canvas bags looking for something of value. The stinking vasculum lay to one side, the fetid pod unharmed. Robert closed the box and surveyed the men. Sing Hoo was topless, his shirt stolen. He had only one shoe. Wang seemed unharmed but sat with his head in his hands and did not acknowledge us. Robert poked the fallen petals with his foot, turning over the dusty soil.

'There is nothing to salvage here,' he said. 'Come on.'

Limping and half-clothed we made it back to the ship. There need be no speculation about the shape of my legs now for we had nothing to cover them save the shredded remnants of my cotton underskirt. Robert tried to shield me. He directed Wang and Sing Hoo to walk one close behind and the other to my left while, proprietorially, he hovered on my right with his eyes to the ground.

'I do see what they meant about your ankles, Mary,' he commented wryly. 'Let us hope the citizens of Chimoo Bay are less observant than the reviewers of Fleet Street.'

I thought it kind of him to try to cheer me up, though we attracted less attention arriving back at the dock than we did departing. At the ship Landers spotted us immediately from his vantage point on deck. He was the only person who appeared to realise that we had been robbed and came immediately to our aid. He ordered hot water to the cabins and covered me in his coat.

'What did they take?' he asked Robert.

'My watch, the clothes and some money.' Robert's voice was flat.

'I will post the news so others coming this way might know of it,' Landers promised.

There was no more he could do. We should not have been there in the first place. The port boundary was our limit. That was the law.

In my cabin I bound my ankle. There was swelling to one side but nothing serious. I wrapped my dressing gown about me and washed myself slowly all over. It seemed to me that we would surely die inside China's borders.

'What have I done?' I whispered.

And I sat on the bed and cried for a long time.

The Buddhists have a meditation upon the subject of death and at length I thought that it might help, or at least divert me. I pulled a book from my trunk and found the page that described this custom. Its purpose, I suppose, was to prepare for the end – to be ready before there was an urgent need. The practice was to think upon three good deeds done. Only three. And yet, when I tried for myself that evening, I found it difficult to choose. I kept thinking that I had left Jane with all my responsibilities. Here I was, moaning about being abandoned when I was not the one in London responsible alone for four children. How many good deeds would it take to compensate for that?

At length, when I considered it, I realised that the best of my actions were small things. Picking flowers and cooking food for my mother when she had been unwell, spending an afternoon with the children, sending money to my sister or kissing goodbye Henry's tiny head as he slept in the nursery before I left. I thought of every detail and afterwards I felt better. Hellfire and brimstone never have appealed to me and I admit I become easily confused thinking of right and wrong. But I do understand kindness.

I had tried my best, of course, but I realised I was not the only Penney woman alone in the world.

The subject of death always brought my father to mind. Now long passed, he seemed a mythical creature to me – a man a poet might describe as being completely insubstantial, constructed only of light and shade. Mother erected a small cross two or three years after he died. She said her delay was to let the ground settle but she need not have left it so long and, as we grew older, both Jane and I knew it. It occurred to me aboard the *Dundas* that night that we had all lived in his dappled shadow long after he was buried. Jane was fleeing from the darkness in his wake and I was running blindly towards any spot of light I could find, dreaming of being dazzled again. One of us his favourite and the other cast out. And here I was in China still searching for my dazzling dream while Jane was in London running from the dark.

We had ten days to Chusan and, confined now to the ship, I endeavoured to learn to use chopsticks. Wang tutored me patiently. I dare say he and Sing Hoo found Robert and me hopelessly eccentric. Between Robert's obsession with plants and my interest in mundane aspects of Chinese life I cannot say I blame them. Lifting the sticks was easy enough but eating with them took longer. Wang set an assault course of empty shells and I practised hard. Landers found this most amusing.

One evening I took my place at table and instead of knife and fork, sticks were laid beside the plate. The captain beamed over the tabletop with his customary enthusiasm. It was time for some fun.

'Well, Miss Penney,' Landers said, 'inspired by you we have all gone jungly.'

Robert looked nervous. He could think of nothing more shaming. He picked up his sticks and dropped them immediately. Landers motioned to the boy attending the table and three steaming bowls were laid before us. They were brimful of noodles of the kind sold on the dockside. I speared a pea with one stick.

'It is a challenge,' I said.

'Quite so. Come along.'

Of course, Landers was proficient and managed the noodles very well. Robert and I were novices. We carefully manoeuvred the sticks in an ungainly fashion.

'I think you will starve if you continue so politely,' Landers laughed, propelling his food towards his mouth Chinese-style, quickly and without ceremony. 'They lift the plates to their mouths, you know,' he encouraged us.

I managed a clump into my mouth. It was soft and delicious. I could taste ginger and garlic. I bit off the end and realised that a noodle was draped down my cheek. Robert motioned to me.

'It is not civilised, that much is sure,' Landers chuckled.

Robert cupped his bowl near his chin and copied the captain.

'Not too poor for a first try,' he pronounced proudly.

After dinner we retained our sticks. One after the other we lifted the salt cellar, tried to pour wine (somewhat disastrously) and held a mock sword fight for the prize of the last orange on board.

'There is a garrison at Chusan,' Landers said past midnight and two bottles down. 'Will Miss Penney continue from there or is she to settle? It is either there or Shanghae that are the last safe places for a lady.'

Robert sobered. He must have liked Landers for normally he would not have answered such a remark. But his views on my behaviour had not changed and our encounter at Chimoo Bay had not put him off hauling me with him on his mission. I was still an embarrassment to be contained.

'Mary stays with me. I cannot leave her anywhere,' he said, his face set very hard.

'I see,' replied Landers, who could, I suppose, push no further.

The mapping inside China was unclear and somewhat contradictory. Many of our vessels sailed the waters between Hong Kong in the south and Shanghae to the north and the maps of the coastline and of those places a day or two's journey from port were excellent. The mystery was further inland. For the tea countries, particularly the black tea region of Bohea, where Wang was born, there was a mere sketch for guidance. Robert's notebook was not only a horticultural compendium and a comprehensive list of all outgoings (including the cost of goods and plants sent home), but also a journal of even the most throwaway remark about the interior. He noted everything. The mention of a great river, another of a canal system, and a rough sketch of a giant, smoke-blue monkey he had been told inhabited the northern forests were all noted in meticulous fashion.

He let me read these notebooks and occasionally, with his permission, I amended or annotated particular entries. We had talked to different people about different matters and therefore sometimes I had details to add to his knowledge. When this was the case Robert leant forward in his chair as I made my comments. Usually it was evening, the lamps were lit, and I was curled up on an upholstered chaise, which Landers had sent along from his cabin for my comfort. It reminded me of nights at Gilston Road, when Jane read by the fire and she and I discussed the passages she had chosen. Robert had never shown an interest then, of course, and invariably retired to the library after dinner. Now he hung on every word of his own manuscript. Going over the diaries made him realise, I think, which details he was missing and what he still had to do.

At Chusan Island he made the decision to stop for a while and gather more information. In Chusan there was great industry and, in addition to filling in gaps in his knowledge, Robert intended to make further purchases to load off for auction in London. After the down-at-heel ports where we had recently disembarked, Chusan raised my spirits. There was the usual raggle-taggle of pickpockets and ne'er-do-wells and notices had been posted of Europeans accosted and robbed in the surrounding areas. We heard that a Mr Martin had recently been quite severely beaten. However, the port at Tinghae itself heartened me with its well-kept warehouses and orderly accommodation. I did not intend to leave it after our misadventures at Chimoo.

A flotilla of small boats ferrying travellers and offering services milled here and there across the bay. Landers' first action at this port was to hop to a barber's raft and have his hair trimmed and his face shaved. Watching from the deck of our own vessel I spotted three of the barber's children watching entranced as their father worked upon the 'white devil'. Most Chinese shave their heads excepting one long ponytail to the rear. To see a full head of hair must have been unusual enough but along with Landers' light colouring and huge frame the children were fascinated. They skulked in one corner of the raft and when the captain rose from the stool they scattered like buckshot, diving into the water.

We departed the ship on excellent terms. Robert shook the captain's hand heartily, commended his courage at the Formosa Channel and gave a present of six bottles of fine port. I had the feeling that, like everything for Landers, we would pass out of his memory immediately he had set sail, or perhaps after the last bottle of our port had been emptied. He waved us off up the dock. The *Dundas* set sail the next day.

Winter drew on and it became colder. By now it was October, almost November. I always imagined exotic locations to be at least temperate, but this was clearly not the case. In the humidity of Hong Kong I had wished often for a biting breeze and now I sorely regretted it. Robert found us rooms in accommodation that was to prove draughty. I never saw a building with glass windows in Chusan, other than the church. Elsewhere the windows were small and either open to the elements or shielded with a thick, opaque paper nailed to the frame on the inside and shutters to the exterior. I had not packed for such exigencies and at the earliest opportunity I bought myself a thick scarf, a padded jacket, a woollen skirt and some gloves. I cannot vouch that Robert did not feel the weather but perhaps his childhood in the Scottish cottage had inured him to such adversity for he never complained of it. Not even when we woke to find frost on the floors inside the house. We had a small iron stove in each room and while Robert made friends at the garrison with the officers of the 2nd Madras I stationed myself in the heat of the fire and ventured out rarely. Even on Christmas Day, invited to dine at the mess, I declined. It seemed wrong and I had no wish to go.

Robert kept to himself and we communicated rarely. I think he came to consider me a strange and solitary creature and I was happy enough with that. I had never spent so much time on my own in my life, and it gave me much cause for reflection. While I was now fascinated by the emerging Chinese world around me and, for that matter, Robert's mission and the attendant details of horticultural interest, I also had time to think about what had happened at home – to pick apart the seams of my story. When Robert did spend an evening in the little house where we were lodged, I related tales about Jane and me when we were children. The summer day we were caught in a storm and how we sneezed for the rest of June. Or of setting the washing out to air on the lavender Mother had planted, and plaiting the fragrant stems, hanging them up to dry so we could sell them come the autumn. My mother had always farmed a little. I conjured up stories of Christmases in the country, presents from my father – toys he had carved from wood. Of him waiting, smoking by our garden gate in the snow, as we walked back from Church. 'He's not a bad man,' my mother said. I had always loved hugging him, sitting on his knee. There was a singular smell of tobacco as I buried my face in his shoulder and a smell of horses too, I suppose, for that was his trade. It seemed strange to me that Robert had not heard these stories before or at least some of them. Jane, I suppose, had said little because, from her point of view, she had nothing nice to say, especially about our father. I was his favourite, though, and he had never hurt me. And there my memories became patchy for I had been very young and, I expect, had not wanted to think too long on my sister getting a hiding and me getting off scot-free. Now, Robert listened eagerly. Perhaps the time passed slowly for him as much as for me and, for my part, I enjoyed telling the tales. I hardened my resolve to try to accept my fate and Robert's part in it as best I could. What use is regret? I was stuck with him and he with me.

On the occasions I did leave the house I went alone. The bustling streets fascinated me. The children in Chusan were bound to their mothers by cloth. Any of Henry's age, that is. On my wanderings I passed many women about their business with a baby clamped tightly to their chest, often as not asleep and always subdued. My son, I knew, was fond of kicking and squirming. He would be walking by now. At home the nanny would have brought him to me daily. I might have told him bedtime stories and visited him at tea. I should have been picking little shoes and caps and robes and buying a bay rocking horse. It seemed so far away now as if I had made it up, a flight of fancy – a little boy made of thin air.

My favourite places in Tinghae were undoubtedly the establishments attached to clothing factories. These manufactured uniforms of all descriptions that they hung outside on display. It seemed all regiments stationed in the region ordered their clothing supplies from the factories at Chusan, and uniforms for all ranks were readily available, from tartan trousers to elaborately brocaded dress jackets. In addition there were magnificent hats and caps adorned with lustrous feathers and ribbons secured with brass buttons. I often saw junior officers going in and out of these establishments, brusque with the elegant shopkeepers who spoke in what, to the European ear, sounded like riddles. The mechanics of any sale were shrouded, I came to learn, in enquiries over the good health of the commander in charge of the regiment and polite good wishes about success in a recent dog race or at cards. I watched and listened and stayed mostly silent. The shopkeepers became accustomed to seeing me now and again with my padded jacket clasped round my frame and my scarf over my chin as I perused the racks of splendid tailoring.

One day, down a side street I found a stationery shop. At the rear there was a shrine to Weng Chang Ti Chun, patron saint of paper makers. I recognised the figure immediately from my studies. Beside an image of the saint with his entourage, incense burned. The smoke was an enticing blend of spices. It made me linger. Most of the goods in the shop were for the purpose of Chinese calligraphy and black ink, thick parchments and sculpted brushes of all sizes were on display floor to ceiling. I used my limited Cantonese to wish the shopkeeper good fortune, congratulate him on his beautiful establishment and then, finally, ask about coloured paints. The tiny Chinese man listened carefully. 'You are welcome to my humble workplace,' he said. 'Ah! I know what to put before you for approval . . .' He nodded so enthusiastically that I wondered if he had misunderstood my request, but when he returned from his storeroom he was clutching a small box of watercolours. I bought them.

I had not painted since I was a child. I purchased a notebook of suitable paper and curled beside the stove in the grey, wintry light, I began to sketch. I chose subject matter from London at first. A blotchy painting of the front door at Gilston Road. A dreadful representation of the children playing in the park and a hobby horse for Henry. Then I took to the swaying outlines of the ships in the bay. British packets and sampans moored side by side, rows of masts like bare winter trees towering over the tiny barks that sold goods between the larger vessels. I showed them about their business, hawking noodles, tea, flowers and haircuts with sailors hanging over the side to buy the wares. Robert, of course, only took an interest when my subject matter moved to his collection of plants. He brought home some small trees with dark green, smooth leaves and tiny, orange fruits that seemed impervious to the cold.

'Kumquats,' he told me. 'They are rather sour but will make an excellent preserve, I should think.'

He sent my sketches of the plants home to the nursery in Wiltshire along with a large consignment of the seeds. And he commissioned me to do more. One of the *poederia* and another of some palms. I was not permitted to initial the drawings but toyed with the idea of scribbling some little sign in the corner as my mark. A star? A circle, like a penny? In the end I dared not risk it; still it was the first time since our embarkation that I felt truly useful. This was something I could do which could not be taken on by anyone else. It was good to be occupied.

I also helped to pick out some clothes to send home. We chose a boxful for Gilston Road. Bolts of satin and splendid brocade. Chinese-style jackets for the children and some lovely blue breeches for Henry and a rather smart cap. (I bought these in several sizes, to see him through.) For Jane I fancied an evening bag of thick silk and a fur muffler. I hoped they would make her happy. I pictured her opening the box and pulling out the items one by one. I could see Helen trying the caps on Henry and holding him up to the mirror so he could see himself as her brother was parading up and down in his smart new jacket and Jane was drawing the rich, dark fur to her cheek, happy with its quality and imagining herself already in her winter coat, her hands safely stowed.

'She will like that,' I thought, as I packed the items, one by one into the wooden cases and slipped in some of my drawings on top, signed with a kiss.

To the auction houses on the Strand we sent boxes of mother-of-pearl buttons, bolts of silk and of satin, beautiful lacquered fans that reflected the light as they moved and intricate ivory fascinators. While Robert could pick and choose for the nurseries and had passable taste in furniture, he had no idea what shades of silk would tempt a lady, and again I found myself competent to help. As I watched the boxes loaded I imagined next season's evening gowns, cut to perfection from the shimmering shades I had chosen. Smooth, white necks arrayed with pearls. The dining rooms of Mayfair lit up.

We rested three months in Chusan and I scarcely saw a soul from England all that time. I cannot remember feeling lonely. The sound of Cantonese with its stretched vowels and subtlety of tone came to rest in my ear. It was as if I was learning a script with its own rhythms and nuances. I dreamt one night, swaddled in quilted satin, of an officer coming to call. I thought of him first as a *Hong-mou-jin*, a red-haired man, what the Chinese call all Europeans. In the half-light, waking to my nose cold and my ears biting, I looked back on the dream and realised I could think in Cantonese. I said nothing to my brother-in-law, for it would only have alarmed him. The barracks were his home as much as our lodging house and I knew he could not read the expressions on Chinese faces or understand the half-caught conversations we passed in the street between the merchants and their customers. His Cantonese was still halting. As far as I could ascertain, he had not bought anything Chinese to wear and only now and again availed himself of the steaming hot food stalls dotted around the town, where gleaming noodles and fried apple dumplings rolled in sesame tempted the passersby.

'Damned odd fare,' he would exclaim, as if he was the colonel of the regiment.

I found it all delicious.

One evening at the end of February I was beside the stove when Robert came back from supper in the mess. I was thinking of a garden. I had read in one of my books that in India there are night-time retreats planted with shimmering white flowers, translucent in the moonlight. They give fragrance in the cool of the evening. A meeting place for lovers. I had been daydreaming of late about the sensation of being held – a woman in a man's arms. I missed that closeness and the feeling, fleeting though it had been in the past, of being treasured. Now I sketched plants around a pond in my love garden. Orange jessamine, star jasmine and seaside daisies. Robert peered over my shoulder raising a lamp to see.

'*Trachelospermum jasminoides*,' he commented.

Why he must always name things in Latin when flowers sound so much prettier in English, I did not know.

'These thrive at home already,' he said. 'The trick is to send back the rare.'

'You are on a mission, Robert. I am not,' I said firmly. 'I may not be fond of plants in general but I like flowers.'

Robert shrugged. Leaving me to my representation of the moonlight on the water he took out his tobacco pouch and rolled a cigarette. He smoked less and less frequently as nothing he could find measured up to the tobacco from Christie's that I had scattered about his cabin aboard the *Braganza* the first day of our voyage.

I had seen Robert's notebook. I read it every few days. The pages were thick now with details of Hwuy-chow – all its mountain ranges, villages and tea factories. He had gleaned all these details in Chusan with the aid of the regiment who had provided a translator whenever he found a Chinaman who came from the region. Bohea, apart from Wang's descriptions, which were mostly of his village, remained a mystery. But there was yet time for that.

'We will leave here soon, will we not?' I ventured.

Robert lit up and licked his lips.

'Too bitter,' he commented.

'It is not long now,' I drew his attention back.

Robert stubbed out the tobacco. He sat forwards, his elbows on his knees.

'How do you know?' he said. 'We might stay longer.'

'They have three harvests a year, Robert. I cannot imagine you will miss them.'

Robert nodded. He seemed amused. It did not occur to him that he might need to tell me of his plans.

'You do know me, Mary. There is no denying it.'

'I like green tea,' I said.

'Well, Miss Penney, you shall have it.' Robert bowed. 'Before Hwuy-chow we shall visit Ning-po. There will be an abundance there. And besides, there is a man I must meet.'

I pulled out our map and laid it in front of me. Ning-po was not far – another British trading port further along the Straits. Robert regarded me from his chair.

'Two weeks, if that, Mary,' he said. 'I have taken our cabins.'

Chapter Six

When Robert and I arrived in Ning-po we were to report to the British Consul, Mr Thom, but he had been borne away on important business. We hovered near his residence unsure what to do. We had no other friendly name to hand and no recommendation to secure us lodgings. Mr Thom's Chinese housekeeper, apparently left alone in the Consulate, did not know when her master might return and had the surly manner of one haughty from being left in charge. Then Wang brought us news of another European who lived in the town's Catholic Mission and we decided to call upon him for advice. It was not far away.

When we arrived at the address we found a rather grand house with a European-style front gate, clustered around which there was a crowd, highly charged with anticipation. We pushed our way through, struck the huge, brass knocker and were welcomed inside by a servant. He showed us into a large, pleasant drawing room. After a minute or two a figure appeared in the doorway. Father Allan was clearly an eccentric. A small man, he had adopted the Chinese way, or so it seemed at first, though quickly I realised that his outfit was, in fact, highly comical. He wore a coolie's hat with a mandarin's robe – something akin to dressing a drayman with a fine top hat. Instantly I understood the reason for the crowd at his front door. If an eccentric such as this lived nearby I would hope to catch sight of him by lingering. Father Allan was unperturbed. His accent was American and his hand movements expansive.

'Welcome, welcome,' he greeted us. 'I am Father Allan, but you must call me Bertie.' He bowed. 'We don't stand on ceremony here.'

I liked him immediately, while Robert squirmed uncomfortably at the priest's open manner. We were in a fix, however, with nowhere else to go and Bertie was well informed and willing to have us.

'You must be the charming Miss Penney.' He kissed my hand. 'And Mr Fortune, of course. News travels here at lightning speeds. Come, have some tea and we will walk in the garden. I have an orchard, you know. It will be quite up your street. You are welcome to stay until Mr Thom returns. We have far too many rooms and I will relish the company. Did you come from Chusan?'

In the end, despite Robert's initial insistence that we take lodgings, we stayed for several weeks in the house and it turned out that Bertie, while audacious in sartorial matters, was a font of knowledge on the subject of the interior. His open manner belied a sharp mind and over the weeks both Robert and I found him an extraordinarily surprising individual. As some kind of hub for the missions Bertie was in correspondence with every Catholic priest inside China's borders. There were communities everywhere, from Hong Kong to locations so deep in the interior that no white man had ever been there. Unlike the Anglicans, the papists encouraged their emissaries to take to the local customs and this secured excellent inside knowledge. Bertie had details of the location of mountain passes and border crossings between provinces in the Bohea Mountains. He had precious news of jurisdictions five hundred miles inland, of local customs and practices that varied from region to region, of

Buddhist monasteries offering shelter to travellers and of areas blighted by disease. In the library Bertie would sit and talk for hours with Robert taking notes all the while.

Bertie had time for everybody and the knack of seeing, somehow, what people really were about. The house was a fine building but it had not given him airs or made him forget the reason he had come to China in the first place. Every evening he had soup served at the back entrance, a huge, steaming pot that was distributed to the ragged crowd who assembled in anticipation at six o'clock.

'I cannot sit down to my own dinner without seeing first to those less fortunate,' Bertie said.

Everyone we had met so far in our adventuring considered the Chinese an untrustworthy race in general, and lazy. Bertie's beliefs ran against this trend. He embraced every soul that he met. The man brimmed with forgiveness. I felt when I sat with him that he could see through me blood and bone, to my soul.

One day Robert went in search of a yellow camellia. The flowers were on his long list of highly saleable plants that he had most hoped to find in China. This colour was unheard of in Europe and yellow, he swore, always commanded a high price so when it was rumoured they grew near Ning-po he took his chances. Bertie and I spent the day on the mission's terrace. Bertie had correspondence to deal with while I attempted to write to Jane. We fell, of course, to talking.

'You are an adventurer, Mary,' he said.

This made me sad. After all, I was not. I'd been forced to take this voyage.

'Robert compelled me to come here,' I admitted.

Bertie leant forward, his grey eyes soft. 'Oh, I did not refer to your journey. Though it is quite extraordinary. No, my dear, I refer to your spirit. You strike me as brave. I hope you do not find me presumptuous, but, well, I am. My guess is that the reason Robert compelled you to accompany him is more to do with Robert than with you. My experience is that two hundred and fifty miles is in general enough to outrun any scandal.'

I laughed. 'It was a scandal, all right. How did you know?'

Bertie shrugged. 'What else?' he said as he rang the bell on the table and ordered the maid to bring us some tea. 'It is my job. Your sister must be very dear for you to bear it,' he said.

I hesitated. 'Bertie, would you, might you, confess me?'

Bertie tipped his hat, which on this afternoon was made of silk in the manner of a mandarin's cap.

'I should have to convert you first and I have no time for a baptism today,' he replied. 'Perhaps it would be more convenient to simply *confide* in me.'

I did not hesitate. Not even for a moment. It was as if I had been waiting for somebody to ask. In Chusan I had spent months alone with no one to talk to apart from Robert, who appeared intermittently in our dingy lodging house. To meet Bertie, with his easy manners and generous company, was like jumping into the ocean after months in the desert. I blurted everything, from my first meeting William to the day Robert and I left Hong Kong. I was so rapt in my own story, I confess, I almost forgot that Bertie was there. It was as if a tide was washing over me and I could not stop it.

'Oh, I know,' I finished, 'it is a hundred sins all at once, Bertie. Adultery, illegitimacy, I have been headstrong and vain. And somewhere I must be proud too for I cannot say I truly regret it all. And Robert will have at me for admitting even the half. I have been utterly miserable.'

Bertie put his hand on mine.

'He has dragged you three thousand miles on account of an illegitimate child and a talent for the stage?'

I burst into tears. Bertie made the sign of the cross before me.

'Hush now,' he said.

And as my tears subsided I had an overwhelming feeling of gratitude that Mr Thom had been called away and I was in Ning-po with someone who understood. To come so far and be listened to felt like flying – a smooth and fluid movement of the soul.

Once I had spoken of my story I found it difficult to lay aside the subject, I admit it. I felt different. Better. The mornings found me on the terrace sipping tea in the Chinese fashion, the leaves floating in my cup, with Bertie patiently listening before he started his religious duties for the day. It was extraordinary, I thought, that he showed no sign of his knowledge to Robert. In fact, if he was thick as thieves with me before breakfast he was no less cosy with Robert after dinner when they retired to the library to discuss horticulture.

'And what of the mandarins?' Robert asked him.

We had Chinese servants and we bought our supplies from Chinese merchants, but Robert was callow in the ways of the ruling classes and I had never met so much as one mandarin.

Bertie smiled and his eyes twinkled. He pulled several books from their places and made a pile of them on the dark table.

'That is a start,' he said. 'But it is only by practice that you will come to understand. They are just men, like all of us, Fortune. Each an individual. They do what they must.'

It turned out that the mandarins were something akin to our own aristocracy or at least our English Ten Thousand – those in charge, those with the power and the money. They were drawn from two tribes with differences in their customs – the Han and the Manchu. The mandarins were known for their barbarity – even to their own people. During our time in Ning-po Robert spent several hours in the library every day and read almost every book on the shelves there.

It was in the library, in fact, that Robert kept his yellow camellias. The flowers had caused great excitement when he had found them, or at least, possibly found them, for Robert had bought the specimens for five dollars, but they were untested – the buds were tight as tiny cricket balls and the prized yellow flowers only a promise as yet unseen. He became quite obsessed, positioning and repositioning the plants each morning so they had the best light of the day. On one occasion when I came into the library, I found him searching with a large magnifying glass around the side of the buds for a mere wisp of yellow.

'They are worth hundreds,' he swore.

'Only if they are yellow,' I pointed out. 'Robert, how could you be so foolish?'

Robert shrugged and settled back down to his book. 'It is a wager. But I think they will be yellow as primroses. I hope so for then when they bloom they will be worth as much as all the tree peonies and azaleas I sent home together.'

Robert had struck a deal that when the flowers came out he would forward a further five dollars to the boy who had procured them on his behalf. One morning I heard the smash of glass as I sat reading on the terrace. I jumped up and ran into the library to find Robert red faced and furious beside the plant pot of offending blooms.

'Damn!' he shrieked, 'the filthy, Chinese liar!' He launched a book he had been reading towards the window, one pane of which was already shattered.

'Robert!' I shouted. 'This is Bertie's house! Calm down!'

'Oh, I will pay for it, Mary. But damn it! Damn it to

hell! These flowers are white – not yellow. Fetch me Wang, will you?'

With our servants dispatched to find the dishonest flower seller Robert's temper eased. He sat on a wicker chair by the camellia, peering at the bloom with his magnifying glass as if inside the white there might be yellow petals yet to come. That evening none of us were surprised that neither Wang nor Sing Hoo could find the young vagabond who had taken Robert's *cash*. He had left town swiftly with the money, no doubt delighted with his scam. Robert clearly thought this behaviour was representative of all Chinese citizens, but for my part, though I left it unsaid, if he had tempted a poor man with a fortune, who would blame the fellow for taking what he could?

'Sorry, Bertie, about your windows,' he said sheepishly over dinner. 'I have instructed the repairs.'

'Ah, the frailty of man . . .' Bertie replied with a twinkle in his eye.

The afternoon after the camellias opened Robert, Bertie and I walked into Ning-po. We had not seen Bertie until after lunch that day for he had been in silent contemplation all morning, followed by his formal prayers, led at a nearby chapel. Bertie's devotion fascinated me. Sometimes he would talk about the time he spent studying in Rome and how the grandeur of the Vatican, all Bernini's angels and Caravaggio's sinners, had seemed at odds to him with what he took to be his own mission. Down by the river we set aside the disappointment of the flowers and Robert and I listened to Bertie talking about the year he had spent in a seminary in Naples as we strolled along the unpaved streets. He talked about his mission in China. At last we stopped on the riverbank and stood staring at the curious bridge across the water. The tide was alternately so high and then so low that the city engineers had built a floating bridge that rested on huge boats. These rose and fell with the tidal flow, leaving the arches of the bridge always high enough for ships to pass underneath.

'It is ingenious,' Bertie declared in admiration. 'It took them months to construct of course, but it is worth it in the end.'

Robert had not been put off his quest for the camellia. He regarded the moving bridge and the persistence required for its construction, as if it was a message.

'I will try again,' he mused. 'It is out there, somewhere.'

We decided to linger for a while, so I set up my drawing stool and made some sketches. It occurred to me that at home we could build jetties on a similar model to allow ships to dock in tidal water. It was in my mind that Robert should send the drawings home to see if anything might come of the idea. Bertie meanwhile was chattering fluently to the small crowd that had assembled to inspect his outfit. He kept a supply of wooden crucifixes in a drawstring bag and gave them out like lucky charms. When I had finished he inspected each sheet, nodded approvingly and then helped to fold my stool. I had found myself all morning wondering what Jane would have made of Robert's behaviour, for his temper had been monstrous. I had never seen him so passionate in London – taken up and bookish, certainly, but not with this fire in his belly – all over a flower.

When Jane had told me of Robert's proposal, all those years before, I had questioned her.

'Are you sure?' I asked my sister, the day before she made her vows. 'Do you love him at all?'

She cast me a glance. To her such questions were a mere annoyance. She wanted to be married. She wanted to be a lady. With Robert these things were possible.

'Oh, Mary,' she shook her head as if I was hopeless. 'I am not afraid of Robert. He is not like *that*.'

An absence of terror seemed a strange basis for a marriage and at fifteen I was still not completely sure what Jane was talking about in any case. I followed my older sister down the aisle and stood by her side. And all I remember is that the bouquet was rosebuds and thistles – a spiky affair.

And now it was clear to me that Robert was *like that*. He had been that way since we left England. Unaccountably, he reminded me of my father, only with Robert it was I who bore the brunt of the man's dark temper and Jane who was illuminated.

'Well,' Bertie said, 'we can't tarry here all day. We are close to a friend of mine who has an interesting garden. Shall we call?'

It transpired that Bertie's friend was a mandarin named Dr Chang. It was characteristic of Bertie not to mention this until we were at the door. I think he must have planned it all along.

'Less of books, Mr Fortune,' Bertie smirked. 'Here we are.'

Standing outside, with hardly a moment to consider what we were doing, I found myself both excited and daunted. There was no question that Bertie's proposition was dangerous. In Chinese law the export of live tea plants is punishable by death. Robert's proposed journey to Bohea and Hwuy-chow constituted a capital offence. Robert said that in the officers' mess he had heard men argue over the Chinese tortures for hours – what was easier to endure and what might kill you soonest. There were tales of barbarous penalties. It made my skin crawl to know they hung men and women by the hair or by the thumbs for days, caged them in metal boxes in the dark, with only one tiny air hole or beat their suspects without mercy till their skin was completely raw. The year before, the authorities had found the body of a man who had died of over three thousand tiny cuts inflicted, they said, over three days and nights. In punishment for treason or murder, as well as this Death of a Thousand Cuts, or *Ling Chi,* there was slow smothering with wet cloths. The prospects at their very worst were terrifying.

While Robert's mission was, I suppose, fairly widely known in the European community, there was no question of confiding it to a Chinese unless he could, of a certainty, like Wang and Sing Hoo, be paid for his allegiance. Even then, Robert still had not been explicit and continued to tell our men that this mission was to collect a variety of new plants on his journey. From his insistent questioning about tea production they knew that tea plants were included in this, but in the time that had passed since we left London, Robert had sent home seeds and cuttings from over eighty other varieties, so it was not yet clear to them that tea was the prize, the whole point of the journey.

On Dr Chang's doorstep, I shifted from foot to foot. My hands were clammy. But with the fear there was also excitement. I knew more of China itself than I knew of her people and here was a chance to learn what the famed mandarins were really like. At first a smartly-dressed servant appeared. He peered at us, betraying only the slightest surprise to see three Europeans standing in the entrance, one of them a woman. I steadied myself, taking a deep breath. The man bowed and ushered us in, showing us through the entrance hall and across a courtyard into a pleasant reception room. He then disappeared and we heard shouting from within the compound. Bertie smiled gleefully. Our arrival was causing a small commotion.

'I do love a rumpus,' he beamed. 'Don't you?'

After a minute or two Dr Chang came. He was a small man with delicate features and was dressed in an embroidered blue robe, which he wore with black shoes and topped off with a cap. Chang's face lit with delight at the sight of Bertie and he started into a babble of Mandarin that I could not follow. All my expertise was in the more widely spoken Cantonese.

'Ah yes, he has heard of you, of course,' Bertie beamed. 'Bow, Robert. That is the way.'

Robert complied, bowing low and then, as if out of nowhere, there were servants bearing trays of tea and we all sat down in the garden, Dr Chang's eyes sparkling as he took in the details of his guests.

It seemed that the Chinese community were as curious about us as I found myself about them. While we were drinking our tea on the terrace, another of the doctor's friends came to call, and then another. Within half an hour we were seated in a veritable congregation of mandarins who had heard we were there and had consequently paid a social visit immediately. As each new guest arrived, Bertie managed a series of sly, cheeky winks in our direction. This I found comforting and I drew myself up, realising how much my experience at Drury Lane stood me in good stead. I imagined every detail of how I would like to appear in such a company and endeavoured to live up to this impression despite my quickening heartbeat. At once it became as natural as if I was often the only woman in a large company of potentially dangerous foreigners.

Conversation was stilted and slow, requiring copious translation, as the language of the mandarins is complex and difficult. It is so different from at home, where one's fellow compatriots might have a different accent but at base everyone has the same words. Here, Chinese society fragmented into class groups, each with a language of their own. The sounds of each dialect has little in common with the others and this made communication difficult between the Chinese themselves, let alone with foreigners.

I listened as one man spun my Cantonese words into new phrases while the others nodded, moving elegantly, their skin flawless and their eyes still.

The mandarins warmed to Robert's occupation with plants. Most of them seemed to have a deep interest in their gardens and one or two had country estates where they grew food for their family's use. The mention of a particular variety of plum, a drawing of baskets of peach blossom and even the cultivation of garden greens sparked animated discussions. At one point, during a heated conversation about the cropping of fruit trees, I realised that the hubbub was almost comical, given the subject of our discussions were so mundane. I swear, these men were as passionate about gardening as Robert!

'You see?' Bertie whispered to me. 'They are just like our own, dear middle classes at home.'

'They'd kill us if they knew, Bertie,' I whispered back.

He eyed me as if I was a child.

'Mary,' he chided, 'and would our own, loyal, white men not kill a foreigner who had come to steal their secrets? Come, come. We have enforced our trade upon them. We have taken their ports under our own protectorate. It is to their credit they are receiving us at all.'

He was right, of course. The men were not evil, only dangerous. If we were ever to understand what was around us we must be more open to it. Bertie was giving us practice, that was all, and making our enemies into real men.

After we had said our long, formal goodbyes we jammed into separate rickshaws. Robert handed me up.

'Well done. Very good, Mary,' he whispered.

'Nothing at all.' I smiled down from my seat. 'Thank Bertie,' I said. 'It was his idea.'

The bearers ran side by side. Many of the stalls in the

marketplace were being packed away as we sped past and animals were scavenging for remains on the dusty ground. There were pools of spilled blood amid the discarded cabbage leaves and slivers of fish skin, but, I noticed, no smell, other than that of cooking in the nearby hostelries. I glanced back but Dr Chang had not followed us.

'This place fascinates me. We must delve into it!' I called over to Robert.

It seemed strange now that all our conversations about the mandarins to date had been on the subject of how to avoid them.

Then, one by one, we were funnelled into a high-sided alleyway where the road was uneven, and I found that I had my head back and I was laughing, exhilarated, walloping along and delighted as I caught sight now and again of a thin stream of blue sky between the high buildings.

Over the weeks, while we waited for Mr Thom to return, I stayed in town while Robert made several forays to the hills. I liked Ning-po and found that my time passed easily.

I had taken each evening to watching the crowd at the back door that assembled for a cup of Bertie's soup. It occurred to me that I rarely saw a woman among them. Usually there were fifty men and always ten ragged children, but hardly ever a woman. When I pointed this out, Bertie explained that for a Chinese lady to be beholden was considered shameful and, it seemed, even the gift of a cup of soup marked an indebtedness considered inappropriate.

'Well then, Bertie, why not let them sing for their supper?' I suggested.

'What do you mean?'

'Well, they can pay by sweeping the floor or polishing a brass,' I replied. 'As if you require assistance and are only paying them in kind.'

143

The light dawned on Bertie's face.

'That is inspired, my dear,' he smiled slowly. 'I am only sorry I had not thought of it before. We shall start with them at the Church Hall then. It is far more fitting there, I think, and there is more to do.'

Within the week a ladies' soup kitchen was set up where the women could come and pay for their meal by offering some small service to the Church. Bertie took to the task with gusto. He supplied squares of paper so the women could fashion pretty flowers from them, and a sewing box so that small repairs might be made to the linen. Robert took no real interest in this, of course, but he smiled indulgently when I was discussing the matter.

'Mary notices everything,' he said.

The soup kitchen flourished and soon was catering for almost a hundred. Many evenings I went to help. Most of the women were very poor. Some toothless. Some balding. Their clothes were worn and grimy. However, I noticed one who was none of these things and I felt for her in particular. She was of my own age. Her feet had been bound so she moved very slowly, and her bearing was that of a fine Han lady. What marked her out were her beautiful eyes. They were deep as dark pools, bright and clear and, however worn the old dress she wore, they showed her as special. Her name was Ling. Unlike many of those who came for free soup, she did not sit ragged on the streets of Ning-po. I never saw her anywhere except each evening at the Church Hall.

One night my curiosity got the better of me and I resolved to follow Ling when she left. The evening streets were busy and it was not difficult to fall in behind her at a distance. Ning-po at night became a bustle of stalls and the town centre smelled of frying fish and steaming tea kettles. As we moved through the alleyways I was aware that I drew far more attention than my quarry. White women did not walk alone, and certainly not in the dark. I ignored the glances and walked very deliberately, as if I knew exactly what I was doing and was meant to be there. Ling continued as far as the riverbank. She intended to sleep there. This shocked me and in all good conscience I could not leave her for the night, but I hesitated a moment, for I was not sure how to approach a lady of honour with my proposition. If the language of Chinese commerce is flowery, the comings and goings in society are even more so. In my moment of hesitation, a Chinaman passed. The man kicked poor Ling – an urchin, only in his way. He walked on. Such unkindness was not uncommon. I rushed forward, words forming in my mind. I hoped I could get them right.

'Please,' I said, 'I have seen your needlework at the Mission and if you might be kind enough to help with the household linen then my friend, Bertie Allan, would be honoured to have you stay. It would be a great help to us all. I hope I do not disturb you.'

'I could not accept such charity,' Ling said as she struggled to her feet.

The man had hurt her leg and she was limping.

'No charity,' I reassured her. 'Your stitching is so beautiful. We beg you to come and help us.'

Ling regarded me slowly. For a moment I wasn't sure what she might do. She was a proud woman, clearly, and my proposition left her torn. There was no question of her accepting charity and, I realised, she was considering staying where she was.

'Please,' I said in a rush, 'the linen is in a terrible state and I cannot manage it alone.'

And then, thank heavens, she relented.

'I will help if I can,' she said.

Ling followed me back to the house with her eyes low to

the ground. Inside, the housekeeper furnished an ointment for her leg. I had one of my Chinese jackets brought down for I noticed despite the mild weather she seemed cold. I picked a bloom from the garden, a Chinese rose, and gestured for her to fix it in her hair. Chinese noblewomen dress their hair beautifully and I thought it might cheer her.

'Don't worry,' I said. 'You are safe here.'

And then we sat in silence and ate peaches on the terrace.

When he came back that evening and saw my refugee, Bertie said he would make arrangements. There was a nunnery at Shanghae if Ling was prepared to go. He would put it to her that the nuns had much good to do and not enough hands to do it, which he promised me 'was not a lie – not even an exaggeration.'

'You have found a favourite, then, Mary,' he said.

My feeling seemed reciprocated, for Ling favoured me too. For three days she stayed at the mission and followed me silently almost everywhere I went.

'What do you think happened to her?' I asked Bertie, when we were alone.

He looked sad but as ever Bertie understood the ways and means of all around him. 'Her feet have been bound – perhaps to assure her a good marriage. Sometimes families do that to their daughters to try to elevate their status. If a marriage doesn't transpire it's difficult. The girl has been brought up above her station and she's crippled, in effect.'

It was true. Ling couldn't do much manual work.

'What happens to those women?' I asked.

Bertie shrugged. 'Sometimes they are deliberately abandoned. That might not be what happened to Ling, of course. Perhaps there was a downturn in the family fortunes – a death or dishonour, and she was left defenceless and alone. She will not talk of it, Mary. Of that I have no doubt.'

I didn't ask. Instead, Ling and I arranged flowers for the hallway, darned Bertie's linen and walked in the garden – such as her bound feet would allow. The maid helped to change her bandages, bathing the tiny, broken stumps at the end of her leg in warm water and herbs. Bertie said that to unbind her feet now would only cause poor Ling more pain and leave her open to infection. Her feet already smelt rotten but when I asked to see them Ling blushed and I did not like to push her. It was plain to see that huge damage had been done, from which she would never recover. Of all the harsh behaviour I had been subjected to, I realised that I had never been so roughly treated as this poor Chinese rose or indeed the millions like her, for foot binding was commonplace among Han women.

When I waved Ling off on the third day, I had the overwhelming feeling that I had been lucky simply to have been able to help her. In London I doubt I would have ever reached out to such a person and it seemed to me that these months of watching and listening, second-guessing words and phrases, seeing so much that was new, had somehow changed me. Perhaps Robert had been right and at home, in England, I had been selfish, unaware of anyone except myself, and anything except my own immediate desires. I had been spoilt.

If our time at Ning-po was one of realisation for me, then it proved so for Robert too. On the evening of the day Ling made her way to Shanghae, Bertie and I were sitting in the long shadows of the fire after supper when suddenly there was a battering at the front door. We went into the hallway where we discovered that the commotion was caused by Robert's early return from one of his forays. It was strange – at this hour the city gates were closed for the night and none should be admitted.

'I climbed over,' Robert explained. 'One look at me,

147

and the sentinel fled. *"Gweiloh!"'* White devil. White ghost. He postured, imitating the man and drawing a mock sword.

Bertie offered a brandy. 'You must have wanted to come back to Ning-po very much,' he teased. 'We have had adventures in your absence. Mary saved a soul, I think. Though it was not her own.'

Behind Bertie, Wang and Sing Hoo were unloading boxes in the courtyard. Robert's journey had been fruitful. I caught sight of hydrangeas and chrysanthemums, some bamboo plants and numerous cuttings. It was not like Robert to forgo seeing these bedded down personally. Something was wrong.

'Are you all right, Robert?' I asked.

Robert lowered his eyes.

'What happened?'

'It was a misunderstanding,' he said. 'In a village. They had nothing.'

We had seen such villages often – muddy houses and a single, dirt track. There were smoke-filled cottages too poor to have a chimney and no livestock for miles. The people were jaundiced and thin. Robert always said that it was the Chinese with their peculiar diet and dirty habits that caused so much sickness. That it was unnecessary. We had passed on loftily, never giving a closer inspection. They were just poor people, that was all.

'They thought I was a doctor. A medical missionary,' he said. 'They came – everyone came to be cured. Out of nowhere. In an instant. And I could not help. I think there were a hundred of them.'

It must have been dreadful to have that descend upon him. The limbless and the old. The blind and the dying. Boils to be lanced, crusted, gangrenous wounds, the sickening smell of putrid flesh and everyone expecting him to help.

Likely the only white men they had seen were the Church's doctors.

'The fools,' Robert shouted, his hands shaking. 'I gave them money. Much good it would do.'

Bertie laid his hand gently on Robert's arm.

'We cannot save everyone,' he whispered. 'We must pray for these poor and desperate people and for you, Robert, helpless in the face of their suffering.' And he fell, there in the hallway, to his knees.

Afterwards we curled up by the fire once more, all of us silent. I noticed, I thought, a single tear on Robert's cheek in the fire's dim glow. I decided not to tell him about Ling. It seemed selfish, somehow, after what he had seen, for me to have helped when he could do nothing. Here, as at home, the poor were pox-ridden, dying and desperate. It was only that in China we had opened our eyes. Bertie put pine cones onto the fire and they crackled and filled the room with the scent of the forest. No one said as much as goodnight and I cannot remember what time it was when we finally retired to bed.

His brush with the unfortunates deeply affected Robert for some days. That such a misunderstanding could occur and that he had been powerless to take any action to prevent it weighed on his mind.

'If I die inland,' he mused, 'no one will know for months at least. If they execute me, most likely no one will know at all.'

'Ah, but when you return unexecuted and very alive,' Bertie pointed out, 'you will swell the Empire's coffers and return to London a celebrity.'

He took a bronze *cash* from his pocket and flipped it.

'Which shall it be?' he asked.

'I think you are both morbid,' I declared.

Robert was doodling on my notepad. He had drawn a tall monument with angels mounted above a grave.

'Lord, Robert,' I said, 'your finds will commemorate you better. Do you think it impossible now to procure what you have been sent for?'

'No,' Robert replied, adding the word 'FORTUNE' to the mausoleum in his sketch.

It entered my mind that there might be nothing left of me for posterity. All Henry had was a photograph, and that was only if they let him keep it. Was he calling my sister 'mother' now? I did not mind, of course, if he was. At least he had her there.

'I wonder what our children will think of us,' I pondered.

Robert flushed, realising that if I had said this, Bertie must know my secret.

'I am sorry. Mary has embarrassed you with her private business, Bertie. Our family disgrace.'

Bertie met Robert's eye. He had great strength, Bertie. Great resources.

'Oh, no,' he said steadily. 'God's will is in everything, you see. I would never blush at the Lord's design.'

And at that, Robert fell silent.

For the first time then I thought perhaps things had happened for the best. For some days after I did not consider myself reckless, wicked or unthinking. It was all part of the Lord's design, after all. Any mistakes made were allowed. In fact, any mistakes made were for the best. I was absolved. I walked with a lighter step wherever I chose to go. I strolled at night in Bertie's garden. The house was completely still, a single light flickering. I skipped between the fruit trees, shadows in the darkness. I slept late and when breakfast came I relished it. I had been forgiven. It felt as if I was meant to be in Ning-po, in Robert's wake, bringing home distressed Chinese gentlewomen and dispatching them to nunneries further north. I was meant to live these days in the house of a Catholic missionary.

'My life here is so very far from home,' Bertie pondered over breakfast, 'I think this place has healed me as much as it is healing you, Mary. We can really help here, you see.'

I squeezed his arm. I suspect that Bertie had ridden out a scandal of his own, though he never spoke of it. In fact, he revealed very little about himself and we knew him far less than we imagined as it turned out, for Bertie had a surprise for us up his long, embroidered, satin sleeves.

Mr Thom, our Consul, returned after some weeks and the news came to us upriver. Bertie had suggested a day trip to watch the fishermen. They had trained cormorants that were tethered to the boat and dived for fish at their master's command. Of course, we wanted to see this for ourselves. To prevent the birds from guzzling the catch the fishermen tied their necks with a length of cord just tight enough to stop them swallowing. The cords were removed only briefly each evening when the clever creatures were fed with eels, by hand. Trained cormorants were worth many dollars and the fishermen were prosperous. Perhaps this was one reason why Bertie had organised the trip. In the nearby villages the children were plump and contented. The old were well dressed.

By negotiation at the river bank, Robert bought a pair of the cormorants for six dollars, and later, together with a tank of live eels for food, sent them to London as a curiosity. As it happened, the news reached us after several months that the eels had spilled out and to save the poor birds starving on the ocean the captain had slit their throats, so London never did see the wonders we had witnessed on the riverbank outside Ning-po.

Wang came towards us with the news we had been waiting for all these weeks.

'Consul Mr Thom is returned to Ning-po,' he announced.

'Oh,' said Bertie in a curious, mystified tone that seemed to imply that he would have somehow expected to know this before anyone else.

Robert meanwhile jumped to his feet enthusiastically. 'At last,' he said. 'We must go back at once.'

He bundled Bertie and I into the small bark we had hired for the trip and then went back onto the riverbank to shout at the servants, who were dismantling our picnic. Bertie and I continued to nibble on the ham, which we had kept in hand. Robert meanwhile practically threw our oarsman into his place and jumped on board with such force that the little bark rocked perilously.

'Lord, Robert. Is this man your true love?' I teased.

'Ning-po,' Robert ordered the oarsman fiercely and then settled down without making any reply.

As we set off I was still licking my fingers clean.

Mr Thom was a tall, languid man with eyes that drooped slightly in the corners. Despite the weather he wore an English suit made of wool.

'Ah, Bishop,' he greeted Bertie warmly.

Bertie bowed low while both Robert and I gaped. Bishop? The truth of it is that had we known we never would have confided our secrets in Bertie.

'Your Honour,' Bertie greeted Mr Thom.

Robert recovered his senses more quickly than I did and shook hands with the Consul, while I was so shocked that I neglected to curtsey, surveying Bertie wide eyed instead.

Mr Thom laughed. 'Ah, it is difficult to believe, I know, Miss Fortune. Our dear Bertie does not blow his own trumpet but he is the man in a crisis. Be it one of the soul or something merely in politics.'

Then Robert disappeared into the Consul's study with some papers that he had promised to deliver by hand from

Chusan. That, it seems, was what we had been waiting for. Bertie and I remained in the drawing room.

'Bishop Allan,' I scolded him and he looked quite contrite, in fact. 'You should have told us. Really, Bertie, you are the end!'

After that Robert started to address him as 'Your Grace', which caused Bertie no end of hilarity.

'The one thing of which I am quite sure,' he said, 'is that the Lord sees me as a man. Not as a bishop. And that is quite good enough for me.'

During our stay in Ning-po Robert's store of information had swelled. He heard tales of natives taunting monkeys so they would hurl tea leaves down the hills, saving them labour in time of harvest. He visited the Chinese bathing houses and came home with stories of steam rooms such as the Turks enjoy, of luxurious, private baths scented with menthol or rosemary, massage beds awash with towels, and gifts of tea and tobacco. He was invited, with Bertie, to dine at Dr Chang's. It was a wonderful feast of thirty courses that they left after four hours, and allegedly only halfway through. But now the maps were in order. Supplies were secured and shipments dispatched. It was clear we were leaving.

Robert wrote three gardening columns, one after the other. On our last afternoon Robert and I planted some seedlings in Bertie's garden. Robert chose strawberry plants as a gift to the Bishop. He had reared them secretly and now laid out the seedlings near the fruit trees. We had never seen strawberries or raspberries in China but Robert was sure there was no reason they would not flourish. We watered the plants carefully and left instructions with Bertie's garden boy. Bertie, though delighted with the gift, declared he was saddened that it signalled the end of our stay. We were all sad, I think.

That night we dined at the Consulate. Mr Thom had

received packet post from a passing navy frigate and he offered Robert and I each a letter and a glass of sherry when we first came into his drawing room. The missives were from Jane. They had been forwarded from Hong Kong some weeks before. She must have written them at the same time we left for Amoy all those months ago. Robert pocketed his and accepted a drink, but I wanted to read what my sister had said immediately. To have news was simply too exciting!

'May I?' I asked.

Mr Thom gestured me towards a side room and closed the door to allow me some privacy.

My Dear Mary,

I cannot say that I either understand or approve of what has happened. You are wilful and seem so bent upon harm that I find myself afraid of what you might do next. It is in your nature to struggle and not in mine. I must urge you now to do your best, my dearest sister. Where is the harm in settling? I am sure Hong Kong will provide a suitable husband and perhaps, who knows, another baby. I hope for no more for you than what has brought me the greatest happiness. I beg of you, my dear, do not vex Robert. He is busy with important business. Let him get on with what he must and do not steal him away with unnecessary drama. You do not realise, I know, the effect you have on people.

Henry is well. He thrives, in fact. He has made his first steps and is quite the terror! I will write at greater length but wish now only to get this to you. Please, Mary, do what is best for all of us and not you alone. Settle. With love,
Your sister,
Jane.

It was a world away. I slipped silently back into Mr Thom's drawing room. How could I write to her about saving a Chinese noblewoman or befriending a Catholic bishop? How could I tell her that I had developed an interest in Robert's foolish plants? That I understood more of them now and that the different seed pods were not as tiresome as I had previously imagined. How could I tell her about Captain Landers and his smashed poop deck or the embarrassment of stars over the midnight straits? That I understood Cantonese now, like a native, and that the barbarian Chinese interested me greatly – I had even taken tea with the mandarins? I loved Henry with all my heart. It would be almost cruel of me to even go back now, I realised. The child did not know me at all and the older he got he would surely find my appearance more and more confusing even if I did turn up respectable and married. Things had changed so much. My sister had no idea.

After dinner, we returned home to sit on the terrace staring at the stars. Bertie had ordered red paper lanterns to be hung from the trees. The garden looked magical. Long shadows cast from the branches, the green lit up against the midnight sky, red cast down the tree trunks. It was balmy as we sipped our brandy.

Robert paced the terrace and lit a cigar. The peppery tobacco smoke wafted back towards us. I felt drowsy. Brandy always makes me soporific and it was getting late. Sing Hoo had made a 'chop', or agreement, with the owner of a barge to take us inland the following morning. He had bribed the man royally, for no European had any reason to head west from Ning-po. There were no treaty towns in the interior. For three times the normal passage the man agreed to take his chances and see us safely along the canal a hundred miles, into Chekiang Province.

Robert puffed with such ferocity as he passed that the smoke hung in a haze.

'Jane tells me the children are doing well,' he said.

'You read your letter?'

He nodded.

'What did she say to you?' he asked.

I shrugged my shoulders. 'To be good, I suppose.'

'Yes.' Robert took a deep breath and made a final perambulation around the terrace before he stopped before me.

'Mary,' he said. 'I have come to a decision. That is, my decision is to allow you to make up your own mind. It is quite up to you. I have no right, I realise, to compel you further. You have faced many dangers coming this far. Ning-po is a pleasant place and I can see you settled here if you wish, or send you back to Hong Kong if you prefer it.'

I sat forward in my chair. My cheeks burned. I cast my eyes down the garden at the orchard lights. Robert moved unsteadily.

'You are giving me leave to stay?'

Robert thought for a moment.

'Yes.'

'And a choice of Hong Kong or Ning-po?'

'Or you could return to Calcutta, if it appeals better, I suppose. It is up to you – your decision entirely.'

'Thank you,' I said.

Robert bowed curtly and turned away, but I was not finished. The sky was inky black and the garden glowed around us. Robert stared into the darkness. I cleared my throat.

'Thank you, that is, for your offer. But no.'

Robert turned back. Over the months I had seen him brave, and what in London had seemed bookish, here

156

showed vision. He lacked kindness, there is no doubt of that. But I trusted him. I remembered praying on the floor of his cabin the day we set out. Anything but out to sea with Robert. Now it did not seem so bad.

'The thing is I do not want to live in Ning-po or Hong Kong or Calcutta, come to that,' I continued. 'If it is all the same to you, the thing is I should like to see it.' I gestured out into the darkness. 'China.'

Robert's face broke into a grin and his eyes lit up. He looked almost relieved.

'I will come with you,' I said. 'If you'll have me.'

The bolts of exotic satin, the fabulous carved treasures, the monasteries in the hills with their shaven headed devotees. All the orange, the jade, the shimmering gold lay ahead of us. It was too exciting to come as far as Ning-po and go no further. I turned to the chair next to mine for reassurance but Bertie, sitting upright, had diplomatically fallen fast asleep. Robert downed his brandy.

'Good, good. I had not thought it, but we leave at six,' he said curtly. 'It will be rough, Mary.'

I nodded, for I knew that already. It would be difficult all right, and dangerous too, but I had survived it thus far and the heady adventure would be marvellous. Jane, when she heard of it, would be furious, I was sure. But I had been given the choice.

'Thank you, Robert,' I said. 'I will have the maid pack for me.'

Then I woke Bertie gently so we could all get to bed.

Chapter Seven

Plain, I swore not to complain. I knew what it would be and prepared for that.

When the dawn broke it was swift as if someone had lit a match. We set off quietly, our goodbyes confined indoors as Robert wished as little attention as possible. The barge had been packed and contracted for a journey of three hundred and fifty li to Hang Chow Foo. This would take several days as it moved so slowly that often we could walk beside the boat. After the confinement of our previous voyages this was a delightful freedom. The barge itself was, of course, very different from any sea-going vessel. The inside was colourful – it had been painted a rainbow of pretty hues – and the cabin was bedecked with an array of luxurious cushions, rugs and curtains. Unlike on an ocean voyage, the canals of the interior varied in width – sometimes scarcely wide enough for two boats to pass, other times the breadth of the Thames at Richmond. I found it most diverting. At first we did not travel due west but a little to the north, as Robert wished to see the lake at Tai Ho where he had heard there were a great many aquatic plants including some spectacular, many-coloured, water lilies.

As we set off I made to unpack, starting with our notebooks. Robert was jumpy, staring out of the low window to see if we might be spotted. I started to flick casually through the pages, picking up a tiny book bound in midnight blue leather that I had never seen before. Inside there was a table of symbols beside words in English that made no sense all together – pig fat, gravel, oil lamp and satin robe. I read no further than that for Robert whisked the book from my hands.

'Whatever is this? Are you conversing in code with someone?' I asked.

He stuck the notebook in his pocket.

'Less we say of it the better,' he directed quietly. 'And, Mary, we cannot have books lying about if they are in English. Pack those away again in the false bottoms of the trunk and if we want them we shall take them out one by one.'

If Robert was a spy I did not consider him a very debonair one, for I had never seen him so twitchy as that first day on the barge, but we made it away from Ning-po attracting no notice and, as I lay in my bunk that night, engulfed in the darkness of the Chinese countryside and its clear, balmy, black skies, I let my mind wander for, of course, to be engaged on behalf of our country was most appealing. I thought of Robert ensconced with Mr Thom the previous day and it occurred to me that the meeting must have been very important for we had held up our mission to the tea countries for weeks on account of it. I imagined Sir Robert Peel himself reading the dispatches and fell asleep daydreaming of daring escapes in the interior, Robert flinging me over his shoulder and riding to safety all the way back to Bertie's house on a piebald stallion eighteen-hands high!

Robert, of course, showed no sign of any such drama or excitement. The next morning we ate a meagre breakfast and retired to the cabin.

'It is good we are the sole travellers here,' he commented.

He proceeded to order Sing Hoo to boil some water on the brazier. Then he brought out a small mirror and began clipping his hair. I hardly paid attention. The peaceful countryside was enchanting now we had cleared the confines of the town. To the north of Ning-po there was great industry in silk, and fields of mulberry trees banked the canal. It was the most verdant I had seen in months and I found it soothing. I settled on some soft, blue cushions by the window to watch the pretty trees glide by. When I turned again into the cabin I had a shock. Robert stood there, regarding himself in the mirror, entirely shorn. He had shaved the front of his crown in the Chinese fashion and had not made too great a job of it, his scalp showing grazes where he had pressed too hard. An involuntary squeal left my lips.

'Well,' he grinned, '*white* men are forbidden.'

I laughed. Robert could scarcely look whiter.

Wang and Sing Hoo were clearly curious about Robert's transformation. Wang offered a putty-coloured cream to ease the stinging of the master's scalp. Sing Hoo arranged Robert's remaining hair with such intense concentration that it was comical, though I must say he made a good fist of it.

'Now,' Robert ordered when he was finally satisfied, 'bring up the trunk I packed in Chusan.'

I had no knowledge of any such luggage and sat forward eagerly as Wang disappeared on his mission, hauling the trunk into the room and opening it with a flourish. Inside I was astounded to see an enticing array of mandarin finery: long, satin jackets edged in rabbit or mink and wide-cut trousers lined with silk. The colours glowed vibrant – peacock blue, vermilion red and shimmering gold. I fell on my knees and began to rummage as Robert looked on.

In one box there was a long, dark ponytail that could be fixed with a comb and another that was clearly fashioned to be sewn into the hair. Robert immediately attached the first to the back of his head.

'Perhaps you could sew in the other for me later, Mary?' he asked.

'Yes. Of course.'

I continued to dig deep, laughing as I pulled each new piece to the surface.

'With these I hope to dazzle them,' Robert said, holding up the finer items. 'It is easy to bamboozle with money, is it not?'

It is true. Many a mediocrity in London found a hit on her hands due to fine lace, an array of marquisette and a good seamstress. Not by sleight of hand but by sleight of wardrobe is it possible to conquer society. Still, this was audacious. Outrageous. And it struck me Robert had not said a thing about it before. He certainly had the knack of playing his cards very close to his chest.

'But this can hardly fool them,' I said in wonder.

'Why not?'

'Robert. You are a white man.'

Robert regarded himself in the glass.

'Thing is, Mary, you know full well China is vast and there is an array of appearance. And deep in the interior they may have heard tales of white men but most have never seen one.'

Robert removed his shirt. The pale skin on his chest and arms was so white it almost shone as he held up the vibrant satin.

'Give me a few minutes,' he said. 'You'll see.'

In the end I had to concede that he made a passable mandarin, and, once he had dressed, the more sallow complexion of his face lent authenticity to the disguise.

He darkened his hair beyond his natural, deep brown (or what was left of it after the shaving). Then he put on the shoes. At first he hobbled in the higher heel, built up an inch or more as is the custom, but after some tuition he could hold himself straight and managed to walk without peering constantly at his feet.

'Excellent,' Robert mused, regarding himself piece by piece, as our mirror was too small to allow a full view.

I continued concerned. The colour of Robert's eyes was too light, but he insisted on claiming himself an official from the far, far north where skin was lighter and, it would seem, eyes might vary in colour also.

'Truly, Mary. I spoke to Bertie.'

This did not comfort me. After all, Bertie's appearance was so eccentric that his support for such a scheme hardly inspired confidence. I said so.

'Not only Bertie,' Robert insisted. 'Some chap from the Royal Highlanders did it last year. He made it five hundred miles to survey the supply lines. I too am of slight stature and my hair is dark. Come, you have transformed yourself far more. I've seen you.'

I had to concede the point.

'But the language,' I started.

Robert's Cantonese was passable, perhaps better than that, but, like me, he spoke with an accent.

'The ruling classes speak one of two or three tongues. Cantonese will be my third language – like that chap at Dr Chang's who translated for us,' Robert pondered. 'The main thing is to stay calm. Autocratic bearing and silence will have to do the job for me.'

'And if you are called upon to speak Mandarin?'

Robert smiled. 'Well, Bertie did tutor me somewhat,' he admitted. 'I can insist the servants deal with this matter, whatever it may be, and I can curse. Besides, Mandarin

162

itself comes in different forms. That will work for me. Come, Mary. Who will call on me to speak and then complain because I have not one tongue or another? Any Chinese man travelling will have difficulty talking to his countrymen and no wonder. There are seven languages at least – all entirely different – and then various dialects on top. It's high-risk right enough, but there's nothing to be done about that.'

Robert was in the right, of course. I stared at him sideways. While in one way he remained bookish and obsessed by his plants, China had brought out new skills in him – an admirable determination, an ability to manage his affairs and a spark of rebellion I had not known resided anywhere in his being. Of course, I had been subjected to the violent side effects of this but it had its estimable qualities as well. Long days of riding out from Ning-po and the physical labour of plant hunting had defined his already muscular frame and now, swamped in the loose-cut Chinese clothes, it was as if this strength had been covered up – another well-kept secret. For it seemed that Robert had more of those than I had ever imagined.

'I have to admit, bar the eyes, you certainly look like a fine mandarin.'

'Exactly,' he beamed. 'And the eyes, well, we can do nothing about those but bluster. I am from the North. The far North. And blue eyes there are prized. Now, tell me, Mary, what shall my name be?'

During much discussion while I sewed Robert's ponytail securely into his hair, I made several suggestions, the more successful of these inspired by the visual aid of Robert striking some most effective poses. Eventually I christened him Sing Wa.

We now presented an extraordinary party – a mandarin, two Chinese servants and a white woman. Robert had no plan for me – he had expected me to stay in Ning-po. I had shocked him by choosing to travel onwards, and, in truth, he shocked himself that he was prepared to take me. His mission was undoubtedly dangerous, but he had given me a choice and now had to stick by his word.

'There is nothing for it but the native garb for you too, Mary,' he pronounced.

But after a short discussion it was clear this would not wash. Robert was dressed as a mandarin of the Han tribe. Among the Han, no Chinese woman above the peasant class had feet larger than her hands and we could think of no disguise that would hide my extremities. A hem the wrong length or a sleeve cut too close could draw the wrong kind of attention, never mind the glimpse of a lady's shoes, which would show her to be low born. Poor Ling came into my mind and I knew there was no way to fake the kind of mutilation she had suffered. Considering the options further down the social scale, a female servant would not be needed on a journey such as Robert's and certainly would not merit separate quarters from Wang and Sing Hoo. It occurred to me that I had only one option: to travel as a man.

'You can be my secretary,' Robert nodded, taken up by my suggestion. 'That will explain your notepads, amply, and allow you private quarters. Your face is small enough. Very slight features, these chaps.' I knew he was echoing something said to him with this bluff, officer's drawl, but I did not comment.

'Me – a Chinaman?' I mused.

The first thing that struck me was that I had never worn trousers before, not even on the stage. To wear male clothing seemed outrageous somehow. But, as I thought on it more and ran through the practicalities, there were, of course, greater considerations than a simple change in costume. Dare I?

I let down my hair and sat staring in the mirror, running my fingers through the strands to the front. I had always been proud of my long locks – my hair fell as far as the small of my back. All the parts I ever played had beauty. A fragile Juliet, or a formidable Goneril. Everything I had ever done was of my own sex and the power of that is in attracting its opposite. Could I give up that power? What was it that marked me as a woman and was I prepared to let it go? As I picked up Robert's scissors and Sing Hoo scampered away to fetch another basin of water, I did not feel the hot tears I might have expected. If I did this I could not go back on it easily. I took one tentative cut – a long tendril at the very front – and tried to imagine what I would look like. I snipped another strand, letting it fall to the bare floorboard beneath me. Of all my foolish, impulsive actions over the years this seemed the most daring. It occurred to me that as a man I could do anything, everything I wanted. The men around me had held sway for so long – my father first, then William and Robert and now I had the chance to become one of them. I'd be master of my own destiny then. A grin spread across my face as I started to snip faster, my hair falling to the ground in a shower.

'Come, Sing Hoo,' I beckoned him when I was almost shorn, 'you must shave the rest for me.'

My eyes were shining. China was turning out to be a grand adventure.

Robert's least fancy jacket, a pair of wide-legged black trousers and a simple cap over the long plait we left to the rear of my head topped off the transformation. I practised walking like a man up and down the cabin, holding my hips steady and striding out straight ahead. It was odd to feel so uninhibited by my clothes and not to be trailing a huge skirt in my wake. Wang made an unction from the dark sesame oil he carried in his cook's pack to yellow my skin and I ran some kohl to lengthen my eyes. Together we applied a paste to darken what remained of my hair. Always slight, my curves disappeared easily. I had to admit that in the mirror I looked like a Chinaman, or at least as much as Robert did. If I kept the tenor of my voice low, I should be fine. I would practise it. The years at Drury Lane had been the perfect apprenticeship for that.

After almost an entire day of transformation we came up at last onto the deck and the bargeman stared at us wide eyed, a squeak emanating from his mouth as the shock set in. Robert comforted the man and some further money set him smiling again. We asked if he had any comment on our appearance but he had nothing to say, only nodded frantically, delighted with his bonus as he inspected us from all angles.

'Just like Chinese,' he said, in wonder.

When we arrived at Tai Ho at the end of the day, we walked from the canal to the lakeside where the shallow water was covered in blooms stretching off into the distance. The place was silent and a haunting fragrance hung in the still air. It was breathtaking. As we noticed our reflections in the patchwork of water both Robert and I burst out laughing. We surveyed ourselves, adjusting our ponytails and fixing our caps.

We were both nervous of what lay ahead. That night we would eat in a Chinese hostelry as Chinese gentlemen. Would we get away with it? Robert cleared his throat and his voice took on an air of formality.

'Mary, you do understand what we are doing, don't you? You do know the penalties for this if we're caught?'

I nodded. He continued, earnestly.

'Should they find us, should anything happen to me, then you must get away. They will kill me if they find out. They will kill you too. So if anything goes wrong you must make for Ning-po. Make for Bertie. Any Catholic priest on the way will help you. There are missions at Hang Chow Foo and one at Yen Chow Foo as well. Don't worry about me. Just run.'

His concern touched me.

'It won't come to that,' I said. 'I'm sure of it. And besides, if they capture me rather than you I will fully expect you to stage a rescue, you know. No heroic stoicism for me. No "just get away if you can", Mr Fortune.'

Robert laughed. 'Of course,' he said. 'I'll come with guns blazing, Mary. You are a lady, after all. I am only worried because, well, I realised today, that perhaps I have taken advantage of having you here – you are so good with the plants and your Cantonese is better than mine. I have often treated you harshly and you have done nothing but help. If I succeed it will be worth it, you know. An Indian harvest will leave England with no need of China. This is my chance to change the world.'

I knew that. Every British household drinks tea. To have a regular supply from our own source rather than a rival nation would make millions.

'It is all right,' I said. 'You don't have to explain. And I chose it, remember?'

Robert's voice softened. 'Yes, but you perhaps did not understand and I wanted to say to you that you do not have to stay if the seriousness of it scares you. We are still close enough to send you back to Ning-po.'

'No. I want to be here, Sing Wa. Truly,' I bowed, cutting in on him. I was surprised to hear him say the words. He had changed more than his appearance today. 'I know what we're doing. Don't worry.'

Robert took a deep breath.

'Well then. Shall we try our luck with these costumes? If we fail at this hurdle it will be back to the drawing board in Bertie's study for the pair of us, I'm afraid. Am I passable, do you think?'

I tried to see him as a stranger. It is difficult when you know someone. A famous actor playing a part is just that. Miss Penney as a Chinese secretary still resembles Miss Penney if she is the familiar face. This kind of charade was about not being noticed. There is talent in that too, I realised, and I knew in me it was untested. I imagined passing Robert in the street in Hong Kong or Chusan. He did not seem extraordinary in any way. I too must adopt that demeanour I decided. I must vanish. Our lives depended on it. I drew up my courage.

'Let's go,' I said.

Wang prepared the way. He spoke for us. In China it is as common as at home for a servant to express his master's wishes. He had a table set and ordered some food. The hostelry was rough but it looked over the shimmering lake with its quilt of green, yellow and white flowers. Inside the place smelt of wood smoke and acrid, hot oil, which wafted from the kitchen. The dining room was half full with perhaps a dozen men sitting at the rough-hewn tables. I stayed mindful that I didn't want to attract any attention and kept my eyes very low. The innkeeper who came to greet us hardly glanced at me but his gaze lingered on Robert's finery as if counting the exact value of the intricate embroidery on the jacket. He was, I noted, just as dazzled by the money as Robert had hoped. As a mere servant, I merited no such attention – I was a man of no consequence. A man.

As I sipped my tea it was the first time in almost a year I had not been stared at. The first time in as long as I could remember that men were not interested in me – not so much as a glance. I watched my dining companions across the room and I mimicked the movement of their hands, the way they held their rice bowls and how they gestured as they talked.

'It is like disappearing,' I whispered, for we were far enough from everyone nearby to be able to speak English, low. Though it made me feel like a naughty schoolchild, I admit it, there was a wonderful freedom too. Here we were.

Robert nodded. I expect for him it was not dissimilar. Such was the attention the colour of our skin had attracted over the months that to fit in was a strange kind of relief and much to be wished for.

At the end of what was, if I'm honest, an indifferent meal, Robert chanced his luck and questioned the innkeeper about the variety of tea he had served us. He took a note of its name – Dragon Keep. With his eyes lowered respectfully, the innkeeper asked about Robert's accent.

'I speak firstly Kwan-hwa,' Robert claimed loftily, warming to his role. Court dialect. The man bowed lower.

'You are very far from home,' he said and Robert nodded sagely.

We were further than the poor man could ever have imagined.

On the short walk back to our barge we were elated. Stars studded the dark sky and the lake glowed a soft, bluish green set off by the low moon. The darkness went on unbroken for miles. Robert caught a firefly and held its glow cupped in his hands.

'Can you believe we got away with it?' I said.

Robert was beaming ear to ear. He set the firefly free.

'We must not be complacent. It may be different in the town. Hang Chow Foo is the capital of the province. There will be guards and they will know more of the world.'

But we were walking on air. For a moment our hands touched and I felt a jolt of electricity snap between us.

'I hope you do change the world,' I said.

*   *   *

Besides the mulberry trees, there were fruit groves that wafted waves of sweet air across the water, for the weather was warm and the fruit ripening. I sat on the deck and sketched everything I saw. A day or two from the town, in the wake of the fruit crop, we passed prodigious bird life. There was a rush of mina with white wings and flapping flocks of white-necked crows. Kingfishers darted in the bushes at the water's edge and I spotted an Indian kite. Robert determined this moment to start the collection of bird skins he had planned. He ordered Wang to fetch the rifle and then conscripted the poor fellow as his hunt dog.

The pace of the barge had not quickened though it was still a stretch for Wang to run and fetch, particularly when Robert shot beyond the immediate vicinity of the river-bank. Sing Hoo concerned himself making congee and blithely ignored the pink-faced Wang each time he returned with the quarry. Robert shot a good pile of unusual birds, though they were thin and wild and none proved easily edible. After an hour he tired of it and Wang came back on deck and sat near the prow recovering his energy.

Robert ordered Sing Hoo to bring the kitchen knives to split the carcasses. He skinned them expertly while Robert and I constructed cane drying-horses and set the feathered skins out in the sun to air. It looked gruesome, I thought, the empty skins along the deck, dead heads hanging down.

'It is like some terrible Red Indian custom,' I said.

It made me shudder. The bargeman was fascinated. He walked past the racks making a minute inspection of each bird, and asked Robert why he had made this display.

'To send to the North,' Robert replied, for after our success at the inn the night before he had taken on the persona of Sing Wa.

170

The bargeman nodded sagely, not questioning Robert's belief in his new identity, while I smiled wryly.

Further inland and south west there were many villages and small towns. The canals brought industry and the settlements were well fortified and in good condition. Robert took notes of everything whether it was of horticultural interest or not, though what he intended to do with the information I could not say. I saw him deep in concentration on two occasions referring to the blue notebook that contained the code. I liked that Robert had a seemingly unbounded capacity and there was constantly more to him than met the eye.

In two days we reached Hang Chow Foo. It was a fair-sized city and bustling inside its walls. At the unloading terminus there were many curiosity shops with stuffed animals, fine blown glass and rough lacquer-ware. It was here that we first encountered Chinese soldiers and had the chance to see if our disguises passed muster among those more in the know than rough country publicans and ill-educated bargehands.

'I shall send news to Hong Kong today,' Robert confided as he surveyed the dockside from the little window in the cabin. Our trunks were packed for we were set to transfer to another boat to continue further inland.

'Is the information you're collecting for Pottinger?' I hazarded. 'For the military?'

Robert nodded solemnly.

'There is no harm, I suppose, in you knowing of it, Mary. They simply wish to be kept informed of any details of the interior, particularly the Chinese supply lines and fortress towns. That garrison we passed on the way in. Two hundred men I think. Vernon did mention here particularly. Hang Chow Foo is one of the closest army bases inland. It is the least I can do for them after all the help they have afforded me.'

'How will you get a message through?' I asked simply.

My curiosity was piqued by this more glamorous side of my brother-in-law's mission. Robert smiled.

'There is an intermediary who can receive it.'

It seemed all those weeks in Hong Kong, Chusan and Ningpo there had been more than planting schedules and lists of horticultural interests organised.

'I cannot believe you are a spy,' I whispered in incredulity, half looking over my shoulder at the feet passing by on the dock.

'Not at all,' Robert said blithely. 'Don't be silly, Mary. I'm just British. It is better though if you do not know the details of the messaging system. Lest we are caught.'

I asked nothing further, though as time passed I came to realise that the information was coded as orders made to Chinese merchants. Robert had Wang dispatch these, addressed in Chinese, of course, with other mail heading for the coast. Robert had no interest in buying pork bellies or need for quantities of fresh soil for planting. Mr Thom, no doubt, would unravel this information, and pass it back to Vernon or Pottinger in Hong Kong. I studiously ignored the Chinese writing on the covering paper – Robert was right, I did not want to be in possession of such secrets, which in the event of our capture might be painfully extracted by the Chinese guard. Though I did wonder if Robert was paid for this kind of thing. I expect, given the circumstances, he took it on out of sheer patriotism – noblesse oblige. If he was captured he stood to be killed for his mission anyway, so why not win the respect of the establishment while he was at it?

On deck, we thanked the boatman gravely and pressed a couple of extra dollars into the man's hand in thanks for his discretion once more. After all, outside our party it was only the boatman who knew our true identities. We had not got away with it yet. As we turned to leave, a small phalanx of soldiers marched towards us and stopped directly in front of the barge. The soldiers were smartly turned out, stony faced and armed to the teeth. They had the right to inspect any of the canal traffic.

Robert and I froze. The captain in charge of the squad saluted and Robert had the presence of mind to nod sagely.

'Foreign goods?' the captain barked.

Robert called Wang forward.

'My servant will help you,' he said, dismissively.

I noticed our bargeman. Unnerved by the inspection, he was trying to back slowly away along the deck.

'You!' the captain insisted, spotting the man sidling away and homing in on him. He pulled the poor wretch forward.

'Your barge?'

The boatman nodded, terrified. I felt my stomach turn over and my hands start to shake. If the man broke down we were dead. I stood stock still and tried to show no emotion.

'Foreign goods?' the captain demanded again and I realised they intended to levy taxes on anything not made in China. This was strictly against the recent treaty.

'No. Nothing. Only to ferry the honourable Sing Wa. I carry no cargo,' the man swore, petrified.

The captain was not satisfied by this and motioned two of his men to board our vessel. They moved ropes along the deck carelessly to see if anything might be stowed under them and then disappeared into the cabin to search. By now my skin was crawling with terror. We had foreign goods, of course, among our belongings, most obviously our notebooks. I thanked my stars that these were safely stowed inside the hidden compartments along with strings

173

of money and our English clothes. For a brief moment I had a vision of the soldiers finding my corset, petticoats and bloomers and wondering what on earth they could be, though of course, all that would have mattered to them was that they were clearly, undeniably, foreign. I held my breath. After a few moments in the cabin, one man came up on deck with two bird skins balanced on his sword and I felt a flood of relief that that was the worst he could find.

Robert, seeming relaxed, motioned towards him.

'Ah yes. To make the journey more bearable for me. I collect these. I shot them on the bank of the canal. Perhaps, captain, you would like to have them, as a souvenir. You are very welcome.'

The man stared. Then he laughed. He ordered the soldier to replace the bird skins.

'Go and help,' Robert dispatched Sing Hoo, who disappeared below deck.

The waiting was agony. We could hear them banging about and only guess what they might find. However, the truth was that the vast part of our luggage was either Chinese or horticultural in nature. The foreign goods they were after were very few and thankfully well hidden. After a few minutes the men came back on deck. They rejoined their comrades. I counted a dozen swords and as many knives. I tried to stay calm or at least to appear so.

'Thank you, sir.' The captain saluted again.

'You are doing a good job for China,' Robert told him.

I felt weak as the soldiers marched off smartly through the crowded dock.

'Blaggards,' Robert muttered as they disappeared. 'They are raising taxes on our goods still. That is directly against what they signed to. Pottinger must know of it. I will write again. Are you all right, Mary?'

I had moved away from the boat's edge so that if I fainted

I would not fall into the water. It was good, of course, that we had got away with it. Our disguises clearly passed muster and our hiding places remained undiscovered. Not for the first or the last time, we had been lucky.

'You don't have a shot of brandy, I suppose?' I asked.

'That, my dear secretary, is a foreign good.'

I could not help smiling.

'We will get some five grain spirit as soon as we can.'

Wang organised sedan chairs to take us through Hang Chow Foo and pick up a further boat on the other side of the little town. I think our bargeman was glad to see the back of us. The soldiers had left him shaken and, of course, had they been concerned more with people and less with excise duties, all our lives might have been forfeit.

Our next destination was Hwuy Chow Foo, more than one and a half thousand li distant – quite a way. Robert left Sing Hoo to unload and see our luggage safely conveyed by the half a dozen bearers he had engaged for the purpose.

'Keep watch for thieves,' he advised, eyeing the thronging crowds warily as we moved off to make some purchases and buy some food.

Wang meantime was sent ahead to agree the chop on our new boat. There would be no need this time for special bribes as we would arrive Chinese and respectable – no one would know us.

In the sedan I found some glances coming my way, much as ill-bred eyes might raise to see the occupants of a smart carriage at home. We passed no more for notice than that, however – our disguises were thoroughly accepted. This set me to wondering what I might try next. Could I stop and buy some of the bean curd dumplings that were being fried on the roadside? Would an inn serve me refreshment if I entered alone? How would they address me if I did? Among the bright market displays and the wafting aromas what did Chinese gentlemen do?

I admit it thrilled me that we were the only white people in two hundred miles or more. That we bore no notice excited me further. That three fine Chinese ladies passed us and bowed coyly to Robert's superior rank when, had they known themselves to be within a yard of a barbarian *Hong-jou-min*, they would have flung up their hands and run screaming, left me in wonder.

Casting my mind back to grey London with all its restrictions I smiled to think of my new-found freedom. Gilston Road was no more than a prison. The tight-laced corsets to which I had once been accustomed were coffin-like in their restriction. By contrast, the loose Chinese trousers let me sit easily in the rickshaw and, if I wanted to descend, I could slip seamlessly through the crowd without having to account for the width of a European skirt. It was like being invisible. Truly I had not realised how much we women are penalised day to day, without even thinking of it. I had never considered these things a kind of punishment inflicted on all my sex. Our customs. Our clothes. Our manners. Women the world over suffer restrictions, I suppose, for think of Ling. Now, free of it all, I was high on the adventure and no matter what the dangers, I pitied my sister for being in London still and smiled that I was a man and in Hang Chow Foo.

The new boat was far larger than our last and had a dozen other passengers. When we arrived at the dock Wang was shouting at the boatman and seemed to be appealing to those around him to agree that the chop suggested was too high. Still, it transpired this was the only barge to leave directly for Hwuy Chow Foo in the next week and, short of changing again part of the way at Wae Ping or Che Kieng (where we knew there was a fortified border crossing), we had little choice. The cabins allotted to us were cramped and the hold was so full that our excess luggage had to be stored in the living quarters.

The boatman, seeing Robert's finery, had some second thoughts about the space he had allotted for our use. He bowed very low and, as is respectful, spoke to Robert through me. He apologised and hoped his humble cabin was not too lowly. He did not reduce his tariff. Robert nodded gracefully. The money was fine. Later though, from a safe distance, I heard the man boasting to another boatman what rich travellers he had aboard and of the large sum of money he had secured for the passage. I thought to remonstrate with him but Robert pre-empted me.

'Take things coolly and never lose your temper,' he advised. 'We will pick our fights, Mary, and none of them over a small sum of money.'

He was right. We had more to lose than a few *cash*.

At last, we checked our affairs were in order before we set off. Robert's trays of plants lined part of the deck, providing a colourful display. The boxes of seeds and bulbs were stowed below. We drank five grain spirit in our cabin, each downing one parting shot from a rough flask that we procured from a public house at the dockside. It made my eyes water.

'Here we are.' Robert toasted. 'A long way to go.'

But in Hang Chow Foo, it transpired, you could count on nothing and we had no sooner set down our cups than Wang burst into the room, with news of a potentially deadly development in our fortunes.

'Master,' he reported, his eyes to the ground. 'There is a mandarin aboard. He has taken the front cabin.'

This stopped us in our tracks – we had not considered such a thing. To be held in close quarters with a mandarin held a real danger of being unmasked. We had anticipated our fellow travellers to be boathands or small merchants – those with business between the two towns – easily cowed by the status of Robert's disguise.

'How long will the man be on board?' Robert questioned Wang who disappeared to find out.

It occurred to me that a party of mandarins at an afternoon tea party at Dr Chang's house in Ning-po was one thing and a party of soldiers for ten minutes quite another, but to travel for days disguised and in the close company of an undoubted enemy was far more serious. How closely our disguises would pass inspection I could not be sure – and then there were our habits. Small details could so easily arouse suspicion in someone truly at ease with the trappings of privilege. Our cover was not designed to withstand such scrutiny and the trip would be horribly risky.

'He will journey with us nine or ten days,' Wang reported back. 'I told his servant you had received a letter and might be called home unexpectedly.'

'Well, that settles it. We will have to disembark,' Robert sighed. 'There is nothing for it. The quarters are too close. It is rotten luck. Even Bertie would not attempt it.'

I agreed. The risk was far greater than any difficulty we might have securing cabins on another vessel. It was a shame for we were all set and ready.

'It will take some time to find another passage,' Robert resigned himself. 'We best find lodgings as far as we can from the garrison. There will be another boat soon enough, I suppose.'

He reached for his notebook and I turned to pack the few items I had taken out on our arrival. Then we left the cabin with Wang ahead of us.

You never can tell, though, when good fortune will give a sudden surge in your direction. As we were about to turn and climb the stairs we all halted at once in the thin hallway, stopped in our tracks by the pungent aroma emanating from the front suite of rooms.

'Opium,' Robert whispered, an idea dawning. 'Are these his quarters, Wang?'

'Yes, sir.'

'Did you smell it before?'

'No.'

If the man had only just lit his pipe, he must be puffing away like billy-o. The sweet smell was very strong and immediately it was clear that the mandarin was an 'opium drinker' – an addict – the kind who had taken the drug too far. I had known one or two actors who had gone that way and more than one or two aristocrats at home – weak-willed, I'd judged them. A grin broke out on my face for this trait in our travelling companion was wonderful news.

Robert motioned us back towards our abandoned cabin and sized up our options as the information dawned on us. The Emperor had decreed that the smoking of opium must cease. It had been made law that addicts in the mandarin class would not only lose their own appointments, but also any appointments or privileges held by their family. This meant that the mandarin at the front of the boat was a renegade the minute he struck a light. He had almost as much to lose as we did. We sent Wang to find out whatever he could.

'All right. Perhaps we can stay,' Robert said slowly. 'I never thought I'd turn blackmailer, but if it comes to that, it comes to it. Besides, if he's an opium addict he will hardly be compos mentis in his duties.'

I nodded. Taken too far, the drug had its devotees cast everything aside, however dear to them.

'Well,' I said, 'at the very least, if he has smoked enough in ten minutes to make the hall stink like that, I warrant that the man will be less dangerous than dodging the garrison at Hang Chow Foo for another week.'

Robert nodded.

'What do you say then, Mary? Shall we stay?'

I said yes.

We found later that the mandarin had almost disembarked when he heard of our passage on board – a high-ranking official such as Sing Wa, after all, would surely uphold the Emperor's decree. Wang, however, managed things admirably, falling into conversation with the man's servants and advancing Sing Wa a reputation of good-natured liberalism in the matter of opium. The situation was, in fact, to our advantage.

With us settled on journeying with this renegade, and him, it would seem, settled on journeying with us, we set off finally, despite all the misgivings, only an hour over time. As the barge pulled away from the city limits Robert received an unexpected invitation to the man's cabin.

'His judgement is clearly out!' Robert swore. 'What is he doing?'

But it seemed the mandarin had ordered a sumptuous dinner to be delivered before we left the city and he simply wanted to share it. Given that our standard rations were rice congee, which we could supplement with meat, vegetables and tea from our own supplies, Robert jumped at the chance of more luxurious fare. And besides, he said, it might seem odd to refuse. Our fellow traveller, evidently an epicure in all respects, had chosen a roasted duck and other sumptuous, speciality dishes – pork dumplings with plums and fried vegetables in bean sauce.

'What will you discuss?' I asked Robert as he readied himself.

He shrugged his shoulders. 'The man has been smoking since he came aboard,' he said simply. 'I can only guess the standard of his dinner conversation. The Chinese do not talk personally, in any case. It will be fine. Between his servants and Wang we will manage to translate.'

As it grew dark I ate alone, spooning in my rice congee with little enthusiasm, knowing Robert was faring far better further along the boat. After I had eaten I sat up reading an extract translated from the *Ch'a Ching: The Book of Tea*. It was a history of tea in China, full of tall tales and excitement. I was tired though. The lamp flickered and my eyes strained but I vowed to stay awake until Robert returned. When he did it was late and he was merry.

'We need not jump ship then?' I checked.

'I could scarcely breathe in there,' he chortled. 'It is a miasma! If that man rises before we reach Che Kieng it will be a miracle.'

It seemed we were set.

Our journey took us through the thoroughfares of uneventful towns: Seh Mun Yien, Yen Chow Foo and Wae Ping. At each settlement beggars appeared alongside the boat, soliciting alms. The boatman always gave them rice after which they would continue to walk beside us for some miles until it became apparent that no further sustenance would be forthcoming. I judged the boatman kind to give alms at all.

On our way Robert collected pine seeds. '*Cryptomeria japonica*,' he proclaimed them. We also found varieties of weeping cypresses, palms, flowers and mosses at the waterside, and a beautiful, old funereal cypress in the garden of an inn. We purloined seeds daily, which I cleaned and dried and sealed up in little bags, for now it was I who did the work with the seeds and Robert who helped with the twine. As an honoured passenger, the boatman was patient with Sing Wa, indulging his obvious eccentricities and waiting until he had collected his fill. I enjoyed helping and found myself more and more interested in the species we encountered. It was easier physically too. I could carry more now as I was dressed in easy clothing and could walk far further afield. Without the whalebone corset to inhibit me, I climbed trees and scrambled up rock faces, often finding at the end of the day that my limbs were sore – I was using muscles I had never had the chance to stretch since I was a child.

'Good man,' Robert said one day when I retrieved a cutting from an out of the way branch by pulling myself up towards it and slipping easily along on all fours like a cat.

'Good man!' I laughed, wide eyed, and he looked sheepish.

But it was easy to let the fact I was a woman slip the mind. It slipped my own mind often.

Further westwards Robert found several varieties of evergreen holly, which caused vicious scratches as we cut them down for the herbarium.

'It is the wrong time of year for berries,' I noted.

Robert nodded. The boughs we had taken were spiky and green, some edged with a lime or a yellow leaf. There was not one splash of red.

'Where do you think we will be at Christmas?' I mused as I carefully placed the cuttings into the basket. It was a long way off.

'St Bartholomew's, Kensington,' Robert teased.

That was the Church we usually attended for the carol service. The choir was quite famous at home and Jane was fond of anything festive, so we always went there in addition to the services at St Mary's, which was nearer to the house. This year, like last, we would miss the graceful harmonies in the freezing transept. It looked as if when the time came we might have holly though.

Robert swore as he grazed himself. He did not excuse his language and I did not pull him up on it. The bushes were treacherous and I had several red, flecked scratches of my own. We treated our skin with lavender oil to help it heal and for days the heady fragrance fought the smell of the mandarin's smoke as the holly wounds healed.

Along the way we stopped for refreshment at inns, in lieu of which I expect the boatman received some recompense from the landlords. Robert's assessment of our mandarin friend proved correct and at each of the stops we made he did not rise but ordered his dinner brought to him on the barge. The dishes arrived laden high with exotic-looking vegetables and some pork or duck, which it seemed, were his favourites. I drew him in my notebook, resplendent like some pasha, on a silk-lined couch, his opium pipe in his hand. Robert found this hilarious.

'His cabin is like our own,' he scoffed, 'there are no satin pillows in there. And the man himself is very thin.'

But I liked the idea of the luxuriating mandarin, plump and hidden, puffing away on his *kong see pak*. If his culinary tastes were anything to go by he had an eye for the best in everything.

In the evenings I tutored Robert in Cantonese, helping him with his vowel sounds.

'Place your tongue here on the roof of your mouth,' I instructed, showing him what to do by holding my own mouth open wide.

Robert peered vaguely towards my epiglottis.

'No, no, further forward,' I corrected him as he tried to copy me, 'and keep the lips still.'

The man was in the terrible habit of moving his lips too much and it was this, I felt, that was at the heart of his struggle to make his Cantonese more fluent.

It struck me as ironic, I must say, that Robert was the

person I was probably closest to in the world. I had despised him in London and truly loathed him as far as Hong Kong. Now, two fellows facing the world together with a single mission, we had become all but inseparable and I could not imagine my days without him. My life in London felt like a curiosity or a vague memory – like a disturbing dream that was thankfully very, very far away. I dreamt of home still, often surprised in the morning to wake alone in my cabin instead of in the four-poster bed I had in Soho, with the arms of a lover around me. Or scrabbling ever after the cloudy memories of my childhood, as if I could not quite grasp hold of the meaning of what had happened – sure that Jane knew something I didn't of the winter my mother died or how the house had been when our father drank and there was shouting and I could not remember why.

I did not discuss these matters with Robert. Most of the time our society was fraternal and based around our common interest in the trip. Sometimes, though, he branched out and we had a conversation or two that he would not, I'm sure have generally had with a lady, but then the boundaries were blurring and we had crossed and recrossed many lines.

'What did you think of the Chartists?' he asked one evening.

'William's father backed them,' I replied, without a shadow of the old bad feeling at the utterance of my lover's name, 'and I think he had good reason.'

'Here,' said Robert, as if we were in the club room at the Carlton 'let me top up your glass. Tell me, Mary, why did you embark on an affair with that man? I have never understood.'

'It is difficult for me to remember,' I admitted with a smile. 'Though 'tis no terrible thing to be a mistress. No one decried Emma Hamilton for her love of Lord Nelson.'

'But to be scorned,' Robert said. 'Like Byron's woman. You take a risk. You take a risk with something very precious.'

'Perhaps in London,' I admitted, 'I did not realise its value. I judged William badly – I truly believed he would keep me. I thought we were in love. Though here, Robert, I feel that I have changed. You were right about me. I was both vain and spoilt,' I laughed. 'I expect I am vain still.'

Robert chuckled. 'Well, vanity is a lady's prerogative, I'm sure,' he said. 'And how many would shave their hair, I ask, as you have done?'

I thought of Miss Pottinger in Hong Kong, of Jane, and of Mrs Hunter, no doubt now ensconced in a mansion in Calcutta with her hateful husband. I shrugged my shoulders.

'They are the ones who have missed out,' I said. 'I wouldn't be anywhere else in the world than here.'

'Honestly?'

I considered a moment. London. With its delicate pastries, smooth burgundy, crisp, lavender-scented linen and hot baths. London with my beautiful baby and even the society of my sister and, for that matter, the acclaim of the critics. I had fought leaving the city for months. Now would I trade it for this adventure?

'Never,' I told him. A whole new world had opened up to me. 'I have changed my mind.'

'You are quite remarkable,' he commented, and that made me ape him.

'Quite remarkable, Miss Penney,' I teased, 'Jolly, jolly, jolly remarkable, in fact.'

Eyes ablaze, he bid me goodnight.

At length we reached Che Kieng. Robert checked his notes and declared that by all accounts the place was very heavily fortified.

'It is a stronghold,' he pronounced. 'There is a huge garrison. I'd like to get a look at it if I can.'

He paced the cabin, checking and re-checking his outfit and glancing out of the window restlessly. The dangers were always on his mind.

As the canal was the main thoroughfare for all goods, most settlements were nearby and on our way into the city we passed what was clearly the main military site for the area. Perched on an embankment to one side, with its own small canal off the main waterway, it was a town in itself. Robert stood on the deck and surveyed the barracks in the distance. They were a good half mile off and were larger, I think, than he had anticipated. He put upon the boatman to draw up under the excuse that he had seen some plants that interested him, and the man, as ever, complied. Like many people we met, the money blinded him, and he was eager to keep in Sing Wa's favour.

Wang fetched the vasculum case and, always patient, the boatman waited. There was clearly no change in the scenery that merited such a stop and I paced the cabin as Robert sallied out, climbing a small hill to one side of the barracks while directing Wang to stop and take cuttings here and there. From my vantage point I noticed Wang pulling the roots of the plants Robert pointed out and Robert ignoring him doing so. They moved out of sight, gone for a good twenty minutes, that frankly felt more like an hour or two to me. Any Chinaman, mandarin or not, caught poking around a barracks might be questioned and this place was large and probably heavily fortified. I paced the barge praying, I admit, for Robert's safe return in short order and I felt a wave of relief when I saw him appear again over the top of the hill, cheerfully making his way down towards us – in fact, I don't believe I have ever been so glad to see anyone in my life. There was a nonchalant look on his face as he strolled towards us. There would, I guessed, be more strange orders for goods going to the Chinese merchants in Ning-po.

In Che Kieng City we docked overnight and, inspired by our mandarin friend, we thought to order a meal to be delivered to our cabin that evening as a treat. There were many hostelries nearby. It was as a result of this that we discovered Sing Hoo's delinquency had taken a turn for the worse and Robert, of course, had to deal with it.

Our money was carried on strings, being minted with a hole in the middle for the purpose. We kept mostly silver dollars that were concealed in our luggage and on Robert's person. However, we had some strings of bronze *cash* for making small purchases and these coins were stowed in a box in the cabin. That afternoon Robert ventured to take a string of *cash* to order our meal and buy provisions. When he opened the box, however, he saw the strings were not equal and that two or three had been 'clipped'. This was a thinning of the metal at the edges and resulted in an uneven string of coins that any merchant would notice immediately. The clipped metal could be fashioned into new, whole coins but what was left behind was almost worthless. Both Wang and Sing Hoo knew where the strings of *cash* were stowed and, as it was clear that this operation must have been undertaken over several days, it was only our own servants who would have the necessary access to perpetuate such a fraud. We discussed this and then summoned the men to the cabin, leaving the money box open on the table.

Wang stood upright, his chest out and his eyes clear. Sing Hoo behaved like a dog, his eyes cast low and his back bent. It was clear where the guilt lay. It was one thing to steal a few provisions, quite another to progress onto *cash* and Robert took it as a grave matter.

'There is money missing,' he said and Sing Hoo sealed his guilt by babbling, 'But I have not been in the box to damage it.' Robert had not yet mentioned any damage, only the theft.

To make matters worse, we were not the only ones checking our money as we came into town. At that very moment our boatman knocked on the door and on entry he furiously swung into the room and grabbed Sing Hoo by the throat. This caused such a commotion that everyone nearby rushed to find out what was afoot (except our opium smoker, of course) and in no time the cabin was crowded with babbling passengers and crew. Upon Robert disentangling the two of them, the boatman claimed that Sing Hoo had asked him to change a silver dollar for *cash* earlier in the day and that, trying to spend it, he then discovered the dollar to be bad. Sing Hoo maintained, screaming, that the bad dollar was not his and the boatman was blaming him, having discovered counterfeit elsewhere in his money. It seemed unlikely.

Robert took charge immediately. I must say he presented a fine figure, barring everyone from our cabin and, saying he would pronounce his judgement from the only area large enough for everyone to witness it, he shepherded the assembled throng out onto the deck. Sitting on a barrel while he pondered, Robert questioned each of the parties like a seasoned judge.

'Sing Hoo is my servant, and I will punish him,' he proclaimed, refunding the boatman's money and telling Sing Hoo that this repayment would be taken over time from his wages.

Robert himself was to flog the man.

I don't blame Robert for deciding on drastic action.

Sing Hoo could have jeopardised our whole expedition with the sheer bad will that his thieving brought. In such circumstances Robert could not let it pass, though the punishment he settled on was too medieval for my blood.

Sing Hoo stood with the crowd around him as Robert readied himself, steely eyed and taut. Then, with Sing Hoo tied in place, he lashed two dozen vicious blows to the man's bare back with a makeshift whip. There was blood running down Sing Hoo's legs and his cries were pitiful. A crowd of passersby gathered beside the boat, anxious to find out what was going on. Afterwards, Robert flung salt on the raw skin to stop any infection and, of course, Sing Hoo wailed even more. The blood dripped dirty onto the wooden deck and Sing Hoo's face twisted with pain. I could smell him – the stench of sweat and blood and acrid fear. And piss too, for when Sing Hoo was let down he fell over and lost all control. The crowd seemed vindicated and almost pleased at what they witnessed – justice done – and people started to disperse. For my part, I felt my stomach turn, my grasp on the rail weaken, and I thought I might be sick before finally everything went black and I was gone. 'What will they all think of me?' the only words that passed through my mind as I tumbled.

When I came to I was lying on the bed. Robert sat beside me. The barge was moving and we had left the town. I cursed my squeamishness and immediately measured myself against my sister. Jane was so stoic, she never would have wilted. I must try harder.

'I did not think myself so weak,' I said, finding my throat dry.

Robert passed me a small cup of tea and I sat up to drink it.

'I forget you are a lady,' he said. 'I should have asked you to leave.'

'Is Sing Hoo all right?'

Robert nodded. 'I had to take a firm hand,' he started as if to justify his actions, but I waved him to stop.

'You did right,' I said. 'You always do.'

That night, I had a dream. I was a child again. I was hidden, for I had been playing a game and was stowed in my mother's crockery cabinet. I could taste bread and lard in my mouth as if I had just had breakfast and it lingered on my tongue. Peering out, I could see that my father was in the kitchen, Jane over his knee as he beat her hard. Her skin was raw pink but she was silent as his hand came down sharply again and again. Her eyes were alight with fury, staring right at the cabinet as if she knew I was there. What did she want of me? What? I woke in a sweat, unable to tell whether it was a true memory or only fantasy. I never remembered Da hurting Jane, though I know he picked on her for half nothing, while I got away with blue murder. I felt horribly guilty. I had a feeling that it was my fault, that Jane was protecting me by taking the beating. I was only a child and she'd been so brave, so silent. If she had cried I would have tried to protect her, I'm sure of it.

The further I got from home the more I realised that I did not remember Da so very much. It vexed me. If he was so vicious, how could Mother have loved him and still been happy that he was gone? Losing a parent is hardly unusual and yet, it seemed to me, I had missed out on something intriguing by simply being so young that I could not quite remember it. People who inspire such contradictory emotions must be worthwhile, I reasoned. Jane, I knew, loved me very much. In adulthood she had protected me when she could have turned her back and yet she found me difficult and frustrating too. What would my son think of me? Poor Henry. No mother nearby and William as good as absent, no doubt. I could not help feeling that both Henry and I deserved better than we had got. And Jane too, perhaps. He had formed us, our father, I realised. He had been the key to our closeness and the source of our differences.

I lit the tallow beside my bed and pulled out a notebook, ripping a page.

Dear Jane,
I am writing to you from inside China. I want you to know that I think of you often. I want you to know, though we are not in the habit of saying such things, I love you very much. You have stood by me always. Thank you.
Mary.

I blotted the ink and folded the paper. I would ask Robert to dispatch it at the next opportunity.

After four more days of journeying, our mandarin friend disembarked at one of the small villages beyond Che Kieng, taking over half the contents of the hold with him. I stood on deck, watching with surprise as the men hoisted three coffins on deck. They loaded them onto a cart and Wang explained that the mandarin was delivering these caskets to his family burial grounds nearby. The delivery of coffins was not considered a priority in Chinese households and often years would pass before the trip was made.

I was to discover that the coffins were often not buried at all but laid out above ground in the family plot. This man might be making a journey that had been hanging over him for some months or even years. On my part, I had not realised we had slept so close to the mandarin's dead relations, stowed directly beneath our quarters. I am sure that I might not have slumbered so soundly had I known. No wonder the poor man did not feel sociable and resided alone in his cabin in an opium haze.

As the mandarin departed I noticed Sing Hoo was dallying on the dockside and, as well as buying some leafy, green vegetables for our congee, he seemed to be selling a small bag of rice to a local village man. He looked shiftily in my direction, hoping no doubt that I had not realised the portent of his transaction. The rice was either ours or belonged to the boatman as Sing Hoo, like Wang, carried no provisions of his own. When the few *cash* were handed over another fight broke out. I could not make out whether it was about the price agreed or some change that was due. Standing beside me, Wang sighed.

'I do not want,' he said, his eyes darting towards Sing Hoo below us. 'He will have us murdered by someone he swindles. I do not want to be murdered.'

I could not help feeling Wang had a point. Later Robert found him packing his things in the hold, intending to leave. By coercion only, Robert bought him out, promising a bonus on the journey's completion.

I, however, was of the view that Sing Hoo was incorrigible. Nothing seemed to make the slightest difference to his behaviour. He simply took whatever punishment was meted out to him, while still selling the contraband nonetheless. We had cast our lot, though. We needed to keep both servants with us, be they bound to the expedition by love, trust or money. Sing Hoo knew our secret and that meant he had to stay. Still, Robert locked the *cash* box, hid the key and it was clear, to the satisfaction of both Wang and the boatman, that Sing Hoo was no longer trusted even if he was not to be dismissed.

* * *

192

As we proceeded onwards the land became hillier and there was a general air of dilapidation. Abandoned pagodas littered the slopes in various stages of disrepair. It was a strange place. Many families seemed to have their burial grounds between Che Kieng and the town of Kiang Nan. It seemed to me we were travelling through the Dead Lands. Some coffins were left above ground and had been there so long that wild roses were growing over them in a tangled mass, as if the earth had come up to meet the dead.

I have never been fond of horror stories or ghosts. Robert had no such qualms and the notion of a good yarn from beyond the grave appeared to boost his spirits. He tried to draw me in, bringing up first the ghost of Hamlet's father and then the story of the Borgias. In these grim and shadowy surroundings, where coffins littered the landscape, I became jumpy.

'Please don't,' I begged like a ten year old, as we walked by the boat in the twilight before supper. 'It makes me afraid.'

'But surely you must enjoy the death pact at the end of *Romeo and Juliet*? I thought that would appeal to you, Mary.'

'It does. But of spirits from beyond . . .' I shuddered.

'So might you be perturbed if one of these coffins was to creak slowly open and the bones of the head of the Dynasty were to sit up?' he teased, his voice low and theatrical.

When he tapped my shoulder lightly I pushed him and, I am ashamed to say, a squeal left my lips.

Thereafter, for several days I confined myself to the barge, declining to take up Robert's offer of a constitutional walk along the bank. I felt as if I left the moving boat the dead would cling to my ankles. It made me maudlin and I thought again of home, my mind drawn back.

'I bought my father a marble gravestone before I left,'

Robert confided one day. 'It is thirteen-feet high. When I ordered it from the mason he tried to sell me something smaller. He said my father was only a servant. But I wanted his grave marked properly. It was the least I could do. He taught me everything. He was the only one ever to teach me. Everything else I have found by trial and error.'

I expect we were both of us thinking very much of home, and fathers too. All those no longer with us, whose influence was keenly felt.

Then after a grim week, slowly the scenery brightened and even the food improved. The hills became more majestic, and I came out of the cabin and sat on deck to enjoy it. Robert apologised for his schoolboy pranks in the Dead Lands and tempted me onto the towpath to walk with him again. We talked for hours. Our conversations were of our days in Hong Kong and our time in Ning-po. Of the day we shaved our hair off and became Chinese. Of the foods we missed most from England (all, we realised, of the sweet and creamy variety) and the sensation of sleeping on a proper bed, with proper sheets. And, best of all, of bathing in an enamel bath with hot water and (oh, heaven!) soap.

'Nettle soap,' I decided. My maid used to buy smooth nettle soap from an apothecary in Chiswick. It left my skin like alabaster.

Over the days, as we went higher, the air felt clear and thin. Time passed and we came closer to Hwuy Chow Foo, following our progress on the map when we started in the morning and before we lay down at night.

I was below deck reading when our pleasant journey was interrupted by an absolute howling. I swear, it was like a banshee. As I jumped up and rushed out to see what had come to pass, I witnessed Robert screaming on deck and jumping up and down. I felt frantic. Had some dreadful new calamity befallen us? As I looked round in panic I checked that there was nothing wrong with any of the men and the boat was unharmed. Then I realised that on the contrary, Robert was not upset. He was in ecstasy. He was pointing ahead.

'My God,' he said, recovering his faculty of speech. 'On the hill. Look, Mary.'

Ahead of us I stared up at the mountains and, realising what I could see, I felt excitement rising in my belly. There on the slopes were the first of the tea plantations. I felt like screaming with exhilaration, as Robert had. It shocked me and I held my tongue. Instead, we stood together on the deck, watching and hardly able to form a sentence between us. Within three li the emerald hills were littered with tiny farms.

'It is here. It is here,' he breathed at last, and I grasped his hand, squeezing it tightly.

The tea countries were upon us.

Chapter Eight

We set up near Hwuy Chow Foo for some time. I was pleased that the dogs in the streets no longer barked at either Robert or me. Our Chinese diet meant that now we even smelt local. Despite the occasional craving for hot chocolate and Welsh rarebit, I had become accustomed to tea with no sugar or milk; to spring rolls and egg rolls and congee; to noodles doused in soya sauce with chickens' feet and to roasted pigeon that arrived with the head on.

Robert took rooms for us at a local inn, having decided that staying in the centre of the town was too risky and we were better out of the way. The inn was dreary. What furniture there was, was worn, but our rooms were large and clean. Sing Hoo cooked for us – his cooking was much more palatable than our first night's meal of over-salted vegetables and fatty pork which we agreed immediately was not to be repeated.

'I'd pay *not* to eat the filthy stuff,' Robert swore.

And, in fact, we did, for the arrangement he came to with the innkeeper allowed Sing Hoo use of the kitchen at a fee roughly equivalent to what it would have cost to order our food there anyway. We deemed it money well spent.

Much of the time we ventured abroad, travelling mostly by bamboo sedan chair, our knees and feet swathed in oiled paper to keep us dry in the rain and our heads covered by an umbrella whatever the weather – for the sun was harsh when it wasn't raining. We were fortunate there was little military fortification in the area and, after our experiences in Che Kieng and Hang Chow Foo, we were relieved to be able to wander easily around the town and up into the farms surrounding it with little threat of a military presence, for it was only the very occasional company of soldiers that marched through.

In the hills we passed streams of coolies carrying wooden boxes full of tea, headed eventually for Shanghae, the main port for the region. There was no better way to transport this cargo along the treacherous mountain paths than on a man's back. Where the path narrowed to a single track the men stood precariously balanced to one side to let us pass. They were perilously close to the edge of the mountain, but seemed unperturbed by the danger.

'Lord, that's risky,' Robert commented, 'but I expect they have it in the blood.'

I drew many of the coolies in my notebook. Some balanced their tea boxes on long wooden sticks when they rested rather than allowing the chest to sit on the damp ground and risk it becoming tainted by moisture. To my mind, the men seemed too old and frail to be carrying the heavy loads at all – so light themselves that a strong breeze might topple them. I did not share Robert's faith in their sense of balance.

Our first trip was made to the hill at Sung Lo Shan. This was a pilgrimage. High above the plains, the hill was where tea was said to have been discovered. I had by now read a good deal of the *Ch'a Ching* and could provide Robert with information from each of its three volumes. Some of the legends were lovely. I especially enjoyed the story of the eighteen tea trees maintained solely for the Emperor's use and also the information regarding the plant's medical

197

applications. Tea was thought to help heart disease, to be good for the kidneys, and to increase fertility in women. The leaves were chewed and applied to chilblains to ease the pain. I passed on all this and Robert made notes here and there, although only if he felt the point in question had a valid industrial or medicinal use.

It was at Sung Lo Shan one bright day that we finally found the yellow camellia. We had passed many tea farms. Mostly they were smallholdings of four or five acres, a down-at-heel farmhouse attached. Near one of these Robert spotted a garden with an orchard and we decided to stop and take a look. The lady of the house, wizened and elderly, lived with her two sons and their families – ten of them crowded into a tiny space. They treated Robert like royalty, maintaining a hunched appearance throughout his visit and addressing him as 'Your Eminence'. We stretched our legs in the garden, the children remaining silent, standing in a ramshackle line and eyeing Robert with awe.

And then I spotted it. To one side, grown quite by chance among the plum trees – a glossy-leafed camellia absolutely covered in yellow flowers. I recognised the plant immediately.

'Robert,' I said excitedly. 'Look. It is your camellia.'

'Oh, well done,' he breathed. 'Stay calm now.'

This made me smile. I was not quite so far gone that I was set to fit over a flower. He casually called the old woman over and said nonchalantly that the plant had caught the eye of his secretary and he would like to buy it. After some haggling, they settled on the figure of two silver dollars – a fortune for the family, but nothing compared to what it was worth in England. Under supervision Wang and Sing Hoo dug it up and placed it into a creaky old tea chest, which had been provided. On the way back to our lodgings it was the camellia that rode in Robert's sedan, with him pacing behind, urging the bearers not to allow it to rock from side to side. We made a curious sight no doubt.

'Be careful. Careful,' Robert instructed the bearers testily, before turning to me and proclaiming, 'Mary, it is a prize. A *prize*. Though I did not find it, Mary. You did. And it is a treasure.'

That night we stayed up past midnight taking cuttings and pressing one or two of the custard-coloured flowers. Robert examined the plant minutely, making plans for when he could collect the seeds.

'This plant is important then?' I asked.

'Of course. It is on my list of the ones most likely to sell well. It is beautiful though, is it not? We have camellias in yellow now! Who would have thought it? I had hoped to find one but I had not been sure.' His eyes were gleaming.

Our stock of plants was growing. Also in Robert's care were a beautiful white gardenia, which smelled of paradise, a sunny, double yellow rose, some cotton plants he had found sown between the tea, a white glycine and some dwarf trees, which in the end, he decided not to keep, as at home these were considered in bad taste and are most unfashionable. The yard of the inn had rich soil and Robert kept the specimens in sundry pots. This transformed the barren courtyard into a thriving nursery so that after a fortnight or two the tumbledown building looked quite attractive from the outside.

Best of all, to our amazement, the local tea farmers welcomed Sing Wa and were completely open about their business, allowing us access to the farms and the processing rooms where the tea was dried and treated. We had not been sure how they might react but in the event it was easy for us, and the men were unfailingly generous, probably due to the lack of soldiers in the area. The Chinese military was notoriously fierce and punishment was uncompromising for common men and mandarins alike. Free from any direct threat, Wang presented Robert as an eccentric, rich Northerner obsessed by tea, who wished to set up plantations on his own land. The farmers had little to do with mandarins, even those in the area (who seemed both few and distant), and they were honoured to have the chance to meet a fine gentleman, especially one so keen to learn their art. We paid a silver dollar or two, greasing palms, smoothing our way.

'*Thea viridis*,' Robert muttered, almost as if it was a prayer.

We had missed the crops being gathered for the first two harvests of the year – the first, tiny, precious leaves in April, which commanded extraordinary prices, and the second, in May, which was the main export crop and had been processed before our arrival. The final gathering, however, was of the lowest quality, picked for the Chinese market and that was underway. We watched like hawks.

All this time, recovered from his beating, Sing Hoo was in good spirits. Hwuy Chow was his home province and he admitted that it was good to be back among everything that was familiar to him. He proposed to visit several of his relations who lived to the south and west of Hwuy Chow Foo, not as far as Mo-yuen. This would take several days' travel and Robert put off the trip, saying he would give Sing Hoo leave to organise a visit towards the end of our sojourn when the work was done. Meanwhile the man struck up a liaison with a maid. One day we arrived back from the tea farms earlier than expected to find him idling with her, a peony in her hair. Robert was furious – such behaviour in London, after all, would throw both parties on the streets. I laughed, ordered tea and dismissed them from our presence.

'Heavens, Robert, let them have their fun,' I said. 'He has done far worse than this and got away with it.'

'If we did not need him he would be gone,' Robert replied irritably. 'I hope that peony was not from one of my plants.'

On another occasion, arriving again early, we disturbed Wang in Robert's room with two men who, we surmised, had paid to see the great mandarin's quarters. They fled on our arrival, leaving Wang shamefaced and Sing Hoo smug. The see-saw of their fortunes seemed to have one up, one down at all times. I knew Wang bargained rice sometimes and had seen him spirit away smaller items though, of course, Sing Hoo was far worse. This time, Wang, to his credit, apologised though he did not disclose the amount of money he had gained from the transaction. Robert blustered but he took no action. The offences were trifling and he had too much else on his mind. The profusion of information seemed to leach his attention and mine. Between us we filled notebooks with drawings and descriptions.

Quite apart from the tea, the colours of some of the hillside flowers were beautiful – green, glossy leaves with deep purple and red petals, the light musky scent of which belied their brazen, exotic colours. Other times the leaves were pale lime and framed lacy, delicate, white blossoms tinged with peach and pale rose. These smelt of the fruit yet to come. I wished I had a greater palette in my water-colour boxes to capture everything.

One night Robert arrived back at the inn with a bottle of rice wine that he had Sing Hoo take to the stream to chill. He was excited, unable even to sit down at first, pacing around the room, full of energy.

'I have bought boxes of tea seeds,' he announced, almost incredulous.

It was exactly what he had hoped for. All the plans were coming together.

'How did you manage it?' I asked.

Tea seeds were like gold dust in the region and their sale was highly restricted, but Robert had befriended a farmer and had sealed the matter by claiming they were for his 'estates' in the North and he could not leave without having them, no matter the price.

'It will take two months,' he declared, 'but the man seems reliable.'

The boxes were to be ready after the harvest and the farmer had given Robert clear instructions about how they should be treated. The seeds were to be sown allowing four feet between each shrub for the optimum yield. Robert, naturally, thrived on these details. From the tea gardeners he found, at last, the answers to the questions he had written in his notebook at the beginning of the trip.

'It is fulfilment, Mary. Completion,' he said eagerly, and this delighted both of us. Robert's mission was rapidly becoming a resounding success.

For my own part, I found myself drawn to the land. We were now set to stay a while and I resolved to enjoy it as if I were on a holiday. The clean air of the beautiful green hills rolled for miles. The sunsets were silent explosions of turmeric and syrupy flame. There was a serene simplicity to this place that reminded me of endless childhood summers. I wondered how I had ever lived in a city the size of London, in a city where it was so grey, and in such close proximity to people. Here I spent the majority of the time on my own by choice. It no longer even surprised me to see the man who stared back from the small looking glass in the corner of my room or who was reflected when I leaned over the still clear water of a hillside pool. It is strange that what seems at first alien becomes second nature in the blink of an eye.

I wished Jane could see this place, though I don't expect she would have taken to it quite as keenly as I. There was part of me that was still childish – that still wanted to swim in the pond down the hill and eat blackberries on the way home until the juice stained my chin. Even at the age of eleven Jane had berated me.

'A lady never rushes her food, Mary,' she scolded.

'Exactly,' I said, not slowing down with the berries one bit.

I wondered if Henry would like it here – now well past his first birthday, no doubt plump and, I hoped, happy. I was sure he would. But I did not dwell on him or indeed on my sister either, and though I thought of my loved ones often, the disturbing dreams stopped and there was no longer a gnawing sensation of regret or discomfort. I found a lightness in Hwuy Chow Foo that allowed me to let them go more easily for a while.

Some afternoons I walked away from the farmed land towards the trees on the horizon. There I climbed up and rested among the shady branches to watch the harvesting far off in the distance. One day I happened upon a pool and jumped in to swim in the icy water, my skin tingling with the cold, my ponytail loose and fanning out behind me like a dark cloud. It was beautiful – a place of heady, simple pleasure.

When the tea was harvested, it was sent to be dried. This took several days and every available space was taken over – cottages, barns and outhouses filled with each man, woman and child, all playing their part in the process.

Robert rose early. He followed the bamboo baskets, brimming with greenery, down to the shallow, iron drying pans, which were set up indoors over furnaces. The barns and cottages were smoky as there were no proper chimneys, only a tiny flue installed in each premises. Even the walls smelt musky.

When the harvested tea arrived the leaves were tossed lightly over the heat for five minutes and then rolled by hand, three or four women to a table. Their nimble fingers danced over the foliage twisting it again and again until a green juice was extracted and the leaves were only a quarter of their original size. Then the tea was left to air outside, shaded if the sun was high and hot for, we were told, it must be done gently.

Once this process was complete the leaves were tossed back into the pans and stirred using bamboo brushes for an hour and then left in flat baskets over charcoal. The tea by this time was not a bright, live green any more, of course, but for their own use the Chinese did not add any additional colour and in this regard they disdained the green tea to which we were accustomed – the kind made for export.

Robert stood over the packing cases watching the even, small leaves of better quality being trod into the boxes by children wearing straw shoes. The farmer was encouraging them to pack in as much as possible. When he spotted here and there an area he felt had not been properly bedded down, he pulled the child across the box to see it was done correctly.

'And of green tea?' Robert asked, 'like the *gweiloh* prefer?'

The man snorted. 'The salesmen add dye,' he said. 'My brother went down to Shanghae once with a big harvest. He sold it to a merchant and stayed to help with the colouring. When he came home his hands were blue.'

'Blue?' Robert tried to question further, but the man knew no more.

'Blue for the foreign barbarians,' he confirmed.

It was a puzzle, though after two weeks of persistently asking every farmer he talked to, Robert was able to procure some samples of the dye. He packed them carefully to be sent to London for analysis. It was some months, of course (and by then we had moved on) but we found out latterly that it was Prussian blue and gypsum that were used. The tea also contained a dye of which Robert had not heard before. It was made from a Chinese plant with beautiful blue flowers, which grew in the foothills.

'*Isatis indigotica*,' Robert chose its name.

It had not been known at home before. Robert, of course, took cuttings and collected seeds.

'This is easy money,' he commented ecstatically, for to find a new species with such a clear application to business was a boon.

Our rooms came to resemble large potting sheds. We pinned drawings to the walls, nurtured seedlings at the window and dried herbarium specimens at the fireside. Boxes piled up full of seeds and heavy papers with specimens between. One evening I counted over a thousand drawings I had made. I packed them in folios, each clearly marked and cross-referenced. In the end there were a total of twenty boxes, like wooden packing trunks, that housed all our goods. Six were filled with carvings that Robert had come across, for up in the hills he had found a mason, working only over the winter months, who wrought extravagant statues, mostly of trees. These were magical, elegant pieces so fine and perfect that they seemed almost like dancers striking a pose. We heard later they had made excellent prices at auction at Turnbull's on the Strand. We wished we had bought more.

To occupy myself over the weeks while Robert laboured, I became interested in scents, making flower oils and combining them in small flasks in different combinations. I fancied myself quite the olfactory chemist and set up a room near the courtyard as my workshop. I installed a long wooden table, some cupboards, mixing bowls and all the apparatus for extracting the oils. In the morning I picked wild flowers and herbs in baskets and even employed three women to help, showing them my preferred plants and then sending them to the hills to pick enough for me to work with. From these I extracted scented oils as my mother had done when I was a child, for where we lived there were meadows of thyme, lavender and mint, which the local women picked and processed for the apothecary in the town nearby.

I thought of myself mixing the fragrance of a certain day – the heavy musk of the hillside after the rain with the lightness of fresh blossoms doused in the downpour. I thought of each little bottle as the essence of a happy day or a sad one. I mixed the scent of a lonely moment – sandalwood and bergamot lingering over a rich, peppery base. As the harvest proceeded I made oil from peaches, apples and melons that added sweetness to my concoctions. Sometimes the scent of the rooms was overwhelming, on a hot day especially.

Robert chose from my collection a gentle, plummy oil as his own and added it to his shaving water. The fragrance lingered. On my part I preferred roses and peaches mixed so that the scent of the flowers just crept up on the scent of the fruit.

Then, one day, some weeks after we had arrived, I was walking back from an excursion on the hillside. I had been lost for some time in my olfactory experiments and was so at ease with life in Hwuy Chow Foo that I was surprised that when I saw the man in the distance, he so drew my attention. My heart began to pound. Although dressed like a Chinaman, I could see from half a mile that he was European. The way he moved was so different. His whole body jerked as he hammered solidly down the hill towards the road. Excited, I began to run in his direction, clasping the basket of herbs I had picked to my chest, ready to drop it if need be. Here was a compatriot – who was he? What was he doing here? And would he bear news? I had not realised I had so missed the company of my countrymen. I did not want to shout, just in case someone heard me screaming in English or in case, just in case, I had imagined the man and he wasn't a European at all. At length he spotted me and I waved to signal to him to stop. He nodded and waited on the track.

'*Waiyee*,' he greeted me as I approached.

And then the sport of it struck me and I greeted him in Cantonese to see if I might get away with the ruse.

'Where are you from, sir?' I asked, carefully modulating the tenor of my voice to sound more male, forcing myself not to stare too closely at his appearance, for in China this would be considered unforgivably rude.

'The hills,' he replied. 'Are you in trouble? Do you need my help?'

Even in a tongue as foreign as Cantonese I could hear his accent was from the North of England – near Liverpool or Cumbria perhaps. His manner was straightforward and he was not the least bit threatened by me, which must be unusual, I thought. Any white man approached so forwardly by a Chinese would be forgiven for being on his guard, but this fellow was at ease completely. I got the impression he was tired – he was a big chap and wore a beard but there was something about his demeanour that made me feel he was truly exhausted. I immediately felt guilty at trying to trick him. He had asked me if I needed help but my instinct was that he was the one who needed assistance or, at the very least, some respite.

'I'm sorry,' I said, raising my voice to its normal pitch and coming clean. I was so glad to encounter a fellow *gweiloh* and was itching to hear his tales. 'I could not help but see if you could tell that I am not Chinese at all. My name is Mary Penney.'

His face lit up. On hearing me speak English he took on the expression of a ten-year-old boy.

'My God,' he peered, 'you're a woman?'

I laughed.

'Yes, and very pleased to meet you, sir,' I held out my hand. 'Who are you?'

'Edward. Father Edward.'

'One of Bertie's priests!' I shouted gleefully, and I was so excited I flung my arms around the poor fellow, who seemed quite bemused by my enthusiasm.

'You must come back to our lodgings,' I insisted. 'My brother-in-law is there – he will be delighted to make your acquaintance.'

Robert took a room for Father Edward at the inn. The man had little money and had been sleeping rough.

'But what are you doing here?' he enquired as we toasted each other with the final bottle of port that Robert had concealed among his things.

'Collecting plants,' Robert gesticulated. The entire inn was packed with specimens.

'What about you? Where are you going, Father?'

'Back to Ning-po. It will take a while, but that is what I have decided. I have done all the good I can in the interior. I was north of here and there were five of us, but the nuns died of typhoid and I am limited as to what I can do alone.'

'We were in Ning-po only a few months ago. I am sure Bertie will be delighted to see you. I can give you some money if you like. It will speed your journey,' Robert said generously.

Father Edward shook his head. 'I am fine,' he said simply.

'I have enough to buy food and that is all I need. A bed for the night is a luxury though. Thank you.'

We spent the evening discussing what we had seen of China. Father Edward told us of the farms where he had come from, about the mission he had set up and the work they had embarked on, helping the old and sick.

'It is so poor,' he said, 'China.'

'Not here,' I countered.

'No. Here there is industry, though the people are taxed too heavily. And the troops are vicious. I saw awful things before the war, when I was nearer the coast. They punished their own people for reporting the white man's incursions. In England a man turning in information is rewarded, but in China, if there is any question of helping a foreigner, even in error, it lays a death sentence on the unfortunate man's head. People giving directions of any kind were killed on the spot.'

'Yes,' said Robert, not saying that this probably worked in our favour. 'What they do to their own people is terrible. And the sickness. I have seen some dreadful things in the villages.'

Sing Hoo cooked a sumptuous dinner and we lingered at the table. I told Father Edward about the Women's Mission in Ning-po and about Bertie's impersonation of a humble priest and how we had been duped. Father Edward was a serious man and he did not laugh when I told the story, only regarded me carefully.

'It made no difference to Mary,' Robert told him, 'though I admit it made me think twice about what I had confessed in Bertie's presence.'

Father Edward sighed.

'You are tired, Father,' I said. 'We are being selfish, wanting to keep you up too long.'

'I am sorry,' he replied. 'It has been quite a time since

I have spoken English. You two have each other and it is not strange to you.'

The next day the priest accompanied Robert to a tea farm and it was there, I think, he realised Robert's true mission. When the men returned there was a strained atmosphere and Father Edward said that he was leaving.

'Oh, please,' I begged him. 'Will you take a letter to Bertie for me? Don't leave yet. Stay another night. It will take me a while to write.'

'Does the Bishop know why you have come here?' Father Edward asked coldly.

'Yes. Of course. Bertie is a great friend. What is the matter?'

He snorted as if my question was foolish.

'The treaty is unequal enough as it is, don't you think? Do you know how poor these people are? Do you know what your actions here will mean? First we make them trade with us so that the mandarin population is slave to our opium and then we steal the only commodity they have to pay for it!'

'I find it difficult to believe you are on their side,' Robert said, incredulous.

It was clear they had started this conversation out on the land and were now merely continuing it.

'I am only on the side of fairness,' Father Edward countered. 'You have been kind to me but I cannot in good conscience stay here. If what you are doing succeeds, these people will lose their livelihood. It is not moral. You are stealing from them, Mr Fortune.'

I hung my head.

'How dare you?' Robert snarled. 'You think they are keeping the treaty? With their secret tariffs and the level of their troops? This is nonsense. You have lost your senses. Every nation must look to its own business and do the best for its people. How long have you been here, Edward? How long did it take for you to forget you are British and a subject of the Queen?'

Father Edward cast his eyes to his feet.

'It is my conscience and I will not lie about it. My duty first is to God's law and not man's accommodation of politics.'

'God!' Robert declared.

Thankfully he did not launch into a discourse on spirituality. Father Edward turned away from Robert at this blasphemous outburst and it was clear he had no more to say on the matter.

'Write your letter, Miss Penney, and I will wait.'

'Do not fret, Father Edward, I will not ask you to carry anything for me,' Robert snapped.

That evening the priest walked out of the town. I had sent Sing Hoo with a parcel of food, but Edward did not take it with him. I watched him leave all but empty-handed from the window of my room.

'He will not report us,' Robert said. 'He may have some strange convictions but he wouldn't dare!'

It had not even occurred to me that there was a danger.

For two days I felt both guilty and disappointed as I debated the storm Father Edward had started in my mind. We were stealing perhaps in one sense, but then, why should any plant belong to one nation? The seeds could as easily blow on the wind out of bounds. Why was it worse to take a tea plant than a yellow camellia? Was it a more serious offence to remove a cutting rather than a seed? Besides, Robert had paid his way amply. I wished Father Edward had stayed so I could reason with him. I wished the original promise of excitement had paid off. Who would have ever thought a white man would come strolling across our

211

path the first time in months and that if he did that we might quarrel? Talking to Robert about it was pointless. We had become too cosy, perhaps, and the shock of Father Edward's intrusion took a good week to subside.

I do not know what happened to the priest. His journey on foot back to Ning-po should have taken two months, maybe three. Perhaps he fell foul of troops stationed on the way. One way or another, my letter never reached Bertie and Father Edward, God rest his soul, never returned to British soil.

Ten days after Edward left, Robert and I made an excursion to the fields and we misjudged our distances. When the sun set it was as if the land simply disappeared and we realised we had left it too late to get back to our lodgings if we were not on the main road already. There was nothing for it, we were caught up in the hills with acres of tea around us, a stream to one side and nothing else for miles. It was next to impossible to travel at night. The tracks were dangerously uneven, there were few landmarks and not one single signpost. That night, in addition, the moon was not out and we were as good as blind men. Luckily there seemed to be few wild animals – the odd fox, perhaps, but little else, so it was not dangerous. Robert had some fruit and bread, which we shared. Then we sat for a while on a large, flat rock, which protruded from a gully. After a while Robert rose. He walked to the running water and bathed his feet.

'Hot,' he explained.

'Well,' I said, settling down, 'if an odd fish like Father Edward can manage this, so can we.'

A bed on the ground is more comfortable than the berth on a barge, I discovered and, having checked for stones and found leaves on which to lay my head, I was comfortable. Even in summertime the night could be chilly and we were on high ground.

'Aren't the stars an astonishment?' Robert breathed, and I could feel his chest rise and fall.

He was right – they were like gemstones scattered across the velvet sky, for it was not cloudy. The hills were so silent that I could hear the movement of the branches off into the distance. To feel so tiny in the face of the wide sky was as marvellous as the anonymity of being unjudged and unnoticed.

'It has become,' Robert commented as we lay on the dark hill, 'most companionable with you, Mary. I could not hope to have such a variety of drawings without your help.'

I smiled in the darkness and realised then that I was committed to this mission. Despite what Father Edward said, I admired my brother-in-law and what he wanted to achieve. Edward had lost himself. He had become confused. A man has to know where he comes from and stick to that. The kind of confusion to which Edward was subject would never happen to Robert and, in that silent moment, I realised that despite my empathy for the Chinese it would never happen to me either. I might think in their language and find myself entirely comfortable in this land, but my loyalty was to the Queen, not the Emperor. I knew my place in the scheme of things.

'I am on your side, you know,' I whispered to Robert.

He did not answer. It was pitch black but I thought I saw the gleam of his teeth as he smiled.

A moment or two passed and I decided to change the subject.

'So, what are we to do with all my drawings, then?' I asked.

'Shanghae would be the best port, I think,' he ventured. 'The *Helen Stuart* makes regular voyages. We shall send them west when we leave for the south. They will return to England. The catalogue will be part of the record of what we have done.'

And I found myself wondering with a tinge of sadness if everything I cared about in China was destined to go home in the end. I certainly did not want to.

'I think,' I said, 'I will never go on the stage again after this.'

I could hear Robert turn. 'Why? What is it that you do wish to do?'

'Be here.'

'Mary Penney! And your boxes of baubles and feather ornaments?' Robert teased. 'Your streams of admirers and fine French lace? All the claret? The slices of lamb and pale Cheshire cheese, my lady? What are you here for, if not to be able to show off in London about it!'

'Better to be a well-kept secret by far. Can you bear to go back and lecture at the Society? To have them think well of you despite your low birth, when here you are free to be whoever you please?'

Robert fell silent for a moment.

'I long to,' he said. 'Both to have their respect and merit their attention.'

'We are opposite in that,' I replied as I stared at the inky sky, my limbs so relaxed that I almost floated. I had never been so satisfied, so happy, in all my life.

Late that night I half wakened and, with my eyes accustomed to the darkness, I noticed Robert had moved off to the side and was sitting against a tree, his knees to his chest, unable to sleep it seemed. I wondered what had disturbed him. It seemed to me that he had been pacing up and down, although now he was still, his back against the bark.

'Are you all right?' I asked. 'Why did you move away?'

'Shhhh,' he soothed, and averted his eyes.

'What is the matter?'

'You sleep, Mary.'

I did as he asked and turned over.

In the morning I woke in the half-light. The dew had come down and the ground was damp. We hiked along the path a mile or so and feasted on wild cherries from a tree by the track. The juice ran down Robert's chin.

'I am torn,' Robert said meditatively, 'between the freedom of this adventure, and the benefits of civilisation despite its constraints. I don't know how yet, but I hope that perhaps I can share my time between both.'

I was glad that he cared for freedom enough to think of it so. For my part, though I was still British, and for all that I had Henry there, and Jane too, London could go hang.

One day, after several weeks in the province, it was finally time for Sing Hoo to visit his family. We had seen the tea harvest in the North and soon we would progress to the black tea countries to do the same, travelling south and then waiting for the spring and the early harvest in April. I knew that Robert had been reviewing his notes, making plans as ever. If Sing Hoo didn't go now it would be too late.

It was difficult to extract information as to the exact location of the man's village as Sing Hoo refused to read any of our maps. This Robert put down to a mixture of stupidity, stubbornness and a vague intention to escape our service if he could by simply disappearing.

'He will want to stay at home when he returns to his village,' Robert grumbled. 'And besides, he may expose us. Had you thought, Mary?'

'It seems to me unlikely he would tell them who we are,' I ventured. 'He has never told anyone before. After all, better servant to a grand mandarin than a criminal in the service of foreigners. He is not reliable, it's true. But he will want to impress his family.'

Nonetheless, Robert insisted that we accompany Sing

Hoo, and we finally established the village was at some three days' distance.

'Perhaps we shall find some interesting plants on the way,' Robert said, trying to make the best of things.

I chose a small carving, a miniature copy of the great stone ship at the Summer Palace, as a gift. Sing Hoo puffed out his chest and grinned openly when he realised that his family were to receive presents. His stock would no doubt rise and he was nothing if not a show-off. In the end we also took some sesame oil, bags of rice, half a dozen phials of my perfumes and some of the dwarf conifers, which we had no use for in our retinue.

'Sing Wa honours my family,' Sing Hoo beamed.

Robert nodded sagely, making his point. 'It is you we are honouring,' he said. 'Your family will be proud of you.'

Despite all his failings we needed to keep Sing Hoo with us. It was far easier that way.

Wang was distraught at all the attention that was being showered on his rival. He served a supper the evening before we set off that belied the meagre cooking facilities of the inn.

'We can visit your family in Bohea,' I comforted him. 'We will bring them gifts too, Wang. Bohea will be our home in only a few months.'

But the man was inconsolable. He hung his head and that evening I saw him sitting on the low wall of the court-yard throwing stones into the inky blackness beyond. Robert gave him a few *cash* with which to amuse himself while we were gone, and a list of strict instructions about the care of the nursery.

When we set off early the next morning, Wang had given himself up entirely to despair. He was already drunk and had a flagon of five grain spirit hanging from his belt. I expect the poor man had been up all night emptying it.

'He doesn't have a family,' Sing Hoo jibed cheerfully. 'Everyone dead.'

I looked back up the road, making out the lonely figure of Wang staring after us from the gates of the inn.

'Poor chap,' I murmured.

'Come along now,' Robert urged. 'I doubt that is true. And besides, we must make our time.'

In the end we did better than planned and our journey was only two days. Sing Hoo became more excited at every turn of the road and spoke so quickly it was difficult to pick up what he was saying. As the hills became less steep and we came to a gentle valley he ran ahead, shouting, and it was clear we had almost arrived.

'Imagine going home after so many years,' Robert smiled.

Sing Hoo had not seen his people in ten years at least. How long might it be for us, I wondered.

The village was tiny, perhaps six or eight houses. Sing Hoo's family lived in the first we came to, which comprised two storeys. They flooded out into the street to his cries and I saw immediately that Sing Hoo looked like his relations, with their small eyes and wide, misshapen mouths. I recognised his expression of delight on their faces as they flung their arms around him and then, the suspicious glances cast as they realised that their relative had arrived with a fine mandarin and his secretary. Sing Hoo wasted no time in showering his relations with the gifts we had supplied and we were duly welcomed. The brother's wives smelt the flacons of perfumed oil and laughed, delighted. The brothers set the carving of the boat beside the door of the dwelling. Sing Hoo, I realised, had saved some weeks' wages and presented them ceremonially to the family. It would be the same with Jane, I realised. We might give her presents, tell some tales, but would she ever be able to really understand what the journey had been like for us?

That evening we ate rice and chicken cooked over an open fire and sat on rough pillows laid on the floor as we listened to the family's babble. Sing Hoo mourned his mother briefly, who had died some years before. He had not known that she was dead. But as the younger children squabbled he was drawn away from any grief and seemed happy again to simply be at home. I watched carefully as Sing Hoo's sister-in-law, with fingers roughened in the fields, served tea of her own picking. It was not long, after years away, to have only one night, but at least for Sing Hoo it was a jolly one. As he babbled his adventures, augmenting the tales to enlarge his role in them, my mind drifted away. My thoughts were already directed to our onward journey.

'Do you think we could leave him here?' I whispered to Robert. 'It seems safe enough and he is a terrible troublemaker.'

Robert considered a moment and shook his head.

'No. We need him, Mary. Who could replace Sing Hoo now? He knows.'

I expect Robert was right.

The next morning I woke to the sound of crying. Sing Hoo brought me some tea and congee and said that his brothers were giving a gift to Robert, who was in the main living room, and that I should not mind the crying – it was only one of the women, an aunt who did not wish him to leave.

It seemed to take forever until we could go. The family fussed around Sing Hoo, clinging to him and wailing as if they were never to be consoled. Eventually Robert, losing patience, practically prised the man from their arms and insisted we set off at once. Sing Hoo was quiet for most of the journey back to Hwuy Chow Foo. He walked behind us at a slow, steady pace.

We slept in the open that night as if we were old hands at it, and rushed the next day to make it as far as the inn, taking the risk of travelling the last mile or so of familiar road in the dark for we were determined to sleep that night in our own beds. Upon our arrival Wang skulked around, making tea and eyeing Sing Hoo jealously as if in his time alone with us he had been up to something underhand. The fires were lit, for it was cold that evening, and I settled under my cover in the glow of it, eating a slice of melon with green skin and rosy, sweet flesh. In the hallway I could hear the muted tones of Wang and Sing Hoo squabbling with each other over nothing, as usual.

After that, our work in the province was done. The harvest was over. The farmers were tending their plants in readiness for collecting the seeds and had directed their attention to wintertime pursuits. There came a week when the weather turned much colder, there was frost sometimes in the mornings and the sky became streaked with winter clouds. I unpacked my padded jacket and my scarves and Robert gave me a fine fur hat, for with my shaven head I felt the cold badly, but still we had decided two days were as long as we could safely leave it. When Robert's tea seeds were delivered he inspected them carefully, making sure they had been properly cleaned and were sealed appropriately in lined, wooden containers.

He engaged seven men to transport the myriad of packing cases and plants in the opposite direction to the one we would take. They were heading to Shanghae, the load at first on their backs, then on carts (once the roads were wider) and lastly by canal boat. The shipment was to be delivered to a local merchant and from there, discreetly, to the British Consul with a letter outlining Robert's instructions for their transport onwards. Some were for the East India Company and others destined for the Royal Society, for auction, or for the nursery with which Robert had his arrangement.

This journey, all to be taken in our absence and mostly over ground we had covered and knew well, was minutely planned. The plants were under the care of Li, a boy of perhaps fifteen years of age, who had often accompanied Robert as a bearer when he had collected specimens in the hills. He had proved a careful and reliable servant and was trusted to tend the plants as his sole duty. The money for the trip was given to his older cousin, also known as Li, who was to oversee the whole operation, organise the carts and the barges and ensure the men were careful with the trunks. Robert outlined exactly what was in each case for the Consul's information and instructed bonuses to be paid to each of the Lis if all was in order when they delivered. Of this they were informed. And, of course, there was the mandatory coded letter too – a rather short one, I imagine, for the tea countries had not provided us with much in the way of military information, though perhaps Pottinger would be interested in the absence of troops all the same.

The tea seeds were to travel with us, such was their value. The penalty for the sale of these to a foreigner was death. It was too dangerous to send these boxes across country. Instead they were loaded with our personal possessions for the journey in the opposite direction – into unknown territory. We were heading over the mountains to the south.

'Like Hannibal!' Robert joked with me as we surveyed our luggage, which was, to say the least of it, extensive.

'I do feel like a Nomad Queen.'

'King,' Robert corrected me.

'You may call me Your Majesty,' I volleyed back.

We would be months in the high ground and as our maps were not detailed we knew there might be surprises on the route. The black tea countries retained a certain mystery despite Bertie's help, which had been considerable, and details gleaned from the farmers at Hwuy Chow Foo, some of whom had visited their Bohean cousins. For this expedition Robert had packed tents and had procured some oil lamps. It would shortly be too cold to sleep in the open and as there were few settlements in the hills we would have to make our own shelter and sleep at least two to a tent, simply for warmth. On the higher mountains there was already snow, although our planned route was over the gentler hills as far as possible. However, there was a large mountain range once we were through Kiang See province that we would certainly have to climb. We took many provisions as it was not clear where we might be able to restock our supplies or how often. Six experienced men from the village were to travel with us and came with two carts and four mules. Two of the men knew the mountain passes well and had travelled there before. Once we reached Bohea they would return home again.

I have never been fond of the cold or the winter. My mother used to open the door and welcome a cold, crisp morning but I was a summer baby. The day we left, Robert and I stood about our empty rooms. He had written a letter home that would return with the shipment. I knew it had taken him some days to compose. Likewise I had also compiled a letter for Jane and had sent some phials of perfume for her. I found it easy to write about the land, the beauty of the place and our strange and exotic food-stuffs. I had described the enmity between Wang and Sing Hoo, the grumpy innkeeper and his pretty maidservant. I outlined our trip to Sing Hoo's village. However, when the missive was sealed I realised that I had not mentioned Robert even once.

The room felt cold despite the fire being laid hours before and set alight while it was still dark. Sing Hoo made hot soup that we drank straight from the bowl, standing close to the flames.

'I hope the black tea countries will prove as profitable,' Robert said. 'There is more industry there, in any case. We might make quite a profit at the silk factories.'

'I think this trip will be difficult,' I replied. 'It will be cold and the going hard.'

Robert nodded. 'Are you able?' he asked.

'Yes. I am well rested, though I admit I am slightly afraid.'

'There are trails through the hills,' Robert assured me. 'We will not be climbing virgin rock. We will be under our own steam, make no mistake. I have a gun.'

This was for protection from animals. High up in the hills we knew there were wild beasts, though the descriptions of these varied tremendously from what sounded like wolves to vicious snow tigers and bears. We had heard stories of dragons too, and, though sceptical of this, of course, it did linger in my mind that the place was strange and that anything was possible.

'Well,' said Robert. 'Until we reach civilisation again,' he toasted, raising his small cup and clicking it against mine.

'To civilisation,' I replied and sipped.

Robert's nose was pink.

'I think,' he said, 'it may be warmer outside. These rooms were not built to hold the temperature.'

'Shall we go?' I laughed.

Sing Hoo's maidservant sweetheart watched him from an upper window as he checked the ropes on one of the wagons. I spotted her as I stepped into the yard. Robert and I had one mule each, both riding on rough saddles slung over their backs. I named mine Prudence. I don't expect Robert gave his a moniker. As we rode away from the inn I admit I had a sense of foreboding, though perhaps it was only the feeling of riding away from a place where

I had been happy. We had no gloves, but I wrapped my hands with two pieces of woollen fabric that acted as mittens, and held the reins to gee Prudence along. Sing Hoo, I noticed, left without any sign of regret. Perhaps his sweetheart had only been a dalliance. Wang was positively eager. After all, it was he who was now going home.

Robert, as ever, was intractable, like a man riding to his destiny. I admired him on his mule, his long ponytail bobbing behind him at every step, his orange robes resplendent, lined with fur and a smile playing around his lips.

Chapter Nine

We moved south slowly. The hills in winter were inhospitable and the journey proved arduous. The bearers, apart from Wang and Sing Hoo, were all natives of Kiang See province. They carried our luggage, our sedan chairs, drove the mules and pitched the tents. In return we fed them generously. Over quarter of our baggage was rice, beans, air-dried meats, vinegars, soya sauce, oils and a large box of carefully packed apples. We also carried some live chickens in baskets, which lasted well the first month. We bought more whenever we came upon a settlement in the hills, though as the journey continued it was infrequent.

At sunset each evening we all retired. The men were four to a tent, which was far warmer but Robert and I had to make do the two of us together – it would not have been fitting, of course, for us to bunk with the men. Mostly we were too exhausted to speak and muffled in furs we fell asleep quickly. I found the sound of Robert's breathing comforting next to me and came to notice the point at which there was a slight change in the movement of his chest and he tipped over into sleep – generally only a moment or two before I did. One morning when I woke we were flushed, hot despite the cold. Our arms were intertwined in a jumble of fur-clad limbs and it took me a moment to remember who I was, where I was and what we were doing there.

Robert fretted over our progress. The mountains were cold and rocky, and the pace was slow. He pored over the maps, reading with the aid of a tallow lamp.

'Barely ten miles today,' he cursed, recording our progress.

Or, when we were travelling in a valley or downhill, 'Easy going, twenty-five.'

The views were breathtaking but at these altitudes there was little in the way of vegetation and what there was, was covered by snow.

Now and again, over a cup of tea we had supervised the picking and processing of some weeks before, Robert talked. He had been accustomed to harsh winters as a child and told me tales of walking the Kelloe Estate in search of lost sheep.

'Without the furs then,' he laughed, 'and never so far from comfort. It is queer, Mary, travelling here. Where we don't even know what it will be like when we arrive. What do we have to look forward to? It could be anything.'

My lips felt dry. I used nut oil as a salve and dripped in some rose so that sometimes I might catch a whiff of it, a barely-there memory of summer.

'I dread to think the state we shall be in when we unswaddle ourselves,' I remarked.

For an hour one night we were indulgent of our fantasies, dreaming of bread and marmalade, hot, fragrant baths and fresh linen – of it being so temperate that we might leave the windows open and enjoy the breeze. Mostly though we were too tired. The hours of sleep disappeared, literally, for they were entirely blacked out. The short, white days dragged on, every step difficult.

In the fifth week one of the bearers turned his ankle and it swelled badly. Wang fashioned a crutch from some wood found by the side of the track. We could not spare a mule for the poor fellow for we needed them to carry provisions. All of us walked. Our sedan chairs were carried empty, loaded up on the carts. It was at this time in the trip I realised that the mules suddenly all looked the same to me, and that I had lost sight of which one was Prudence.

At Hokow we stopped to rest with the intention of leaving the injured man in lodgings with enough money to speed his recovery and see him home. The town was tiny but to sleep behind solid walls and dine on roasted meat was a luxury after the open hills. News of the rich mandarin and his entourage spread through the tiny community and we put out word that we intended to restock our supplies. This might take some days as we knew the locals would be careful to sell us only what they didn't need themselves. In winter, in the hills, it is an easy matter to starve if your reserves are low, and we knew it was likely several of the farmers would sell us nothing at all. We hoped, though, to manage something. We were not low on food but, as Robert observed, we should stock up wherever we can. It was also a chance to bathe and change – the clothing I had been wearing needed to be burned and I did not waste time trying to salvage it, instead seeking warm enough replacements among the trunks, which were difficult to open as the locks had frozen fast.

It was at Hokow, however, that danger came our way and in the end we had no chance to spend our time negotiating for chickens or dried beans and little enough time to procure extra furs where we could. It was all down to a slip of the tongue. As Robert went to check the mules were properly stabled, he came across Wang, who had picked up a village girl. She seemed too delicate to live in the frozen hills and not much more than fourteen or fifteen if his judgement was right. Wang was regaling her with tales of

226

big cities, of sailing the Chinese Straits in the service of a foreigner. The girl was stunned and excited. He had clearly impressed her.

'A foreigner!' she squealed. 'A barbarian?'

Then she looked at Robert, he said, and somehow, where others had failed to see it, this girl knew.

'What nonsense,' he blustered – a show for her. 'When we return to my estates in the North I shall see you punished for talking such nonsense to a poor, village girl who knows no better.'

And with that Robert bore Wang away, before he could say more.

Safe in our rooms he berated the man.

'What the hell were you thinking, Wang?' he shouted, furious. 'It is difficult enough to stay alive in this weather without alerting those around us to the illegality of our trip!'

The green tea countries had inured us, made things too easy, and I think until that moment even Robert and I had let down our guard a little. I had not seen him so angry since his venom was directed at me over a year before, and he was barely holding himself back from laying hands on Wang. His fists clenched and unclenched and if there had been something to throw in temper I am certain he would have.

'Do you know what they will do to us, all of us, if they find out, Wang?'

Wang hung his head while Robert embarked on a lecture on the law, self-preservation and the penalties the man would face if the authorities found that he had aided our journey and how it only took one pretty girl to tell her father what she'd heard and who knew what might happen?

In his defence, when he could get a word in, Wang protested

that the foreigner he was talking of was some other master and swore that somewhere in the nuances of the language Robert had lost this thread.

'Nonsense!' Robert ranted. 'Do you think I am a fool? You better pray you have not sunk us, Wang. You better pray!'

He clipped Wang's ear soundly and dismissed the man, telling him to forego supper and that he must keep watch all night in the hallway of the inn, for he had put every one of us in danger.

I thought myself that Wang's explanation was possible and perhaps Robert had overreacted but, as it turned out, the indiscretion was not to pass. So, in this inhospitable place, the very next day, with Wang bleary eyed from undertaking his punishment, we received an unwelcome visit. In fact, it was as well that Robert had set Wang to keep watch for he darted into the room and warned us just in time.

'*Loi-yu!*' Watch out!

I jumped up and stood behind Robert, thanking my stars that the room was dimly lit. I had not yet shaved my head and the colour was coming through too light for a Chinaman, and I was not properly dressed, though not so uncovered as to make my femininity clear.

The man wore a fur coat and carried a muff that matched. He bowed low as did Robert in return. Then, in Cantonese, with all the ceremony of that flowery language, he enquired as to our purpose. Robert embarked on his usual cheerful story of horticultural obsession and his wish to collect plants for his estates. This generally provoked a delighted response – stories of the horticultural interests of others, polite questioning about the manner of the estates and expressions that any humble help that could be supplied would be forthcoming. This man stood still and silent for a long time. When he spoke, each word was deployed as carefully as pieces are moved during a game of chess.

'Perhaps,' he said at last, 'you would like to avail of our free service. I can offer you safe passage.'

Robert thanked him but said he was most willing to travel at his own expense, and indeed, risk.

'I think free passage to Hong Kong may be more advantageous to you. Or perhaps Shanghae? Ning-po?'

The offer was made politely but the three ports named were all British. Robert stiffened. The gun was in our luggage but I knew Robert also carried a knife upon his person. My hands were cold and quivering, I wished now that I had a blade of my own to wrap them round.

'I have never been to those places,' Robert answered carefully. 'We have travelled overland from my estates in the North.'

I felt my stomach turn. The mandarin was dispassionate, of course. He did not threaten directly but nonetheless his air was sinister.

'I have lived in Shanghae,' he stated simply. 'I think the city would suit you better. I will take the liberty of sending for an escort.'

He took his leave and in the event we, of course, took ours. Robert jumped up and pored over his maps, estimating the man's journey time and, indeed, routes and times for our own escape.

'To get an escort,' he said, 'he will have to send a messenger. The nearest garrison we know of is over a week away and it is tiny. That is on our side. In two weeks we can cover a lot of ground.'

Here he stopped and considered, shaken but not panicked, though his lips were pursed and his shoulders hunched.

'But if we can dissuade him from even sending the

messenger . . .' he mused, pausing for only a moment before he roared, 'Sing Hoo! Pack everything!'

Then Robert roughly pulled Wang to one side.

'We can all die here, Wang. You as well, by God,' he said. 'You will find that girl. You will tell her that your mandarin master is offended by the visit he received. Tell her you like the look of her. Tell her you are sorry you have to go. That your master is ordering his retinue to move on tonight. Tell her we are heading east. For the coast. East. That I am shaken, but determined to continue on my own, *back to where I came from*.'

Wang, his eyes darting, repeated the message to Robert and then quit the room hurriedly. I felt sick.

'Come on, Mary,' Robert said. 'We must all lend a hand.'

I began to pile papers speedily into one of the cases.

We left the village at nightfall with two extra mules, the man who by rights should have rested his ankle astride one of them. The bearers were disgruntled but had not as yet understood the full import of what was going on. After two miles travelling eastwards, Sing Hoo was ordered to clear our tracks as we changed direction. He hovered in our wake, brushing the powdery snow clean as we moved ahead to the south once more.

'Will the mandarin follow?' I asked Robert nervously, as we continued in the dark.

Robert shrugged his shoulders. 'If Wang has done his job it is likely the man has had no time to inform anyone that he knows of our presence before he hears we have left. This might discourage him from sending a messenger. He will not want to admit we have slipped through his fingers, Mary. That's what I'm hoping. He might comfort himself we are heading for the coast anyway.'

'And if he sends a messenger?'

'The garrison is miles away. And if they follow I hope

that in the first instance they will keep on in the direction of the tracks we have left and head east. It will give us an even longer head start.'

'You think the mandarin will know we are gone?'

Robert looked at Wang who was leading the party.

'He heard of our presence quickly enough. His easiest course of action is simply to forget that we were in his village and to comfort himself that we have left. Failure is judged harshly by the Emperor's men. If he reports that we fled and he did not hold us, then he may be punished. Him and his family.'

We continued in silence. About half an hour after we turned to the south we heard Sing Hoo howling behind. Robert rode back and he swore we were being followed.

'He has sent a scout.' Sing Hoo was beside himself and it took us a while to calm him down but, when we did, the man was adamant that he had picked out sight of a torch some way behind.

Robert and I doubled back but there were no fresh tracks and at first we couldn't find a soul. Then, as we turned to rejoin the party, we heard a snapping sound. Robert took his torch over to a thicket of bushes. He put the flame to the driest of the twigs and set it alight. We waited, our breath clouding before us as the dry sticks caught fire in the snow. Through the licks of flame, after only a few moments, we saw a figure, a frightened pair of eyes. The man bolted through the undergrowth but Robert was too quick for him. He wrestled the spy to the ground.

'Douse the fire, Mary,' he shouted and I stamped on the lower branches and piled snow onto the flames until once more it was only our torches that burnt into the night.

The man had been sent by the mandarin to follow us. He was to return before morning and, if he could be sure of our route, the troops would be sent to track us further.

Clearly, this fellow knew we had gone eastwards and then to the south. To send him back would be madness.

'*Gweiloh*,' he spat, defiant, in Robert's face. 'They will come. They will find you.'

Robert's eyes blazed furiously. I did not see that my brother-in-law had drawn his knife and I did not realise that, without any hesitation, he had stabbed the spy in the stomach. The first I knew of it was the blood that dripped in a pool onto the snowy ground as the man's body opened and his insides spilled out.

I covered my face with my hands. This was murder. And yet what choice did we have? Robert had done the right thing. There was a terrible bravery to it. My breath became short in the freezing air as the man died quickly and Robert flung him to the ground. We stood apart for a moment, our minds racing and our faces pale with horror. I was not afraid of Robert – the morality of what he had done did not shock me. It was kill or be killed in these harsh hills. I wondered for a moment if I could have thrust the knife into the man's body myself. I was glad I had not had to make the choice.

'We cannot bury the body,' Robert said. 'The ground is far too hard. But we must get rid of him.'

I looked back down the hill. Sing Hoo was hysterical enough as it was.

I cast my eyes about, remembering passing this way earlier. We had had to steer the mules carefully for there was a frozen pool further along.

'Come,' I said. 'I know what to do. We will lift him together.'

We dragged the body a hundred yards and stripped it. The man was still warm beneath his padded coat and sheepskin boots. He was neither stiff nor heavy and easy to manoeuvre into position. Robert was staring at me. The shock of what he had done was setting in.

'Give me your knife,' I said, and from the edge of the pool I hacked a hole through the ice.

It was not frozen too deeply and the ice came away easily from the surface of the water below. Without question the hole would freeze again, covering our handiwork overnight.

'You had to, Robert,' I comforted him.

He nodded. 'I know,' he said. 'This is a good idea.'

And together we slipped the man's body into the water.

Up the hill, returning to the place we had found him, Robert bundled the clothes together to take back down with us and piled snow on top of the blood while I covered the traces of fire on the bushes as best I could. We were careful, almost businesslike – working as a team. I could find no tracks and surmised that, experienced in the hills, the man had covered his way. We were safe enough now.

'They will follow our tracks eastwards if they come to look for him but that is a mile from here.' Robert was thinking out loud.

His face looked pinched. I wondered if mine was similar.

'If they fan out they may find this, but they will not know where we have gone on to and we will have the whole night or more of a lead. We must cover our tracks back to the others and then go as fast as we can. Will you be all right, Mary?'

'I am alive,' I said, 'and I hope to stay that way.'

Together we checked for any last traces of the spy's trail and then made our way back to the company, who were waiting ahead to see if we would return. We were silent. There was no need for words anyway – we knew what had happened and we knew we agreed.

Wang looked relieved as we emerged out of the darkness, but I saw hatred in the eyes of the bearers. The pieces of the story were fitting together slowly and they were furious. What would they do if they knew there was a Chinese man murdered, hidden behind us, under the ice?

'Hold your nerve, man,' Robert admonished Sing Hoo as we passed for he looked terrified. 'There are no ghosts in the hills and no one living that I can find either. We are not being followed. Stay firm.'

And Wang was sent to sweep our trail the rest of the night.

We continued to alter our route, and, rather than travelling directly south, we zigzagged through the snow. Although exhausted, we made a good pace but the men muttered angrily, feeling betrayed. Now they knew we were not mandarins from the north they had to be compensated for our secret. Robert promised them a bonus on the journey's end. We walked through the dawn and the weather hardened. I felt horribly lonely. Only greed, and fear of having helped us now bound the men to the party. I shuddered to see the previously friendly faces regarding me plainly with disgust and fury.

At nightfall we stopped. My mind raced. Robert sent Sing Hoo to scout the area and, stiff as statues, we ate only for fuel, while Robert kept his eyes about him, grasping his gun and watching over the men as they huddled round the fire and, after a night and a day on the road, slept, exhausted.

'I will keep the vigil, Mary. You sleep if you can.'

I was surprised that I wanted to, but my mind was settling down. These were vicious times and they had brought out the animal in me. I would eat and sleep and kill if I had to. Anything to stay alive. I had discovered more about myself in the last few hours than I had the whole of the rest of the trip. With a sudden clarity, I realised that this determination had always been inside me and my past fears and dependencies had been unfounded. I was always set to survive.

Three hours in and I had dozed. The sound of Robert shouting woke me and I stumbled to my feet, running to his side, ready even half-asleep to do whatever I must. He was a few yards from the campfire.

'What is it?'

Robert pointed. One of the men had tried to leave the camp. He had stolen supplies and clearly intended to return to his home village. I shook my head. I knew what this required and so did Robert. In front of the others, he beat the deserter and then hauled the man back to the campfire in a fury, while the poor soul crouched, bruised and fearful. Robert needed to impose his will. He struck the deserter on the mouth so that for the second time in as many nights blood fell on the snowy ground. I was not sure if he might go further. Robert had never killed before he had had to, and I hoped the experience would not make him blood-hungry. His face was stony and he fiercely brandished his gun. I told myself I was behind him whatever he chose to do though it was with a tense kind of relief that he stopped well short of really harming the man.

'You cannot desert,' he told the huddled crew, like a general marshalling his army. 'You have no choice, but this: see us to Bohea and there will be rice wine aplenty and a fat bonus for every one of you. Think how you will spend that money. Your wives and your families back in Hwuy Chow Foo will appreciate your wages. But if you flee now, if you break our agreement, you get nothing. If you go to the authorities they will torture you. You have to stay and see it through. This man I will forgive. But I swear, the next man who leaves, I will shoot him dead and if the mandarins find him before I do, they will do worse.'

For the merest second I thought that they might pounce. Six strong men together might gain the upper hand. But Robert was formidable and they only sat on the ground dejected. Soon, one by one, with us watching over them, they settled to sleep. They might have been afraid of what they had discovered but Robert's ferocity had made them tame. They were, after all, only tea farmers – not warriors – and all had families to return to. Before dawn Wang returned from his watch with the news that we were not being followed. Robert woke the group and we set off once more.

From that evening on, Robert took to checking the rear in the afternoon before we camped and then sending either Wang or Sing Hoo to check again at night. No one could survive easily in the freezing hills without setting a camp-fire and we never saw one behind us. It seemed that the mandarin had given up the trail and we could only hope that his missing scout delayed matters enough to make him quit entirely. Each day that passed was good news.

All this time, Robert was like stone, his conversation terse. I knew that in this state of mind there was no margin in trying to comfort him and mostly I kept my silence. The man he had beaten bore the marks for many days but what Robert had said was true – if any of our party returned they could be captured and tortured both for what they knew and in punishment for the help they had given us. We applied ourselves to getting on. Robert had several books on military strategy. We consulted them by candlelight each evening. These gave good information about the length of time it was possible to track men in snowy conditions, and how to plan a route that was difficult to follow. After ten days we concluded that this and Robert's basic good sense had borne us away quickly enough to avoid capture in the first instance and keep us safe on the longer term.

'It seems we have got off lightly, Mary,' he said.

'We got off, that's the main thing,' I replied.

It did not seem so lightly to me. Still, now we were sure

we were not being followed, the men relaxed. It had been a close call. Our escape had not been certain but our route was so erratic, they would have some job to find us now if they had not sent a party to tail us already. Still Robert continued to check our rear and we never rested for more than five hours – all of us pushed to the limit.

The days felt long, though I suppose it was really only a fortnight more of biting cold until the temperature rose and the altitude dropped and we found ourselves, quite miraculously, in the grounds of a Buddhist monastery. Here it was still winter, but the site was sheltered and, when we came across the place miles from everywhere, it was like a gift. To find civilisation in such a remote corner lifted my spirits after what had been a frightening ordeal.

'Can we stop here?' I asked Robert.

'Yes. We need the supplies,' he said simply.

Bertie had told us of the kindness and acceptance of the monks who ruled themselves separately from the mandarins and were independent of mind. I was glad to be somewhere spiritual, in any case, and from the first the monastery certainly felt that way – a retreat from the world.

'They will consider you a gift from the heavens. If you are in the interior and in a fix, the monks are a good bet. They will tell no one,' Bertie had promised.

Trusting this was true, Robert and I climbed towards the building like pilgrims, on foot. After months of rough inns, buildings with floors of trampled dirt, poor lodgings when we were lucky and camping rough in freezing conditions when we weren't, the temple seemed miraculous, set, we realised, at the head of a valley of clear streams.

'Good monks,' Wang smiled. 'Make all better.'

At the top of the steps our party was greeted by a boy swathed in orange cloth. He caught sight of us, hesitated nervously and then fell to his knees and bowed very low. We were later to learn this was the custom with new recruits, who were enjoined to learn humility by bowing to everyone they came into contact with. Robert and I bowed in return and asked if we might avail ourselves of the monastery's hospitality.

In the courtyard our men stood in awe. The square was peopled with gilded statues of wood and clay. They shone golden in the sunlight, almost glowing as they held the light, towering over us thirty or forty feet in the air.

'This is beautiful,' I whispered.

We could hear men's voices raised in prayer and were led past an open courtyard where the monks were chanting, meditating on beads, like rosaries such as the Catholics use. A bell chimed a slow rhythm. It had a peculiar, clear tone that struck me as restorative and as we walked through the myriad courtyards I came to anticipate it. Each successive yard we passed through was littered with shrines around the walls, one for each of the priests, we later discovered. The stones were inlaid with incense, which burned constantly, sometimes billowing skywards, other times smouldering, the tiny puffs disappearing immediately. The whole place smelt of sandalwood, but here it was not a lonely scent.

At last, the boy bid us wait before two huge, wooden doors and disappeared for a few minutes.

'Deluded,' Robert commented, shrugging towards the shrines.

'I think they are lovely,' I said, still listening for the chime of the bell far off on the other side of several walls.

I do believe in kindness, if not in God, and this was the closest I was likely to come in a holy place to not being a blasphemer. I breathed in deeply and wondered if my soul might ever recover from what Robert and I had done in the mountains.

At length another monk appeared. He bowed low.

'We offer all travellers rest,' he said. 'You are welcome here. You are safe.'

These were just the words I wanted to hear. After almost four weeks fleeing through the hills I felt my body involuntarily weaken and my arms flop by my side.

We were allotted quarters – simple rooms that were clean. The monk who welcomed us had a stillness about him that reminded me of Bertie when he was listening. He spoke clearly with an air of reverence and was enormously kind to our injured bearer, helping him to the hospital. He invited us to dine at sunset, saying we would be collected from our rooms when the time was right. I lay for a while but I was curious and felt drawn to wander the courtyards. The chimes of the bell had ceased and prayer time was over. I surveyed the enormous statues, exotic Buddhas towering over the height of the walls. Hardly anyone was about: most I expect seeing to their business, for in monasteries such as this, each devotee has his chores. The beaten earth beneath my feet was a bright orange, darker than the novice's robes. This earth in China is called Dragon's Blood and is believed lucky.

After a while Robert came to join me. He surveyed the large, golden Buddha and then kicked at the dusty ground.

'We can stay here some days,' he said. 'I think it will do no harm, Mary. I imagine it is Christmas by now, you know. I should have counted the days more carefully and then we would be sure. But by my reckoning it is very close.'

I had forgotten. Our world had come to be regulated by the natural rhythms. Harvest time, planting time and the time for snow were more our measure than any specific day. All that was more than a thousand miles away. I thought now that in London there would be a stocking at the end of Henry's bed for this year he was old enough. Jane must have had the hallway decked with boughs and the children were surely singing carols. It struck me as strange.

'Henry will enjoy it,' I said.

Robert eyed me. He never mentioned his own children.

'Yes, Henry will be almost two, Mary. He will be walking. Talking perhaps.'

A tear trickled down my cheek. Robert reached out and touched me gently on the shoulder.

'We could have died,' I said. 'That's why we had to kill him.'

'We have been very lucky. I am sorry, Mary. The last days I have been thinking I should never have brought you.'

I shook my head.

'I chose it, remember? You let me choose.'

'Then we must put it behind us. Can you do that?'

'I will try,' I said.

Among the many plants they cultivated, the monks farmed bamboo and at dinner that evening they confessed that they had great difficulty with packs of wild boars that from time to time devastated the crop.

'We have sound alarms rigged in the fields,' one monk explained, using hand movements to illustrate his point.

'When the bells go off, we have squads of young monks with pitchforks who chase the animals and sometimes kill them.'

It struck me as amusing that these gentle people, who would never consider eating an animal, would slaughter any found among their crops and it transpired they even dug pits for the boar, with deadly stakes pitching up from the base.

'But if an animal dies we bury the carcass,' the man explained, seemingly unaware of the ethical minefield he was trampling. To be among such gentle men was heartening.

'I can hunt down some boar, if you like,' Robert offered. 'I have a gun.'

This caused a deal of excitement and it was agreed that any animals Robert killed could be eaten by our bearers on condition they cooked the flesh outside the monastery grounds. The monks had never before seen a firearm, of course, and some of the younger men in particular were eager to witness what such a weapon could do.

The next morning, wrapped against the winter weather, we set off across the hills with the gun. Beneath us we could see villages scattered in the monastery's wake and lakes on the valley floor where the locals fished for ling, using tubs rather than conventional boats. The tubs bobbed on the water, although they appeared tricky to steer, causing one or two crashes, which we witnessed from a distance.

The hills near the monastery were verdant even in winter and it was clear to see that in summertime it might be difficult to pass in some areas, the plants overgrowing the pathways. There were Japanese Cedar trees, figs and camphor plants. Sing Hoo dutifully took cuttings for the vasculum case while the three young monks who were accompanying us, keen to see Robert's gun in action, directed us along the best paths in search of the boar. After we had been out for three or four hours we stopped to refresh ourselves with fried vegetable dumplings that the monks had carefully packed in a wicker box. The men prayed before eating, simply thanking their god for the sustenance. Sing Hoo bowed his head and joined in.

'We never say grace these days,' I said as it occurred to me.

'You? Grace?' Robert teased.

'I know, I know. It is a nicer custom here though. I am at home with it.'

I was making my penances, I suppose.

I took my dumpling and wandered towards the edge of

the slope to peer over onto the pass below where I fell low to the ground, motioning to the others. Beneath us, a short way off, there were half a dozen boars, black and grunting quietly as they foraged in the undergrowth below. We had a perfect shot.

'Shhhh.' I motioned the others over.

Robert took aim. He fired twice quickly, killing one animal and wounding another as, squealing, it tried to run off into the trees. The other beasts fled. Beside me one young monk was jumping up and down with his hand to his mouth. The others looked equally shocked at Robert's crack shot and stared on in admiration. Although Robert had explained what would happen when he fired his weapon, the effect was far more exciting than they had evidently expected. The bearers also looked impressed and I thought it was no bad thing that they should see Robert's prowess with his weapon. Having made the kill we were too far away to track the boar any longer, for the herd had a head start on the lower pass, but Robert let the monks fire the gun into the earth, all being unwilling to fire it into anything deemed to be living, even a tree.

Sing Hoo and one of the bearers went to fetch the kill, stringing the carcass onto a stripped bough and carrying it over their shoulders. Hiking home, our men made for the wood outside the monastery and started a fire on which to roast their meat. Robert and I left them to this feast and proceeded inside where a vegetarian dinner was prepared and we were welcomed. Fragrant rice and a dozen exotic-looking vegetable dishes lay on matting alongside cups of hot tea flavoured with flowers. I sank down and was passed a bowl and chopsticks, ready to eat after a long day of walking and a welcome return to normality. The young priests chattered with their friends, eager to share their news and mimicking the gun's action. Robert sat directly opposite, already deep in conversation with one of the older men. This fellow, it turned out, had started his religious life at Tien T'ang Monastery, where many centuries ago tea was first exported to Japan by travelling monks who had tasted it on a pilgrimage.

'To Japan?' Robert was saying. 'What manner of tea was it?'

As I felt the hot drink revive me I found that I could follow Robert's thoughts, his line of questioning. What had the Japanese monks discovered? How did they process the tea leaves? I could anticipate each question before he asked it, and listened, rapt, to the old monk's replies. The image of the map we carried appeared in my mind's eye and I found myself wondering how long it might take us from Hong Kong to Japan when Robert met my eyes, seeing my idea clearly, and shook his head, smiling at my enthusiasm.

'Not this trip,' he murmured.

We passed a week at the monastery. Our bearer's leg finally recovered properly and, in fact, so did our spirits. Robert itemised his plants and, along with the tallow, figs and camphor from the hills, he found other fine specimens in the monastery's grounds.

'I think these will be the first plants to go to the west from this particular region,' he said. 'No one else has ventured here.'

Foraging daily, he found thistles exactly like those in Scotland, and also abelia, red spiroea and some more hydrangea to add to the other seeds, cuttings and herbarium specimens. Between us, we put everything in a special case and then duplicated it so that when we came to send it home two ships would bear the responsibility and the risk would be halved.

'You have become adept,' Robert said.

I certainly knew what I had to do. I liked that now I could set up a vegetable garden or a flower plot if I wanted. I liked that I recognised the different varieties of seed and could find the North Star, or even on a cloudless night tell which way was home from the lichens growing on the bark of the trees.

'Do you think it really is Christmas?' I asked.

Robert considered. 'Very close. I wish I had kept a log in more detail. Last year we never marked it together. I ate at the mess in Chusan. This year it is your choice, Mary. We can have Christmas here any day that you like. In fact,' he smirked like a schoolboy, 'we can have several.'

As I laid out the specimens I sang carols: 'God Rest Ye Merry Gentlemen' and 'Silent Night'. Robert joined in, his voice strong and cheerful. When we had finished with the plants, he stood up and bowed with a flourish.

'Might I ask for the pleasure of this dance?' he said. 'It is the Christmas Ball, after all.'

'At the Royal Horticultural Society?' I teased.

'Is your card quite full?'

'Of course. But I do happen to have one space. Now, in fact.'

He took my hand and led me to the 'dance floor', pretending to listen to the music.

'Ah,' he said to my giggling, 'a waltz!'

And we careened around to Robert humming an orchestral waltzing tune, which had been a particular favourite before we left London. We must have looked a sight. Two Chinese gentlemen waltzing around between the herbarium specimens. When the Chopin waltz had finished I was quite flushed. I curtseyed low, imagining myself in a beautiful, wide skirt that billowed around me, more fancy and fitting for the occasion. The clink of champagne flutes and the diamond brilliance of the chandeliers seemed not far off.

'Thank you,' I said.

Robert helped me up and kissed my hand before he led me back to the fireside. 'You looked radiant tonight, my dear,' he jested.

I pretended to take a fan from my pocket and spread it over my face so only my eyes could be seen.

'You are too kind.'

'You have been so brave, Mary,' Robert said. 'And I want you to know that I appreciate . . . Well, I appreciate it all.'

From his pocket, he handed me a box, a small ebony one.

'Merry Christmas,' he said. 'I had brought this to give you anyway. It seems the right time.'

'Robert.' I was shocked.

I had not thought to celebrate and the idea that Robert had even planned a Christmas gift showed unexpected foresight. I had never known him to care for such personal touches before. I fumbled to open the little box. Inside, nestling against a small piece of fuchsia silk there was a freshwater pearl mounted on a gold chain.

'I thought you could wear it. Underneath,' he said, gesturing with some embarrassment at my mandarin-collared silk top.

I put the chain round my neck. It was wonderfully kind of Robert.

'*Door jair*,' I said. Thank you for the gift. And I bowed, tears thickening the back of my throat. I would be dead if it wasn't for Robert, I was sure of it.

'Don't cry,' he reached towards me. 'It is only to thank you.'

'I am honoured,' I said, taking his hand. 'Truly. It is beautiful. I will wear it always.'

I wiped away my tears. Things had certainly changed. For better and for worse.

*   *   *

I loved our time at the monastery, short as it was. I spent my days talking to the monks and helping where I could with their tasks. One named Tang, an elderly priest with a fat belly and sparkling eyes, particularly interested me. He spent a large portion of his day meditating, rocking as he prayed, but when he was not engaged in such spiritual pursuits his main duty was to plan the monastery's meals. As such he knew the stores of rice and flour, what vegetables and fruits were in season and the traditions of feast and fast days and how to accommodate them. This seemed to endlessly delight him and when he received news of the day's production of bean curd, the preservation of eggs daubed in flavourings and buried, or how the soya sauce was fermenting, he would joyfully reel off the dishes that were soon to be prepared from each ingredient. The monastery fed hundreds each day: quite apart from the monks themselves and the occupants of the monastery hospital, alms were given usually in the form of rice to the poor who came to beg at the gates. Tang surveyed our supplies and ordered some sacks from his storeroom to augment our provisions for the journey. Robert offered to pay him, but it seemed the monastery was happy enough to gift us the food and see us on our way.

When it came time to leave I was sad, for unlike Ningpo or Hong Kong where I might well return, I knew that in all likelihood I would never see the monastery again. Robert had spent two days on the monks' farm and presented the gardeners with various seeds. These were for fruit trees they had never before cultivated. He also discussed with them at length an irrigation programme they would put into action in the spring and drew diagrams to help with the process.

As we wound down the tree-lined avenue in the early morning sunshine the monks rang bells in our honour and the crisp winter breeze invigorated our stride. It had been a wonderful Christmas but we still had a long way to go.

The sedan chairs had been strengthened, for the hilly ground was harsh on them. The joints had been reinforced and the sticks doubled in the monastery workshop, but due to the terrain I had not expected that we would use them routinely until we were well inside Fokien province. However, Robert had other plans. On the third day he stopped the party and insisted that we make a show to approach the border crossing between Kiang See province and Fokien up ahead, where there was an armed guard. Most people travelled on foot unattended, so our party, with two sedan chairs in use, would make quite an impression with the soldiers and the plan was that thus intimidated they should allow us to pass unmolested.

Robert and I mounted the chairs and covered ourselves in two sumptuous rugs which he had stowed for the purpose. Slowly our party limped towards the outpost.

'This will work well,' Robert said proudly.

In the event I wonder if the guards noticed us at all, for one was asleep at the crossing station and the other was engrossed in conversation with an older lady I assumed to be his mother.

'We might as well have ridden through with a company of the Highlanders!' I joked when we stopped two li up the road and loaded the chairs back on the carts.

'Lazy!' Robert snorted. 'Lucky for us.'

It still seemed to me comical that he considered laziness normal in Chinese soldiers as if our solid British troops never idled, all for duty and honour instead. I think it is true to say that in all our wanderings Robert never lost his sense of the Chinese being a different species and never saw them even as people really. It was not in his nature to identify the common concerns rather than the obvious differences.

Perhaps that protected him, I am not sure. But however different he considered the Chinese there is no question that their knives were sharp enough to pierce our skins and, had they known of us, those very same soldiers would have tracked us down and killed us.

In Fokien province there were a deal of hostelries by the roadside and when we reached the Bohea Mountains, which ran like a spine across the north of the region, we knew that we were over halfway. By Chinese New Year the weather had eased once more and we celebrated in a tiny village on the north side of the mountain range where there were musical entertainments and a procession with beautiful red and gold lanterns.

Never had I been anywhere so bleak and so wild. As the weather became warmer the snow and ice began to drip, shifting uneasily against the emerging earth. We were travelling over perilous ground. The thin, sludgy paths were overhung by snowy outcrops and we had to make progress carefully every step lest the snow should shatter above us and fall in deadly shards. One mule was almost swept away in this manner and it was only the sheer speed of one of the bearers' wits that saved her. It took half an hour to induce the terrified animal to move on again. I was shaken myself.

Most nights we camped, with the men mounting a watch by the fire, a shift of two hours' duration from which both Robert and I were excused, though for his part Robert still got up two or three times a night to check our safety. He slept with the gun loaded beside him and scouted for animal tracks rather than flowers. In the lowland safety of Ning-po I had wished for snow tigers and mountain bears. Here in the cold, cloudless nights I shivered at the thought. We seemed isolated and vulnerable. An animal could rip through the party with vicious ease and we had only one rifle and a roaring fire to protect us, for I was sure that the sabre-like knives carried by the men would be little use against animal ferocity. To get close enough to strike would mean fierce injury at least.

Robert found animal tracks all right, though always mottled at the edges, days old. Once we came upon a grisly, blood-stained, bone-strewn arena in the snow where two creatures had fought and one had been eaten by the other. It would take some time, I realised, before the evidence of the massacre either melted into the earth or became over-grown. The winter, it occurred to me, held on to atrocities, which lay unhealed and silent till the spring could melt them. We had left one of our own in our wake.

Now and again we came across a settlement with an inn. At Chin-hu it was the custom for men to bring their animals inside and the rooms were packed with goats and hunting dogs and even a cow or two. There was little food and no choice on the menu. I found it difficult to stomach the whole roasted pig – an animal cooked with its entrails intact, the belly sliced open with a flourish. I longed for the simple dumplings that Tang would have ordered at the monastery, for his spring greens and snow peas which had arrived piled on blue plates, steaming and delicious.

As we came, finally, to the south side of the slopes the trees were in bud and the earth waterlogged with melted snow. The carts got caught in the mud and we slowed even further, each mile an enormous effort. We berated the mules, pleaded, cajoled and beat them. We had to stop to mend the wheels at least twice a day. It was exhausting and very damp. My skin began to itch and my feet, already blistered and painful, felt as if they were set to melt into the sludge. It was miserable. Nothing we possessed was dry and we smelt of sweat and mildew. Each day I woke believing we would reach our destination by the afternoon. I dreamt of bathing, stepping out of the warm water and patting my skin dry. I dreamt of sleeping in a warm bed. Hill after hill, slope after slope, step after step.

Mostly we pressed on no matter the rain but once or twice we stopped and sheltered, for it drove too hard and we could thole it no longer. During one storm we came to a halt under the trees and found a band of other travellers – impoverished migrant workers heading south for the tea season where they might pick up casual work on the farms. Some travelled shoeless with a blanket slung over the shoulder. All were thin and cold. Travelling by foot, with far less to carry, they easily overtook us on the road and Sing Hoo informed us one man had told him the farms were a good week's journey and for us, of course, longer.

We rose in the darkness and made camp in the darkness, pressing on absolutely determined. Robert pushed me to travel by chair but the men were so exhausted that I would not hear of it and, besides, it would only slow us further. Every inch of me ached, every step an effort. By the last days I tasted nothing and I did not dream. We became a silent band of travellers for there was nothing to say and words were only an effort. Wang and Sing Hoo had long since ceased their usual bickering.

Then joyously, on the ninth day after we sheltered, we came upon a rice paddy cut into the hillside. By the tenth day there were several. Robert consulted his maps and announced we were very close. By our best reckoning we had left Hwuy Chow Foo in early November and it was now almost March. We had wintered for four months in the hills and were worse the wear for it. But our ordeal was almost over and, in another two days, at last we made it to Tsong-gan-hien, a small town beneath the great mountain of Wuyi.

We took lodgings, arriving like a rough crew, soaked in mud, the men irascible and the mules bony. The inn was built of wood, a huge dining hall with a balcony around it and, in another building behind, with suites of rooms for hire. Our mules were stabled and fed, our luggage stored safely, the men ordered hot baths and five grain spirit and, thank God, Robert and I were allocated rooms. We were given the best there was on offer – two tiny, wooden bedrooms. The small windows looked out onto the mountain, though on our arrival neither Robert nor I noticed the view.

We oversaw the stowing of the luggage and made sure the men were provided for. Then, at the peak of my exhaustion and on my way to see to myself, I tripped over the step at the very front door, falling hard onto the wooden boards. It took a second or two before I even registered the pain, hauling myself up and staring, disbelieving, at my ankle as if it had betrayed me. Robert came up behind me.

'Mary! What happened?'

I turned my eyes towards him and motioned, exhausted, at my foot. It was obvious.

'Help me up,' I asked, though as he did so it was clear the ankle was swelling and I could not put any weight on it.

'Here,' Robert offered and he pulled me into his arms. 'Come on,' he said, and carried me to my room, laying me on the bed. 'I cannot believe you made it over the hills and that the front step of the inn defeated you!'

We inspected the injury and, after moving my foot one way and another, realised that there was thankfully no breakage. I lay back and was glad that I was safe at last and that we had nowhere to go.

'I will bind it,' Robert offered. 'You must rest and in a day or two it will be fine. You only knocked it, that's all.'

I had no objections to resting. He must have been as

exhausted as I was but he found some muslin to use as a bandage and carefully wrapped my foot and ankle so they were supported.

'Thank you,' I breathed.

'Do you think you can sleep?'

I giggled and nodded. I was glad to be lying on a proper bed at last and I could already feel I was slipping away.

'Don't worry about me, Mr Fortune,' I murmured.

I slept for two days. When I woke they brought a tray of food. The stove in the corner of my lodging had been stoked and my luggage brought up. I ached when I moved but thankfully my foot was no worse than any other part of my body and I was ravenous. As I ate sitting up in bed there was a knock at the door and Robert entered. He had on fresh clothes and had made his toilet, looking fine, I thought, with a thin moustache in the Chinese fashion. When I moved I could feel the pearl he had given brushing against my skin on its thin gold chain. I was delighted to see him.

'I can scarcely believe we are here,' I cried out. 'We shall have black tea and in abundance. And the food is fine. Here,' I gestured a small bowl towards him with some kind of fish cooked in spices.

Robert waved it away. 'I have eaten. And eaten.' He smiled. 'I am glad to see you up. Since we arrived it has hardly rained at all. Not a drop. The soil is draining already. Are you well, Mary? How is the injury?'

I nodded. 'My foot is much better. A few days' rest and I will have recovered. How are the men?'

'Mostly drunk,' Robert admitted. 'They leave to go back in the morning. They think now the ice is almost melted and with less to carry they will be home in six weeks, in time for the second harvest. I have paid them a bonus, reminded them of the danger if they report us, and, all in all, they seem well pleased. They want to get back to their families now.'

'I could not imagine another step, I swear,' I said. 'Harvest or not.'

'We will rest,' Robert promised. 'There is much to see here in any case.'

'More specimens?'

'Oh, perhaps. But the hill itself will be a find. They say there are legends of lost spirits. I want to climb it.'

I cast a glance outside at the mountain. It was a lovely view – the slopes were green and the day bright.

'Robert,' I said. 'I just want to sleep.'

He took away the tray and I lay back on the cushions and closed my eyes. Robert sat by the window and I heard a book open as he settled to read. I could smell the plummy oil he used. His favourite. He could take Wang, I thought sleepily, and climb the mountain. I would wake later and we could dine then. I was already looking forward to it. I pulled the satin quilt around my shoulders and as I slipped again into unconsciousness I thought I heard him murmur something. Sweet dreams or somesuch. Then I heard him adjusting the position of his chair. He is going to watch over me, I realised as I drifted off. He is going to sit here while I sleep.

Chapter Ten

When I woke again it was dark, my room was empty and the hostelry silent. I crept out of bed barefoot, pulled a blanket around my body and sat by the window. I pushed back the screen and the view took away my breath. The full moon was low, silver and bright. Beneath it Wuyi Mountain was lit up, all green shadows. The scene was perfect, nothing out of place. There was not a breath of wind, so the faultless landscape stood unmoving and silent. The town seemed deserted. The houses and shops were closed for the night and there were no lights from any of the buildings and no one abroad on the streets. Everyone was asleep.

'It's magical,' I whispered under my breath.

In the morning the coolies rose with the sun. Our settlement lay along the Great Imperial Road and as soon as light dawned the thoroughfare burst into life with frenetic activity. It was easily as busy as Piccadilly.

Early, a maid came into my room to stoke the iron stove and, finding me awake, she hastened to fetch tea. This was different from the black tea one might expect at home, I noticed, and upon enquiry I found it was known as Luck-cha and was a mixture of the green and the black varieties. Commonly used in the region, it was never produced for export outside its borders and was quite unknown even elsewhere in China. Robert had clearly procured pure black tea for our use the other day but when I asked her the maid knew nothing of it. The Luck-cha was pleasant enough, however, and it suited me well. After all, I was between green tea and black tea myself.

After the maid left I hastened to make my toilet – finding a razor and shaving my head again, I sorted through the clothes laid out behind the screen and found something clean and suitable for the day. Then I donned a cap and a coat and, checking myself over in the small glass, I resolved to explore the settlement for myself.

It was cold outside but there was spring in the air. On the street, bright braziers were already alight and the shops and stalls were opening. I followed the dirt-paved thoroughfare, setting off in what seemed the most promising direction. As I strolled through town the buildings became larger and I found a *Tsin-Tsun*, a tea market, among the warehouses. This was an open marketplace with a small raised platform such as is often found in cattle markets at home. It was too soon in the season for even the earliest crop but still there seemed a good deal of trade in sealed boxes, which I assume were packed with seeds.

I passed through the warehouse district and, buying a bun from a stall with rickety bamboo wheels, I carried on my journey to the edge of town where the tea fields started on the slope of the mountain. The soil, I noticed, was very clay and a browny, yellow colour. Such a location was well suited to the cultivation of tea and the plants were coming along well, given the harsh winter they (and we) had endured. I noted that the drainage seemed excellent, given the conditions, and then I laughed at myself, for in my head I sounded like Robert. I licked the last crumbs from my fingers and proceeded to climb the hill a little way. The town receded and became quite picturesque, the smoke from its fires snaking upwards in pretty spirals. Bohea was certainly charming.

As I climbed I tried to make out our lodging house and to ascertain which window was my room. I found a large, flat stone on the path and sat to contemplate the settlement. Up on the hill one or two women were checking their crops but it was too early for the harvest and they merely nipped a dead bud here and there and moved on through the rows of plants. As I had seen in Chusan, one was carrying her baby all swaddled and bound round her with a long, brown cloth. Another kept her hands busy, weaving a length of matting from rushes she carried in a bag over her shoulder, only stopping now and then when she had need of her agile fingers to tend to a plant.

At length I walked back down and picked my way through the crowded streets to our lodging. Robert was up, eating fried eggs and sipping tea. As I entered, Sing Hoo placed a steaming cup in my hands and I wound my cold, pink fingers around it.

'Good morning,' I greeted Robert. 'I have been on the lower slopes this morning.'

'Did you see?' he asked.

'What?'

'You were in the tea fields? What did you notice?'

'That the women of Bohea are never idle,' I joked.

Robert slurped his tea. This habit of his used to annoy me, but curiously I had become accustomed to it.

'I realised yesterday,' he said. 'It took me a while too. Mary, it is extraordinary. They are the same plants. Exactly. I can find not one single variation from Hwuy-chow. Last night I cut up the roots, only to be sure that there wasn't any difference there. It's *thea viridis*. And all this time we believed there to be two species. But the difference between green and black is only in the processing. That is all.'

I cast my mind's eye back to my stroll on the slopes – of course the plants looked similar but I had not truly examined them.

'But then,' I concluded, 'we are here for nothing. For no reason at all.'

I sank down beside the table in a state of distress. I felt completely despondent – our long journey had been endured only for this.

'On the contrary,' Robert said cheerily. 'We are here to see what they do with these plants that results in tea that is so very different from the green variety. But it's true we will need little for the herbarium. Most of our time will be spent in the factories. I have had our sedans brought around and yesterday I sold the mules.'

'How long have we been here?' I asked, suddenly aware that I felt most disoriented.

Robert's eyes became gentle. 'Oh, Mary,' he said, 'this is our fifth day.'

As well as spending long hours at the local tea factories, Robert quickly made it his business to investigate the military garrison in the area, which was based over twenty miles from Tsong-gan-hien, away from the main stretch of farming land. The military presence in Bohea was far greater than we had had to endure before but it also seemed more self-contained, for the garrison did not use the town's facilities. Under the cover of an excursion with both Wang and Sing Hoo by his side, Robert collected plants from the fields around the barracks and returned with excellent drawings of the buildings and the means to calculate the numbers of men and horses, as well as the level of armament at the garrison's disposal. In Hong Kong they had very little detail available about the military this far inland and were not sure how the Chinese supply lines operated so Robert's information was no doubt invaluable, although here, certainly, the soldiers' main function appeared to be to keep the peace and enforce the law. The barracks was not at battle stations and, as far as we could tell, was not directing either troops or supplies towards the coast. By now, of course, Robert and I were both more confident in our disguises, and, having come through so much and having scared Wang and Sing Hoo sufficiently with our past experience, we felt ourselves equal to handling a garrison at a good distance. A wary kind of confidence in our survival had become the habit and, though it was more dangerous in Bohea than in Hwuy-chow, we were circumspect.

One day, highly excited, Robert returned from a surveillance expedition to the north of the garrison.

'There are soldiers' houses up by the river. I cannot work out what on earth they are used for,' he said.

'We could take a stroll nearby,' I suggested.

Robert hesitated. Thus far he had kept me well away from his espionage activities. While I guessed what he was up to and often saw his drawings or calculations, I still had no idea of the details – who the intermediary was who received his reports, or the precise meaning of his coded letters.

'You don't have to tell me anything,' I assured Robert. 'But a stroll by the river together can do little harm. Please take me with you this time. It will be exciting.'

We set off the next morning, taking Wang and some bearers, for it was best to travel by sedan chair on these longer journeys. It took two hours to reach the spot and, sure enough, there were a dozen strange conical huts scattered along the riverbank.

'*Ping*,' the chief bearer announced.

Soldiers. But there were no soldiers to be seen. We ordered to be set down and, taking Wang, we wandered in the general direction of the little settlement, discussing loudly the kind of plants we hoped to find. There was no activity around the huts – no coming or going and no sign of any cooking facilities or other habitation. The bearers settled down to wait, unimpressed by our little show. They drank some water from the stream and crouched by the sedan chairs in the shade while we walked on, picked some wild flowers and circled the huts at a distance.

'It is eerie,' Robert said. 'There is not a soul. Do you think they are storage huts?'

'It is odd to store supplies so far from the garrison and with no guard,' I pointed out.

'You stay here,' said Robert. 'Dig up that plant.' He pointed randomly to a berberis bush, which was growing a few yards away.

'Don't go,' I whispered nervously, realising that he intended to approach the huts.

He turned and gave me a stern look.

'Keep a look out, Mary, and get off sharp if you have to.' He winked and proceeded carefully towards the river, disappearing from view.

Wang began to move the soil around the berberis. The buds were formed and already they smelt lovely. I stood over him as he worked, in what might be termed a supervisory position, and glanced intermittently towards where I had last seen Robert. The place was indeed deserted.

To my relief, after ten minutes Robert reappeared, tearing up the hill towards us. He had a broad smile on his face.

'Mary,' he said gravely, when he arrived, 'do you think that the word for soldier might have another meaning too?'

'Why? What did you find?'

'Nothing Pottinger will care for! They are full of ice. Quite clever, in fact. The stuff must be brought down from the hill in the winter and then stored. There are troughs at the back for the melt to run off into the river. They are crammed with blocks cut from the hill over the winter.'

'Blocks of ice?'

'Yes. And there is a seal on the door, like a coat of arms. The huts belong to a mandarin family.'

Our eyes locked and we laughed. Wang regarded us plainly as if we were mad.

'Wang,' I asked him, 'did you know these were not soldiers' huts?'

Wang nodded. 'Yes, Master. They are for ice.'

Even as he pronounced it, the two words were so similar that it was obvious where our mistake had come from.

'And you thought we wanted to see these ice houses? Full of ice?'

Wang looked vacant. 'Yes. Masters always want to see everything Chinese. Masters like Chinese.'

I hesitated. I took his point. Such was our interest in the mundane details of Chinese life that it must have seemed not the least bit strange that Robert was excited at the idea of viewing storage houses for the local estate.

Robert smiled. 'We have wasted our day today.'

'Well,' I remarked, 'not if we remove this berberis. Look, Robert, it is quite exceptional.'

And between us we dug the plant from the soil and carried it back to where the sedans were waiting.

On our journey back to town we passed half a dozen officers riding towards the barracks. They nodded curtly as we passed, and Robert adopted the haughty expression that had served Sing Wa so well. Ordinary Chinese men were always nervous of soldiers, and our bearers stiffened as soon as the riders appeared. I kept my eyes straight ahead and did not acknowledge the men. We later learnt they had arrested some poor soul at the tea market and beaten him soundly for purporting to have tasted Dragon Well, the Emperor's own tea. Perhaps it was for the best that we had gone to see the ice houses that day and we scarce saw a soldier other than that.

Wang, having done his duty with regard to unpacking our things and settling us in, now requested permission to visit his family. We were stationed at quite some distance from his village, which he had pinpointed on our maps as being, by our reckoning, perhaps a week's walk and would take him across the path of the Wuyi River. Robert was not keen to give the man leave of over a fortnight, but to me it seemed only fair.

'Sing Hoo has given us far less service and we let him go home,' I pleaded.

Robert adopted an amused expression. He was not in the habit of caring about people. It is not that he was deliberately unkind, he simply did not make human considerations.

Over dinner, some days after the outing to the ice houses, we came to discuss it.

'Do you think Wang will return if we give him leave?' Robert threw his hands in the air. 'Do you?'

'Yes,' I said solemnly. 'If he gives his word, I think he will. Just as you would. And if you are so worried perhaps we should accompany him as we did with Sing Hoo.'

'A fortnight at least, Mary. How can we?'

'Well, I could go.'

Robert stared forlornly at the map.

'Alone?' he said.

'No. With Wang, of course. And an entourage.'

Robert considered this. 'No,' he said slowly. 'If anything happened to you . . .' His voice trailed.

'We should send him with gifts then, and some men to make him look grand. Give him an outfit, perhaps.'

261

'It is,' Robert raised his eyes heavenwards, 'as if you are staging an Easter pageant, for heaven's sake. Must you look after everyone?'

We argued on over the meal and it was only in the hallway at the very end of the night that Robert finally agreed that Wang could be given leave to make the trip. He was equitable by nature, only sometimes he took coaxing.

'All right. The man can go,' he said.

'He will thank you the rest of his life for that, Robert. Imagine being so close and not going, poor Wang. In the rush to change the world I would hate to think that he was trampled.'

Robert paused for a second.

'You know, Mary, in making me do all this, you make me a better man.'

He spoke slowly and then he bowed, acquiescing to me. 'Thank you.'

'Oh, nonsense,' I dismissed him, 'don't beatify me for something that should be normal. Your conscience would never let you behave any other way, if only you thought about it.'

I smiled though and, I admit it, felt rather saintly.

The next day Robert made the arrangements, sending Wang with a couple of local men who would certainly want to return to their families. I noticed that in giving Wang the good news Robert emphasised the bonus the man would receive when we reached the coast at the end of our journey.

'You are wily, Mr Fortune,' I teased him.

Robert only smiled.

'For your information, Mary,' he continued, 'I am writing to Dr Jamieson who will be in charge of the tea gardeners that I am engaging to take with me to India. I will leave them there in his charge. I am insisting on excellent terms for the fellows. I thought it would save us a spat.'

My face cracked into a grin that I could not contain as Robert continued.

'They will be away for at least five years by the time their skills are no longer needed. Knowing your views on India,' he paused, 'having avoided it yourself at all cost, I thought it only prudent to make arrangements of which you would approve before you came to champion their cause. Not that I don't enjoy our discussions.'

I let him tease me.

'I'm proud of you, Robert,' I said.

The six tea gardeners (all single men) and two lead men (both married) who were engaged for the posts were given assurances and a substantial advance to compensate their families.

We gave Wang leave to be away for seventeen days. I organised a new outfit for him and sent plants (some fruit trees this time), money, perfumes, an excellent soapstone carving of a dragon and two baskets of live chickens for his family. As Wang packed, Sing Hoo skulked, sneering poisonously. 'Master came to my village,' he said as Wang organised his provisions onto a cart we had hired for his journey. To his credit Wang ignored his rival and, as we waved the cart off, Sing Hoo's toothy grin seemed to linger, like a grotesque.

'Never coming back,' he whispered.

In Wang's absence we continued our work. Robert completed his study of the production of black tea, noting that the difference between black and green was particularly in the fermenting stage, as the leaves in Bohea were allowed to fully break down in the storage baskets before being heated, rolled, dried and then sorted for quality. This process took longer than for the green variety, with the rolling and airing method lasting anything up to three days before the leaves were fired on a slow, steady heat to remove the last of the moisture.

Many of the tea farmers also owned fields of scented flowers, and these we decided to visit. The flower plantations were set on low, flat land and were somewhat haphazardly laid out some two days' journey from the hilly country where the prime crops were planted. The scent as we approached was marvellous, wafting from miles away before the trees themselves even came into view. I lay back in my sedan and breathed in. As we got closer the sight was breathtaking – there were acres and acres of flowers – I had never seen anything like it. The blooms from these farms were in their turn dried and added to the final tea to make varieties such as Pekoe and Jasmine, which are both, of course, very popular in England.

'If I had to pick a job to do out here,' I said to Robert, as we walked through the banks of jasmine, 'I would choose to work here.'

When the first tea harvest of the year was finished and the precious leaves processed and packed, Robert had all he needed and our time came to remove. Wang still had not returned from his village and neither had his escorts. The men had now been away from the settlement for more than three weeks and the second crop of leaves was unfolding on the tea plants. The weather was fine and we could see no reason for the delay.

Sing Hoo took to pointing out Wang's absence by lingering by the window or the doorway as if he was eagerly checking for his rival's homecoming.

'Not yet,' he said, peering into the distance, affecting to be dreadfully troubled and concerned for Wang's safety.

Robert said nothing, although he had begun checking through what needed to be packed. We would travel eastwards to the coast now and make for the nearest British port. We wanted to make the journey in the mild weather if possible, rather than once more facing a winter caravan. Organising bearers, transport and the packing of our not inconsiderable baggage could not be achieved in the allotted time by Sing Hoo alone, who, despite both men sharing all the duties we could provide them, was more of a gardener and cook than a logistician. I began to worry that I had jeopardised our mission and that Robert had been right, but there was nothing for it – we simply had to wait.

I passed my time as usefully as I could and while Robert was taken up with the last of his investigations I wandered the outlying areas to see what I could find for myself. High up in the hills, where the tea farms tailed off, one day I found myself at a small dwelling. The layout of it intrigued me – there was a tiny house and much larger outbuilding but no sign of the tea processing that was taking place further down the hill. I knocked on the door but there was no reply so I made my way over to the large shed and, as I approached, I could hear that there was some activity inside.

The farm was peopled by three very elderly ladies who were most perturbed when I came to the door. They shouted at me instead of speaking normally. I reassured them that I was lost and only looking for directions back to the town. Still, one of them tried to shoo me away, waving her hands in the air as if I was a chicken who had strayed. I did not move and glimpsed inside the shed where I saw to my delight that the old women had a press for making oil. This was quite up my street.

'Will you sell me something to eat, perhaps?' I asked over the din.

I thought it would engage them, at least. Two of the women were now squabbling over my presence and one

265

was loudly telling the other off for shouting. I drew a string of *cash* from my pocket that stopped them in their tracks, elicited toothless grins from all three, and sent them scurrying into the house to make rice and tea and even provide some strips of mango.

As I ate at a small table out in the yard, I asked a few idle questions of the sisters. Once they had established I was not a threat, they became quite helpful. They were pressing tea seeds to make oil, they said. Further up the hill a variety of closely related camellia plants grew wild and the old ladies harvested these. The oil was used for cooking and they let me taste a little.

'Ahhh. My master does not use this oil on his estate. I have not come across it before.'

I bought a flask.

Having, as they saw it, nothing else to sell, two of the women retreated into the shed, bored with me and clearly intent on getting back to work. They left open the door and, I noticed, were employed packing the dry, crushed seeds that had been mangled by the press into rough burlap bags. These they stored at the end of the warehouse.

'What are they for?' I pointed, asking the remaining sister who lingered at my side.

'They buy it down the hill over the winter,' the old lady explained. 'For the tea plants. It is good for the soil. They mix, mix, mix and then the next year it makes a good crop.'

Something stirred inside me. This was certainly something Robert could employ.

'I'll take a bag of that too,' I said airily, pulling out my *cash*.

That evening I arrived back at the inn with my purchases and breathlessly explained to Robert what I had found. The oil was of less interest, but Robert's eyes lit up when I opened the small burlap sack and showed him the powdered tea seed.

'Perhaps it is this that makes the Chinese tea bushes thrive where the Indian plantations have so far been unsuccessful,' he mused. 'We never would have found it for we have not been at the tea farms over the winter.'

'It was only a press,' I said. 'Easy enough to manufacture.'

'Well done, Mary,' Robert grinned. 'This is invaluable. Invaluable.'

I am sure I glowed.

As Robert considered our immediate practical plans and the logistics of our caravan, and we waited for Wang's return, I ran out of little trips of my own and came to linger at the lodging house. Being unoccupied over several days, I soon turned my mind to what was going to happen on the longer term. After all, what was I to do? Our journey would soon be over.

Staying close to the inn, I climbed Wuyi Mountain and surveyed the emerald hills and the tiny town below. I swam wherever I could, enjoying the icy mountain water, cool against my skin. When we arrived back in a British port must I again grow my hair and adopt the life of the respectable, unmarried lady? Would I return to Hong Kong or, as an English woman, travel to India with Robert's entourage and our beloved plants? Might Robert consent to take me to London and, if so, did I want to accompany him? There was a life for him in Kensington, with his newly-developed trade concerns and the horticultural lectures that would doubtless be demanded of him, but for me the thought of London was intolerable and I was all too aware that back in England I would find myself alone, passing my days reading and staring at the back garden. That is, if William even consented to my presence. To return in secret to the shallows of Drury Lane left me equally as horrified now. Either way it was to be half dead, surely. And I knew my sister would not understand any of it. Indeed, I wondered if it was because she had everything she desired that she could not see what was now so clear – I needed to fulfil my own nature. For Jane, I thought, it was like how, with a full belly, it is hard to appreciate another person's hunger. Whereas, to my own mind, I was not bad any more or wild either – I was merely different.

After a week of considering this for myself, I chose to broach the subject with Robert one night over dinner. Sing Hoo had procured some duck and roasted it, serving the aromatic, seared flesh with a delicious, spiced-lychee chutney and wilted greens. We ate slowly, savouring the dish and sipping hot Jasmine tea. Robert murmured with each new mouthful. He had spent the day up on the hill and was duly ravenous. I was taking tiny bites because I did not want to become too full and have to stop eating. Sing Hoo had truly surpassed himself.

'So. We have triumphed,' I started.

Robert grinned openly and took his teacup in hand, by way of a toast.

'Maybe,' he said, and then, smiling, 'Almost. We certainly have everything we need – apart from Wang, of course. All that remains is to leave Chinese borders.'

'A trifling detail!' I waved my hand.

Joking aside, it is true that neither of us were concerned with this particular journey. After all, we had travelled four times the distance inland that it would take us to get to the British port of Foo Chow Soo on the coast. The terrain was not as rough as the mountains had been or, indeed, an unknown quantity, such as we had encountered when we started our trip. It was still dangerous, of course. We remained in breach of Chinese law and would be on our guard until we left Chinese waters entirely, but we both felt confident that we would make it.

'In all I have bought over a thousand pounds' worth of goods and they are all dispatched,' Robert said. 'Quite apart from what we have collected for free. I'd say we are well in profit, Mary.'

He had only the day before done his accounts. Although some of the money used to purchase the goods was borrowed, the profits would be grand enough to pay back these debts and still make a tidy sum.

'And you are for Hong Kong and then to India?'

'For a short while,' Robert agreed. 'Certainly.'

I laid down my chopsticks.

'And, Robert, what of me?'

There was silence. I had taken him by surprise. Robert tried to speak but no words came. He stumbled. I could not believe that he had not thought of this. Once or twice he raised food to his mouth, but he could not bring himself to eat it. At length he blurted.

'Well, Mary, it will be up to you, of course.'

I sighed and tried to hide the tears in my eyes.

'Back in a corset,' I burbled.

It was not what I wanted, but what else was there? I felt both hopeless and helpless. Robert leant over, offering me his handkerchief to dry my tears.

'No. No, Mary. We will think of something,' he tried to comfort me. 'You have looked after everyone else. Now it is *your* turn.'

'But what can I do?' I sniffed.

'Well, first, I think we must know what you truly desire. For then our plan can as closely resemble your wishes as we can manage. I know you might not like to return to London – but you could. You would be able to lecture at the Royal Society as much as I am, you know. I mean, they will certainly want you to. And I intend to write a memoir of the journey and will need an editor.'

The tears were coming fast now. I did not give a fig for lecturing at the Royal Society or tidying up Robert's notes. What I wanted was to do this, to travel and adventure while still having a mission. To be free and yet feel worthwhile. I could not manage to say so, however. And besides, I thought it impossible. How could I travel as a mandarin alone? And what would be the point? I would have nothing to do!

In the absence of any real solution Robert disappeared into his room and came back with a hip flask of spirits.

'I stowed this in Ning-po. It is the last of it,' he said, tossing out the tea and pouring a measure into the porcelain cups. 'Now, Mary, we will find you a plan. Never fear. Let's drink to it.'

I sniffed and put the brandy to my lips. It smelt good and tasted very smooth after a long time of nothing but the occasional dose of rice wine and five grain spirit. I could feel it travelling down my throat and lighting a fire in my belly.

'Thank you,' I smiled.

Robert touched my hand. 'I can't imagine what it would be like, if you were not . . . had not accompanied me.'

This, for some reason, made me calm again. Perhaps it was because I knew that he understood what I meant; that is to say, what the journey had meant to me.

After dinner we decided to walk around the town to pass the time and soothe my nerves. We strode out, soon finding ourselves at the very fringes of the place, where the farms spread out from the buildings. At this end of the settlement there was a rough inn, which seemed uncommonly busy that night. The end of the first harvest had seen many of the farm workers paid their first proper wages and the men were out celebrating. In the courtyard there was some kind of cock-fight taking place with gambling on the outcome. Inside the men were gaming with dice. Spirits were high. Around the bar loose women, wearing red satin with their glossy hair piled up, were plying their business, accepting drinks from the men and, I was sure, taking them upstairs to one of the beds for hire if they would pay for it. It was greatly in contrast to the majesty of the hills, which spread out into the darkness. To one side was all that light and warmth and life, and on the other the majestic, black depth.

'Let's climb up here,' Robert suggested, hauling me up the first hillock, which had a pippala tree at its peak. I followed him, and we sat on our haunches side by side, staring down at the settlement and the activity at the inn.

'From a distance it is difficult to believe anyone has any troubles at all, isn't it?' he said.

I nodded. I had been climbing the mountain for days now for that very reason.

'We will think of something for you, Mary. I promise. Please do not feel that I don't consider you. I do. I know in the past I have failed in that. I realise now that I should have stood up for you. Even as far back as London. I should have challenged that man. He behaved disgracefully. But you know that. You always did. And you had no one on your side. Not really. I'm sorry for that.'

'Thank you,' I said. 'But you took in Henry and I, Robert. You and Jane. There was no need to duel on my behalf as well. And now I cannot even wish that I had not been banished. For look at all we have done. I don't know what we will find that will replace these wanderings, but if anyone can think of something, I know that with our heads together, we will.'

Robert smiled. 'Yes,' he said.

Beneath us, the light glowed golden from the buildings and we sat for a while watching the scene at the inn unfold as if we were giants looking down on a tiny village for our amusement. We could see several workers we recognised and had fun picking them out. One man was very drunk and blundered around near the bar while another was regaling one of the prostitutes with a story. It pleasantly diverted my attention from my predicament, until we both observed that there was a commotion in the courtyard and quite suddenly the tone of the revelries changed. I stood on tiptoes to get a better view while Robert hiked up on a rock nearby. Two men who had been gambling on the birds were now fighting each other. A circle formed around them.

'I swear,' said Robert, 'the Chinese will bet on anything!'

But the tenor of the voices as they wafted towards us soon demonstrated that the fight had become particularly vicious. We heard screams and then one of the men struck the other, who fell over, covered in a dark slash of blood. A wailing set up as the men realised one of their own had been killed and the murderer dashed from the inn with a bloody machete in his hand, chaos in his wake, and a man I recognised from the fields set off in hot pursuit of the murderer, who disappeared into the inky blackness on the other side of the inn. Without stopping to think, I moved towards the settlement.

'Come on,' I said. 'We must help.'

Robert grabbed my arm.

'No,' he said firmly. 'It is too dangerous, Mary. This is not a time for your soft heart. Lots of people witnessed what happened there and at closer quarters than you or I. They will deal with it. Come. We can go back to our lodgings along the hillside. It is a long way but it will bear us from the scene of the crime.'

I hesitated a moment, but I followed Robert into the blackness. How quickly, I noted to myself, things can go wrong. Your own problems can seem serious but measured against events they pale into inconsequence. A man had died right in front of us, for nothing or next to it – a gambling debt.

Sure enough word spread quickly, for along our dark and circuitous route back to the lodging house there soon came galloping horses. Soldiers from the barracks, we guessed. They must have been summoned by fire signals or drums, for there had not been enough time for a messenger to make the journey out past the ice huts bearing the news. We could hear the riders from half a mile off, hammering along the track at a gallop.

Once more, Robert's wits were about him and he pulled me from the path.

'Out of the way,' he said. 'If they see us they will stop us. Better by far to dodge them.'

We pulled in under a strangely shaped rock with an outcrop, bundled out of sight. It was a very small space and we were jammed in tightly.

'Quiet!' Robert motioned as the riders came closer and we froze, hardly breathing, listening as the horses passed on the road, catching only a flash of military uniform and the smell of the stables as they pounded past.

When they had gone the sound of galloping receded into the blackness. Neither of us moved. That night things changed quickly and forever in the cool air of the Bohean Hills. I have no idea how long we stood, Robert and I, closely packed against each other. My heart was pounding, not from the soldiers or the murder, nor the brandy, come to that. Or even my silly plans. For time seemed to stand still and I was lost. Close all of a sudden, I could smell him. I could feel him. And we were looking straight at each other, eyes bright in the darkness. Completely still.

For sometime now I had known that I cared for Robert, of course. But here, in this very small space, I realised that my emotions were those due to one who was not only a friend or a brother, but a man. Someone who listened to me, helped me, inspired me and guided me. Who'd saved my life.

After an agonising time, Robert took my hand, and I gasped. He ran his fingers down my face. And I knew that it wasn't only China, or the freedom or the adventure I had fallen in love with. All these months it had been him. The revelation was more shocking to me than any murder. I thought of the night I had woken to find him sitting against the tree or the evening after I had first shaved my head and our hands had touched, sending sparks of electricity through my body. The realisations came fast and there were many of them. The way Robert had watched over me as I slept through the first days in Bohea, the joking and the kindnesses. My mind was crowded with tiny signals I had not even registered at the time and yet, here, I could see and feel him and I knew that this had been coming, even if I had not known it was on its way. Now he leant his forehead against mine and all thoughts disappeared. I so longed to kiss him that I could hardly breathe. Everything else was gone from my mind except his heartbeat and my own. I searched his eyes to see if he felt it too.

He nodded.

I brushed my lips against his, slowly, and I felt myself melt. He took a long, agonised breath and pulled me closer before kissing me hard. Passionately. For a long time. Over and over. His hand cradled the small of my back and I could feel how strong he was. I brushed my fingers over his cheek and then he kissed my neck, sending shivers coursing through me.

'My God. My God.'

At length he pulled back. And only then we realised what we had done. We were caught, both of us, between ecstasy and horror.

'For months now,' he started, but could go no further, his agonised face lit up in the moonlight. 'I think you are the most beautiful woman on earth.'

I could feel my skin flush, still tingling from his touch. My heart was leaping somersaults. I knew Robert. I trusted him. My whole body was quivering with desire. What is there in the world if love is not possible? And yet, how could we?

'We will never speak of this,' I decided, pulling back. It was impossible.

Robert nodded. 'Yes,' he said. He knew it was wrong as much as I did. 'Quite right.'

But I would have given anything, that moment, for him to have been free.

As we walked towards the road I saw him reach out and touch the side of the rock where we had been pressed as if he wanted to take the sensation with him. I could not meet his gaze. I always thought of love as it had been with William. Flowers. Baubles. Promises. The glamour of a title and a string of private carriages. My world had been shallow, I admit it. China had brought me greater depth. And now I had, for once, no stomach for adventure, though I was already pining to touch him again despite the shame of it. In truth, I was afraid even to look at him. God knows where that might lead us. I was walking on air, stunned. This would change everything, and I knew I had to be strong. Already the thought of lying in the bedroom next to his had me half-terrified, half-elated. Robert had taught me so much, brought me so far and set me free.

'I must ignore it,' I swore to myself.

But all I could think of was the pounding of my blood and the way I had melted, looking into his beautiful eyes.

Along the road, acutely aware of each other and only a

foot apart, we tramped in sullen, agonised silence. The pearl he had given me for Christmas seemed hot against my skin now. I could not look to my right at all – could not as much as turn my head towards him. Oh, Jane! The shame! That night, I swore, I would pray. I would get on my knees beside the open window and beg for the strength to make everything as it had been before. All the months, we had had so much together. Surely that would be enough. For what had happened with Robert, even a glimpse of it, was an adventure too far.

Chapter Eleven

The moment I woke the next morning it seemed like any other day until the memories flooded back. I could hear Robert moving in the room next door to mine, and I pulled the cover tightly around me, my eyes darting. I felt a deep yearning for him, just as much as the night before, only as the pale light fell in streams through the window my shame was even greater than it had been in the dark.

I was determined to ignore what had happened. Trying to hold onto my memory of what it had been to wake on any other morning of our journeying together, I jumped out of bed to the small mirror on the table and desperately attempted to arrange my features into a cheerful countenance. I imagined blithely discussing the route overland to Foo Chow Soo, or enquiring after a consignment of pretty lacquer boxes I had chosen to dispatch to the auction house. It was useless. All I could think about were the kisses. They were vivid in my memory. Divine – or rather, satanic. I cursed myself and once more threw poses in the tiny mirror of the easy intimacy we had enjoyed for so long. Each made my heart sink further. The longer I dwelled on what had happened between Robert and I, the more I realised that we had had a great deal more than a mere friendship for a long time. I had been a fool.

'Whatever I feel, I must mask it,' I swore, reaching for my clothes.

As I completed my dress I was startled by a rapping at the door so urgent it made the hinges shake. My brother-in-law was clearly not for ignoring what had happened and was in some kind of passion. My heart beat faster.

'Oh, Robert,' I whispered, intent immediately on composing myself.

I swore inwardly that I would say as little as possible.

'Come in,' I called nervously, my voice high.

Such was my relief when it was Wang alone who entered the room that I sank onto a little chair behind me. Wang bowed very low. He had left the door wide open in his wake and through it I glanced into the hall for any sign of Robert. I was on such tenterhooks that I neglected to ask poor Wang where he had been all this time, or welcome him back from his weeks of absence. After a moment or two, Wang realised that he would have to commence any exchange and, I suppose, took my silence for fury. He fell to his knees and kowtowed at my feet.

'Please, Master,' he started. 'So sorry. Please.'

'Oh, yes, Wang,' I motioned him to rise. 'Of course. Get up. Get up.'

He did so sheepishly.

'You are late returning to Wuyi Mountain,' I said without feeling. 'It has inconvenienced us greatly. Where have you been?'

In truth, I couldn't have cared less. My eyes were fixed on the door of Robert's room – I could not tear them away. Wang looked as if he might fall once more to his knees.

'Bridal celebration,' he murmured shyly, his shoulders rounding in.

'Ah. Blessings on your clan,' I replied, as was the custom. Wang smiled.

278

'Master,' he said. 'It was a celebration for my bride.'

'Oh,' I exclaimed in surprise.

It occurred to me that there was perhaps something in the Bohean air that had ignited romance.

'Oh, Wang. *Gong-tsi*.' Congratulations.

I took my eyes from the hallway for a mere second in surprise and, of course, it was then that Robert emerged from his room and, seeing Wang bowing down in thanks to me, he burst into a rage.

'Where have you been, Wang?' he shouted as he advanced into my bedchamber without so much as a glance in my direction. 'You have held us up intolerably! You are over three weeks late.'

'Robert,' I smiled, though it felt as if my heart had stopped at the sight of him. 'The man has married. Wang is in love.'

This took the wind out of Robert's sails and he glanced awkwardly at the floor.

'Oh, very well, Wang,' he mumbled. 'But your private affairs,' here he paused, suddenly gauche, 'your private business can hold us up no longer. We are packing to leave. You must be about it, Wang.'

Wang nodded and made for the door, only halting as I called him to enquire, with seeming lightness.

'What is your lady's name, Wang? Where is she?'

Making such an enquiry felt better than having to face Robert. I was keen to calm my nerves and let him relinquish his passion and anger before we had to speak. The best way to achieve this was polite small talk, though I could not think of a single pleasantry I could direct towards Robert. Now, by the door, the man looked flustered at my question. In China there are many superstitions regarding pride in achievements or family. Parents often demean their children so the evil spirits will not take an interest in them. To a European such reticence denotes gaucheness, but for the Chinese it is self-protection. Wang did his best to shield his bride's identity.

'She is a simple woman. She was widowed and when we were children we knew each other. She is at my home village still.'

'Good, good. What is her name?'

He paused for a second, glancing to his left as if checking for a malevolent Chinese sprite who would bear the news away to the underworld.

'Soo-yi,' he said in a low voice.

'May she bring you great happiness and many sons. I expect you would like to know we will have only a few more months together. You will be dispensed of your duties at Hong Kong once everything is embarked. You will be able to return then to your village and you will be a rich man.'

Wang could not contain the grin that broke out on his face.

'Thank you,' he said gratefully, and quit the room to turn his attention immediately to the caravan of boxes and packing cases that was forming in one of the stables.

Robert and I were alone. We stared at one another. I hid behind the mask I had composed.

'Mary,' he started. 'It is I who should be on my knees before you, not Wang. I am sorry. I apologise absolutely for my dishonourable behaviour.'

He regretted what had happened. My stomach sank.

'For many weeks,' he continued, 'many months, in fact, my regard for you has grown.'

He was short of breath and I could see tears in his eyes. This was sheer torture.

'The truth is that what we have shared is something I do not wish to be without. Ever. And yet . . .' His voice trailed.

'Please,' I cut in on him frantically. To see him moved so made me panic. I had to stop him. The truth was that in my heart I regretted what we hadn't done as much as what we had. Now I had given vent to my feelings, I did not want to let them go, even though I knew I must. I would. But the words were too difficult and I did not want either to hear them, or say the cursed things myself.

'Please. Stop.'

I gesticulated and as I did so I knocked the mirror behind me and it crashed to the floor, shattering and making me jump.

Robert smiled. His shoulders relaxed and he laughed.

'Look at us,' he said. 'We are both so nervous and you look like a frightened child.'

'How can you?' Tears of shame filled my eyes.

I felt so foolish. So exposed. Though I knew the affair was impossible, it still felt like a rejection to have him here, apologising for loving me, and jolly at my expense. My emotions were in a jumble and suddenly I was angry as much as guilty or repentant or desperate for his touch.

'How can you laugh?' I snapped.

Robert was beside me before I could protest and took my hand. I pulled it away again, though my temper was subsiding into a morass of self-pity. Why did everything I touch turn into such a mess?

'This whole thing is impossible. We have spoilt it all,' I murmured.

'I am sorry.' He tenderly wiped the tears from my cheek.

'I just don't know how to bear not having you,' I whispered.

We weighed each other with our eyes. It felt as if I had lost everything. I realised now that the intimacy of our journey together could never be the same as it had before. Everything was changed and in its place a dangerous depth we were forbidden.

'I have nothing worthwhile to offer you,' Robert breathed. I sank back onto the chair.

'Robert, you have given me the greatest freedom and adventure I have ever known. I cannot regret that gift. Coming to know you, well, I have never had such a friend.'

'And then I dishonour you,' he berated himself.

'It is no dishonour.'

'But I cannot marry you.'

That he had thought of this caught my breath. No one before had ever wanted to. My eyes fell to my ring finger. If he had been unmarried, would he have slipped a ring onto my hand?

'But Henry,' I whispered. 'Even if you were free . . .'

Robert shrugged his shoulders at the disgrace of a child born out of wedlock.

'I do not care what you have done, only who you are.'

He surprised himself with this statement. His face looked shocked as he knelt in front of me.

'Damn it. It is *I* who is unworthy of *you*. I am a married man and yet I have never wanted anything for myself as much as I want this,' he said. 'And you are the very person I cannot have . . .' His voice trailed.

He gave up trying to explain himself and laid his head in my lap, like a child seeking comfort. I stroked his smooth scalp, winding my fingers through his ponytail. How could I have been so blind with all my worldly ways, not to see it? And if I had would it have mattered – this man was married to my sister. My own, dear Jane.

'I cannot wish away my children, my responsibilities,' he whispered, 'but this is my life now. You are my life, Mary. I do not know what to do.'

At length he rose.

'I must see to business,' he said brusquely, as if it was an apology.

I nodded, disappointed. Robert turned and quit the room. I hadn't the heart to clear up the shattered glass at my feet and instead moved to the window. I positioned myself in sight of the mountain, though I admit my eyes fell and I watched when Robert left the main building and made his way towards the stables where Wang had already put several bearers to work, moving our preparations up a gear. Robert turned and looked up at me as he reached the open wooden doors across the yard. My heart was pounding as he disappeared inside.

I stayed in my room all morning. There was a great deal to blame myself for. I did not want to feel pulled towards the window in case I should catch sight of him again but I rose every few minutes just to see. I did not want to look at the family photograph I kept inside the front cover of the *Ch'a Ching* nor did I want to hide it away. I did not want to give up my wonderful adventure and yet it would never be the same again. Things had been blighted, without any question, and yet I had never felt so truly alive. What had happened was no midnight mistake and a night's sleep had brought no respite from it. I had spent my entire life, I realised, emulating feelings, acting not only on stage but off it too. What had happened up on the hill was a result of my first real feelings. Anything else I had ever experienced shrank in the face of them. I cursed the whole, damned drama of it.

Early in the afternoon Robert returned.

'Business go to hell,' he said, 'I cannot concentrate, Mary. It is as if there is a cord tied between us.'

We stood then for a while on each side of the room, in silence. After a while he moved forwards a step. So did I. Each glance, each unashamed, slow blinking, stare was like a caress.

'We are doing something very wrong,' I said. 'Even looking at you, Robert, seems indecent.'

'Jane must never know.'

I nodded.

'We will never be able to marry,' he breathed.

'The need for that is all very far away, Robert.'

'I swear I will love you forever. I swear I will never let you down. It is death alone that will part us, whichever path we follow. There is a cord between us, Mary.'

He did not need to say it, spoken or not, I knew. We were giving ourselves up to this, one way or another, for the rest of our lives.

We kissed for hours, though it seemed mere moments from the time his lips touched mine, until Sing Hoo knocked on the door and brought in the dinner as the light faded from the sky. Robert was tender and slow in his attentions and this lit a passion in me beyond anything I had ever known. I can truly say we left the world behind and what passed between us in that little room was our own whole universe. Nothing else mattered. His body was strong and I ran my fingers along his arms and down his chest. It felt so different from the softness of my own form – his lines angular and mine curving gently. We were still clothed when we ate dinner slowly and in silence, feeding each other roasted meat and ripe peaches and unable to look away. This passion was unlike any other I had known. My lovers before had been directed towards only the end of their satisfaction. Now, me touching Robert and him touching me was satisfying in itself.

After the food was gone Robert closed the shutters and fetched thick, satin quilts from his bedroom, which he laid over the mattress, the bright colours shining in the golden glow of the oil lamps. He lifted me up and lay me on the bed he had made, kissing my lips, my eyelids, the crook of my neck.

'My wanton love,' he murmured.

I longed to feel his skin against mine, and, enjoying every second, we undressed each other slowly and explored, kissing everywhere till we became so entwined that there was scarce a difference between one body and the other, and I was lost in ecstasy.

It was like floating on a high cloud. Like flying. My limbs felt light and my spirit soared. We stroked each other, confident and gentle. When we had kissed so much that my lips tingled he pulled back for an instant and then lay on top of me. I moaned with pleasure and gently, with mounting intensity, he tupped me till the sweat dripped from us and I was screaming his name. Afterwards he held me close and kissed my hair, breathing in deeply and taking in my scent. He pulled a quilt to cover us and we were almost asleep when a maid came with some tea and buns.

'What is this?' Robert roared at the intrusion.

The girl kept her eyes on the floor and, I must admit, looked horrified. To her, I suppose we were two gentlemen, and though such things were accepted in China they still merited a level of shock, especially, I suppose, in one so young. The girl silently crossed the room, opened the shutters and then scampered out again, her hand to her face. The sun had risen again, in fact, it was quite high. We had been up all night.

As she closed the door we heard first whispering and then giggling outside. A moment later I heard Wang telling Sing Hoo. After the giggles there was a whispered 'they both look like men – poor girl!' and then another rattle of laughter. This is the first time they have been united in anything, I thought to myself.

Robert and I ate breakfast in bed before exhaustion took us.

'I have never known such passion,' I whispered to him.

285

I felt shy.

'I have never known such love,' he returned, a cheeky smile on his face.

I thought of my mother and my father, rolling downhill together. I thought of how lucky I was to have found my match. I thought how Jane did not like what Robert did to her, and I was glad of it. I'd never have another man again. One night with Robert was worth a thousand shallow suitors with their tawdry desires or a million declarations of devotion from those titled tomcats I had been accustomed to. I was utterly contented. Such a night cannot be shaken from a woman's memory. Such a night changes one's life forever.

When I woke it was the afternoon and the tousled bed was empty beside me. I stared at the dark wooden ceiling and reached out my hand without looking to feel the indent where he had laid. Then slowly I rose and threw open the window to air our room. I found a small bottle of lilac oil and lit a tallow in it to scent the place. Then I called for the maid and ordered a bath. The tub arrived and two maids brought hot water to fill it, in buckets they had heated over the kitchen fire. This took a long while and in the meantime I sprinkled rose oil on the water and made ready drying cloths and my clothes. For the first time since we had left Ning-po I wished I might dress in a European outfit to show off my waist and my cleavage. I wanted to move sinuously and swing my hips. But, of course, that was out of the question. Instead I chose a long Han jacket of a delicate green and gold, which I laid out ready on the stool. I sent the maid to fetch cut flowers and put them into a pale yellow painted vase on the dresser. I, myself, made the bed. When Sing Hoo arrived with some items he had washed, he showed no sign of his bout of giggles with Wang outside the door.

'Master,' he bowed.

'It is all right, Sing Hoo.'

When all was ready I dismissed everyone from the room. I know the servants at the inn found it strange. A mandarin would surely visit the town's bathhouse to complete his ablutions. I expect I had the reputation of a strange, shy gentleman. The scented water was luxurious and relaxing. As I dropped my clothes to the floor and slipped into the bath a feeling of complete ease came over me. I floated in the old tub, surveying my body, admiring myself as I truly was. I let my dark ponytail fan out and drew it through the water behind me as I bobbed on the surface. I did not hear Robert enter the room for my head was ducked under. He pounced on me playfully, and I screamed, splashing out.

'This room smells like a boudoir, Mary,' he teased.

'That is because you have made a woman of me,' I said, and I kissed him deeply.

Settling beside the tub Robert languidly stroked my skin, smooth in the hot water, and I drifted this way and that, turning so he might lay his hands on my back as easily as my front side.

'You are reckless,' he said with a celebratory tone in his voice.

This made me laugh, for in London he had uttered exactly such words but in derision. I pulled off his jacket and he slipped out of his clothes as I drew him into the water with me, causing a spill over the high sides of the tub. The perfume of the room was intoxicating and the light breeze from the open window was refreshing as Robert and I moved together, kissing in the water. The intensity of the night before returned and I clung to him as he mounted me, biting his shoulder so I wouldn't scream, for now it was daytime and such cries would surely bring the servants running.

'I love you,' Robert breathed in my ear. 'I have never felt this before for anyone. I never will again.'

To hear these words only increased my passion and I found myself swinging round in the water, positioning myself on top of him and kissing his mouth deeply. We moved together frenetically, excited, unable to stop ourselves. It was unbridled and I wanted to devour him, to be only one rather than separate. Like Robert, I had never had such feelings before. We spent ourselves and then sat back at opposite ends of the bath. My lips were swollen and my colour high. Robert's cheeks burnt too and he eyed me with a lazy satisfaction.

'My God,' he said. 'I never imagined.'

He crossed the bath and kissed me before reaching for the soap and washing himself in the water. I watched as he lathered his body. I enjoyed every movement, such was my languid desire.

At length we clambered out and dried ourselves. I blew out the flame in the lilac oil and threw my silk jacket over my nakedness, leaving the ties unfastened, knowing that he might peek at me as I moved. I wanted to afford Robert every pleasure I could. I sat by the window and he called for the bath to be removed, which was a laborious process as the water had to be taken away in buckets before the tub could be lifted. I hid myself while the work was done. Around the bath, the wooden floorboards were sodden and the maids were busy mopping up the puddles. Outside the farm, workers were coming down from the mountain for the night, their baskets piled high. It was almost dark.

'Mary,' Robert said from the other side of the room once everything had been cleared. 'Wang has made great progress.'

In truth, we had been almost ready to leave even before Wang returned, and his skills had all but completed our preparations. The distance to the coast was several thousand li and we would travel for two months at least. Eight weeks. My last weeks of freedom, camping at the roadside discovering tiny villages and bustling, dusty towns. I thought of the cramped tents. I imagined waking with the sun, in Robert's arms, or staying in the hostelries we would find by the road, sneaking under the covers and relishing each other. This was worth becoming a woman again and eight weeks felt like a long time from where I was sitting. I even felt excited that I would see the sea again after so long. The Great Water. I was immersed in the present now, unworried about what was to come. The impossible choices. They'd have to wait. We had promised each other this time and we must take it.

'Let's make no decisions, my angel,' Robert soothed me. 'Let us only enjoy it.'

'When do we leave?' I asked.

Robert smiled as he crossed the room. He took my hand and pressed it to his lips.

'Two days.'

The road for the most part was in good condition and the weather fine. The highway was busy all year. It was, after all, the main road to the coast and as such it was peppered with inns and other stopping places so that by Robert's estimation we need only make camp with the men one night in three. We were a large party. In addition to the tea gardeners, who acted as bearers for the journey, we had another six men to help with the loads and the animals. Our company was both animated and highly organised with Wang and Sing Hoo clearly in charge and a hierarchy that quickly established itself under their lead. The men ate two meals a day, both of rice congee. The first was served just after sunrise and the second at sunset, which was accompanied by tea and a rough rice wine we carried with us as part of our provisions. This stuff was a fearful brew, native to Bohea. It stung the mouth and brought tears to the eyes. The men seemed to like it, though I must say it brought out the best and the worst of the petty rivalries and friendships that were bound to flourish in such a tight-knit group. Managing so many bearers was the only difficult task, for in every other respect this journey was considerably easier than any of our other wanderings, the road being in good condition, the weather warm and the direction clear.

At night Robert and I took to the countryside alone, walking hand in hand under the vast sky, away from the camp. This time was, I suppose, our honeymoon. Each night was different – each special in my memory, for as we explored each other and our new situation, our love deepened and grew. Once we came upon a pool and swam naked under the bright, low moon, our skin almost luminous, translucent in the pale light, and shining as our limbs splashed in the cool, black, satin water. Another time we entered a wood of fig trees and Robert pressed me against the rough bark in the darkness under the canopy and took me where I stood. I was eager for him, always soft, always yielding. The most intimate thing now, I realised, were the silences, desirous, comfortable and intense. A glance was enough to express concern or interest. A smile enough to denote pleasure or desire. I loved the way his eyes moved over my body in the daytime, surveying his territory. I loved the way my mind could wander. We both longed for the end of each day, as the tents were pitched, the darkness fell and the men cooked dinner. The camp was lit by firelight or the occasional torch of rags and we would eat and leave, eager to be alone.

While Wang and Sing Hoo certainly marked the change

in us, the bearers were oblivious. They had not, after all, known us before. They believed me to be a male secretary and Robert my master. On the road eastwards I heard more than once Robert and I referred to as 'brothers'. I suppose it was not uncommon for the higher classes to separate themselves from the lower. Even had they thought us male lovers I expect it would have made little difference to them. What would hang you in London would excite mere comment in the Orient. Nonetheless, I admit there was a certain frisson, which I enjoyed as a secret woman, a secret mistress, sharing a forbidden love with Sing Wa, my secret mandarin.

On the road the inns were variable. Some were so dirty and flea-ridden that we would rather camp for the night than stay indoors. Other times the hostelries were luxurious, with their own restaurants, theatre and a suite of rooms that was bright and pleasant, the beds hung with buttercup-gold awnings that cast a glow upon our private nakedness, marking our lovemaking even more brightly in my memory.

'You are blossoming, Mary,' Robert flattered me, though I admit I felt more confident and secure than ever before in my life.

Robert for his part seemed taller, somehow, and happier. He approached each day with a passion that surprised me. It was as if his ardour leaked into all his pursuits. Before, his organisation had always seemed obsessive, if effective. The mark of a man taking his duty beyond the call of the ordinary. Now, without doubt, he had a new vibrancy to his vision. He ate to enjoy the taste of the food. Robert had become hearty.

Within a week we found that riding in the sedan chairs was tedious. Even side by side with the curtains drawn so that we could converse, it proved tiresome. To address this, Robert bought horses when we came across an inn with a stableyard. They were ponies really. A chestnut for me,

291

a wonderful beast whose veins stood up on her neck and legs when I cantered her. She came with an embroidered leather saddle that fitted perfectly. This made us think she was far from home, for Robert was sure such fine work was from the north, perhaps Mongolia. My eyes narrowed as I pictured the map.

'Near Russia,' Robert proffered, and so I named her Romanov.

Robert's steed, on the other hand, was a dirty white pony he named Murdo, after the bully in his class when he was at infant school in the village where he was born. This animal was as much a thug as his namesake and would snap at my poor Romanov if he felt she was getting too much attention.

Aside from Prudence the mule, whose top speed was a smartish trot, I had not ridden since I was a young girl and I was nervous. However, both Robert and I were keen for sport. Our caravan moved slowly and we found we could canter a long way for our amusement, thundering along the road or crossing the country at a gallop, clearing fences, chasing the clouds. This way we could be alone. The road was safe, our provisions plentiful and we were mostly not needed. Occasionally we would come across an unusual ficus or olea and interrupt our race to take cuttings. Mostly though, we explored, the wind in our faces. The caravan's pace was so steady that after several hours of a detour we would always find it exactly where it was expected on the road. Wang and Sing Hoo, both with their eyes on their promised bonuses, proved more loyal and steady than at any other time, and, while I have no doubt that Sing Hoo traded some of our provisions of rice wine, there were no serious incursions.

A month from the coast Robert and I came across a village on our daily excursion away from the caravan.

We stopped and spoke to the headman. It was an ordinary enough place – a few scattered huts and some fields that had been cultivated, rice paddies cut into the hillside. It did not seem to me, however, that there were enough people there. Perhaps, I hazarded, the majority were away, working part of the land we had not ridden through. I thought no more of it.

Beyond the village the soil changed and it was difficult for Romanov and Murdo to keep their foothold. The land was steep and the earth seemed to fall away, as if it was not bound properly together. The going was treacherous and we tried to loop round the patch but it went on for quite a while. As we proceeded over the crest of a hill there was a large lake. It was unusual to find this, rather than a spring or waterfall, and the pool itself was flat and deep. Frustrated with our lack of progress, Robert and I dismounted and checked over the horses. Both animals drank deeply from the pool and Murdo wandered off to make a meal of the nearby vegetation – he was the kind of pony that ate anything, we had come to realise.

Robert sat at the water's edge but soon moved on, slapping his skin.

'Midges,' he swore. 'I have not seen the like of it since my last summer in Kelloe and then I cannot have been more than thirteen.'

The little dots skimmed the top of the water. They were far more interested in Robert than in me, I noticed.

'Come on, let's keep going,' he said. 'This will drive me mad. I cannot believe I am a Scotsman and bothered by midges. Why aren't they going for you, Mary?'

I shrugged my shoulders and laughed.

Past the pool we came upon a burial ground, mostly overgrown, though there were new coffins placed off the earth to one side in the traditional manner. Some of these,

I realised, were children's caskets. I wondered if here were the missing villagers. I counted upwards of ten, not an incidental number for a village of perhaps thirty souls, and all dead within months of each other, if the encroaching vegetation was anything to go by.

'Could be anything,' Robert said sagely. 'An attack, an accident or some sickness or other.'

I laid a stone on each of the coffins in remembrance and we moved on.

By the end of the day we had rejoined the caravan at a small town on the main road and instructed the men to make camp and see to our horses. While the mules needed little attention, Romanov and Murdo were ridden hard daily and required rubbing down and a careful feed. All this was done for us while Robert and I took rooms. I could already see that Robert was not quite himself, but it did not overly concern me. By later that evening, however, I noticed he had become jumpy and his skin felt clammy to the touch.

'You should lie down,' I ventured. 'I am worried that you have caught some kind of infection.'

'Don't fuss, Mary,' he insisted, 'I am fine,' and he unpacked the small overnight valise Sing Hoo had brought from the servants' camp.

When it came time to order dinner Robert was indecisive and had little appetite. I ordered for myself and suggested some chicken soup for him. Something light. By the time the soup came his skin was hot to the touch and he was running a fever.

'I'm fine,' he murmured once more, but I could feel the burning and insisted on taking command.

'Is there a cold stream?' I asked the innkeeper, a fat man in the habit of carrying a knife with him, I noticed, though I only ever saw him use it to carve meat off the joint.

He nodded and pointed away from the settlement towards the higher ground.

'Have them bring me a bucket of water from it,' I directed. 'Cold.'

When the maid arrived with the bucket it was icy enough to bring Robert's temperature down if I doused him in it, I was sure.

'Come now.' I took him by the arm and guided him to the bed.

He seemed confused.

'But dinner . . .' his voice trailed.

He was getting hotter.

At first I had no other thought than perhaps this was a chill and that with a good night's rest and some cooling he would recover. I knew what to do. Jane and I had made cold compresses to ease Helen's fever when she was little. The freezing flannels had broken the child's burning overnight. I started to cool Robert's skin with the spring water and, after protesting at first, he let me.

'Bring me another bucket of this water,' I directed the maid.

After some time I realised that Robert's fever was not breaking and the cold compresses were curiously ineffective. By midnight he was all but delirious. The sweat dripped off his pale skin and the cloth of cool water became hot in my hand almost immediately I held it to his forehead or swabbed his chest.

'Doctor?' Wang offered.

'No. No.'

I forbore to call a Chinese doctor, trusting instead to my own nursing skills and being unsure what might be prescribed, for what little I knew of Chinese medicine seemed to me more outlandish than wise. The cuts and strains and scratches we had suffered over the whole journey had all been mended in our own keeping – there was no need to turn to native superstition. I dismissed our servants back to their tents and continued in my nursing activities. As the hours wore on I forgot my own exhaustion, continually dousing Robert, blowing on his face and watching for any sign of a recovery.

At two in the morning or thereabouts I had an idea. I left him only a second, running to the fireside and waking the inn's servants who slept there.

'Come,' I ordered them, hauling them behind me back up to the room.

'Move the bed. Over to the window,' I shouted.

Sleepily they hovered in the doorway.

'Come along!' I released the catch on the window to let in the cold, night air.

Then I returned to the foot of the bed and hauled the frame myself until they realised what I wanted and put their backs into it.

'And fetch me another bucket of water from the stream. Cold as you can,' I barked at one poor girl. 'Now!'

As the night wore on, Robert called out, very loud, and in English. He shouted the name of a dog he had as a child.

'To heel, Tuppence,' he yelled. 'To heel!'

Once he gave instruction as to the care of different specimens of orchid I knew he had grown at Kew. A few times he said my name and for an instant I thought perhaps he knew I was there, but it was not so. As the dawn approached, I worried that his shouting would carry and perhaps be recognised as English. As the maid brought bucket after bucket of icy water, one each hour now, there was fear in her eyes at this strange screaming. I explained Robert's cries away.

'He is a scholar,' I said. 'These words are from ancient texts.'

The screams got worse. I tried to hold his jaw but he bit me, hard. I was so concerned I thought of gagging him, but a few minutes of that, achieved with a length of muslin from our packing case, seemed only to make him more agitated and I could not bear it and loosened the cloth immediately.

As dawn broke he was no better. In fact, my guess was that his skin was hotter still. Sing Hoo and Wang came to the rooms as they did every morning when the sun rose. They shifted, immediately worried. Robert was such a force to be reckoned with that to see him delirious and vulnerable was disturbing for us all.

'Doctor?' Wang offered.

I declined.

'No. Sing Hoo, you must tell the men we will rest here. Have them guard the camp in shifts and dispense a little money – perhaps two *cash* each – for their amusement.'

It was important to consider our charges, no matter what else was going on.

'Go!' I urged him.

Wang stayed with me.

I had not slept and I was clearly exhausted.

'You rest,' Wang motioned. 'I will do this.'

I curled in the chair by the bed but such was my worry that I only dozed fitfully. By late morning Robert's limbs were twitching in spasm. His skin was pink and his mouth became dry within seconds of swabbing his lips with a sponge. He had stopped shouting, but his silence now seemed worse to me than the uncontrollable screams. I was frantic. The sweat was still running off the poor man's body and I wondered fearfully how much more he could stand.

'What shall I do, my love?' I muttered under my breath.

After all the commotion and entreaties of the long night, Robert sat up, his eyes open. He stared at Wang and I distractedly, unable to stay still for a moment as his arms twitched at his side. Then with a focused determination he reached out and grabbed my forearm.

'Get the tea, Mary,' he said breathlessly. 'Whatever happens to me. You must get the tea to the port.'

And then he let go of my arm and fell back, lying with his eyes closed and his body convulsing. It was terrifying.

'My God,' I started to cry. 'Robert,' I called, trying to bring him back. 'Robert.'

The tears were pouring down my cheeks. He did not speak. I grabbed him by the shoulders. His arms were completely limp as they jerked, and I shook him hard in desperation.

'Robert,' I screamed, letting go in horror as I realised from the feel of him that he was going, that he had given up. I slapped him on the cheek, a fury rising in me.

'Don't leave. Don't leave,' I cried.

Wang was standing beside me silently, a look of terror on his face.

'Master,' he started.

'Yes,' I shouted hysterically. I was absolutely desperate. 'Fetch the doctor. Fetch him now.'

I don't think I stopped crying from that moment until Wang returned almost an hour later. In the meantime I swabbed Robert's body and dripped water into his mouth constantly, but there was little change in his condition.

'If he is still moving, then he is alive,' I told myself. 'Don't you dare leave me,' I entreated him. 'Don't you dare.'

This could not be what our love was destined for. I refused to think it.

When Wang opened the door at last, the doctor entered and bowed to me. He was a fit, jolly-looking, old man. I must have looked a fright – up all night and half frantic. He stared past me though and, seeing immediately Robert's distress, he went directly to the bedside and got straight down to business.

'How long like this?' he asked.

'He has been hot all night,' I replied. 'But twitching since this morning.'

I felt relieved to have some help, although this man, I noticed, had broken nails and a ragged hem to his gown. My heart fluttering, the doctor examined Robert quickly and brought from his case two long, thin needles and a jar of evil-smelling unction. This preparation he smeared on Robert's lips and on his fingernails. I sighed with frustration. Surely this could have no measure of success. I could bleed Robert myself, I realised. Yes, I would have Wang fetch leeches. This Chinese medicine was hokum and this country doctor a fool. I must try myself. Why had I not thought of bleeding him before?

The doctor raised the needles, clearly about to apply them. Horrified, I flung myself forwards.

'No!' I shouted. 'You'll hurt him.'

The doctor moved back calmly.

'Your master has a reason to die?' he asked.

It was a callous question.

'You want him to die? You are prepared to answer for it?'

I almost spat with fury. How dare he? What kind of medical man worked by fear and threat? If I lost Robert I would die myself. I would have to.

'Leave him alone,' I said and I turned to pick up my dousing cloth.

The minute my back was turned the doctor moved quickly once more to the bedside. He inserted his needles deftly into Robert's left ear. Then, as I realised what he had done and was about to turn on him, he bowed, stepped back and sat to one side. I had no truck with this and immediately dipped my cloth in the bucket and went to remove the stupid pins and douse Robert again. Clearly this man had been a false hope and I must continue to look after him myself. As I approached the bed, the doctor held out his hand to stop me.

'Twenty breaths,' he said.

The man was mad.

'He has been like this for hours,' I shouted, dismissing him.

Without a further word the doctor grabbed me. He was far bigger than I and rough-handled me over to the chair easily.

'Fifteen breaths,' he said.

I hammered on his shoulders. Robert continued to twitch on the mattress.

'Wang,' I shouted furiously. 'Get this man off me!'

Wang cast his eyes around the room, unable to come to a decision about what to do.

'Ten breaths,' the doctor said calmly.

I loosened my grip on him. I'd whip Wang myself for ignoring me. Robert was lying there dying for all he cared. I tried to stay calm and counted the doctor's slow breaths until there were ten.

'See,' I shouted without even looking. 'Useless!'

At this the doctor stepped back, turned to the bed and bowed graciously. Robert was pink but still. His chest rose and fell calmly with each breath. There was a change in his state, and it was certainly for the better. It was a miracle.

'Oh! Oh, thank you. Thank you,' I cried in shock, as my anger fell away and I realised, shamefacedly, that I had panicked.

I grasped the doctor's hand but he shook me off disdainfully and only moved to the bed, took out the needles in Robert's ear and inserted them instead near his collar bone.

'You people know nothing,' he muttered.

Then the old man sat patiently on the chair to wait out the fever. A shocked laugh left my lips.

'Bring the doctor something to eat and drink,' I ordered Wang as I peeked at the needles, wondering if they hurt.

On either side of the bed, the old man and I watched carefully the rest of the day. The doctor drank some green tea but would not eat anything. I sank down on my knees and thanked God that Robert's condition was improving. I reached out and held his hand and I swear, he squeezed my fingers. I had not lost him.

'*Nue*,' the doctor said, without looking at me. 'There have been outbreaks in the hills.'

Nue, I later learned, was a kind of malaria. No doubt the disease that had carried those villagers away.

By the evening Robert was asleep, his skin was cool and his breathing steady. I had washed and changed and taken time to eat. As the sun sank, the doctor left. I paid him twice what he had asked, such was my gratitude. He left instructions as to Robert's diet and suggested not moving him until he was fully recovered. Judging me of an independent mind despite his advice, he said the next hospital on our route was at the Shan te Maou temple. If we did continue on the road it might be as well to know that help could be found there. For me, however, there was no question of it. I was taking no chances. We would stay as long as Robert needed.

I spoke to the landlord to secure our room and then had a small bed made up on the floor where I slept at last, waking twice in the night, frantic. Once I was in a sheer panic and the second time I dreamt we were in Scotland, a place I have never been. There were midges everywhere and Robert said to me, 'I had rather die than have to leave you, Mary.' And I could not reply. I could not form the words. As I woke, I jumped from the little bed and checked on my patient.

He was fine, of course, the dream only a foolish fancy. When I opened my eyes the third time it was morning and Robert was sitting up. I rushed to his side and flung my arms around him.

'You scared me,' I said.

'What happened?'

'You almost died,' I cried.

He had no memory at all of the fever though he still felt weak. In a babble I told him everything that had happened and of the doctor's treatment and instructions.

'It will set us back to tarry,' he objected.

'Lord, Robert, I thought I would be ordering that monument you drew. Your own mausoleum with Fortune carved over the gate. We will stay here until you are completely well. And you, my boy, will eat fish and vegetables as instructed.'

Robert laughed.

'You are clearly in charge, then,' he teased me. 'I take it that you would have been upset at my demise?'

I shuddered at the thought. He was weak still, dizzy when he tried to rise.

'If you had gone, that cord that runs between us would have pulled me over the divide,' I swore. 'I could not bear it.'

I brought flowers to the bedside and read to him from one of my books of Chinese myths. For days my patient fell asleep to stories of warriors who could fly and of spirits who returned to earth to haunt their dishonourable relations. The threat of separation, even separation by death, had scared both of us and, as what had happened sank in, Robert became tender with me once more, strong enough between restorative naps, to take me in his arms and kiss me.

Meanwhile I resolved as Robert slept to keep his journal up to date and make pencil sketches of the countryside around the inn. It had been some time since I had paid any attention to the notebooks. Leafing through the pages I could see his mind had wandered of late and I was flattered to read that he had taken notice not of the properties of the soil or the acidity of the water, but of me. The flowers by our bed at Wuyi Mountain had been pressed dry and kept between the pages, and Robert had written of our lovemaking, the taste of my mouth and the softness of my skin. I was touched. He had drawn me naked as I slept and written wistful lines of our chase across country one day when the horses had taken off and we had wheeled towards the hilly ground to the south of the Great Imperial Road. He had written my name over and over and then: 'What will I do without her?' And here I stopped. Without me? What horrors was he planning?

I furiously flung the book down and then bundled it back in its box and thrust the whole caboodle beside the door, eyeing it angrily from my chair across the room as my mind raced. How dare he? For my part I was not naïve but I simply had ceased to think so far ahead. My whole world was in our summer caravan, with no thought to its destination. We had promised each other that. No choices, no decisions, he had said. And when it came time we would do so together. And yet, here was Robert, in advance of me, wishing our time away. Worse, coming to a conclusion alone. He had decided on rejecting me, it seemed. Of course, from our situation, some things were clear – after all, how could I return to London now? But then again, how could he? Still, it was unforgivable. It was like William all over again. By Hong Kong I would be inconvenient and Robert would slip back to London alone.

When Robert woke I was sitting cross-legged on the chair with my arms also crossed before me.

'Oh, dear,' he said, for it was clear all was not well. He sat up with some effort.

'You are for leaving me behind, I read in your journal,' I said coolly.

He did not berate me for reading his private papers, but sat up squarely.

'What do you mean?'

I tramped over to the box and pulled out the pages.

'What will you do without me, Robert?' I said, throwing them haphazardly on the bed. 'Without me?'

He lifted the page.

'I don't know what I will do,' he said sadly, 'for I love you completely. But what else is there? I am contracted from here to India and then to London. Will you come with me and kiss your sister hello?'

I kicked the chair so hard it buckled. I knew I could not go home again.

'And must you go back?' I asked, tears welling in my eyes. 'You cannot avoid it? What of all your promises, Robert? This love of ours? Your intention is to abandon me, is it not? I am convenient here – a bit of fun for you – but come Hong Kong you will head west and scarce look over your shoulder.'

'The last part of the money is due on return,' he said. 'I must collect it for the children. For Jane too, if it comes to that, Mary. I must go home and see to my duties. The Company will pay me over a hundred and fifty pounds in London. I cannot set that aside.'

It was a huge sum of money.

I nodded sadly. 'It seems too easy for you,' I said, the tears welling. This felt horribly familiar. A man returning to his wife, abandoning his promises. I had no doubt that I had uncovered Robert's secret intentions. The truth was he had everything on his side. He could do whatever he wanted.

The patient picked up the papers on his cover.

'Easy for me?' he retorted, casting his eyes on the sheets before him. 'How could it be easy for me?'

I followed his gaze. The page or two I had not read, the last entry, was before me.

'And I had rather die,' he had written. 'It will be agony. But I swear I will return three thousand miles to her. I will come back. Whatever it takes.'

I picked up the page, my heart quickening, 'And if I stay here and wait then, you will return?'

'How could I not?' he said and reached out to touch my arm. 'How can you even think it?'

I knelt down. It was as if China had healed me of all my hurts from before. In that moment my faith was truly restored and I knew, absolutely, that I was loved. Robert might be rushing towards London but it was only so he could settle his business there and return to me the quicker. We had a month till we reached the coast and a few weeks more until Hong Kong. But we would be together no matter what, and that was all that was important.

'Then I will wait for you, wherever you leave me, however long,' I promised.

Robert reached out, putting his arm around me.

'We are home to each other now,' he said. 'There is no other way.'

Chapter Twelve

Foo Chow Soo is Britain's most southerly port in China, but it is a small place and not at all popular. In good health and set on each other for life, Robert and I approached the settlement in the middle of the day, dirty from the road and with a full three tonnes of luggage. It was four weeks since we had left the inn and the journey had been glorious. Now, as our party crested the hill leading to the little town, the tea gardeners caught their first, bright glimpse of the sea and a wild wail started. The strangeness of the shimmering water shocked them beyond all belief. Two men burst into tears. Another fell on his knees and begged Wang to send him home again for he was too afraid. Robert looked down amused at this commotion from the sedan chair he had adopted for our arrival in the town. It had not occurred to either of us that the sea would be such a shock.

'The ocean will not be their only surprise in Foo Chow Soo,' he said lightly.

We, after all, were set to lose our disguises once we were safe on British soil.

To allow the bearers to get used to the scale of the water, we chose a slightly longer route into town that brought the men to a shingle beach about a mile to one side of the port. There we stopped so they could take in the view and, we hoped, compose themselves. Together in a line they walked hesitantly towards the little waves breaking on the pebbles as if the water might surge forward and engulf them. For me, it was lovely to be near the sound of the surf again and, despite my misgivings about what the coming weeks might hold, I felt exhilarated. This was not only Robert's achievement, it was mine as well, and I wanted to see the completion of it, even if it meant Robert would be gone a year or more back to Europe. And then, of course, we were anticipating treats – British food, ample wine (French, we hoped), fresh books to read and news of home.

While the bearers moved gingerly up the shale, Wang and Sing Hoo stood beaming. Both had spent much of their lives by the sea and were basking in the cosmopolitan air this now afforded them in the eyes of their compatriots. Also, I expect, our arrival in Foo Chow Soo clearly marked the last stage of our journey and as they reached the sea their promised bonuses drew yet closer. This proximity, however, did not seem to help the rest of the men come to terms with their amazement at the vast expanse of blue water before them. Sing Hoo laughed, mimicking their wide eyes and distraught expressions.

'Stop that,' I told him. 'Look,' I explained, jumping off my sedan and splashing my hands in the surf to demonstrate. 'There is nothing to be afraid of. It will not come to you any further up the beach. It's only water.'

Still, the men clasped onto each other as they moved forwards, though all of them wet their fingers to taste it. Laughter broke out and it wasn't long before they were splashing like children and eagerly asking questions of Wang and Sing Hoo about the size of this 'lake' and why the water tasted of salt.

'We will leave on a ship,' I said, pointing towards the port in the bay where a smattering of sampans were moored and only one vessel, I noticed, of a British bent. Robert took a deep breath of salty air. The breeze off the ocean was certainly stirring.

'Come,' he roused the men. 'Let us get on.'

Inside the city wall, it was strange to see that there were no European-style buildings. Foo Chow Soo did not resemble any other British port we had visited. The Consulate was a small, wooden building with a diplomatic staff of three. Aside from that there were only two British merchants in the town – both opium traders, of course – and a small barracks for the military contingent. This meant that while Foo Chow Soo was nominally British, there were scarcely fifty Europeans stationed there, and they were out-numbered easily a hundred to one by the native Chinese in the area. We had not expected so small a presence or anticipated what it might mean. From the start it was clear that the local Chinese were hostile to anything foreign – even the graffiti down by the docks proclaimed it. Unlike in Hong Kong or Ning-po or Chusan, the British were not welcome here, even on a superficial level for trade, and we passed no shops selling goods for European tastes or even those where allowances had been made for the British market. All in all, there was an unpleasant atmosphere of contention that we had not counted on. The place felt on the very verge of mutiny. This crept up on our own feel-ings of celebration the minute we entered the settlement and made us wary.

As we picked our way along the main street our entourage caused quite a stir. Not one single merchant tried to sell us goods but many came to ogle as we passed. Our bearers were jostled as they carried our trunks and I heard swear words muttered behind us – not from our own men, but from those who had come to inspect the caravan. Though on our sedans we were untouched, we were certainly noted. Two mandarins, clearly friends meeting by chance outside a shop, stared and then haltingly followed us at a distance.

'Lord,' said Robert, thinking on his feet. 'Strangers are not welcome here. I had thought it would be busier and there would be more of our soldiers.'

He eyed the mandarins, who were pointing and whispering to each other before he continued. It reminded me of our time in the hills before Chusan where we were attacked by the crowd who had come to inspect us. This time, however, Robert was not for pressing on and ignoring the unfriendly stares.

'Well, I do not judge it wise to march up to the Consulate and knock on the door, that is for sure,' he said. 'I think we might be better advised to stay Chinese for a while until we have assessed this place. It is most odd.'

I agreed.

Warily, we directed the caravan towards the port and when we got there a small phalanx of British soldiers marched towards us and ordered us to halt. This was to be expected. In every settlement it was at the port that the troops had their main presence. Here though, there were perhaps only six men on duty, the first European faces we had seen in two years, or at least since Father Edward had left us. I was excited to see these men, though it struck me that the soldiers seemed so much hairier than the Chinese appearance that I was now used to, and their faces were so unusual – another species indeed. It was surprising how strange my own countrymen had become to me. Quite apart from this, the men were armed to the teeth with knives at the belt and guns they thrust out before them. They looked like they would strike any moment.

The captain motioned our sedans to be set down so he could interrogate us.

'Name?' he roared in Cantonese. 'What is your business here?'

Robert smiled. He knew he was being followed by the townsfolk and that we must be careful; here though was the definite chance for some sport. He reached out a long-nailed finger and motioned the officer closer so that none could hear what the grand mandarin was going to say. The man moved towards the sedan warily, his soldiers ready with their arms if need be.

'Come along then,' he barked. 'Name.'

Robert leant towards him.

'They call me Sing Wa, old chap,' he whispered in his best English drawl. 'And by my judgement we had best stick to that name in these parts, but we are headed for Hong Kong and Sir Pottinger. Treat us as you would any Chinese merchant, arriving in town. We will take rooms here.'

The captain stood upright. He stared first at Robert and then at me.

'I say,' he muttered.

I adopted a haughty expression and hid my smile as his eyes searched my face momentarily, to see what might be beneath the surface. Then he rallied.

'Right, men, look at the luggage here!' he shouted. 'Hop to it!'

The troops fanned out and checked over the cases, shoving our men out of the way where need be, while the young captain whispered something to Robert I did not catch. Once our inspection was completed he waved us on.

'They are often under attack here,' Robert relayed to me. 'The man says that if we unmask ourselves it is his view that there will be an uprising. He said the situation is very hostile.'

'Then let's stay hidden,' I agreed.

Right on the bay we took rooms in a newly-built complex

that we discovered was to let. The place smelt of freshly sawn wood and new paint. There was a courtyard to the rear that backed onto a pristine warehouse and Robert also let this accommodation for our luggage and, of course, the men. While Wang and Sing Hoo busied themselves wrangling our entourage into their quarters, we took tea upstairs and assessed the situation. Outside, the mandarins had gone, but there were two Chinese servants loitering nearby in the street with instructions to take note of our activities no doubt. In a town the size of Foo Chow Soo our arrival constituted an event and our new neighbours were nosey. This wasn't British territory or at least not as entirely as British as we had anticipated. In fact, it was a good deal less welcoming than either of the tea countries we had come from. It felt as if the place was under siege.

'I am looking forward, Mary, to seeing you a lady once more.' Robert regarded me.

I blushed. 'Not in Foo Chow Soo,' I said.

At length, Robert called Wang and instructed him to enquire about sailings to Hong Kong on a ship that could accommodate us.

'Leave by the side door,' he instructed. 'Be careful, Wang. They are watching.' Robert gestured vaguely out of the half-shuttered window where the men outside were standing together.

'Yes, Master.'

'And how are we to let the Consul know we're here?' I asked.

'Did you notice there was a little theatre? I think we should attend, don't you?'

I turned in surprise. This was most unlike Robert.

'The Chinese Opera?'

'Yes. We have made our own fun, far too long. Let's see what is playing this evening.'

'What are you up to, Robert Fortune?'

'Oh, everyone goes to the theatre, Mary. I should imagine that even the Consul may be there this evening.'

Here then was the subject of the whispering I could not catch between Robert and the captain of the guard. I stood up and stared down into the street, the teacup to my lips. This town felt murderous. We would be lucky to escape with our skins.

'Have there been many attacks here?' I asked.

'I should think so,' Robert put his hand on my shoulder. 'Try not to think of it. We shall be gone soon enough.'

In the meantime we set about providing for the men and seeming as Chinese as we could. Sing Hoo was sent for provisions – all of a Chinese nature – and everyone was confined to their quarters. We did not want word getting out about our intentions.

That evening, with our charges settled and a watch set up, Robert and I ventured out. We both carried knives beneath our long silk jackets. The streets around the theatre were lively after dark, the smell of cooking and the sound of high spirits pervaded the muddy alleyways. The candle-lamps set in the doorways gave the shabby street stalls a golden glow and, though it was small, the commercial heart of Foo Chow Soo bustled the hot, dark evening long. Still, in the street, we were followed. Wang led us, sure-footed, and we ignored the stares. These servants could not trail us into the theatre, in any case. There was an entrance fee, for a start.

We entered as the huge, carved doors were opened by a burly doorman. Inside we were greeted by a man dressed in black, and asked if we preferred the gallery (where one must stand) or a table by the performing area. The six-man orchestra was already playing mesmerising Chinese music that I knew Robert would hate. Caterwauling he called it, and he had never got used to the Oriental rhythm or the high, haunting tone. We decided, however, upon a table, which was the choice most consistent with Robert's rank as Sing Wa. Robert stood for a moment, considering what was on offer and then he directed us silently with a long arc of his finger to the other side of the room.

There was a table of off-duty Chinese soldiers a few seats away, and they shifted to get a look at us. Robert had worn a jacket studded with crystals and, sure enough, it was this that caught their attention and in my plain, dark secretary's outfit I happily paled into insignificance. As I sat down on a mound of bright, satin cushions, and a pretty waitress in a plain yellow robe with a red sash served little cups of *sham shoo*, I realised that when we were seated the soldiers were obscured from our view and, more importantly, we were obscured from theirs. The fact there were Chinese troops, off duty or not, in a British port was unheard of, and it made me even more uneasy as if I had to keep checking around to see who might be looking or what they might guess.

'Well, now,' I whispered, trying to put us at our ease, 'I never knew you were a lover of Oriental music, Robert.'

He knew I was being facetious and didn't reply. Instead I surveyed the crowd in the gallery, brightly dressed women with intricate hairstyles standing demurely with their men. Some of these ladies no doubt worked at the town's brothel and were being paid (well, I hoped) for their attendance. Robert noticed my line of vision.

'At home the audience is no different, Mary,' he smirked.

I smiled. At home the programme at this time of year comprised of new plays and some classics. Congreve, often Marlowe, and sometimes a production in French.

'In that case, the ladies will be scurrying around back-stage. Completely engrossed with their make up.'

'And at the Royal Society,' Robert mused, 'there may be a lecture.'

'Oh, yes. Mosses of the Highlands?' I ventured.

'Mosses and lichens, more likely.'

'Of course.'

'Well,' said a deep, unfamiliar voice, 'I can't imagine why you would want to tarry here, then.'

I spun round. A tall, fair man with a grin on his face had taken a place at the table behind us. He seemed too large for the cushion he was seated on. I was immediately reminded of playing with the children, when we might seat a teddy bear, far too large, at a table with some smaller dolls and serve them all tea. It is odd how unfamiliar the sight of a white man had become. I marvelled at him.

'Rum game this,' the large man smiled.

'Mary,' Robert whispered, leaning towards me, 'you must take that look off your face and turn towards the stage.'

Quickly I pulled myself into check.

Major Gilland introduced himself properly and then apologised.

'Couldn't resist it,' he explained. 'I must say, your disguises are excellent.' He peered over.

We did not turn around. Seated at the table directly behind us with Mr Morrison, a secretary from the Consulate, and I suppose it would appear that Gilland was talking to his companion, and that Robert and I were talking to each other, when in fact we were, all four of us, engrossed in conversation together. Or at least three of us were, as Morrison remained silent throughout the meeting. I was so unused to congenial company that it was like daydreaming and I said so. Gilland laughed.

'Fun and games, eh?' he observed. 'Mind you, I can't imagine them not spotting you in the interior, ma'am,' he continued. 'If you don't mind me saying so.'

'Let's hope they will not spot me here, Major.'

'We had given up on you for lost, Fortune. Had notice almost two years ago now that you might come this way. Plucky expedition of yours and they did not mention you had a lady in your party. Wish I could hear all about it. Good show.'

'Thank you. But the show is not over, is it?' Robert chipped in.

'We'll see what we can do. We'll come up with something.'

'I hope so. Don't know how you are managing here, Gilland. It's dreadful. Not come across the like of it before.'

The major did not answer this.

'Well, we have a plan of sorts for you, in any case. The boat leaves in three days,' he said. 'It's a shoddy bucket, but the best we can muster on this notice. Captain McFarlane is a good fellow though plagued by his crew, I should imagine. Chinks to a man. They will get you to Hong Kong in something over a week. We are hoping Pottinger will send us reinforcements. I am not sure how long we can hold out, to be honest.'

My blood ran cold. Only ten days now. Only ten. Robert pressed his leg against mine.

'Well, I'm looking forward to some decent English food,' Robert said. 'We thought we'd be able to unmask here. Don't worry – I will see Pottinger myself, Gilland. I am sure he will send what you need.'

'Good thing you turned up,' Gilland said. 'Is there anything else I can get you?'

'You wouldn't happen to have any marmalade, would you?' I blurted. It came out of the blue.

'They are set to cut us to pieces and the lady wants marmalade!' Gilland hooted.

I felt ashamed for asking but everyone laughed.

'I'll see what I can do, ma'am,' he swore.

At this moment the actors came on stage and we fell silent. The main female character was clearly played by a man, who lumbered unconvincingly around the platform.

'The provinces!' I joked and we settled down to watch the show.

'See, my love,' Robert whispered, 'we will be fine.'

That night I sat up by the bedroom window. There remained a watch over us in the street below – two Chinese house servants huddled in a doorway opposite. We had set up a vigil of our own at each corner of the compound. I was glad the warehouse was to the rear of the property and not easily accessible, for this would make it difficult for our adversaries to find the nature of our cargo. With our men confined to quarters we were confident that no one would give our game away and it was only a matter of passing the time, staying safe until we could leave. To keep the bearers occupied Wang ordered the repacking of all the boxes one by one and the construction of Ward's cases from glass and wood, which Robert had ordered from a local merchant and which had been delivered at the end of the day. The intention was once more to bolt the portable, sealed glasshouses to the deck and cultivate plants during the journey – this time the seedlings would be tea, of course, interspersed with mulberry bushes.

'Never been done before,' Robert had told Gilland that evening, when the entertainment had ceased, 'but it will work, I am sure of it. If the tea plants thrive, then we will have a way to transport any fragile seed – you will have chestnuts in the tropics, Gilland, and oak trees too, I'll warrant.'

'Ingenious,' the major had replied. 'I miss the trees at home.'

I had felt sorry for him and admired his bravery too, for he was risking his life every day here.

The night was colder than usual and I pulled my loose silk gown around me as I watched the men over the road, silent in the darkness.

'You cannot sleep?' Robert asked from the bed, waking as he turned.

'No. They are still watching.'

'Come here, Mary.'

I crossed the room silently, let the gown fall from my shoulders and slipped naked back under the satin sheet. Robert's body was warm and he wrapped himself around me.

'It is the last hurdle,' he whispered, 'and we will take it flying, Mary.'

He had a gun, I knew, next to the bed. I tried to forget everything that was going on. And when I fell asleep I swear I was kissing him still.

The next day we decided to explore the town. There were some supplies we wished to procure and, with our Chinese shadows in tow, we made our way along the main street, inspecting the shops one by one. The weather was stormy now and the daylight marred by heavy cloud. We found some interesting antiques along the thoroughfare – small wood carvings and lacquerwork. Robert bought them and dispatched Sing Hoo home to the warehouse, hauling them on his back. As we strolled on we passed several mandarins, all peering more closely at us than was remotely polite. One said something in a strange tongue, trying to address us. With Sing Hoo gone, Robert gave the man a condescending stare and then retreated, hurrying me onto my sedan and back to the house. It felt very dangerous.

'Damn!' he said as the front door closed behind us. 'It is a treaty port and they can do nothing. After months in the interior we will not be stopped on our own soil. This is preposterous.'

But we both knew we simply didn't have enough men on our side here to enforce our will if push came to shove and things turned nasty. We stayed in for the rest of the day.

That evening Mr Morrison called at the house. He had been soaked in the rain but refused the offer of a sheet to dry himself. His thin lips pulled back from his teeth as if they were fitted too tightly, and I thought that in his dark suit and with such odd features, he looked like a strange kind of animal – perhaps a vole fresh out of the water. He bobbed from one foot to the other as if he was about to take off at a sprint.

'They have made an official complaint,' he said. 'They are on to you. It is signed by three mandarins.'

My skin felt icy. Robert's eyes flashed at this news.

'And you coming here probably confirms it,' he replied acidly. 'Whatever are you thinking?'

'It's too late for all that, Fortune. Gilland has a plan.' Mr Morrison's tone was flat. 'But you must leave as soon as we can get you away. Captain McFarlane is ready but the ship is poorly supplied – you will have to make do with what is on board already. We do not have the luxury of properly fortifying her. The Chinese do not like to do things openly, so this is a huge declaration. In the normal run of things, not that this can be called remotely normal,' he commented to himself, 'but usually they would find a way to save face, you know. This is uncharacteristically direct. Gilland is concerned. Very concerned. We must get you out now. We will stow all our valuables on the same boat and hope that we, ourselves, last long enough for the reinforcements to arrive.'

I thought of the mandarin in the mountains and his offer of safe passage – the oblique way he had avoided accusing us of anything. Safe passage was probably the last thing the mandarin's countrymen wanted to offer us here. I was struck by the bravery of those we were leaving behind. Morrison continued.

'At midnight tonight the tide will be perfect. While Foo Chow Soo sleeps, you must load your cargo and sail on the *Island Queen* before there is time to do anything about the complaint. We are merely holding it at present, but we cannot do that for long without a riot breaking out. We must act swiftly. At eleven Gilland will send fifteen soldiers to provide safe passage to the dock. They will nab the Chinese lookouts and hold them until you are gone. Our men can help with the loading. We have a contingent at the Consulate now as a precaution – later tonight the rest of us will retreat there and must be armed all round. It is a last stand, I expect.'

'Mr Morrison!' I did not know what to say.

Robert thought for a moment. 'And the major does not want to ship you all away? Come, there must only be fifty.'

Morrison shook his head sadly. 'Our orders are to hold the port. Our military are quite determined on it.'

I could see the man was frightened, and there was nothing he could do. If I had the measure of him Morrison was an administrator, not a soldier. He was being as brave as he could.

'I'm so sorry,' I said.

He shrugged his shoulders.

'Oh. And, ma'am, he sent you this.'

The man pulled a jar out of his pocket. It was a little pot of West and Wyatt's Best Marmalade Preserve.

'He said you might as well have a decent breakfast.'

I took the jar and thanked him sheepishly.

'We will set to it, Morrison,' Robert shook his hand. 'We will be ready at eleven.'

Morrison slipped back into the storm and Robert

immediately ordered two of the upstairs bedrooms to be lit with an array of candles and their shutters left unfastened. This show of light would distract our lookouts across the street. A man was to walk between the two rooms from time to time and provide some additional interest for them to monitor. Meanwhile, in the rooms we truly inhabited, we packed the cases by the light of a single, dim oil lamp and fastened our shutters tightly. Wang brought everything downstairs to wait in the hall. I was nervous, but excited too. We had never had an armed escort before – until now we had always been on our own wits.

'It is no night to be sailing,' Robert commented. This was true. Outside it was practically typhoon weather.

'*Dai-phoo*,' Sing Hoo said sadly, for he had never got over his voyage sickness and in this weather he knew he was set to suffer. I patted his shoulder to comfort him.

'Better this than what might happen if we stay,' I told him. I was not sure how much Sing Hoo or Wang had understood, except this was an unfriendly port and we were leaving.

Come eleven there was a sharp rap at the door and Robert himself went to greet the troops. The officer in charge was the captain who had stopped us in the street the day before. He shook hands with Robert enthusiastically. It struck me that he was terribly young, perhaps only twenty, and I noticed his eyes shone with excitement at the escapade. He was a Home Counties boy, raised, it seemed to me, with exactly this kind of adventure in mind.

'Captain Peverill,' he introduced himself. 'We have the sneaks tied up.'

We had not told the main body of our men what was to happen, for we wanted no show, noise or commotion of any kind for the lookouts to interpret. Everything in the warehouse was packed already so there was no measure in giving them advance notice. Now Wang and Sing Hoo went to rouse the gardeners and, under cover of darkness, on carts drawn not only by mules but by a dolorous Romanov (who considered the task well beneath her) and a furious Murdo, we made our way to the port in the rain, through the two dark, sleeping streets between us and the *Island Queen*.

McFarlane, a ruddy-faced Scotsman, waited up the gang-plank and saluted as we came aboard. The ship was grubby and worn – hardly the Royal Navy vessel we had hoped for, but it would do the job. It was good to have so many men behind us and I was glad to be getting away. We were the lucky ones, no question.

'I hear you're from my neck of the woods,' McFarlane said to Robert. 'Well, there's no such thing as bad weather to a Scot, Mr Fortune. It's all in keeping your pluck and having the right equipment.'

This man would do fine.

'Ah, Mrs Fortune,' he bowed towards me.

And neither Robert nor I corrected him; instead we saw the boxes aboard and made sure the plants were secure in the cabins. The Ward's cases, only half-made as yet, we stowed below decks, for there was no time to bolt them in, and in this weather it was only madness to delay.

But we were not to get away as easily as all that. The loading, haphazard as it was, took close to an hour and in that time we were spotted. Three mandarins arrived on the dock to challenge us. They were armed to the teeth with knives and backed by another twenty servants, all fortified with pitchforks and machetes. The leaders bowed very graciously but their intent was clear enough. Peverill's men stood to attention with their captain to one side, who was poised and clearly hoping for a confrontation. His eyes shone with anticipation, like those of a little boy playing soldiers, but the sight of the Chinese party made my stomach turn. I had no desire to see brave men die but it felt as if there was nothing for it. They were a rough crew and determined. Still, with the advantage of the soldiers' guns, I calculated that our side would win if it came to the bit. In truth, I just hoped that we would get away.

'You leave late,' one of the mandarins said passively in English, shouting from the dockside up to the deck. 'Sneaking like vermin.'

McFarlane ignored the insult. He bowed and walked down the gangplank steadily. We were still loading the final boxes.

'When the wind will take me I will go,' the captain said nonchalantly and he stood his ground.

'It is not honourable to leave with unpaid debts,' the man protested.

'I owe you nothing, sir.'

'This crew,' the mandarin screamed wildly. 'They owe money in this town. All this crew. They must settle their debts. Only wait until the morning and we can sort it out. Our brothers are coming. We have come to confiscate your sail, as is the custom for debtors. You cannot leave tonight.'

Gilland's judgement had been right. More were on their way, and the army no doubt as well. The accusation of the debt was only a pretext. I clasped Robert's hand tightly behind my back as the mandarin pushed past McFarlane to carry out his threat and strode up the gangplank towards the sail. The others surged behind him, muttering threats. As soon as the man set foot on the deck, Peverill sprang into action, shouting at his men, who took aim all at once with a precision and discipline that was most effective. The noise of the guns being raised stopped the mandarin in his tracks for a moment, but he glanced towards the sail,

322

his prize, hesitating only a second or two, his knife drawn to cut the ropes and disable the ship. I knew once the violence started each side would fight to the last man. I could hardly breathe.

Robert dropped my hand and I looked to see where I might fling myself, thinking to pull him beside me out of the firing line, when to my astonishment, instead of falling back in the face of the fracas, Robert stepped up between the mandarin and the bank of guns on the dock, and held up his hand while he addressed the Chinaman.

'You say this crew owe you money. I am most interested in that. What are these debts?' he asked the man. 'How much?'

I could not believe Robert was bothering with this. It had been laid as a red herring, surely. The Chinese simply wanted to stop us leaving. Peverill froze, holding his men at action stations while Robert called the man's bluff.

'Many *sycee* dollars,' the mandarin said, moving very slightly towards the ropes again. The *sycee* was the currency of the opium traders – a form of silver dollar.

'How many?' Robert enquired.

'Twenty,' the man spat.

This was a lot of money. More than a ragged crew of Chinamen could easily spend in their few days at port. Even the most degenerate of them.

'Ah, my friend. Twenty *sycee* dollars.' Robert languidly waved Wang towards a chest and had him open it. He pulled out a bag of money and nonchalantly dropped it into the mandarin's hand.

'Twenty,' he said, 'and no need to take the sail or fire a single shot. We do not want your brave men to die here.'

A grin broke out on Peverill's face. Robert had called the Chinese's bluff. The young captain was enjoying this. All eyes were on the mandarin, of course, who hesitated, halted in his tracks. He was not sure what to do. His followers had their knives still drawn and in turn the guns of Peverill's men remained trained upon them as Robert bowed deeply and moved to walk the mandarin off the ship.

'Thank you for allowing me to fulfil this debt with honour,' he said graciously.

The mandarin did not reply. There was a mere, mean incline of his head, his still eyes trained on the sail behind him. If a single shot were fired, that would be it. Open warfare. Robert put out his hand and lowered the man's knife.

'It is settled,' he said. 'With honour.'

Robert hoped that without an excuse he might win us the few minutes we needed to get away. The man's jaw twitched a second. If the ship sailed he would no doubt know the wrath of his own country's soldiers when they arrived in Foo Chow Soo the following day to discover he had accepted twenty dollars rather than halting our expedition. He had to do something. I saw his body tense, all at once, and then he dropped the bag of silver and bolted, screaming, towards the sail, with his knife held high. One clear shot rang out. It was Peverill who had taken aim. The man dropped to the ground on the deck and the soldiers trained their guns on the mob immediately. Everyone froze. Everyone that is, except McFarlane, who bounded back up onto the ship as two of his sailors pulled up the gangplank smartly behind him, and, in less than a minute, the fracas was isolated on the dockside.

The Chinese stared, calculating what to do. The truth was that they would be crazy to take on an overexcited Englishman with fourteen guns at his disposal, despite their greater numbers. McFarlane's men were already casting off and there were bullets trained upon the little group at close quarters.

'Put down your weapons,' I heard Peverill shout and the

two remaining mandarins, presumably making a swift calculation of their odds, dropped their knives to the ground, followed shortly by their compatriots. I could hear the metal clink against the stone of the dock.

Peverill nodded up at us. We were already a few feet away and it was so dark we would not be able to see him much longer. I was sad to leave such brave men behind. For my part, I thought the army's orders were wrong. Foo Chow Soo was hardly a place worth defending and it was certainly not worth dying for. These men were soldiers, though, and orders were orders.

'Send reinforcements as soon as you can!' Peverill shouted up. 'Safe journey, McFarlane!'

I waved. And the last I saw the Chinese were being rounded up as the soldiers disappeared into the darkness.

Sailing away, I was overcome with relief almost immediately, and grief too. There would surely be a confrontation in the little town, if not today, then tomorrow. I hoped they would stave it off with as few casualties as possible.

'Nice try,' Captain McFarlane said to Robert, dropping the bag of silver into his hand. 'We were lucky it was not worse. I will have the men drop that blaggard's remains overboard when we get out to sea.'

'A stiff breeze we have behind us, Captain McFarlane,' Robert said. 'One close call and now another.'

He had a good point. It was the wildest weather I had seen for two years. Out of the sheltered bay, the waves rose twenty feet in our wake. Robert and I stayed with the captain, soaked, on deck.

'I hate to leave Gilland in charge of such a mess. It's a pig's ear,' Robert sighed.

I expect our thoughts were all still there.

'God knows if it will come off without incident in the end,' the captain shrugged. 'The Chinese know they cannot retake the port from us, when it comes to it. That would mean another war. And you are gone now. There is no measure in a fight, Mr Fortune,' he replied. 'But it's been stewing for weeks. We must look to our own troubles, I think, and let the consul deal with his. Best to sail up the coast a little, or rather, ride the tide, and then dock if we can. For only a madman would hazard open water in this weather! I do believe it's getting worse.'

'Will they follow us, do you think?'

'They will be shot trying,' McFarlane swore. 'Peverill will cover for us. No, we will set ourselves to it. We just have to make it through this storm to one of the bays further up the coast, as far off as we can.'

Below decks, Sing Hoo's customary moaning had started up only to be drowned out by the howling of the wind. The rest of our men crouched terrified in the stew of vomit and piss that quickly collected below decks, each one convinced that death was to hand.

'Do you think you might ride the storm better on deck, Mary?' Robert asked kindly. 'I know you hate being shut in.'

I admitted that being stowed below with our rancid gardeners was not an appealing thought. As the ship pitched and the crew tried to set our course, McFarlane barked orders from the poop deck, shrouded in his sou'wester. Robert kept his arm around me.

'Come,' he said, 'let's try it,' and he secured our waists by rope to the vessel before handing me a sturdy-looking knife.

'If the ship breaks you must cut yourself free, Mary,' he said, 'or be dragged down with her.'

'All right,' I replied and stowed the knife in my pocket.

This was a contrast to Robert's demeanour the last time I braved a storm in his company and for that matter, a contrast to the last time he had tied me to a ship.

On deck the water was everywhere and there was little

time to think or worry what was going to happen. Every second was taken up in itself and it was enough to stand, the waves breaking over us and the ship pitching hard. The ragged crew knew their business, and we haltingly moved up the coastline as my heart pounded. I never lost my terror after the *Regatta* but being out in the heart of it, I realised, was a far better way of dealing with a storm.

'Come on then!' I shouted at the water. 'Come on!'

Robert and I clung to each other, falling more than once onto the deck and scrambling to our feet together. Many hours of soaking later, the ship finally found a sheltered bay and McFarlane dropped anchor. It was dawn and the rising sun lit the storm clouds over the open ocean. The storm was failing now in any case. The wind had almost blown itself out.

Robert and I retreated to the cabin, soaked to the skin, and crawled into the hammock, which was the best the *Island Queen* could afford. We fell fast asleep and when we woke the ship was moving steadily ahead and the sun was high. Robert dropped his feet to the floor and peered out of the porthole.

'I'm hungry,' he announced. 'Let's hope the ship's provisions will run to something.'

I leaned over and lifted my sodden coat. From the pocket I withdrew Gilland's present – the jar of marmalade. The label slid clean off the glass.

'I will see if there is any bread,' Robert promised and he disappeared out of the room to rifle the galley.

The fishing was fine that trip. We caught both shark and tuna. There were hardly any provisions on board, bar some ship's biscuits and a rough corn bread that the cook baked each morning. Nonetheless, we had tea and rice of our own and with the daily catch this proved adequate. McFarlane was a rough fellow. His usual cargo was opium and he looked most bemused at the array of plants that appeared on deck the first morning after the storm. Robert set Sing Hoo and Wang to complete the construction of the Ward's cases he needed for the long, onward journey – sixteen by his calculation. We could not plant them up as we had no soil, but at least they would be ready. McFarlane's crew, Chinese to a man, were taut, thin fellows with sharp teeth like street dogs. I noticed that neither Wang nor Sing Hoo even attempted to sell them any of our provisions – a mark no doubt that they were feral men and would take what they wanted at knife-point the second it was offered on the black market, for they knew there could be no appeal against it.

Our men kept below deck and together. Robert and I visited them regularly. On the first day we spent over two hours calming them and by means of drawing a rough map helped them understand the route of our journey. I described Hong Kong and made promises of a fine feast once we had docked.

'Dim sum,' I promised, 'and roast pork.'

Most recovered their stomachs as the storm subsided and the promise of a square meal heartened them.

'You are good for morale,' Robert said.

'They are afraid. We must promise them the familiar as a comfort.'

Robert nodded and later I heard him in conversation with one of the lead men, discussing the germination of the tea seeds in the cases, and expressing his own preference for black tea rather than green.

It was on board the *Island Queen* that I took the decision on our first day at sea to allow my hair to grow back. It was a landmark, of sorts, for in that I recognised my travelling was soon to be over. Late that afternoon, when we were underway, I had Wang bring up my case from Ning-po. Slowly, I pulled out all my silks, my bodices and corsets. The colours were pale compared to the attire I was now accustomed to – brash Chinese shades that shone in the sunshine. As I drew one gown and then another to my face my skin seemed to lighten and I looked like a woman once more. I scrubbed myself clean and then stood for an hour piling up my hair and securing it with combs and pins until the shaved part of my scalp was obscured. I looked elegant, even sophisticated, as I slipped on my lace-up boots and a plain, cotton day dress in the palest blue. My waist was tinier than ever, I warranted myself. And yet in the mirror I was a stranger.

When Robert came to the cabin his face broke into a grin. 'You look beautiful, Mary,' he said. 'I must transform myself now or we will be an odd pair, don't you think?'

He slipped his arm around me and inspected my form more closely as he kissed my neck. I said nothing.

That evening Captain McFarlane jumped up and held out my seat at the dinner table. The candles were burning low but even in that odd light I could still make out the cramped shabbiness of his quarters, though, I admit, they were comfortable enough.

'Please,' he gestured, and I sat down.

Robert had found a pair of breeches and a jacket.

'We are all dressed for dinner, eh?' he grinned at himself in the glass before he took his place.

'You do appear quite different,' McFarlane commented, and then he rang the bell and they brought the fish. The boy who served it glared at me in this new incarnation but I merely glared back at him. Lord knows what our tea gardeners would make of me.

'A toast,' McFarlane raised his glass. 'Before we sup. To the brave men we left at Foo Chow Soo. May they last until we can send comrades to strengthen their numbers! Our prayers are with them, every one.'

We drank to that and then had a moment's silence. We were the lucky ones, there was no doubt.

'Come now,' said the captain. 'We must enjoy our meal and a week or so's company.'

And we set to.

I was no longer accustomed to eating with my waist pinned and given the tightness of the stays I managed very little. Robert wolfed his food and engaged McFarlane in some talk of Edinburgh and the gardens at Inverleith where he had worked as a boy when first he left his father's house. McFarlane's father had been a fisherman at Granton.

'Changed days,' he sighed.

'And you ferry opium?' Robert enquired.

'Yes. Five years in the navy, of course. And now, all this,' he gestured around him, a twinkle in his eye. 'Two years ago I went to London,' he continued. 'I visited the theatre and there on stage they portrayed an opium trader. Their notion was rather far from the truth, I'm afraid. It is as profitable as they showed it, but, well, some of the other advantages were rather poorly imagined. I am not a man of the world really. I could have a far finer ship, but this old girl sees me right.'

'Ah,' Robert's eyes glinted, 'what they say in Drury Lane matters little. Many things on the stage in London are not as they seem.'

After dinner McFarlane brought out a box of cigars and he and Robert puffed away over an excellent port, while I went back to the cabin. On the way I passed one of our gardeners. Our eyes met and he caught his breath, surveying me as if I was a strange curiosity.

I smiled. 'You may still call me Master,' I told him, and hearing my voice seemed to confuse him further and he rushed off to tell the others what he had encountered.

Back in the cabin, my fingers fumbled as I undid the laces

330

and took down my hair. I climbed into the hammock and blew out my candle but I could not sleep despite the comforting rock of the ship on the water. Tomorrow I would face them and answer all the questions. Perhaps Wang would answer them for me – he was probably facing them now. The ship creaked. I told myself it was only a week or so.

When Robert returned he did not realise my eyes were open and he sank into the chair by the door, saying nothing. He and McFarlane had finished the bottle and now, as ever, with his mind working ahead, Robert pulled out a book and began to read. Through the ropes that secured my bed, I saw he had picked up a directory of Indian customs and practices. It was only then I think that it ceased to be words and I truly knew that he was going. My mind flitted ahead from India to London. Gilston Road, to be precise. With my thoughts wandering, I decided I could share him with Jane if I had to. The truth was my sister hardly knew her husband. It was not such a bad arrangement. She would never know of it anyway, and, besides, this way we could both get what we wanted. My conscience pricked only slightly, and I glossed over it, telling myself that she would never know, never mind. Never.

When Robert came to bed an hour later I feigned sleep, turning over to cling to him and sighing as if deep in a dream.

'I adore you, Mary,' he whispered and kissed my cheek.

I wound my fingers through his hair. It was very difficult to let him go, to share him with civilisation or anyone else. When he kissed me he tasted of tobacco and wine, the inside of his mouth hot. I fought the sadness that was at the fringes and told myself that I had never done anything yet that was conventional – why should the love of my life be any different? Besides, I knew the deal I was making. I would have China. China was all mine.

Chapter Thirteen

Five days from Hong Kong and I was woken by the sound of scurrying on deck. I turned over sleepily in the hammock to find that Robert was gone. Yawning, I swung myself to the ground as I heard the hammering of feet pass the doorway, the whole crew it sounded like, running below decks screaming '*Jan dhou!*' as they went. I had not the least idea what this meant and the only thing that came to mind was that for some reason they were set to molest our gardeners. In a panic, I pulled on my clothes and went to investigate.

On deck in the blazing sunshine, it was clear that the cause of the shouting was not the enmity between the two groups of men on board. The gardeners were nowhere to be seen and the crew continued rushing this way and that all over the ship in an absolute panic. They were a rough lot and I could not imagine there was much they might be afraid of. McFarlane stood on the poop, shouting over his men's raised voices in a strange version of Cantonese that I had difficulty understanding. Between these bouts he swore in English.

'Bloody cowards!' he screamed.

'Captain McFarlane,' I said, as I approached him, 'whatever is the matter?'

McFarlane drew himself up. His lips were pulled tightly

across his face and he was agitated. He gave a cursory nod towards the line of the horizon. Far off in the distance there was a peppering of ships, but I could not make them out clearly.

'Here. See for yourself, ma'am,' he said.

I put my hand out for the spyglass, which he stoutly handed over and then strode off, no navy officer, still shouting incomprehensible insults at his men. I drew the glass to my eye. Magnified, I could see that the ships were Chinese junks but beyond that I could not tell what the fuss was about. The little fleet was coming from the direction of Hong Kong so, I presumed, had not pursued us from Foo Chow Soo. We had often passed junks on our travels before – as many Chinese ships as British traded up and down the coastline and along the main rivers, if not more. McFarlane was at the other end of the deck by now and the panic was worsening. My hand, I noticed, had started to quiver. It was most alarming to have such un-controllable anxiety all around and not know what we were facing.

The next minute Robert passed me. He had a look of intense concentration on his face as if he was considering a particularly thorny conundrum. The crew had mostly disappeared now, though I could still hear their shouting from below decks.

'Robert?' I caught his arm.

He swung around. He did not realise, I suppose, that I was lately risen and had no idea what was going on.

'Thank you,' he said and removed the spyglass from my hand. 'Good idea, Mary.'

He drew the glass to his eye.

'An hour at least,' he said, 'and they have clipper-built hulls, I think. Makes them damn fast,' and then McFarlane strode back towards us.

'The men have stowed themselves below deck and are tearing their clothes to shreds to look poorer. I will whip them for this. It is no help.'

'Gentlemen,' I burst out, 'will you tell me please what is going on?'

Robert's eyes softened. 'Mary. There are pirates,' he said.

I had heard tales of Chinese pirates, from the legend of Chen Chih-lung on. There were regular attacks on British and American trading boats, opium clippers mostly, and there had been since Chen's days almost two hundred years before. On our voyages to Chusan and Ning-po there were so many naval vessels on the straits that we had not been easy game and the scoundrels knew they had less opportunity of a safe catch on those more crowded and well-defended waters. Pirates near Hong Kong were not a huge problem. The sea around Foo Chow Soo afforded more isolated game, however. We had been spotted and were being pursued. Chinese pirates were known for their viciousness and this, I suppose, accounted for the desperate state of our crew, who were preparing for their imminent slaughter and tearing around the ship, blindly. We were not well armed and certainly, if they boarded us, we would be done for. During the war there was a high bounty set on British ships and I had heard horrifying tales of vessels captured and the crew all beheaded, for the bounty on men was paid by the head, so why, in the eyes of the pirates, would they bother to keep the rest of the body?

The six pirate vessels pursuing us were in the main about the same size as our own though, McFarlane said, the cut of their sails was marginally better than that of the poor *Island Queen*. On top of that the wind was in their favour. Such ships did not venture onto the open ocean, but scouted around the coastline and their tactics were directed to boarding their targeted vessel, rather than to open combat.

They had no interest in sinking us – and their weaponry reflected that.

'They will have small bombs and perhaps mines. I cannot see yet if any of the hulls are defended by spikes. If so, they may ram us. We must turn back,' McFarlane said. 'It will be difficult with all hands below decks but we are three. We can tack. It is not all lost – we have a head start and with the same wind conditions as they are enjoying, we might have a hope of losing them if we can keep ahead until darkness. It is our only chance.'

Robert shook his head. 'Back towards Foo Chow Soo? A rock and a hard place, don't you think, McFarlane? And we have no friendly port beyond that. Not until India. We will be turning ourselves to sea, as good as a void. And Gilland is counting on us, don't forget.'

McFarlane considered this. 'We will not outrun them in Chinese waters, never mind further,' he mused. 'We will not outrun them even as far as Foo Chow Soo, Fortune. Our only hope is the darkness, if we can keep ahead long enough and then lose them when they cannot see our course. We cannot help the others at Foo Chow Soo if we are captured.'

Robert let this point sink in.

'They have made up a few hundred yards since the first sighting. There is no measure in running, surely. Do you really think we can outrun them till darkness? It is hours away, McFarlane.'

'Would you take them on then, the blaggards? Fight them just the three of us? What options do we have?'

Robert shook his head. We were in a shabby position for a battle, there was no denying it.

'We could treaty with them,' he said. 'I have money.'

McFarlane laughed. 'Like gentlemen? They will board us, slit our throats and take everything without a by-your-leave. The ship is worth more to them than a few *sycee* and they will have your *sycee* and mine, anyway. If they get close enough to treaty we are all dead.'

Robert drew the spyglass to his eye once more. The junks were still not close enough to make out much in the way of detail beyond the shape of the hull and the cut of the sails. I felt my throat tighten. From what I had heard I could only surmise that our plan was to try to outrun the ships pursuing us and that we would probably fail. I considered that, if I had to help turn the *Island Queen*, it would then be my duty to go to our own men, take my gun and any knives I could find, and stay with them until these beasts came aboard. I was steeling myself for it.

Robert had not given up so easily.

'They are directed to boarding us, you say?'

'Yes,' McFarlane snapped as if Robert was an imbecile. 'They are pirates.'

'They do not have cannon or guns?'

'Not many. Perhaps one cannon on deck. We cannot see yet, but I doubt it. As for guns, they will have what they have captured before, but probably only a few, if any, and little shot. They will, however, have bombs, though they will have to get close enough to throw them by hand. Fortune, you are wasting time talking, we must turn and get off.'

Robert ignored him. 'So they would not take on a naval vessel? The white devils. They would turn tail at that.'

'Certainly. Or at least be put on the back foot. Do you think you can magic HMS *Fortitude* and all her guns from thin air? There is no one here but us.'

Robert grinned. 'Not HMS *Fortitude*. But HMS *Island Queen* we can manage. We cannot make out more than an outline now. Neither can they. They do not know who we are. We have one cannon at the helm, but it's better than nothing and between us we have some guns. Five, I think.'

McFarlane's face froze for a second.

'Three of us,' he said slowly.

'We have nine men below decks quite beside the crew.'

'Chinese.'

'Oh, that is all in the appearance,' Robert waved his hand. We had both proved that point. 'We will wager they will not get close enough to inspect the cut of our jib or the slanting whites of our eyes too closely. How many British clothes do you have, McFarlane? Are you game for it?'

McFarlane thought for a moment, surveyed the advancing junks.

Then he nodded.

'All right,' he said. 'Truth is they will butcher us anyway.'

It was, perhaps, not quite the spirit we might have hoped for. Robert squeezed my hand as we sprang into action.

'We'll fight them,' he marshalled me. 'Scare them,' he promised. 'It's all in the show, Mary.'

We fell to the job and, quickly, from the cabins, McFarlane and I mustered six full English outfits between us, and the guns. Robert went below decks and sent up Wang and Sing Hoo first, who gingerly picked jackets and breeches from the pile we had laid on deck, and examined them. 'Either breeches with a loose shirt or a jacket done up over your own clothes,' Robert directed. Sing Hoo smiled.

'Quickly, Sing Hoo!'

'I am to be *gweiloh*?' he said with delight, and needed no further instruction, eagerly pulling on the breeches, fumbling over the buttons. It was not military attire, but it was Western and, I suppose, if the pirates got close enough to see the details too clearly we were probably done for anyway.

Wang chose a greatcoat that belonged to McFarlane. I inspected him and Sing Hoo, topping off Wang's outfit with a hat and binding Sing Hoo's head with a piece of linen

337

cloth, as I had seen English sailors do. It hid his Chinese baldness and his queue admirably. The two men eyed each other and then burst into hysterical laughter. Then, berated by Robert for wasting time, Wang fetched the tea gardeners on deck and between us we arrayed them as best we could. From a distance they could have been from Southampton as much as Foo Chow Soo by the time we'd done.

Up at the helm, Robert and McFarlane loaded the guns. The cannon it transpired had come from Chusan and there were only a dozen balls for it. With the men attired, we sent Sing Hoo to fetch anything sharp or jagged that he could muster from below decks. We could fire kitchen knives if we had to, the ship's supply of nails for repairs and even, we supposed, the crockery would injure if pitched at a high enough velocity.

'They will aim here first,' McFarlane instructed us, pointing out the key points of the pirates' tactics. 'If they can knock out the helm we are disabled. The shot will set the deck ablaze whether it hits home or not. It will be close quarters.'

'Right,' said Robert and set our men to drawing buckets of seawater ready for this contingency.

'Have you ever been in a battle?' McFarlane asked Robert.

'No,' Robert admitted.

'Me neither,' I said, which made the three of us giggle.

'So,' McFarlane confirmed, 'they will fire. I hope it does not shock you too much. With me, I find, it makes me angry. It's the best you can hope for. Ma'am, I cannot help but think that perhaps you should be below deck. You are a very brave woman to stay.'

I did not know about that. I cast my eye back over the tea gardeners, who a few weeks before had never seen the sea, never mind heard of pirates. I had known I was heading into dangerous situations when I took my place at Robert's side. They had simply thought they were earning some extra money for their skills on another plantation.

'I would rather be fighting,' I told him. 'In the eye of the storm, Captain. Truly, I would prefer it. Besides, there is a more fearsome crew below decks than above at present. I cannot imagine me, your fierce men and all our plants, happily stowed together for the duration of this. So, it is best that I know what is to happen. Explain more to me. We must hit the deck and hope it goes over our heads,' I said. 'It is not a course of action for the faint-hearted, eh? What then?'

McFarlane resumed. There was no measure in squabbling with me about the niceties of a lady's place in battle.

'Well, ma'am, then it is a matter of putting out the fires and shooting back if they don't hit the mainsail or the helm or plain sink us, that is. Though it is to our advantage that sinking us is not their aim and they are not armed for that. We can shoot back as they are reloading whatever guns they have at their disposal. Mostly though, they are set up to board us and take the ship, not fight us from a distance. They may have no guns at all. It is quite likely we have the advantage there.'

Here McFarlane pulled out his pistol and his bag of shot. Robert surveyed our men. I knew exactly what he was thinking. They were hardly competent.

'I can fire a gun,' I offered.

Both Robert and McFarlane hesitated.

'But, Mary—' Robert started.

'Oh, please, Robert,' I dismissed him before he said it. 'I have been a man the last eighteen months. And I can fire better than any of those poor souls.'

I grabbed a jacket, a hat and a gun and took my place.

'Some woman!' McFarlane said with delight.

'Stop fussing, Captain,' I sounded like a nanny. 'We have

only a few minutes left to make our preparation – let's get the best out of them!'

Robert placed the men at intervals and said he would signal them to show themselves when he was ready. The poor souls were terrified.

'You will follow the captain's orders, my orders and the master's,' Robert told them. 'Just do as you are told, whatever happens.'

I suppose if we three all died, the men would be sunk anyway. Not one among them knew anything of battle. Despite this, they certainly looked stout enough. I thought they were bearing up very well and that Sing Hoo and Wang had done a good job of rallying them, explaining what would happen as best they could. Still, I saw one had already pissed in the fine pair of breeches we had dressed him in and it did not take a great judge of human nature to see they were afraid.

'We are fighting for our lives here. Shout "Yes, sir!",' Robert admonished them.

The crew tried this without much success but after several attempts they did sound like English sailors, albeit drunk ones.

At this point I saw one of McFarlane's men sneaking up on the deck. Our own crew looked chipper in comparison, for the sailor was filthy and had ripped his clothes like many of his fellows when the pirates first came into sight. He surveyed the gardeners' outlandish attire with wide eyes without stopping in his tracks, and continued to move, smoothly, across the deck, almost sliding towards the side of the ship, ignoring our newly formed crew. McFarlane spotted him just as he was climbing over. He grabbed the man by the hair.

'Thought you'd slip overboard, did you?' he spat viciously.

The man struck out, but McFarlane felled him swiftly. He was a big chap and clearly adept in a fight.

'There will be no swimming to the safety of the shore, you sneak. We are on navy rules now. Bring me that rope,' he snapped at Sing Hoo.

He deftly tied a hangman's noose and it was only then that I realised his intention. Navy rules, I suppose, were navy rules and deserters would be hung. We could not have one coward giving others ideas. With a brutal efficiency, the man was noosed, the rope slung over part of the rigging and the sailor hoisted high as McFarlane himself secured the cord.

'No deserters,' he shouted at the crew, as the sailor's legs thrashed and his eyes bulged. I had never seen a hanging at such close quarters but, truth to tell, I had no objection to stringing up such a coward. He threatened us all. A sharp pull on the man's calves quietened his thrashing to a mere twitch.

'He will hang there until the fight is over,' McFarlane announced. 'And the next man who goes over will be treated likewise. You will fight here and some may die, but none of us have any chance if we do not all fight together.'

'Yes, sir,' the men shouted and I could see, oddly, that Sing Hoo's eyes were alight.

With everything else ready, McFarlane raised the Union Jack and some other flags that he happened to have stowed in a box in his cabin.

'Not quite the right thing for a navy vessel, but close enough and we are clearly British,' he said. 'Now we can only take our places and hope.'

'Do you think this will work?' I asked as I crouched by the helm.

McFarlane smiled and shrugged. 'I think we have a shot,' he hazarded, honestly. 'They are terrified of the navy in these waters. It is not so long since our boats decimated them. We cannot outgun the six of them but if we put up a decent show we may hold off until nightfall. If we are lucky they will not be able to follow us and we can change course and sail without lamps. Fortune is right. We cannot outrun them in daylight and if they see us as we are then they will know we are easy game. This is the best we can hope for. That and a dark night.'

I looked at the sky. It was the early afternoon at latest. The junks were only a few minutes away from firing range. We would have to fight them off for hours before dusk. McFarlane saw what I was thinking.

'I've had better odds, ma'am, but I have had worse too,' he assured me.

I felt sick to the pit of my stomach. Each time I peered over the side the ships were closer, looming into view with dark sails. When we could make out the men on their decks, Robert marched our crew at action stations so the pirates could see we were British. He even managed to get one or two of McFarlane's men back up on deck to join in – a godsend as it was proving difficult to sail the ship using the gardeners as the only crew. The poor men had no idea of the logistics of unfurling a sail or tying the thick ropes in place as they were required.

McFarlane stood with his spyglass in place and surveyed the pirate vessels relentlessly. He said nothing of what he saw, unwilling, I expect, to make clear how many men we were taking on or how well they were armed. It was daunting enough as it was.

After what seemed like a longer wait than it probably was, the junks sailed into range and swung into action. They lobbed over their bombs, all together.

'Hit the deck!' McFarlane screamed and everybody dived.

The shot passed over our heads but the ship took the brunt of it. There was splintered wood strewn everywhere, much of it alight. Many of the men were caught in the shrapnel

342

but none were floored by it. Sing Hoo's face was peppered with tiny, bloody cuts, but he rallied the men. At intermittent gunpoint our gardeners doused the deck in seawater while Robert, Wang, McFarlane and I returned fire across the water. Our sniper skills were not too shabby and we hit half a dozen men between us on our first two or three volleys. The pirates returned once more and again, we hit the deck and, on rising, found all round us aflame. Sing Hoo rallied the men once more, drawing water on board and raking the deck where he could to douse the flames. This time I saw one man had been hit badly in the side with a sharp shard of wood. He was screaming over and over again. McFarlane, I saw, also had a huge splinter of what I took to be the yardarm in his leg. The wood had not shattered completely and the sail was still in place and useable. He removed the stake from his thigh and bound the bloody gash without even wincing. We reloaded. This time with four volleys from each of the three of us we hit only four of our marks. Their men were lying low now, as were we.

McFarlane changed tactics. He took a careful shot at one of the junks and managed to hit a rope that secured one of the sails. This caused a huge commotion aboard the junk as the cloth crashed onto the deck and the ship foundered.

'Ha!' he shouted triumphantly.

'Good shot, Captain,' Robert grinned.

In this way we fought for what seemed like a long time, the *Island Queen* moving alongside the pirate vessels but maintaining a good enough distance to keep them from boarding. Our deck was littered with burnt wood but the helm and mainsail were safe. The same could not be said of our men. Not one of us was intact and there were streaks of blood across the wooden deck. We gave as good as we got, though, if not better sometimes, and each time we volleyed fire we caught one or two of them fair and square – and importantly, we seemed to hit one captain, for that junk, along with its sister whose sail McFarlane had disabled, fell behind. For our part I consider that we were extraordinarily lucky with our injuries.

Well into the battle I managed to tend the first man who had been hit in the side and he quietened, even rising shakily to his feet to help again after a while. Our only fatality was one of the feral crew who came up on deck about an hour in and whom McFarlane shot himself when it became clear that the man intended jumping ship and swimming towards the shore rather than helping us. It seemed the example of his fellow, now a very bloody carcass, swinging from his rope, had not been enough to discourage him.

'Shame to waste the bullet,' the captain muttered as the man fell.

I have to say, McFarlane was formidable in action.

Robert's skin shone and he proved an excellent sniper, following McFarlane's example and felling one more mainsail.

'You are in your element!' I accused him.

'If we survive you can say that,' he volleyed. 'But if we fail or are hit then, Mary, this is not my element, no doubt about it.'

I was sorry then to have accused him. It was in the heat of the moment and, in truth, I liked taking aim myself. If you didn't think about it too much, it was exciting, and I realised quickly that it was far better not to think.

At the end of the afternoon we had them down to only two ships and I think neither we nor they had ammunition left. We had fired every piece of offensive wood, glass, pottery or metal we could bring to hand including some stone carvings we were carrying, which, while not worth our lives, would have made a pretty penny on sale in the

Strand. Safe to say, we would be eating off a bare table with our fingers if we were lucky enough to survive.

When the sky finally melted into a peachy haze, the clouds dark against the failing sunlight, we had kept well enough ahead. The pirates put on one last push, but it was half hearted and we held them off. I think they had thought us an easy prize and we had proved we were no such thing. Still, a prize we were and they wanted our skins. As the dusk turned to blackness, I was both exhausted and relieved. McFarlane sent for his remaining sailors who appeared sheepishly on deck. There was no measure in berating them now. To manage in the darkness he needed a fresh crew of men who knew the ship and what to do with her. The pirates lit lanterns but we had no such luxury and set off as night fell, all of us silent, and praying that the cloud would hold, for there was little light from the moon.

'Not a breath. Not a word from anyone,' McFarlane swore. 'They do not need light to follow us. Voices will do.'

And our Chinese sailors, cowards every one, slipped around the deck of the *Island Queen* like ghostly shadows. We cut further out to sea. For a while the pirate junks still followed us, managing by instinct to tell our route, but after an hour or so the lanterns disappeared and McFarlane changed direction, arcing a loop to bring us eventually in the direction of Hong Kong. It was a roundabout course to take and would add two days, but we were safe.

'Might we run into them again?' Robert asked as McFarlane pored over his maps.

'Unlikely,' he said, 'though not impossible. They have no way to plot what we are doing. If we do meet again it will be mere chance and they will not want to head close to Hong Kong themselves, for there is the real navy.'

We collected the British clothes, ordered all wounds

345

doused in seawater and then I myself soothed them with warm water and lavender oil. We had all sustained injuries, McFarlane the worst. He was brave with it, though for the rest of the voyage he walked with a crutch. Later the men were issued with extra rations, such as were available. Nothing could be cooked so it was ship's biscuits, stale corn bread and *sham shoo* for supper. They were ravenous and it would do. Our last duties were to throw overboard the bloodied bodies of the two deserters.

'Thank God,' Robert breathed, as we sank into seats at the captain's table, close on midnight.

McFarlane found a decent bottle and uncorked it in the pitch black, passing it to each of us in turn. The glasses were long gone. The bottle itself was the only one that had escaped being used as ammunition. The rest of the case had become splinters and shards in the pirates' sides.

'Thank God for this refugee. At least I know my way around a cork and bottle,' McFarlane joked. 'After that long day, we deserve more than slops from a barrel of rice wine. I propose a toast to us all. Quick thinking, Fortune. And, Mrs Fortune, might I say, not many ladies would manage as you did. You are a crack shot, madam.'

'Mary,' Robert admitted, 'is a treasure. Once she was even shipwrecked, you know. But, Captain McFarlane, I must tell you that Mary is not my wife. She is my wife's sister.'

McFarlane downed his drink. I heard him gulping.

'Really?' he said. 'I would never have guessed you were not a love match.'

I knew Robert probably smiled here, but could not see it. For myself I held the secret to my heart. I would, I knew, have to get used to that.

When Hong Kong appeared on the horizon I was on deck. It was early in the morning and I was taking a turn. We knew we were close – there had been seabirds wheeling high in the sky the whole of the night.

Robert and I had stood at midnight on the deck. The *Island Queen* was a sight – like some kind of zombie, still moving despite her bones being exposed, she glided through the darkness.

'I promise you, Mary—' Robert started.

'Hush,' I said.

He did not need to say it. We both knew how we felt. We both knew it must be a secret. Things would appear quite normal but we would have each other despite that. Now we held our bodies close knowing our next night would be on dry, English soil.

When Hong Kong island came into view I jumped up and down with the excitement of it. The Peak towered, lush and green over the bay and in the two years we had been absent there had been a lot of new building. Even from a distance, parts of the city looked quite fine, I thought, the houses painted white, standing out against the jungle. I pictured myself the last time we had been here – a well-dressed woman, seemingly sophisticated but callow in the ways of the world, with all the shallow concerns of a privileged European close to her heart. An observer would probably doubt I could have survived on foot in the Bohean Hills in winter or raised a rifle against a pirate attack sustaining the injuries that still nipped my skin. I had loved poetry and the theatre. Now I loved adventure more. And, of course, the man who had adventured with me.

McFarlane anchored at the dock, his battered ship drawing much attention. A friend, another opium runner, strolled over and called for permission to come aboard.

'What the hell happened to you?' he asked, flinging his arms around McFarlane's frame in greeting and almost knocking our brave captain over, for he still was not entirely steady.

'This,' McFarlane turned, 'is Robert Fortune and this Mary Penney. We fought off a pirate attack together as well as if we were a navy frigate!'

The man laughed delightedly.

'Now that story merits a side of ham and some burgundy,' he said.

'I would kill, Captain, for some steamed pudding,' I admitted.

'Or some cheese and chutney,' Robert chimed in.

The captain laughed. 'How long have you been away?' he asked.

'Two years,' I said. 'Heavens. Do you think there may be chocolate?'

And a mere ten minutes later we were aboard the *Oriental* with warm, delicious chocolate streaming down our chins and an advance message dispatched to Pottinger about the state of affairs at Foo Chow Soo, to be followed in short order, or as short as we could, with a visit in person from Robert and myself.

It was in this state that she found us. Aboard the *Oriental* there was a window in the captain's cabin that oversaw her approach. I saw the figure, but I did not properly register it. It was so entirely unexpected, you see. A minute later there was a sharp knock on the captain's door, the sound of our laughter wafting out, I expect, as she burst in. Jane Penney. Mrs Fortune. My dear sister. In her navy dress with the red buttons and a parasol at her side. She must have been waiting at the dock to find us so soon after we had arrived. She had been poised and ready for some time.

'Jane,' Robert stuttered at the sight of his wife.

My sister glided to my side. Oddly, I was glad to see her.

I had no time to plan my reaction. It just happened. My mouth twitched, the start of a smile on my lips and my arms reaching out to hold her, completely uncomprehending as she raised her arm and struck me a blow on my face that had me reeling.

'How dare you?' she spat furiously. 'Do you think I am a fool? Did you think I would bide at home with your bastard son while you steal off with Robert? Dear God, Mary, what will it be next?'

We had our chests unloaded and the men housed. Wide eyed and shocked, we dispensed *cash* at the bustling port and, as I had promised, supplied a feast for our tea gardeners that, under Sing Hoo's watchful eyes, lasted three days. Jane had, it transpired, been six weeks at port, waiting. From London she had sent letters that were forwarded to Ningpo and as a result she had been in correspondence with Bertie for over a year. Alone for the first time, we were all in a carriage, bound for the house Jane had let and where we would now be staying together. There was no point in denying her suspicions.

'How did you know?' I asked.

'It's you!' She was venomous. 'You disappear off with a man, my man, I might add. What else would happen? You are nothing if not predictable. You steal everything, Mary. Being married is the only thing that I ever wanted! The only thing that mattered.'

There were tears in her eyes.

'Jane, it is my fault, not Mary's,' Robert cut in.

'You!' Jane snapped at him. 'I thought you were a gentleman, Robert Fortune.'

Robert's eyes fell to the rush matting on the tiny floor.

'No,' he countered his wife. 'You wanted to make me a gentleman. And, Jane, that is what I have been doing.

349

Elevating us. It would not have been possible without Mary. It is what you wanted, is it not?'

'Money! Pah!'

Truly, I had never seen my sister in such a temper. Her pale skin was shining.

'We have ten years' worth of money sitting in the bank and it means nothing. I hate you. I hate both of you! How dare you!'

She broke down furiously. 'It is not for money!' she kept saying over and over. 'Not for that.'

My heart ached to see my stoic sister so upset. I swear, not when our mother died or when, once, she lost a child in her belly, had she cried like this.

'Jane,' I reached out to comfort her, to try to explain, but she pushed my arm away and with her eyes hard, spat back at me.

'Don't! Just don't!'

As we dismounted and entered the house I thought we might perhaps be able to talk. In the event, both Major Vernon and Sir Pottinger were waiting with another man, an East India Company representative called Thomas Gerard.

'A great achievement, Fortune,' Pottinger blustered as he burst out of the drawing room towards us and grabbed Robert by the hand. 'Congratulations!'

Jane hovered in the hallway, barely controlling herself. It was clear there had been an upset. Her cheeks were wet. Our guests ignored it, pulling us into the drawing room with good-humoured bluster.

'And I hear, Miss Penney,' Major Vernon said, 'that you were invaluable. Quite the lady in a fight. That's the spirit! You must be so proud of them, Mrs Fortune.'

Jane bit her lip and I saw her fingers twitch but she kept her silence.

That afternoon there was little time to be had alone together. Closeted in the study with a set of maps and endless bottles of port, we poured out our story. Pottinger dispatched three ships of recruits from Happy Valley to Foo Chow Soo on the next tide and wrote an emergency dispatch to London to be taken by Captain Harper who was due to sail westwards that very night. I hoped that it saved brave Major Gilland and his men.

All the while, Jane sat regally on a red velvet chair by the window and listened silently to our tales. For the most part she knew our route, for the goods dispatched home had made that much clear. Still, Robert's espionage activities were all news to her, as were the full extent of our dangers and successes. The account of our flight through the Bohean Hills and escape from Foo Chow Soo provoked a spontaneous bout of cheering from Vernon. The fact that Robert had procured boxes of precious tea seeds elicited a quiet smile from Mr Gerard. That he had almost died of the fever, I noticed, moved Jane, and I took it from that that all was not lost. It was a glimmer that forgiveness might be possible. But it was not offered yet.

By the time the men left it was late and we were all of us drunk, I think. Pottinger promised a grand reception at the Governor's Mansion and Vernon, kissing both my hand and Jane's in taking his leave, swore to dance with both of us. As the door of the house closed behind our guests, the three of us on our own at last, Robert turned.

'I hope there are three bedrooms in this house,' he said to his wife.

Jane, like a child, pushed him.

'You think I would share a bed with you? I despise you,' she said.

I caught his eye. We were unrepentant, we sinners. Neither of us had apologised, I realised, and neither of us would.

351

'Come on,' Robert said. 'I am exhausted. Jane, it is for you, I think, to allocate the sleeping quarters.'

And that night, between heavy, cool sheets, I slept in a room to one side of the house where, I noticed, the floorboards were creaky. I slept alone.

The next day brought gifts delivered before breakfast and a flurry of invitations. Our arrival in the colony had caused much excitement. Pottinger was as good as his word and had set an evening aside for an official reception. We were quite the celebrities. Slight acquaintances from our last docking at Hong Kong had written notes of congratulations, many enquiring if my plan was still to settle here for they had a position I might like to consider. I left the letters by my bed.

When I came downstairs Jane had not yet risen and Robert was in the study. He was surveying an accounts book when I entered although he had been up for hours reading his correspondence, the piles of letters on the study desk attesting to it. Robert's editor at the *Monthly Review* had sent two missives tersely enquiring why he had received no more reports about the plant life of China. There was a letter from a colleague from the Royal Horticultural Society who had written with some questions about the care of a particular orchid. There was confirmation of some of the new species that we had found – it was like a strange kind of dream – all these people carrying on their normal lives, with queries and problems addressed thousands of miles away as if their small London lives were of paramount concern. Robert had read all these and then turned his attention to the auction reports and the ledger Jane had kept. She was, of course, an excellent administrator.

'Dear God,' he said, looking up. 'She was telling the truth about the money. Mary, we are rich! Or rich enough! And we are carrying goods to the value of the same as all this again in our retinue at present – bar what we had to fire overboard, of course. But still . . . I had no idea we would do so well! The gardenias alone sold for fifty pounds! Those large soapstone carvings have raised three hundred between them.'

I slipped into a chair on the other side of the desk.

'That is good news,' I observed, 'but Jane is very angry.'

Robert nodded. He laid down the book at once. 'I am sorry for that but I think it changes very little,' he said solemnly.

It was not fair, I knew it. But he was right. We must just try to get through it.

Over breakfast Jane perused the invitations, all addressed to us in trio, Robert read a newspaper from London that was only three months out of date, and I stared out of the window at the house's pretty little garden.

'Your plan is to stay here, Mary?' Jane enquired.

She was, I think, assessing the situation. Getting rid of me once more. I nodded. Robert lent over the top of his paper.

'Mary will stay here. I will return with you via India, to London. Then, Jane, I will come back to Hong Kong.'

Jane laid down her butter knife.

'You have everything planned to perfection,' she sneered. 'Well, everyone will know of it, Robert. I will divorce you, you know.'

Robert betrayed no emotion. 'That is your prerogative,' he said.

'And you,' Jane spat, turning to me, 'you would just love that! Playing into your hands!'

'I don't want you to divorce your husband, Jane,' I said. It was the truth.

'Oh,' Jane squealed in frustration. 'It is not up to you! You are always the golden girl. Well, it's not up to you!'

The fact was that Jane would never divorce Robert. It would taint her children's reputation and, however angry she might be, she would never do that. None of us said so, however.

'You feel trapped, don't you?' I started. 'Jane, neither of us planned this. But it has happened.'

'And you,' Jane raised her voice, 'I suppose had no hand in it? It happened! You really expect to get away with this, don't you? The same as you get away with everything and I am the one who is hurt and punished and has to put up with it?'

'Stop it!' Robert stood up. 'Stop it at once! You will not blame Mary. I will not let you.'

I held up my hand, motioning him to retake his seat. 'This is my fault as much as Robert's but it is honest. These are honest feelings. You are my sister and I love you and I can see that what we have done is wrong, but we have done it anyway. You have every right to be angry, Jane. But things have changed here. They have changed forever. The truth is though, that there is no punishment in this for you. None whatever.'

'I can never have him again! Not now! You fool!' she screamed at the top of her voice.

Robert turned pink with anger.

'Please do not pretend that I am a loss to your bed! Tell me, did you want me inside you even once while I was away? My arms around you? Once?'

Jane's eyes were blazing.

'And that is what this is all about. Your disgusting, filthy, animal habits! That is all you care about!'

Robert turned to me. He took a deep breath.

'Mary,' he said. 'Would you mind if I had a word with my wife, alone?'

I was glad to get away and I suppose that the discussion

that ensued was of a private nature. We still had privacies from each other, despite what had happened, I assured myself. I left the room and descended to the kitchens where I asked Wang to climb the Peak with me. I never had achieved it when we were here before. It was, after all, the site of the beginning of his adventures with us, that rainy day when he brought me home. For this trip I attired myself in a Chinese outfit with stout shoes – far more suitable for such a climb than a lady's get up and, as it was still early, we started out before the sun was high and the humidity oppressive. When we left the house, Jane and Robert were still closeted but their voices were no longer raised. I was glad of that.

The Peak rose behind us. The overgrown tropical plants were no longer alien, but the view still took my breath away. From the top I could make out the garrison at Happy Valley and the shanty town at Wanchai. We found birds of paradise and double-headed roses in among the lush, green vegetation and, as we were accustomed, took cuttings of course. Coming back down to the busy streets easily this time in my Chinese shoes, I bought dumplings and there I spotted the old lady who had so admired my Lady Macbeth when we had dinner the night before we left on our adventures. She was travelling in a sedan chair. When I greeted her, poor thing, she was quite confused.

'It is I, Miss Penney, Robert Fortune's sister,' I explained, as I waved her down.

She looked at me aghast.

'Have you not heard? Robert and I were in the interior. We travelled as Chinese, you know.'

'My dear, of course,' she smiled, 'but how very convincing you are! And you are promised as my Ariel, are you not? Though this outfit will never do! My, my.'

'I think I must memorise my lines again,' I admitted.

'It has been some time. I am so sorry that I never replied to your note.'

The old lady eyed me. 'Well,' she said, 'perhaps you should come to tea and you can tell me what has knocked our precious Bard clean out of your head! Was it not terrifying?'

'Edifying,' I assured her. 'I shall call later in the week.'

'When will you leave for Ta Eng Co, Master?' Wang enquired on our way back to the lodging.

'You shall be dismissed very soon, Wang. Very soon.'

'And you will see a steam ship?'

'No, Wang. Mr Fortune is leaving, but I will stay here.'

Wang looked confused.

'We both have business to see to,' I explained.

I did not want to think about it too closely.

On our return to the house, Jane completely ignored me and I half-wondered if she even recognised me in these clothes. She stormed past and disappeared into the morning room.

'Mary, come with me,' Robert directed.

My palms felt sticky with fear, for I did not know what had happened while I was out. Robert anticipated this and whispered kindly, 'Don't worry. She is impossible, but she will come round. She has to. For now we must pay off our men, don't you think?'

I nodded.

'We must make it as easy as we can for her, Robert,' I said. 'Promise me.'

'Of course,' he put his hand on my shoulder. 'I promise. Of course.'

We saw to our business. Robert called Wang and Sing Hoo into the study one by one and gave each a bag of silver coins (a small fortune for two years' wanderings and easily five years' salary had they stayed at the docks). He also offered them their choice of gift. Sing Hoo said he wanted gold. Wang smiled. He asked for a necklace for his wife. Both these I arranged that afternoon and delivered to them personally, with my thanks.

That evening, Wang set off. The journey back to Bohea would take him until the winter at least and he was keen to make it before the snows. He had made a grand profit from the escapade. As he said goodbye I sensed no unhappiness, only excitement. He thanked both Robert and I profusely and bowed coldly to Sing Hoo before leaving the house with one small bag of clothes and all that money. I saw him proceeding down the road, as jolly and capable as the day he had first found me and I was glad we had climbed the hill that morning together.

Sing Hoo by contrast, lingered. He too had been paid but it was clear he had nowhere to go. With no duties he inspected the tea gardeners' quarters and double checked the arrangements for Robert and Jane's passage on the *Lady Mary Wood*, due to sail within a fortnight. Each morning for the next few days I saw him sitting on the kitchen steps and each evening he took his place in the servants' quarters. Between times I suspect that he frequented the brothels at the dockside.

'Perhaps you should take him to India, Robert?' I suggested.

'So he can vomit the whole sea voyage and steal a percentage of my supplies once ashore?'

'He is good with the men.'

'Why do you think he stole all that money if he had no purpose for it?' Robert pondered.

But then, of a sudden, after perhaps three days, Sing Hoo simply disappeared without even saying goodbye. In due course we heard he had departed on McFarlane's ship once more, taken on as a hand and bound this time for

Shanghae. I expect he intended to make his way home at last from there. Perhaps he had decided on the spur. Who knows?

Jane was silent with me all the while. Each day we welcomed visitors and each night we all dined out. Robert and I laid not a single hand on each other. It would not have felt right. He told me that he had made it plain to my sister that she was free to do as she pleased, but all he could offer her was a marriage on his terms, which, he pointed out, were not much different from the marriage they had had all along. He would support her and the children, love them all, and dedicate his time to his work, which now meant spending much of his time in China, building their rising fortune. Jane had ranted, he said. She had screamed and cried, but there was no measure in that.

'You can be a scandal,' he had told her, 'if you wish it. Or you can be a rich man's wife and no one will know. I will support you either way, Jane, but the latter will be better for our children.'

In her temper, I wondered if my calm, practical, usually compliant sister might lash out, consult a lawyer, scream it from the rooftops or worse.

Meanwhile the dinners and afternoon teas continued. I visited my old lady and promised to recite, I gave a short talk to the ladies of the colony on the subject of our adventures and answered interminable questions about the ways of the natives in the interior and how awful it must have been for me. Jane emerged only for the larger social functions. She had some lovely new dresses, I noticed, and a fine collection of fans. Often congratulated on her husband's success and her sister's unusual character, I could see that she found her time in Hong Kong wearing. I would have found it so myself. I tried to talk to her several times, but she continued to ignore me, on one occasion rapping my fingers with a closed fan when I reached out to take her by the arm. She spoke to our society friends, of course. Once, when someone had congratulated her on having such a spirited sister, I overheard her say 'Yes. Most masculine. Mother always said that Mary took after our father, you know.'

From Jane, this was an unheard-of insult. I hung back then. If she did not wish to talk to me there was little I could do.

My time with Robert was now pitifully short. The passage to Calcutta would be five weeks or so, and from there the journey on to Ahallabad and the Valley of Deyra had been organised. To get to the Kaolagir tea plantations would take several weeks. Jane would not make the journey with her husband, but would stay in Calcutta and wait. Mr Gerard knew the city well and organised lodgings for her and introductions. With Robert now a luminary, she would spend her time lavishly among the company's wives. Meantime Robert wrote ahead to Dr Jamieson at the plantation once more so that he would know the men were set to sail.

One morning a closed carriage was sent and Robert proposed we take a trip together, out of the blue. It was pleasant to be alone and we held hands, side by side.

'I feel like your betrothed,' he admitted.

'Don't be shy,' I told him. 'We will be together again.'

As the horses trotted on, I noticed we headed towards the new houses at the base of the Peak. Here as the carriage drew up Robert gave me a key, which he drew from his inside pocket. Understanding dawned upon me.

'A whole house,' I breathed. 'Robert, I have no need of that!'

'It is not so large. Besides, I have taken it for you. If you are lonely you must take a lodger! I hope you do not mind me moving you, but I thought a fresh start . . .' he stuttered.

I unlocked the front door. Inside the air was cool and I could see a beautiful garden to the rear. I ran through the rooms like a child at Christmas. A small kitchen, a dining room, a drawing room and a sitting room. Upstairs three fine bedrooms with balconies and dressing rooms besides. To the side there were some maids' quarters. Robert was proud of himself. He strolled behind me pointing out the features.

'Look, Mary, such a large bath. And won't you like this view? You do like the view?'

I couldn't say anything. He had tried so hard to please me. I never dreamt I'd have such finery to myself. And yet he was leaving.

'I thought you would want to engage your own servants,' he said.

'You are right. Thank you.'

I stood before him and reached out my hand, trailing my long fingers down the front of his shirt.

'I will wait for you here,' I said.

He bit his lip. 'I will hurry.'

The next day we dispatched most of my boxes of clothes from one house to the other and Robert set up a line of credit. It was more money than I had ever imagined. These new-found riches were a boon. A home is a rare kind of pleasure and, after so many months at berth in one boat or another or quartered in provincial inns, it was time to be a woman again.

'You will have a porcelain service,' Robert promised, eager to please. 'Oh, Mary, what of this linen? You do like it, don't you?'

'I do. I am happy,' I told him.

'And you will stay here? You will wait?'

I smiled. He was as nervous as I was.

The days passed regardless. Then, almost at the end, I was

360

packing the last of my things before I finally moved myself over to my own little mansion, when I came across a box in the study. Robert's correspondence was piled up, being catalogued. The Royal Horticultural Society would inherit it, in due course, I had no doubt. I fingered the pages, reading a line here and there. And then I noticed there was a small pile of unopened letters. I lifted one. It was addressed to me in Jane's hand. I realised these were the missives that had been sent to await my return, before she knew what we had done, what had happened. My sister had written over twenty letters until some eight months before we arrived back, when the correspondence had abruptly ceased. I sank into a chair by the empty fireside.

The sound of the wax seal breaking on those letters was agonising. She had written to me of Henry, of course – his first words, his first steps. He had been teething. She described the sunny nature of a happy infant and said that William had called on his son twice and sent gifts at Christmas. She loved my son, there was no doubt of that. In another of the letters she thanked me for the consignment I had chosen – recognising my eye in the gifts and writing at length how the children had played dress up. She told me of the seasons in London – a wet spring, a glorious summer and John, her eldest, who had returned from school for the holidays. Should she plant laurel in the back garden or a clematis – which would take longer to grow? The later letters sounded worried and contained less news – only that Thomas had begun his Latin and that she had had the drawing room redecorated. Robert was silent and I had not written in so long that she was afraid, she said. It was a lonely business, being in London, her companions abroad. Please, please, she entreated me, would I send some word? She was worried. The words resounded – an echo of the sister I had lost, the love and care that I had gambled.

361

I sat silently. The staff moved through the house. I could hear them. The letters lay on the side tables to the left and right, like an abandoned meal. I kept thinking of those last few weeks, of Robert and I riding together on our way to Foo Chow Soo. Of the golden countryside and our lovemaking in the fields. And then the clear image of Robert taking aim at the pirate junks and the day we had had chocolate again, the sweet, rich texture. I wished I had kissed him afterwards, the taste still on our lips. I loved Jane very much. We both did. And we had hurt her.

As if floating, I left the study and climbed up the stairs towards my sister's room. I knocked on the door and entered. Jane was sitting alone by the window and looked up as I came in, her enquiring look turning to a withering glance instantly when she saw it was only I. I crossed to her chair and sank down onto the floor beside her.

'Jane,' I said, 'I just read your letters.'

She remained silent, her small fingers fluttering to the collar of her gown, thinking through, no doubt, what she had said in each note.

I continued. 'You are angry, I know. You have every right to be so. But . . .'

I got no further.

'Don't! Don't!' she shouted. 'I do not want an explanation. I do not want your pity either.'

'Listen,' I entreated her. I had to take her on. 'I have been looking forever for something that I want. All that time in London, all those plays, that silly house near Soho Square, damn William and his wooing. I was searching, Jane. And quite by chance I have found what I was looking for. Here.'

'My husband,' she sniffed.

'No. No. Robert is incidental. You don't understand. I found a country that fascinated me. I found something I was good at. I found a vocation, an interest, a calling.

362

And yes, all right, I found him as well. I hated Robert in London. You know I did. And the truth is, I will never go back there. But here in China, Robert and I, we have this together. It has sparked something that is amazing in every way. And however much I don't want to hurt you, I cannot regret it. Nothing will make me regret it.' I was crying. 'But you and I may never see each other again, Jane. And you are still my sister. I do not love you less than before and I do not want to lose you. Even if you are angry with me, let's make it up. Let's cobble together something. Please.'

My breath was heaving. Jane was having none of my sentimentality. She fought back.

'So you want my love while you share your bed with my husband? That is not possible, Mary. You have made your choice. Take him then! I will not divorce him. But know that you have humiliated me. And that's what you will have left of me because of this. A façade. A pretence. I will play my part. No one will know. I will be your housekeeper, Mary,' she spat sarcastically. 'I will look after your mistakes and back up all your endeavours. I will invest your money. I will auction your goods. I will be Mrs Fortune for you and they can all tell me how marvellous you are. How wonderful. How extraordinary! You show-off! You have to have everything. You have found what you wanted. Well, bully for you. For in taking it you have got the only thing I ever dreamed of since I was a little girl. He is my husband.'

I felt for her. 'We will never agree,' I said sadly. 'But Robert is hardly gone from you. You did not really have him in the first place, Jane. Everything that you liked is yours still. All that time in London you preached acceptance to me. You told me that I had to do what is best for my family. Well, perhaps things haven't turned out just the way you'd like, but now it is your turn to play the hand you're dealt. And it is not as easy as you thought, is it?'

My sister lashed out. It was a surprise and her blow sent me flying. She jumped up from her chair and kicked me hard in fury when I was down. I grabbed her by the foot and wrestled her to the floor.

'How could you? You are so like him! You beast! You foul, foul monster!' she shouted.

Her hair had come loose and fell about her shoulders like a madwoman's. I held her down.

'That's it, isn't it? It's Da! He hurt you and he never hurt me. And now it's not that Robert loves you less that kills you, it's that he doesn't hate me any more! You can't bear that. Because you thought you were his favourite. You can't bear having to share him!'

The commotion of our tussle had brought a maid from downstairs. The door clicked open and the girl stood there, her mouth open at the sight of my sister and I, hair flying, fighting like street urchins. We both sat up, suddenly well behaved, as if we were children caught by their governess. I laughed.

'Get out!' Jane screamed at the girl, who fled immediately.

'I thought all you wanted was to be Mrs Fortune,' I muttered. 'And you are. You hate the part of Robert that I have. I have no desire for the part you like. We can both have him, Jane. It's not like Da at all.'

'Convenient,' she snarled.

'You have always been good to me but, Jane, I never had what I wanted. I have it now and I won't give it up. '

Jane thumped her hands flat on the floor in frustration.

'And there is nothing I can do! I just feel so helpless,' she howled.

All at once I realised that I remembered that feeling. Other people making decisions for me – things I did not want at all and had no choice in. It was not so long ago that, frustrated, I had hit the floor myself. I stroked the back of her hand.

'We are family,' I told her. 'And we must stick together, Jane. You know that. My son, your husband, all the responsibilities. We are going to share more than most, I suppose. And I know it is wrong. But I will not steal him from you, not like you are thinking, and no one need know. Truly. The only difference is that I am happy here and that Robert, some of the time, will be happy here too. It is not perfect for any of us, but it is what we have.'

Jane's eyes were hard. There was no resolving things. Not now, anyway. Forgiveness takes time.

'You are Mrs Fortune,' I promised her. 'And I am Fanny Kemble, I suppose.'

On the next night, their last, we dined at the Governor's mansion. The guests toasted Robert at the table, all twenty of them. During the pudding Pottinger received the news that Foo Chow Soo had been relieved, thank heavens, and we all toasted that as well – both the success and to the memory of the men who fell.

'And Major Gilland?' Robert enquired.

'Sent the news himself. Gilland is indestructible, I think,' Pottinger joked.

I was glad of it.

Afterwards I recited Juliet and received a standing ovation, Robert joining the applause and Jane clapping politely at his side.

'And what will you do, Miss Penney, now you are set for the quiet life?' the Governor enquired.

'I have not the least idea, though the capital profit Robert recently made does have me inspired to trade. If I can make for Ning-po and perhaps Chusan from time to time I am sure I can find exceptional goods to send for sale in London.'

Pottinger raised an eyebrow.

'Miss Penney,' he said, 'you are full of surprises, but I suspect we would have you no other way. There is a reliable fellow I can perhaps recommend to you as an agent.'

That night I did not sleep at all. I could not bring myself to it. I had been feeling ill of late. At first, I thought it was my troubles. The difficulty with Jane, and Robert leaving. Already I was beginning to recognise that it was more. I did not say a word.

The next morning on the dock the *Lady Mary Wood* was loaded, the tea gardeners in their quarters, the sixteen Ward's cases sown with germinating tea seeds on the deck. I sat in Robert's rooms, books piled to one side, his notebooks in the trunk. Jane had said goodbye to me already, kissed my cheek coldly and removed to her own cabin. It was, I realised, a start, albeit a small one. Now my darling sat staring at me and I at him.

'I love you,' I said.

He must go. He must go.

When the tide was ready he walked me to the gangplank, hugged me and I left the boat just before the anchor was raised and the ship cast away. Robert stayed on deck, staring back at me. I was not empty without him, I noticed. Perhaps that is the measure of a true love. I thought I saw the small figure of my sister come to stand at his side just before the ship finally disappeared. I hoped so as I turned towards the town. There were camellias growing in front of some of the houses. I wondered if I might spot a yellow one.

Epilogue

My second son was born in Ning-po the following April. Society was, oddly, not scandalised at all, at least, not that anyone showed it, when I returned to Hong Kong with a baby in my care. Money, I realise now, buys many things that are not the least bit material. And the colonies, I suppose, are different. The greatest shock was Robert's, of course. I had decided not to tell him by letter. I wanted him to return to me, not out of duty, but out of love.

The baby has a slash of dark hair and my lover's shy smile. I have called him Albert Gilland Penney and Sir Pottinger has said he will stand as godfather to the boy, who was baptised, of course, by the Bishop. Robert does not know this yet. He has only just arrived. He is on the verandah in the shade, with his son in his arms.

'I am going to keep this child at home, myself,' I told him. 'I will not lose another little boy.'

Perhaps, I daydream, they will be friends one day, these half-brothers, Henry and Albert. Perhaps John and Helen and Thomas will find out they have, well, we will call them cousins, I suppose. It is strange to love one's children so, without even knowing them. I cannot help myself and I daydream that there will be more.

For now, Robert has brought his maps and we are set for Japan. Another adventure, just the two of us and more riches to be made, no doubt. Albert will stay in the care of a governess I have employed – a lady who arrived in Hong Kong some months ago in the wake of a scandal. I employed her immediately and I am happy to say that I am paying her far too much.

'Two hundred and fifty miles will outrun almost anything,' I said. 'I think you have overshot the mark in coming this far, but I do hope you will stay.'

She has not as adventurous a spirit as I, but her company is very pleasant and she knows the part of Ariel by heart.

I notice that there is a letter in Jane's hand addressed to me. It is the first I have had of her since her leaving and I smile at the very thought. I will read it later, curled up on the balcony, tomorrow morning, or perhaps afternoon – whenever I emerge. Now, though, I stand at the garden door. Robert has been crying. There is no need for either of us to say a thing about it.

'I think there will be tree peonies,' he remarks. 'In Osaka.'

'Tell me,' I enquire, as I put the baby in his basket and slip sinuously onto Robert's lap, 'how much does a new species of tree peony sell for in London, these days?

Historical Note

The Secret Mandarin is what Truman Capote called 'Faction' - a mixture of reality and fiction. I freely admit to putting the needs of a good story before anything else, but I have retained historical accuracy wherever I can. Fortune made several well-documented trips to Asia and wrote his own accounts, which mostly focussed on his horticultural discoveries. The Secret Mandarin contains episodes from all of them. His books were bestsellers in their day (though rather dull if you aren't a botanist). Between the pages and pages on different species of plants, they offer tantalising glimpses into what might be considered Fortune's more exciting adventures. He mentions only in passing that he spoke to a Mandarin or went to stay in a local farmhouse, for example, and devotes only a few paragraphs to the pirate attack I have reproduced on Captain McFarlane's ship (on the way to Hong Kong rather than on the way out). In many places I have simply 'rcsited' events. Robert did not live at Gilston Road, for example, until later in his career, but I have moved the Fortune family there earlier (from staff accommodation at Kew Gardens) to accommodate the needs of Mary Penney. Wang and Sing Hoo both served Fortune during his trips, but their time in his service was not contemporaneous. During his time in the tea countries Fortune stayed with the Wang Family, rather than taking a trip of only a couple of days to visit (as in my account). I hope that these changes do not distract - 1 tried to write a story that was in the spirit of the times, based around what really happened, taking guesses at what might lie in the gaps between the documentary evidence available. Likewise, there is no concrete proof that Fortune spied for Britain, though it seems very unlikely that the military commanders in Hong Kong would not have asked him to keep an eye out, given that he was one of very few Europeans who made their way into the interior of China. I found myself in awe of Robert Fortune - a truly adventurous man - though very aware of his shortcomings. He really never understood the country that brought him so much prosperity and fame. The omissions in his own accounts were telling of both his character and his understanding. It was for these reasons that Mary Penney, a character entirely of my own invention, seemed to fit in like a jigsaw piece. It was as if she had always been missing.

There is very little documentary evidence of Fortune's private life, as Jane Penney burned all his letters and some of his papers after he died. A horticulturist told me that she had done this at his request, but of course, of that we can never be sure. As a novelist this left an enticing gap that once more, the invention of Mary Penney seemed to fill seamlessly. I hope you enjoy the book and forgive any liberties I may have taken in creating the story.

Further Reading

I found the following invaluable in the course of my research:

Non-fiction:
The Victorians by A N Wilson (Arrow)
The Victorians by Jeremy Paxman (BBC Books)
Victorian London by Liza Picard (Phoenix)
The Suspicions of Mr Whicher by Kate Summerscale (Bloomsbury)
For All the Tea In China by Sarah Rose (Hutchinson)
The Age of Wonder by Richard Holmes (HarperPress)
The Scottish Enlightenment by Arthur Herman (Fourth Esate)
The Plant Hunters by Toby Musgrave, Chris Gardner and Will Musgrave (Cassell Illustrated)
A History of Hong Kong by Frank Welsh (HarperCollins Publishers)
Chinese Mythology by Derek Walters (The Johns Hopkins University Press)
1421 by Gavin Menzies (Bantam Books)
The Chinese Opium Wars by Jack Beeching (Harcourt Publishers)
The Opium Wars: The Addiction of One Empire and the Corruption of Another by W. Travis Hanes and Frank Sanello (Robson Books)

The Honourable Company by John Keay (HarperCollins Publishers)

Fiction:

Water Music by T C Boyle (Granta Books)

The Crimson Petal and the White by Michael Faber (Canongate)

Jonathan Strange and Mr Norrell by Susanna Clarke (Bloomsbury)

The Star of the Sea by Joseph O'Connor (Vintage)

Fingersmith by Sarah Waters (Virago)

The Journal of Ore Damage by Belinda Starling (Bloomsbury)

Points For Discussion

I spent almost eight years, on and off, writing *The Secret Mandarin,* and in doing so I never once planned a theme for the book, though it transpires it has several. When I was asked to write some questions for reading groups I was surprised that firstly, *groups* of people might read the story and secondly that the book could be analysed in any kind of organised way! In writing them, I have found myself considering many issues raised by the book for the first time and that has been a pleasure. I hope you enjoy them as much as I have.

1 Mary Penney discovers an alien and exciting foreign world thousands of miles from everything she has ever known. In today's world, is this still possible? Despite higher levels of education, ease of travel and the access to information available to us, how alien is modern day China or India to our Western minds? Have you ever felt (on holiday or elsewhere) that you were alien to everything around you?

2 The book is written from Mary's point of view, do you feel you have also followed Robert's journey? What might he have said differently if he had been given his own narrative voice?

3 The book chronicles the development of feelings between the couple from loathing and fear on both sides, to a burning love. Where are the key shifts in this change? When did you first realise what was happening?

4 Mary and Robert are travelling in the early 1840s – before the advent of modern psychology, Era One medicine or Darwin's theory of evolution. How would these advancements help or hinder what happens in the story?

5 Even travelling as a Chinese secretary, essentially a servant, Mary finds she has more freedom than she ever did as a free British woman. What must living in Victorian culture have been like for most women? In over 150 years how much has changed? If a woman were to disguise herself as a man today, what freedoms might she discover?

6 Robert on several occasions clearly feels highly constricted by society too. How does this contrast with the terms of Mary's social imprisonment? If you could choose to be in either Mary's position or Robert's, which would you decide on?

7 Robert's trip inside China changed the landscape of the tea industry. Morally should he have done so?

8 The book contains glimpses into the lives of many 'supporting' characters – for example, the Hunters, Bertie Allan, William, Father Edward, Wang, Sing Hoo, Simon Rose, Captain Landers and Ling. Which characters did you enjoy most and why? What other adventures might they have had?

9 Any historical novel relies heavily on the atmosphere of the time it is evoking – in this case an early Victorian London, a new British Colony and post-Opium War,

Imperial China. What made you feel you had experienced these places? How was the atmosphere communicated to you?

10 There is a strong bond of love and loyalty between Jane and Mary Penney. What do you think happened in the Penney household when the sisters were growing up?

11 *The Secret Mandarin* is 'faction' – a mixture of fantasy and reality. Are you aware where one ends and the other begins? How valid is this way of learning about the past?

12 When you picked up the book to read it was it what you expected? How much can a front cover and a few paragraphs on the back communicate the contents of any novel?

What's next?

Tell us the name of an author you love

| Sara Sheridan | Go ▶ |

and we'll find your next great book.

book army

www.bookarmy.com